THE TRAIL WEST
MONAHAN'S
MASSACRE

THE TRAIL WEST
MONAHAN'S MASSACRE

WILLIAM W. JOHNSTONE
with J. A. Johnstone

PINNACLE BOOKS
Kensington Publishing Corp.
www.kensingtonbooks.com

PINNACLE BOOKS are published by

Kensington Publishing Corp.
119 West 40th Street
New York, NY 10018

PUBLISHER'S NOTE
Following the death of William W. Johnstone, the Johnstone family is working with a carefully selected writer to organize and complete Mr. Johnstone's outlines and many unfinished manuscripts to create additional novels in all of his series like The Last Gunfighter, Mountain Man, and Eagles, among others. This novel was inspired by Mr. Johnstone's superb storytelling.

All Kensington titles, imprints, and distributed lines are available at special quantity discounts for bulk purchases for sales promotions, premiums, fund-raising, educational, or institutional use. Special book excerpts or customized printings can also be created to fit specific needs. For details, write or phone the office of the Kensington sales manager: Kensington Publishing Corp., 119 West 40th Street, New York, NY 10018, attn: Sales Department; phone 1-800-221-2647.

PINNACLE BOOKS, the Pinnacle logo, and the WWJ steer head logo, are Reg. U.S. Pat. & TM Off.

ISBN-13: 978-0-7860-4073-5
ISBN-10: 0-7860-4073-4

First printing: March 2017

10 9 8 7 6 5 4 3 2 1

Printed in the United States of America

First electronic edition: March 2017

ISBN-13: 978-0-7860-4074-2
ISBN-10: 0-7860-4074-2

PROLOGUE

Naturally, Dooley Monahan had never cared a whit for Nebraska. After all, when a man is born in Iowa, he frowns upon that great state due west that lay just across the Missouri River. Come to think on it, Dooley never liked Illinois much, either, over to the east. And especially not Missouri, what with its bushwhackers and outlaws such as the James boys and the Younger brothers and that crazy governor named Boggs the state south of Dooley's home state had once had elected. Had he ever really given Wisconsin or Minnesota much thought, Dooley might have decided that he didn't care much for those places, either.

But Nebraska had always been something of a rival of Iowa, at least from what Dooley had been reading in the *Council Bluffs Journal* that he had found accidentally put in with his mail at the general store in Des Moines. Well, actually, it wasn't so much all of Nebraska that the editor, one Jonas Houston, waxed most violently against with his poisoned pen. Just Omaha, which lay just across the wide Missouri River from Council Bluffs, Iowa.

When Dooley crossed the ferry and landed in Omaha, he didn't see what all the ballyhoo was about. Nebraska, and Omaha, looked fine—maybe even, Dooley had to reluctantly admit—a sight better than rickety, ramshackle, and rank-smelling Council Bluffs. But not Iowa, overall, with its rolling hills and verdant pastures and corn and mud and everything that Dooley had grudgingly grown to like over the past two years back on his farm.

Omaha, Nebraska, was all right, Dooley had decided as he loaded up his supplies into the saddlebags, gave his blue dog a bite of biscuit, and swung into the saddle on his bay gelding.

A minute or two later, Omaha and Nebraska—and Dooley Monahan's life in general—went straight to hell.

CHAPTER ONE

As he rode west down the wide, muddy street, Dooley Monahan felt content. He had a belly full of coffee and biscuits and gravy, a newspaper article—torn out from page three of the *Council Bluffs Journal*—and enough supplies, or so the merchant at the general store had told him, that would get him to the Black Hills of Dakota Territory, where Dooley had decided he would make his fortune at that gold strike up yonder. And a fellow he had met at the Riverfront Saloon had sold him a map that would take him to the Black Hills and avoid any Sioux warrior who might be after a scalp or two. Two blocks back, he had even tipped his hat to a plump blonde who had not only smiled at him, but also even offered him a "Good morning, sir."

"Yes, sir, ol' Blue," Dooley told the blue-eyed dog walking alongside his good horse, "it sure is shaping up to be a mighty good day."

That's when a bullet tore through the crown of his brown hat.

A couple of years had passed since, as best as

Dooley could remember, somebody had taken a shot at him—but Dooley had not been farming for so long that he forgot how to survive in the West. Ducking low in the saddle, he craned his head back down Front Street where the shot had come from while his right hand reached for and gripped the Colt .45 Peacemaker he wore in a well-used holster slickened with bacon grease.

On one side of the street, that plump blond girl dived behind a water trough. On the south boardwalk, a man in a silk top hat pitched his broom onto the warped planks, slammed one shutter closed, and dived back inside the open door of his tonsorial parlor.

What looked to be a whole danged regiment of cavalry charged toward him, the hooves of wild-eyed horses churning up mud like a farmer breaking sod—but only if that farmer had Thoroughbreds instead of mules, and a multidisced plow that could rip through the ground at breakneck speed.

"The James boys!" came a shout.

"It's the danged Youngers!" roared another.

"The Reno Gang!" yelled someone.

"We're the Dobbs and Handley boys, you stupid square-heads!" shouted a man with a walrus mustache. He rode one of those wild-eyed horses that were coming straight for Dooley Monahan; his dog, Blue; and his gelding, General Grant.

"Bank robbery!"

"Murder!"

"St. Albans!"

Dooley had read about St. Albans—not in the *Council Bluffs Journal*, but some other newspaper, maybe one in Des Moines back when he was living with his mother and father and long before he got the urge to ride west and find gold and had made a name for himself as a gunman who had killed a few outlaws. St. Albans was a town in Vermont or New Hampshire or Maine or maybe even Minnesota—but not Iowa or Nebraska—where Confederates had pulled a daytime robbery of a bank during the Civil War. So whenever the James-Younger boys or the Dobbs-Handley Gang or some other bunch of cut-throats or guerillas robbed a bank in daylight hours, folks still cried out . . .

"St. Albans! St. Albans! Foul murder! Robbery!"

Or:

"Get your guns, men, and let's kill these thievin' scum."

The men of Omaha, Nebraska, had taken up arms by now. Bullets whined, roared, and ricocheted from barbershops and rooftops, from behind trash bins or water troughs. Panes of glass shattered. The riders thundering their mounts right at Dooley Monahan answered in kind.

General Grant did two quick jumps and a stutter step, which caused Dooley to release the grip on his walnut-handled Colt. His left hand held the reins. His right hand gripped the horn. And seeing his dog bolt down the street, leap onto the north-side boardwalk, and move faster than that dog had ever run gave Dooley an idea.

He raked General Grant's sides with his spurs and felt that great horse of his start churning up the mud of Front Street himself.

Later, when Dooley Monahan had time to think everything through, when he came to realize every-thing that he might have done—*should* have done—

Dooley would realize that perhaps his best move would have been to dive out of the saddle and over the hitching rail and fall onto his hands and knees on the boardwalk. Then, he imagined, he would have crawled rapidly east—toward Iowa—until he reached the water trough, where he gallantly would have dived and covered the body of the plump blonde, shielding her with his own body, earning much praise for his heroics and chivalry from the editor of the *Council Bluffs Journal* and maybe even Omaha's *Weekly, World, Herald, Register, Call,* and *Mormon Prophet.* General Grant, most likely, would have galloped off after Blue, found shelter down an alley, and Dooley Monahan would have avoided confusion and near death. A parson would have found his horse and dog and led them back to the saloon on Front Street where Dooley would have been talking to the plump blonde. She would have kissed Dooley full on the lips for saving her life, Dooley would have been given a couple of cigars and a bottle of whiskey, and he would have continued on to the gold mines of the Black Hills—if there were mines—or maybe he would just have filed a claim on some creek. Either way, he would have been well on his way to a fortune, and not running for his life.

Yes, that is what Dooley should have done.

But when a man is mounted on a fast-running horse and facing a charging horde of rough-looking men, with bullets slicing dangerously close, even an experienced farmer turned cowboy turned gunman turned gold seeker turned amnesiac turned recovered amnesiac turned farmer turned fortune hunter does not always elect to do the smart or proper thing.

Instead, Dooley did what came to him first. He spurred his horse, and General Grant led him westward down Front Street. He leaned low in the saddle, and almost not low enough, for one bullet grazed the skin tight across his left shoulder blade.

The frame, sod, and bricked buildings of busy Omaha seemed blurry as Dooley glanced north and south. He saw the flashes of guns from a few windows or doorways, but none of the bullets came that close. Still, he managed to yell, "Don't shoot at me, you fool Nebraskans! I'm just trying to save my own hide!"

They couldn't hear him, of course. Not with all the musketry and the pounding of hooves and, perhaps, even Dooley's own heartbeat.

General Grant had always been a reliable horse, and as fast as many racehorses. But Omaha's streets had become a thick bog after a bunch of spring rains, and the fine bay horse had spent the past couple of years on an old farm a few miles outside of Des Moines—so he wasn't quite up to his old form. Before he knew it, Dooley felt riders on both sides of him. He wanted to slow down, but even as he eased off his spurs, General Grant kept running as hard as his four legs could carry him. And Dooley understood that the bay gelding really had no choice. Too many horses were right behind him. Even if the horse or Dooley could have stopped, they would have been trampled by outlaws and bank robbers trying to get out of Omaha as fast as they could. Dooley could not go to the left, because a bearded man on a buckskin mare blocked that way. Dooley could not veer off to the north side, either, because a tobacco-chewing man wearing a deerskin shirt and riding a black stallion held Dooley and General Grant in check. There wasn't much Dooley could do except ride along with the flow of the outlaws and pray that he didn't get killed.

Of course, later, Dooley thought that maybe, had he drawn his pistol and shot one of the bad men riding along either side of him, he might have been able to leap General Grant over the dead man and save his own hide.

Which never would have worked in a million years.

On the other hand, had Dooley possessed the sense of mind to draw his hogleg and put a bullet through his own brain, that might have been the easy, if a coward's, way out.

The man with the deerskin shirt pulled ahead of Dooley, but a rider in striped britches on a pinto mustang quickly filled the opening. The man in the deerskin put his black mount right in front of Dooley and General Grant.

That, Dooley decided, wasn't such a bad thing to happen. No fool Nebraskan would now be able to shoot Dooley dead, mistaking him for one of the bank robbers. At least these men of the Dobbs-Handley Gang were protecting Dooley's life.

By now, Dooley was sweating. His lungs burned from breathing so hard. His butt and thighs ached from bouncing around in the saddle. Mud plastered his face from the black stallion galloping ahead of him. Mud splattered against his denim trousers and stovepipe boots. He glanced to the south and saw the bearded man riding the buckskin mare stare at him. Dooley tried to smile. The man turned away, raised the Remington .44 in his right hand, and snapped another shot toward some citizen and defender of Omaha, Nebraska.

Then the outlaws, with Dooley right among them, turned north.

More gunfire. More curses. More mud and shouts.

Dooley glanced up at a three-story hotel. A man on the rooftop stood up, did a macabre dance as bullets peppered his body. The Winchester rifle—or maybe it was a Henry—pitched over the hotel's façade, and the protector of Omaha—for Dooley glimpsed sunlight reflecting off a tin badge on the lapel of the man's striped vest—followed the repeating rifle and crashed through the awning and onto the boardwalk in front of the hotel.

That caused Dooley's stomach to rumble. He thought he might turn to his side and lose the whiskey he had downed at the Riverfront Saloon and the biscuits and gravy and coffee from Nancy's Diner. But he did not vomit, and he thought that power might have saved his life. For surely had he sprayed the man on his right, the man in the deerskin shirt on the black stallion would have shot him dead.

And that man was a mighty fine shot, for he was the one who had killed the lawman on the rooftop of the hotel.

The horses kept running, though by now the gunfire was dying down. And the buildings weren't so close together anymore. Before long, the Dobbs-Handley Gang had put Omaha, Nebraska, behind them.

They kept their horses at a gallop.

And Dooley Monahan had no choice but to keep galloping with them.

CHAPTER TWO

Eventually, the lead rider's horse began to tire—as did the mounts ridden by the other outlaws—and the pace slackened, but did not stop. Dooley wanted to say something, but, on the other hand, he really didn't want to get killed. He swallowed any words he thought of, especially when the men to his side began shucking the empty shells from their revolvers and reloading. They filled every cylinder with a fresh load—most men, including Dooley, usually kept the chamber empty under the hammer to make it less likely to blow off a toe, foot, or kneecap. When they had their six-shooters loaded, they began filling their rifles or shotguns, too.

They did this while their horses kept at a hard trot.

Which took some doing.

Dooley kept both hands on his reins. He didn't even look at the Colt in its holster. At least, Dooley thought he still carried the revolver. For all he knew, it might have been joggled loose during that hard run and was buried in Omaha's mud or the tall grass they now pushed through.

They turned south, swung a wide loop to avoid any trails, farms, travelers, or lawmen, and kept their horses at that bone-jarring, spine-pounding trot. Dooley felt, more than heard or saw, a couple of the riders in the rear pull back. Most likely, he expected, to watch their back trail and let them know if any posse took off after them. From Dooley's experience, posses could be slow in forming—especially when that posse of well-meaning but not well-shooting citizens knew it would be going up against the likes of Hubert Dobbs and Frank Handley and the murdering terrors who rode with them.

South they traveled without talking. General Grant, though, kept tossing his head back, hard eyes trying to lock on Dooley, and probably cursing him in horse-talk for running him like this for no apparent purpose. Dooley wondered what had happened to that blue-eyed dog of his. Well, Blue wasn't actually Dooley's. The dog didn't belong to anyone, as far as Dooley knew, but he had more or less adopted the dog some years back. Fed him. Befriended him. He sure hoped he hadn't lost him again. Good dogs—any dogs—were hard to come by.

Of course, when the outlaws finally stopped running, Dooley would be able to go back to Omaha and maybe find old Blue and—

When they stop, most likely, they'll kill me.

The thought almost caused Dooley Monahan to pull back on the reins, but he quickly stopped an action that would have caused quite the horse wreck. And if spilling members of the Dobbs-Handley Gang, maybe laming a mount or two, and busting collarbones and wrists and arms of outlaws, didn't incite murder among those owlhoots . . .

Ahead, he saw the river, and now all of the horses slowed down. Oh, no one stopped. The leader jumped off what passed for a bank, and Dooley and the men riding on either side followed.

The water felt good as it splashed over Dooley's wind-burned, mud-blasted, sweaty face. General Grant's hooves found solid bottom, and the gelding pushed through the water toward the shore.

This, if Dooley had his bearings straight, would be the Platte River. Wide, but not that deep, even after all those thunderstorms and being fairly close to where the river flowed into the Missouri. It was wet, though, and Dooley took a moment to scoop up some with his right hand. He splashed it across his face, repeated that process, then found another handful and brought it to his mouth. There wasn't that much to swallow, but what did go down his throat felt good, replenishing, but most of the wetness just soothed his dried, chapped lips.

The two riders on his left and right pulled ahead of him, but Dooley knew better than to try to escape now. He tried to think up various options, but no matter what idea came to him, the end result most likely would lead to Dooley Monahan's quick and merciful death. Unless Handley or Dobbs decided to stake him out on an ant bed, cut off his eyelids so the sun would burn his eyeballs out before the ants started eating him alive. Then that death wouldn't be anything close to quick or merciful, but it would most certainly be eternal death.

Those three riders had reached the banks about twenty yards ahead of Dooley now. He heard horses snorting, and men grunting behind him.

Water cascaded off the horses as they climbed up

the bank. The riders—that bearded man on the
buckskin mare, the man in the deerskin shirt, with a
cheekful of chewing tobacco, on the powerful black
stallion, and the puny gent in the striped britches,
who rode a brown and white pinto mustang—turned
around, drew their revolvers, cocked them, and
waited.

The Platte began to get even shallower, and soon
General Grant was carrying Dooley out of the wide
patch of wetness. Behind him came the other riders,
who grunted or cursed or farted. Dooley let his bay
horse pick its own path up the bank until he reined
in in front of the three men. He stared down the
barrels of a Smith & Wesson, a Colt, and a Remington. Behind him he heard another noise.

You never forget what a rattlesnake sounds like.
Maybe you think you know how it sounds—or how it
makes you feel—but once you hear that rattle, you
know exactly what it sounds like and you know it will
practically make you wet your britches.

Quite similar to the whirl of a rattler is the cocking
of a single-action revolver . . . the thumbing back of
two hammers on a double-barreled shotgun, and
the levering of a fresh cartridge into a Winchester
or Henry rifle or carbine. Those were the sounds
coming from behind Dooley Monahan.

Not the rattlesnake, of course. Not that sound.
Though right then, Dooley would have preferred it
to those metallic clicks.

Dooley eased the reins down, letting them drop in
front of the horn. The horn he gripped with both
hands, and leaning forward, he nodded his head at
the men in front of him.

"Who the hell be you?"

That came from the man in the deerskin shirt. He wore a wide-brimmed dirty hat that might once have been white but had been dirtied up and sweated through over some years. Or it could have been gray, but had been faded from so much alkali dust and the blistering sun of the Great Plains. Dooley didn't think the hat had ever been black.

Brown juice came out of the man's mouth like he had opened a spigot, and he wiped the tobacco juice off his lips with a gloved left hand. The right held a large Smith & Wesson pistol that looked just a tad smaller than a cannon. He was the biggest of the men, which explained why he rode that giant black stallion. Dooley couldn't quite guess, but he had to figure the man stood six-foot-four in his boot heels, and had to weigh around two hundred and forty pounds. Maybe more.

"Name's Dooley," Dooley said. "Dooley Monahan."

The bearded man on the buckskin mare pursed his lips as if in deep thought. Thinking did not mean the man took the .45 caliber Colt away from Dooley's chest. He just thought.

He appeared to be more medium size, maybe not even as tall as Dooley, but tougher than a railroad tie and maybe twice as solid. Muscles strained through his muslin shirt, and Dooley couldn't quite remember when he had ever seen a beard that long on any man. There had been that woman back at that circus in Davenport that time, but you expected that when you paid two bits to see the bearded lady at a circus in Davenport. Her beard didn't seem real, though. This gent's certainly wasn't glued on.

"We ain't got no one goin' by Dooley in this gang,

does we?" the man on the massive black mount finally asked.

"Ain't got nobody usin' the handle Monahans, neither."

That sentence came from the third cuss, the one with the striped britches. He was puny. A spring wind might have carried him off like the furs on whatever those weeds with the furlike tops were called. Puny, and pale, with the coldest blue eyes Dooley had ever seen, sunk way back in his head. His blond hair, soaked by sweat and some Platte River water, hung like greasy rawhide strings. He was even uglier than that bearded lady back at that circus eighteen months back in Davenport, Iowa.

The man seemed so sickly, the big Smith & Wesson never steadied in his pasty white hand, but neither did it ever exactly not aim at one of Dooley's vital organs.

"Monahan," Dooley corrected. "No *s*. Just Monahan. Dooley Monahan."

He thought if he kept talking, they might not kill him.

"Shut up," barked the man on the black horse.

"Kill him, and let's ride," said the one on the buckskin mare. "Posse'll be chasin' us directly."

"How did you come to be ridin' with us?" asked the sickly one on the pinto. "Dooley *Monahans*." He stressed the last name and especially the *s* on the end of it, even though it wasn't Dooley's name.

Dooley shrugged, but kept gripping that saddle horn. If he let go, those men would think he was going for his Colt, and he'd be plugged before he could explain by a .45, .38, and .44 bullet—and no telling what calibers or gauges from the men behind him.

"Came to Omaha to stock up," Dooley said honestly. "Was riding out down that main street when you boys started whooping and hollering and riding."

"And shooting," said someone behind him.

"And shooting," Dooley added.

The men behind Dooley chuckled. The ones in front of him did not even blink or crack a smile.

"Y'all kind of swept me up," Dooley went on. "Wasn't anything I could do but keep riding. If I stopped, you would have run over me. That would've caused quite the spill. Probably got one of you boys caught, if not killed."

"We're obliged to you for that," said another voice behind him.

"Do you know who we are?" asked the tobacco-chewing man on the big black.

Dooley's mouth went dry. He could only shake is head.

"Hubert," came the first voice behind him. "My horse's gone lame."

"Now do you know who we are?" The man spit out more tobacco juice and shifted the quid to the opposite cheek.

Dooley just swallowed, but what he swallowed was mostly air. His mouth felt dried out like his skin did when he was farming. And his muscles did not respond when he tried to shake his head.

"C'mon, boy," said the man with the long beard. "How many bank robbers you ever heard called Hubert?"

"Shut the hell up, Frank," barked the tobacco chewer. "Hubert ain't no name to be ashamed of.

Belonged to my grandpappy on my ma's side, and his grandpappy's long before that."

The bearded man grinned. "And now you know my name, Dooley Monahan." At least he pronounced Dooley's name correctly. "Frank Handley."

"Which," said the big man on the big black, "makes me Hubert Dobbs."

"Which makes us," said the thin man on the pinto mustang, "the Dobbs-Handley Gang."

"A pleasure," Dooley managed to say.

"Step down off that horse," said the man who had not introduced himself.

"But first," added Frank Handley, "pull that hogleg from your holster . . ."

"Real careful," warned Hubert Dobbs.

"Real careful," coached the second voice behind Dooley.

"And," said Handley, "drop it to the ground."

Dooley Monahan obeyed.

"Let go of the reins and step away from the horse. Kinda in my direction." The tobacco chewer spit again. "That way. That's good. Two more steps. Now one more. Now don't move. Good. You take directions real good."

"Thank you," Dooley said.

The puny man leaned over in his saddle, and now managed to steady the .38 caliber Smith & Wesson. "Do I kill him now, Hubert?"

"No, Doc," Hubert Dobbs said. "Gunshot would draw a posse."

Which meant the sickly-looking man on the rangy pinto would be Doc Watson, the coldest and most vicious killer to ride with the Dobbs-Handley Gang.

"I can slit his throat," came a new voice behind Dooley Monahan.

"You could," Frank Handley said, "but Dooley Monahan rode with us. Maybe by accident. And maybe for just a few miles. But he rode with us. And we don't murder men who rode with us. It ain't in the code of the outlaw."

Dooley's heart skipped a beat. His mouth started to open to thank, to praise, Frank Handley.

Then everything went black.

CHAPTER THREE

Somewhere in the depths of dreams, delirium, or death, everything struck Dooley Monahan with perfect clarity. But that was the way things had been the past couple of years. When he was sleeping—and being clubbed over the head with a shotgun stock and left unconscious, not to mention for dead, on the far side of the Platte River, which was a form of sleeping—Dooley Monahan could think clearly and remember clearly. Awake, even after four cups of coffee, Dooley's mind tended to fog over.

"Thinkin'," the circuit-riding Methodist minister who rode and preached on the Des Moines–Corydon–Accord–Lamoni–New Virginia–Old Albany City loop had often told Dooley, "ain't your strong suit, son."

But he was asleep now—technically, unconscious—and he could remember. Everything.

"I should have told Hubert Dobbs that I once rode with Monty's Raiders," he muttered in words that would have been unintelligible had anyone other than a jackrabbit been around to hear him.

Riding with Monty's Raiders, of course, had been by accident, too.

Way back in 1850, when Dooley was but twenty years old, his pa, the now dearly departed David Monahan, had sent Dooley south to fetch a cow. The cow he had procured, but afterward he met some boys who seemed friendly enough but turned out to be part of Monty's Raiders. Of course, by then, Monty McHugh, who had formed the raiders, had given up robbing pig farmers and corn farmers in Iowa and had made a fortune selling soap to miners in Hangtown, California. But the new members of the gang, liking how Monty's Raiders sounded so gaily on one's tongue, had kept that handle.

The new Monty's Raiders put up with Dooley for a while, then knocked him senseless and left him for dead—much as the Dobbs-Handley boys had just done—and Dooley became a drifter, turned cowboy, and wound up playing poker in a bunkhouse in the Dakotas when he had gotten into an argument with Bob Smith.

Well, whiskey, and not blows to his noggin, fogged much of what happened, but the long and short of things said that Dooley Monahan put one bullet through the heart of Bob Smith, who, the law soon learned, was not Bob Smith but one Jason Baylor, who had posters on him planted inside every lawman's office between Missouri and Montana.

Then, in 1872, three years after Dooley had plugged Bob Smith né Jason Baylor, Dooley had drifted into the Arizona Territory, where he had found a newspaper article that told him he ought to be heading north. California? Or was it Alaska? Someplace like that. Dooley still had trouble remembering everything. Although he did remember why he was drifting. Jason Baylor had some family, and that family did not like having one of its own killed by a cowboy who nine times out of ten could not hit a barn door six feet away with no wind, no noise, and a fence post to rest his gun on. Between 1869 and 1872, Dooley had been carrying around the voucher the lawman had given him after Dooley had plugged Jason Baylor. All Dooley had to do was turn in the voucher at an accredited bank and he would be presented $500 in cash money. Enough for Dooley Monahan to make it to a booming gold town and strike a fortune. Dooley had been heading to that gold strike, as soon as he found a bank to cash in on his reward, and that's where he was going to when he camped one night in the Mogollon Rim—he could still smell those pines in that mountainous country—when he had first found that blue-eyed dog.

"Where are you, Blue?" Dooley muttered as he rolled over on the Nebraska plains. The rabbit did not hear him this time as the rabbit was desperately trying to avoid becoming a hawk's supper. The hawk did not hear Dooley, either.

The dog was one of those merle shepherds. No. No, merle was the color. That's right. Somewhere between blue and gray, with patches of black tossed about. White feet. White chest. And some copper spots on his legs, muzzle, and a couple of dots, also copper, over his eyes. An Arizona shepherd. Because Dooley had found the dog somewhere between Payson and Show Low. Had Dooley been in San Francisco, it would have been a California shepherd. Had he picked up Blue in Australia, it would have been an Australian shepherd. Had he been in Iowa, it wouldn't have been anything but a mutt, and, most likely, a mutt with the mange.

Blue had belonged to a family of settlers. Dooley remembered that. It caused a tear to run down his cheek as he rolled back over. Apaches had massacred the family. The blue dog was an orphan, so Dooley, after burying those awful bodies, had let the dog tag along with him. He was a good dog. Made Dooley feel like he really wasn't traveling alone.

So Dooley had been heading to Phoenix. Maybe Tucson. He didn't think it was Flagstaff, although it might have been Prescott. He ran into a sheriff named Carmichael who was traveling with a red-headed cowboy Dooley had worked with in Utah before he had even shot Smith/Baylor deader than dirt. Butch Sweeney was a kid, but a cowboy to ride the river with, and before Dooley really understood why, Butch Sweeney had been with him. So had a girl.

What the Sam Hill was her name?

It wasn't Sam Hill. Judith? No. Judas? Don't be silly. Jennifer. No. You were closer with Judith. Judy? Julie. That was it. Julie. No. No, it wasn't. Julia. Yes. Definitely. Julia. Julia Arizona, because he had met her in Arizona.

He laughed and rolled over, slid down the embankment closer to the Platte. Julia Arizona. That was a joke. She wasn't like some shepherd dog. In fact, now that things began clearing up a mite, he saw her face. She was a pretty girl. Maybe even beautiful or would be in a few years. Back then, Julia Cooperman—that was her name. Not Arizona.

Julia Cooperman, thirteen years old. Sweet. Spunky. But tortured. Pained. But a good kid.

And they had taken care of those other Baylor boys, too. So Dooley's $500 reward had turned out to be worth $1,625. In gold.

Which would have staked Dooley and Julia and Sweeney to a trip to Alaska, where they would make even more money.

So they had ridden from Phoenix all the way to San Francisco, California, with plans to board a packet and sail north to Alaska.

Yet something happened. He remembered rubbing General Grant's neck, then felt as if someone had just taken an axe and split his head clean in half. Dooley fell into that dark, dark void, and when he finally woke, to a splitting headache but at least his head remained intact, he couldn't remember much of anything. Including his name. That much he learned from his wallet, and he also realized he had more than $1,000 in cash. Whoever had clubbed him good had not been intent on robbing him. He knew his bay gelding was General, but General what? And he had no idea what the Sam Hill he was doing in San Francisco. In fact, the only reason he knew he was in San Francisco was because of so many signs in that big city saying it was San Francisco.

SAN FRANCISCO MORNING CALL

CAFÉ SAN FRANCISCO

SAN FRANCISCO'S BEST LIVERY

SAN FRANCISCO'S LARGEST WAGON YARD

SAN FRANCISCO'S GAUDIEST WHOREHOUSE

The dog, which at that moment he figured to be a California shepherd, seemed to be his. So Dooley Monahan mounted his horse and took his wealth and his merle dog and rode out of the big city by the bay and decided to head to Virginia City.

Obviously, the memories came back to him, by and by.

In Virginia City, for instance, he started saddling the horse in Virginia City's Best Livery Stable when he just said as he reached under the gelding's belly for the cinch . . . "Grant."

He blinked, brought the strap up, and blinked some more.

"Grant. General Grant. That's your name."

The bay gelding snorted and even seemed to nod its head in agreement.

Which told Dooley Monahan something else.

"I must be a Yankee."

Southerners, he knew, would not likely name their horse after Ulysses S. Grant.

If, indeed, he had named the horse General Grant after the Union Civil War hero and president—that's right, Grant was now president of these United States. He remembered that even before he saw an article in the *Virginia City Enterprise* that had a few choice comments about President Grant's policies and choices for political offices.

He lost $233.76 of his more than $1,000 at roulette and blackjack in Virginia City, so decided to take his shrinking fortune and his blue-eyed shepherd dog and bay gelding named after a Union war hero (and disaster of a president) toward Montana.

Somehow, he wound up in Cheyenne, Wyoming, instead.

By then he had begun to call the dog Blue, and the dog wagged his tail and the bay gelding nodded its head in agreement.

In Cheyenne, he heard a couple of cowboys brag in a saloon that they had lynched a damned old sodbuster. Dooley dropped his beer—half-full or half-empty, depending on your point of view—and said out loud, "Iowa."

At Fort Bridger, Wyoming, he had paid four dollars and thirty-five cents to a doctor, who had treated Dooley, given him a tincture of some medicine that tasted most foul but caused Dooley to sleep like a baby and gave him some of the wildest dreams. The doctor said that this amnesia—which was the word he used to describe Dooley's loss of memory—could end, could be permanent, and even could cause Dooley to die an early death of a stroke or aneurysm or suicide.

"But it doesn't appear to be that bad of a case," Dr. Smoker had said, and he smoked like the 2-4-0 locomotive on the railroad tracks nearby. "You remembered the dog's name. You remembered your horse's name. You assumed you are Dooley Monahan and that is likely correct."

"Assumed?" Dooley had asked.

"You could have stolen the wallet from the real Dooley Monahan."

"Nah." Dooley shook his head. "I think I'm Dooley Monahan."

"Why's that?"

"Who the hell would call himself Dooley Monahan if that wasn't his name?"

Dr. Smoker, between coughs, went on to say that various things would cause Dooley to regain most of his memory. And that's what happened.

In Cheyenne, he understood that he hailed from Iowa. The word *sodbuster* jogged that memory back into place, and Dooley remembered he was a farmer. So he rode back.

Other memories would come back to him—but some of those he didn't care to remember. Besides, he was sleeping right now—unconscious—and wondered if he would remember anything when he woke up. Right now, though, he didn't care if he ever woke up because he was having a mighty fine dream. And he had used up the last of that opium or whatever the sawbones had called it years ago.

It was the plump girl from Omaha. And Dooley had saved her life. And now she was showing proper respect by kissing him all over, and Dooley's hands were going to some places on her body that were plump where they should be plump and felt mighty fine. But then the plump blonde started licking his face. And she kept right on licking. Wet, sloppy licks from a tongue that felt like coarse leather. And Dooley had no choice but to open his eyes and say . . .

CHAPTER FOUR

"Damn you, Blue, stop licking me!"

He rolled away from the merle-colored dog, who was sopping wet, and shook his head. That was a mistake, he learned, as he lifted his body off the ground and vomited. Then his arms gave out, and he planted his face in the weeds and sand and everything his stomach had just purged.

Beside him, Blue whimpered.

Eventually, Dooley rolled over. He waited for the dizziness to pass, then wiped his face with his hand. Blue came over to help, and licked his face again. This time, Dooley did not complain.

"How'd you get here, Blue?" he asked the dog, who did not answer, but backed away a bit, shook more Platte River water off his body, and lay down, head up, staring at his master.

"Good boy." Dooley managed to smile, even though stretching his lips caused his head to ache.

After about an hour, or maybe a day, he managed to push himself to a seated position and looked across at the cranes and the coyotes along the far bank of the Platte. It was morning. He must have slept through the rest of yesterday and all of last night. Eventually, he lifted his left arm and tested the knot, about the size of a goose egg, on his head. Dried blood matted his hair, but at least the blood was dried. He wouldn't bleed to death.

He didn't know where his hat was, but figured he would find it when he climbed back up the bank. He moved his right hand toward his gun belt, surprised to find his shell belt but remembering that either Dobbs or Handley or maybe the pale Doc had ordered him to drop his Colt. Most likely, one of the outlaws had taken possession of that .45.

And General Grant?

Slowly, carefully, Dooley turned and looked up at the cloudless sky and the tall grass. He wet his lips, then tested his voice:

"General?"

No answer.

"General Grant?"

A crane flapped its wings.

"Horse?"

Well, he figured as much. The outlaw whose horse had gone lame had taken General Grant. And probably they had taken the lame horse with them a ways.

He checked his vest pocket where he found his pocketknife, his pocket watch, and even his billfold with thirty-two dollars and seventy-two cents in change. The robbers hadn't robbed him. Even better, they hadn't killed him.

In the last pocket on his vest, he fished out a piece of taffy and a hard bite of beef jerky. So he would not starve to death, at least for a little while, and he even had water from the river to wash down both the candy and the dried meat.

He returned the food to the bottom-left pocket. No sense, he told himself, in testing that stomach yet.

All in all, this morning was not as bad as he thought it could have been.

Well, he was horseless, but he did have his dog. He looked at the shepherd.

"How'd you find me, Blue?"

Silly question. Obviously, Blue had followed the outlaws from a distance. He had swum across the wide river. Dooley was horseless, but at least he had his dog back.

And his memory.

He smiled. He knew his name without having to check his wallet. He knew the dog's name. He remembered his horse's name. He could recall everything that had happened, except some parts of those wild dreams he had been having—but that was usually natural. Never had he been very good at remembering his dreams, especially when he had just awakened.

After about an hour, Dooley decided to stand. He weaved and staggered and even collapsed to his knees once, but eventually he reached the edge of the Platte. Lying on his belly, he reached out into the river and washed the vomit off his face and the blood out of his hair. He drank, and the stomach accepted the offering. His tongue reduced in size. Rolling over and sitting up, he soaked his boots in the cool water.

When he decided he could stand again, he did. He moved downstream a few yards and looked at the tracks in the sand. A posse must have crossed the river here, but turned back and recrossed the Platte.

Maybe the men decided to return home. He saw one stick that had been used for a torch. So they had come across the river at night. Dooley nodded, and surprised himself when he did not irritate his head or stomach.

"If they came at night, maybe that's why they didn't see me," he told Blue.

Blue wagged his tail.

He drank more water, a lot more water, and climbed up the bank to the general area where he had talked a bit to Hubert Dobbs and Frank Handley and had been buffaloed by a mean hombre from behind and left horseless on the far side of the Platte River.

Dooley looked across the river again.

"That posse," he told Blue, "crossed the Platte and almost immediately recrossed the river."

He rubbed his chin.

"Maybe that river's the boundary of their jurisdiction," he told Blue, who had lost interest in anything Dooley Monahan had to say. Dooley looked west. The grass had been pushed down by the horses of the bank robbers. Even Dooley Monahan could follow that trail, so certainly a posse from Omaha could have done it. But the lawmen had not. Another thought entered his head and came out of his mouth.

"Cowards."

Not that Dooley Monahan could blame them. He remembered reading that story in the *National Police Gazette* back on his farm that said Hubert Dobbs had personally murdered fifteen men; Frank Handley had gunned down at least twelve, plus two mules, a goat, and a Canadian; while Doc Watson had plugged five men with pistols, two with shotguns, one with a rifle, ten with knives, three with his bare hands, and one with a pitchfork. The article had not counted up the murders done by the other men who rode with the gang.

"Or," Dooley said, trying to say something nice about Nebraska and Nebraskans, which came hard for a man from Iowa, "it could be that they mistook the Platte for the Missouri." He nodded. "And if they thought this was the Missouri, that would mean that the outlaws were in Iowa, so they'd have to turn back."

He smiled. His head shook. He looked at Blue and said, "Even Nebraskans ain't that stupid."

After another minute, he said again, "Cowards."

Dooley found his hat, carefully knocked off the horse apple on the brim, and even more carefully placed it on top of his head. The sun had warmed up considerably since Blue had licked him back into the real world. So now Dooley Monahan had to make a decision.

He could walk back to Omaha. It would be a considerable hike in wet Wellington boots that would be even wetter because he would have to cross the Platte River to get there. Or . . .

Dooley gazed down the trail of bent grass.

Some no-account coward who rode with a bunch of murdering thieves had put a knot on his head and had taken, most likely, his Colt .45 and the best horse he had ever owned. And the men had left a trail a blind man could follow, at least for the time being. Dooley Monahan wasn't a lawman, or a gunman— even though he had had a bit of success with the latter—but nor would anyone ever call him a coward.

He reached into a vest pocket and brought out the

taffy, which he stuck in his mouth. The jerky he tossed to Blue, who gobbled it up without even tasting it. As he chewed and sucked, Dewey put his right foot in front of his left, and followed with the left in front of the right.

It made sense. After all, Dobbs, Handley, Doc Watson, and the boys were riding west. Dooley needed to go west at least for a spell, too. Eventually, he would have to turn north and find that gold strike in the Black Hills of Dakota Territory. He stopped, found the back pocket on his canvas trousers, and felt the newspaper clipping he still carried with him. The outlaws had not stolen that, either.

He walked. And Blue followed.

At first, the trail proved easy enough to follow— even if he didn't have bent and crumpled grass, and plenty of horse apples, to guide his way. Handley, Dobbs, Doc, and the others just rode along the Platte River. When it dipped south, they dipped south. When it bent to the north, they bent to the north.

For two or three days, Dooley Monahan and his shepherd dog walked along the banks of the Platte. Blue managed to catch a rabbit and devoured it, but Dooley had little to eat except the taffy that he had finished before he had traveled a hundred yards on the first day. On the second day, he found some quail eggs in a nest near the river and had eaten those raw. He had not gotten sick, either.

On the third day, however, the Platte River turned west, but the outlaws rode north. That meant Dooley would have to ford the wide river on foot. Or turn back like the cowardly posse had done and make his way back to Omaha. Or find another city.

He thought about that because by now his feet really ached. Wellington boots were not meant for walking across Nebraska. Probably, he later decided, he would have done just that, and then another thought came to him.

He could have gone back to Omaha three days earlier, bought a horse and saddle with the money the outlaws had not stolen, maybe even managed to buy a used pistol that would fire the .45 bullets in his shell belt. Then he could have gone chasing after Hubert Dobbs and his fellow horse thieves and scoundrels.

"Why," he asked Blue, "do I come up with better ideas after I've already implemented the stupid one?"

Blue walked to the bank.

"Yeah," Dooley said. He crossed the river. Everyone said the Platte could be a mile wide but rarely an inch deep. That wasn't quite the case, but never did the water reach above his knees.

It wasn't so much the anticipation, or the vague notion, of catching up to a bunch of riders on horseback that led Dooley and his dog to ford the wide river. It was the smoke.

CHAPTER FIVE

The smoke led Dooley and Blue to the sod house about two or three miles northwest of the Platte. The smoke wafted white and gray from a stovepipe that rose above the weeds that grew from the roof.

Dooley swallowed. He had always thought his farmhouse, which had been his parents' home before they had been called to Glory, was as hardscrabble as any place on the good earth until he saw this dirt home cut into a hill. A mule stood in a small corral near the small sod hut. An outhouse stood a few yards behind the corral. On the other side of the corral, Dooley spotted the well. Behind the sod house, some ground had been turned over, but most of the land around the farm—if you'd stretch your imagination and actually call this a farm—remained prairie. But Dooley kept walking, no longer drawn by the woodsmoke but the smell coming out of the open door in the little hill.

Salt pork frying in an iron skillet, mixed with the aroma of coffee boiling.

When he came about twenty yards from the doorway, Dooley stopped, swallowed, and whispered to his dog, "Sit."

Blue actually obeyed.

Dooley sucked in a deep breath, exhaled, and cupped his hands round his mouth.

"Halloooo the . . . uh . . . house," he called out. His throat ached. He tugged the holster on his hip toward his crotch, just so the farmer could see that Dooley was unarmed, and he spread both hands far away from his side, just so the farmer could see that Dooley meant no harm. Besides, after so many days walking across Nebraska, Dooley figured he must look pathetic. Even a Nebraska farmer would take pity on any critter that looked half as wretched as Dooley Monahan did right then.

A big man in dirty denim britches and a homespun shirt filled the doorway, studied Dooley, then Blue, and after a moment stepped into the light. His hands, like Dooley's, remained empty.

"Howdy," said the man. The greeting was country, American, Nebraskan, farmland, but the accent came from Europe. Norwegian, Dooley guessed. Or some such place.

Dooley lowered his hands and smiled. "Howdy," he returned. "My horse got stole a few days back."

The big farmer took another step and looked at his mule before he turned his big head back and locked his gray eyes again on Dooley.

"I'm not after your plow mule," Dooley said. "Just was hoping for some water for my dog and myself. Maybe some coffee. And . . . well . . . I have had one piece of taffy in three days."

The farmer waved his big hand.

"Come," he said. "I have plenty. Feed you. And dog. Good dog. Come."

Rancid bacon burned to a crisp so it wouldn't make a fellow sick, and coffee so strong it went down about like the bacon filled Dooley's stomach as he sat in a chair, a real chair, and stretched his boots out underneath the rickety table. The farmer, whose name was Ole Something-another-dorf, turned over a keg to use for his chair. Obviously, Mr. Something-another-dorf was a bachelor.

The big farmer listened as Dooley told him what had happened in Omaha, and why he was walking across eastern Nebraska. The man blinked but said nothing, and Dooley figured Ole Something-another-dorf had never heard of Hubert Dobbs, Frank Handley, Doc Watson, and maybe even Omaha. It was obvious the man did not read newspapers.

In fact, the man took pride in pointing out two things in his home, and neither was the blanket in the corner near the fireplace that served as his bed. One was a Bible, a lavish, leather-bound beauty that appeared to be twice the size of the Bible Dooley's mother had read. The other was what appeared to be a copy of the claim Ole the Farmer had gotten when he had filed for his 160 acres under the Homestead Act of 1862.

"Is there a town nearby?" Dooley asked.

The man made a vague gesture northwest, which was the opposite direction of Omaha.

"Dutch Bluff," he said.

"How far?" Dooley asked.

"Fifteen miles," Ole answered. "Maybe thirty."

"Oh." He wondered how far away he was from

Omaha. Maybe Ole the Farmer would offer to take him to Dutch Bluff in his . . . buckboard? Dooley had seen no sign of any wagon, any means of transportation, other than the mule.

Ole the Farmer, however, did not offer the loan of the mule, but he did pull from the water bucket near his smelly bedroll a jug, tore the cork out with his teeth, and handed the earthen container to Dooley.

Hospitality. If every Nebraskan showed this much cordiality, Dooley Monahan, as a native of Iowa just across the Missouri River, might have a higher opinion of the state. Of course, Ole wasn't really from Nebraska—was anybody, other than maybe some Pawnees and Poncas?—but he hung his hat here, and made some potent but quite tasty liquor made from potatoes. Or so Ole had told Dooley.

Over potato liquor, and potato bread, and peeled potatoes fried in bacon grease, and coffee, Ole and Dooley talked about this and that, farming and outlaws, Nebraska and Iowa, homesteading and the book of Genesis, which, turns out, was as far as Ole had gotten through that ornate Bible.

Dooley liked talking about his farm. A hundred acres in corn, forty in oats, forty in hay, thirty acres of cow pastures, and the rest for horses, the barn, the pigs, a garden, a well, a cistern, and a fishing pond. When he had been a young buck of right about twenty, he had owned half of that. Now that his mother, Janine, and father, David, were walking the Streets of Glory, it was all his. His parents, and a baby sister that never lived to see her first birthday, and an older brother taken by the croup or something when he was three years old, about two years before Dooley entered this world, were also sleeping their eternal sleep on his farm, on a hill that overlooked the cow pastures.

"You?" Big Ole leaned back on his bucket and stretched his powerful arms. "You leave farm . . . farm like . . . that?"

Dooley tried to focus on the big Norwegian. Liquor made from potatoes packed quite the wallop. "I didn't actually leave it."

The farmer studied Dooley. "Then . . . why . . . here . . . you be?"

Dooley smiled and slid his right hand into the trousers pocket on his hip. Carefully, he withdrew the clipping and held it across the table, careful not to let it fall into the bacon grease or dregs of coffee.

"Gold," he said. "A fortune. Just for the taking in the Black Hills."

The man did not touch the worn piece of paper, but did lean his head close to the eight-point type. Dooley didn't know if the man could read English. For all he knew, Ole's Bible was printed in Norwegian. But in about the time it would take most people to read the article of six paragraphs and six decks of headline, Ole leaned back and shrugged.

"And . . . farm?"

Dooley thought he understood what the Norwegian meant, and Dooley felt a little bit shamed. He hadn't meant to brag about those just a tad under two hundred acres north of Des Moines. After all, a farm that size was a dwarf compared to most of the neighbors Dooley had grown up around. Farming might have taken hold of Dooley had his father not sent him down toward Corydon to buy that Jersey cow and bring her home, but instead Dooley had become affixed to things like wandering and drifting and cowboying and chasing after gold.

"There was a blackberry patch," Dooley told Ole. "That was the best thing. But the blackberries were usually bitter."

The farmer nodded.

"It was hard work," Dooley began, but stopped. Hard work? Some dust drifted from Ole's roof and settled into Dooley's cup of potato whiskey.

"Didn't mean to be bragging," Dooley said. "It wasn't brag. It wasn't much of a farm, really, and I certainly wasn't cut out to be a farmer."

"No," the big man said. "You brag no. You talk of home just. Talk home . . . is . . . good thing. No?"

"I guess so." Dooley felt relaxed again. "I guess Iowa was my first home. And . . ." He started counting. Kansas. Arkansas. Texas. Kansas again. Texas again. Kansas again. New Mexico Territory. Colorado. Utah. Nevada. Utah again. Idaho. Montana. Dakota. Iowa. Kansas again. New Mexico again. Arizona Territory. And even a few stops, though usually just riding the grub line or helping mend or fix or chopping wood in California and Nevada again, and Wyoming, and Kansas again, and Arkansas once more, and back on the farm in Iowa. Now he was bound for the Black Hills of Dakota. He wouldn't count Nebraska as one of his homes, even if Mr. Something-another-dorf asked him to chop some firewood. There was no firewood to chop, unless one walked down to the Platte and happened to find some scrub. That might have explained why the coffee and the bacon and even the potatoes tasted slightly of dried buffalo droppings.

A lot of the money he had found on his person after he had lost his memory in San Francisco had gone to pay the back taxes he owed to the state of Iowa to get his farm out of receivership. He had wised up, though, after two years of farming almost two hundred acres. This time, he had offered Mr. Cahill and his twelve sons the opportunity to lease his farmland and take over his pig and cow operation, while Dooley was off to the Black Hills. They had shaken hands on it.

"I work . . . hard," Ole told Dooley.

"Farmers do," Dooley agreed, "but I don't think anyone I've ever met—especially not Mr. Cahill, because the littlest of his brood is barely smaller than an ox—works as hard as you do, Ole. Takes a lot of work to make a place like this go. It's going to be a fine farm one day."

"Fine now," said Ole. "Home it be."

Dooley laughed. "It is fine. And it is home now."

He took another slug of potato whiskey, all the while trying to think of how he would get to Omaha or Dutch Bluff. How he would ever catch up with Dobbs and Handley and that fine bay gelding named General Grant.

With a belly full of potato liquor, fried taters, fried bacon, and potato bread, Dooley Monahan slept soundly. Even Ole's deafening snores did not disturb his sleep. One typically slept well when he was fairly drunk and had spent the past three or more days walking in the Nebraska sun and Great Plains wind with nothing to eat but one bit of taffy candy and some quail eggs.

He did not dream that night, so that plump blonde from Omaha was not barking like a dog when he awakened. It was Blue that was barking, growling, backing up from the door the big farmer had left open to catch a breeze and cool off this furnace he called home. Dooley rolled off the dirt that was his bed onto more dirt that was the floor, and reached for the Colt that he did not have.

From the glowing embers in the fireplace, Dooley could just make out Blue, so while he could not see that the dog's hair shot out like bristles, he heard the dog barking again and scratching hard against the floor of dirt.

On his bed, Ole Something-another-dorf just snored.

Dooley carefully came to his feet, inched his way to the right side of the open door, and groped against the wall until he found Ole's grubbing hoe. That was the only weapon in the house.

"Come here," he said in a tight whisper, and Blue obeyed, dropping onto his belly at Dooley's feet.

Dooley listened, waited for Ole to stop snoring, and as soon as silence filled the sod hut, he strained toward the darkness. Someone . . . or some thing . . . was outside, clopping around. Ole resumed his snores. Dooley tensed, waited, and when Ole fell silent again, he listened. A second before Ole started sawing logs once more, Dooley caught something deep and throaty and natural. The snorting of a horse.

He picked up the hoe, and waited.

There wasn't anything he could do until the sky began to lighten and the sun started to rise.

"Hell," he said as he twisted the handle of the hoe in his hands. "When it gets full light, there still won't be nothing I can do."

CHAPTER SIX

Ole Something-another-dorf stared long and hard at Dooley and the grubbing hoe and shook his head when Dooley mentioned the clopping of the hooves in the pitch-blackness of night.

"Mule," Ole explained.

Dooley shook his head. "Not unless your mule got out of that corral. Listen."

Frowning, the big farmer bent forward toward the door that remained open. The mule brayed. Dooley nodded. "That come from your corral. Now listen . . ."

They waited. The horse snorted again, then clopped along a couple of steps, blew a long, loud fart, and began munching on the potato peels the farmer had dumped on the side of his sod home last night after supper.

"Ack," said Ole, and he stormed out of the house. Dooley quickly followed, holding the hoe like a war club, and Blue darted out between Dooley's legs, no longer growling, but yapping happily. The farmer stopped quickly, and stared, but said nothing. The dog danced around the horse.

Dooley lowered the grubbing hoe, and a moment later leaned it against the hillside that served as the farmer's south wall.

"General Grant," Dooley said, blinked his eyes, then wiped them, then even tested the subsiding knot on the top of his head.

The farmer turned back and studied Dooley with some suspicion.

"That's my horse," Dooley said.

Ole decided to reach for the grubbing hoe, just to play everything safe.

"I swear," Dooley said, "I don't know how he got here. Or how he found me. Or how he escaped from the Dobbs-Handley Gang."

The saddle—Dooley's saddle—lay askew, bringing the Navajo saddle blanket Dooley had won in a poker game near Fort Wingate over to the side, as well. A hard lope, and most likely the saddle would be hanging underneath the bay's belly. Dooley saw the shotgun's butt sticking out of the scabbard. Dooley's Winchester carbine was gone, and the butt of the shotgun had blood and hair on one corner.

Which is how Dooley determined that the man who had hit him from behind and dropped him to the grass a few days ago on the other side of the Platte River had used a shotgun's stock to almost shatter his skull.

Slowly Dooley withdrew the shotgun, and, seeing the fear in the farmer's eyes, he opened the breech, pulled out both shells—buckshot, twelve gauge—and slid those into the nearest vest pocket. After snapping the breech shut, he tossed the scattergun to Ole, who caught it and studied it.

That farmer was so big, the shotgun—a sawed-off Greener—resembled a toothpick.

"Take it easy, boy," Dooley whispered, to the horse and not the farmer. He went to work, removing the saddle and placing it in the sun and placing the blanket on top so it would dry out. The saddlebags he laid near the doorway. He led the horse to the corral, introduced General Grant to the mule, which he called "Mule," opened the gate, and brought the tired gelding to the trough. He rubbed down the animal, checked over his head and hoofs but saw no signs of abuse, removed the bridle, and left the corral.

Ole just stared at the empty Greener in his big hands.

"So . . . ?" Ole began.

"I don't know." He hoped the saddlebags might hold an answer. "How about some coffee while we sort out this puzzle?"

"Coffee." The big farmer leaned the empty shotgun against the hillside wall and went through the doorway first.

Inside, Dooley opened one of the bags, hoping he would find his spare clothes and shaving kit. He did. He also found his .45 Peacemaker, with all six chambers filled with bullets. Naturally, thinking about his own safety, he pushed out one bullet so the chamber would be under the hammer.

The big farmer stared hard as he began getting the fire going again.

"My pistol," Dooley said. He laid the Colt on the table and opened the other bag. That side should have held his grub and cookware, but he knew that wasn't the case because the handle of the skillet wasn't sticking out from the leather and the cup he used to make his one cup of coffee did not rattle. What he found inside, however, caused him to blink.

"Well," he said softly, and smiled. "I guess whoever stole my horse decided he didn't like my skillet and bacon and taste."

He dropped the saddlebags by his boots, wet his lips, and looked at the big farmer.

Dooley sighed. He couldn't lie.

"I don't know how much greenbacks there are in there, but it's a right smart of money," he said. He added, "I did not steal it."

"Greenbacks?" Ole asked.

"Money," Dooley explained. He reminded the Norwegian about the bank robbery in Omaha that had started all of this, including how Dooley had wound up outside Ole's front—only—door.

"But how horse here come?" Ole asked.

"That's the question, ain't it?" Dooley slid out from the chair and came over to the fireplace. "I think better with coffee in the morning," he said. "Don't you?"

With a wide grin, Ole Something-another-dorf poured Dooley Monahan a snootful.

Blue fell asleep at their feet, but Dooley couldn't blame the dog for that. That old shepherd had spent the whole night growling and barking—which never had shortened the farmer's sleep or stopped his snores—at the horse outside. Although Dooley wondered why the dog had not recognized the gelding's scent.

No matter, Dooley had been reunited with his horse.

"The way it might have happened," Dooley said after his second cup of coffee, "is that General Grant tossed his rider and took off back to find me."

Ole slurped, wiped his lips, and nodded.

"Smart horse."

"Smart indeed."

Dooley sipped, and thought some more.

"It wouldn't have taken that much brains, though," Dooley said. "Just backtrack his way here. Here?" He looked at the farmer. "Did you see a gang of riders come by here a few days ago? Riding hard? One man on a big black stallion? A real skinny gent, more cadaver than rider, on a pinto mustang? And a mean hombre—well, every mother's son of them is a mean hombre—on a buckskin mare? And I don't know how many other men on other mounts, but a lot of them. And one guy with a shotgun who was riding that there bay of mine?"

Ole did not have to think for more than a second.

"Sure. They ride. I wave. Not notice your horse, though. Much dust. Much dust. No wave back them men."

Dooley lowered his cup and stared with incredulity at the big man.

"Why didn't you mention that to me before?" he asked.

Ole did not answer. Because something else took his attention, and Dooley's, too. Blue woke up and began growling.

"Easy," Dooley said urgently. "Stay, Blue. Stay still and shut up."

A man in dirty clothes with a bandage over his right ear and a brown leather patch over his left eye stood inside the sod hut. He held the shotgun at his waist, those two cannonlike barrels trained in the general direction of Dooley Monahan and Ole Something-another-dorf.

"Nice of you to take care of my horse," the man said.

"My horse," Dooley said softly.

"I was plumb sure I bashed out your brains, mister," the man said. "You must have a skull harder than granite."

"It hurt," Dooley said.

Ole muttered something in Norwegian. It did not sound like anything from the Bible, even Genesis.

Dooley did not remember the man from the banks of the Platte River south of Omaha, but he knew he would never forget the man for the rest of his life. Of course, as he stared at the big barrels of the twelve-gauge, his life expectancy for another few minutes didn't look promising.

The man's face had been well chewed up with pellets from shotgun, blades of knives, knuckles, fingernails, and who knew what else. His black hat had been ripped a few times, too, and the brim hung limp over his big ear and the bandage covering where the other ear would have been. Dooley had seen junipers that weren't as twisted and misshapen as the man's nose. He wore black striped trousers and a blue shirt with the sleeves ripped off above the elbow to reveal his muscles. The boots the man wore, brown and rough, had been scratched up on the uppers as well as the feet, and his pants legs were coated with dirt, grime, grass, and cockleburs.

"The money?" the man said. "Where is it?"

"Saddlebags," Dooley told him, thinking that maybe the big man would let them live if he got the saddlebags and made off with the money. Dooley tilted his jaw toward the leather pouches.

The man did not let his eyes off either man, but backed away, still training the shotgun's barrels in the direction of his prisoner until he could see both the saddlebags and the men he held at bay.

It was hard to believe, but Dooley saw relief sweep across the man's face, and his eye—the one not covered by the patch—appeared to even tear up.

"Thank the good Lord!" the man said, and let out a breath of utter relief. He stepped toward the bags, keeping his eyes and shotgun on the prisoners, grabbed the saddlebags, and tossed them out the door. Then, looking relaxed and confident, he studied Ole, Dooley, and the blue-eyed shepherd.

"Mister," Dooley said, "what happened?"

"That danged horse threw me," he cried out, no longer looking relieved but speaking as a man who had been beaten up by life and was ready to take revenge on anyone who happened to be close enough to kill. "Took off. Took off with half the money we took in Dutch Bluff."

"Do you mean Omaha?" Dooley asked.

"I mean Dutch Bluff, you ignorant fool. We robbed it yesterday."

Ole blinked and said, "Money much they have at Dutch Bluff bank?"

The one-eyed man stared in disbelief, trying to

rearrange the words and grasp what the Norwegian had just said.

"Yeah," he finally answered.

He straightened. "So Dobbs sends me back to fetch the money. Says if I ain't back with what I lost, he'll kill Artie."

"Artie?" Dooley asked. He kept thinking: *Keep this guy talking and you have a chance. When he stops talking, he'll kill the both of us. And most likely Blue, too.*

"My brother, you ignorant sodbuster!"

Dooley tried to think of something else to say, but couldn't. Luckily, Ole had something to add to the conversation.

"Man threaten brother. Boss you like?"

"No," the big man snapped. "No, I don't like Dobbs. I don't like Handley, either. Doc, well, he ain't that bad unless he's in his cups and cutting off some hombre's head. Hell, I don't even like Artie that much, but he's my brother."

The big man shook his head, waited a moment, and then said, "Dobbs wouldn't even let me take a horse. Made me walk."

And that got Dooley mad. "You walk fifteen or thirty miles in a day. Mister, I had to walk four days to get here. That's right, mister, I've been chasing you. Nobody steals my horse and bashes in my head. I'm glad my horse threw you. I'm glad General Grant came back here. And I'm most glad that you got sent here. Because now I'm going to tear you from limb to limb."

The man with the eye patch didn't even consider the big farmer. He swung both barrels at Dooley Monahan and squeezed both triggers.

CHAPTER SEVEN

Click.

Both hammers fell simultaneously, making one sound that soon was drowned out by the roar of the man with the eye patch.

At that moment, the outlaw started to put one hand behind his back, stopped, and quickly reached for Dooley's Colt that still lay on the table. Dooley, Ole, and Blue raced to stop him.

It had been a gamble, of course. Dooley knew he had unloaded the sawed-off twelve-gauge, but for all he knew, the man with the eye patch and brutalized face had filled the twin barrels with fresh loads of double-ought buckshot. Dooley figured it was a bet worth making. It was his only chance to get out of this fix alive.

The dugout was small, but the big brute reached the table well before Dooley or the Norwegian. Keeping the empty scattergun in his left hand, he picked up the Colt with his right, slipping a finger—missing the top joint—into the trigger guard while his thumb began pulling back on the .45's hammer. The gun came up, and as the brute turned around, Blue's teeth clamped onto the man's wrist.

"Arrgghhhhh!!" he roared, and the Colt .45 dropped onto the table, which overturned, kicking up a cloud of dust from the dirt floor.

His left arm rose, intent on braining the shepherd with the stock of the shotgun. That's when Ole and Dooley slammed into the outlaw.

Dooley took the man low. The giant farmer took him high. The man grunted, Blue let go of his arm, and the dog disappeared in the dust. That happened in a second. Then they slammed into the wall, sending mounds of dirt cascading like a Rocky Mountain waterfall.

The farmer's home turned into choking torture. Dooley came up, but had to use both fists to push the dirt and grime from his eyes. A second later, he felt the big outlaw's boot smash into his chest. The blow sent him backward, crashing over the farmer's chair, rolling to the wall. He hit it hard, causing more dirt to rain from the ceiling.

Up he came, now spitting out dirt. Somewhere in the swirling dust, he heard Blue's growls, and curses, grunts, and punches from Ole and the badman.

Dooley stepped out of the falling dust and charged into the cloud. It hurt to breathe. A fist grazed his cheek, but Dooley responded. He made contact with flesh and bone, pulled back. That boot found him again, and he landed, rolled over the dog, who cried out, and darted into the debris. Ole cried out in pain, but Dooley couldn't see the man. He couldn't see anything but falling dirt and clouds of dust. Dooley charged into the maelstrom, lowered his shoulder, and—though he saw nothing—knew he had slammed into the outlaw's gut. It had to be the outlaw. He didn't smell like a farmer.

He braced himself for impact against the wall and figured he would most likely be buried alive with Blue and Ole and that scoundrel, but to his surprise he kept going and going. He no longer felt so hot, so dirty, and the air turned fresher. He could breathe, and his eyes, though burning from the dirt and debris, seemed to find daylight. He felt the wind, too. Then he landed. The outlaw grunted, and Dooley rolled off. He scrambled to his feet. His lungs worked hard, taking in the fresh air, and tears washed dirt from his eyes. Dooley couldn't see clearly, but he saw well enough.

The outlaw stood, coming to his feet, coughing, and wheezing, before he straightened. Dooley heard something and saw the big farmer crawling out of the dugout, which appeared to be collapsing. When the big Norwegian pulled himself to his feet and leaned against the hill, dust bellowed out of the shrinking opening like smoke from a horrid house fire. Dooley grimaced, but felt relief when Blue darted from the tumult.

Dirt coated the shepherd so much he no longer looked blue, but the dog did not bother to shake off any grime. Instead, he growled and began approaching the outlaw.

"Blue," Dooley said softly, and coughed. The dog stopped.

"Stay."

The merle-colored dog obeyed.

Wetting his lips, Dooley tried to think of what he

should do. This appeared to be a stalemate. No weapons to speak of. Dooley's Colt was by now buried under about five hundred pounds of dirt inside what had been that farmer's home.

"Take your money," Dooley said. "That's what you come for. Take your money . . . and go."

The man brought his left hand to his mouth and wiped the dirt from his bloodied lips.

"And the horse?"

Dooley considered this, and it didn't take him long.

"Take General Grant, too," he said. The dog, as if he understood English, turned toward Dooley and uttered a little whimper.

"It's all right," Dooley told Blue, although the words were more for Dooley Monahan than that dog. He told himself, mentally, that if General Grant was smart enough to buck off that beast of a killer and make his way back to find Dooley once, well, he certainly could do it again.

"Take the horse," Dooley said. "Take your money. Just leave us be."

Everything might have worked out. But the roof caved in, and the door exploded out of the opening, and Ole Something-another-dorf let out a roar as he turned around, backed up a few paces, and watched his home destroyed. Then the big man turned savagely and charged the outlaw with the eye patch, scooping up the grubbing hoe that had been knocked into the yard as he moved.

He moved gracefully for such a big, powerful farmer.

"No!" Dooley shouted.

Blue jumped out of the farmer's way and looked at Dooley for some command, but Dooley was already running. Out of the corner of his eye, Dooley saw Blue charging, too. He also spotted the outlaw as the big cur reached behind his back, and knew the man most likely had a revolver tucked inside his waistband. He remembered seeing the man make a move behind his back before, most likely deciding that Dooley's .45 Colt on the table would be easier to reach.

The pistol the man grabbed and brought up in his giant right hand was ancient.

No wonder, Dooley thought later, he wanted my gun instead of his.

Right then, Dooley did not get that good of a look at it, but it was an old Smith & Wesson rimfire, with a five-inch barrel and no trigger guard. He lowered his shoulder, but knew he had no chance of reaching the one-eyed killer before a bullet was fired.

In fights like these, where a man has to kill to stay alive, things happen, and once you try to sort through why they happened, you might go crazy. The outlaw had to make a choice, and the big man with the eye patch chose to shoot Ole first.

Which probably made sense. He was the biggest of the attackers, and the closest, and probably looked the most dangerous, although he had already felt Blue's fangs.

A big thumb cocked the hammer, and a massive finger squeezed the tiny trigger. Dooley heard the .32's pop, but didn't see Ole go down. By then, the outlaw was turning, ducking to one knee, bringing up his free hand to fan back the Smith & Wesson's hammer. He was aiming at Dooley when Blue's teeth ripped into the man's flesh. That was a glancing blow, for the man cursed, turned, dropped the pistol, and sent Blue sailing toward the prairie Ole Something-another-dorf was trying to turn into a wheat field. Or potato patch.

Then Dooley slammed into the big beast and knocked him onto his back. Dooley rolled off, came to his feet, and caught just a glimpse of Ole, the big Norwegian farmer. What he saw enraged Dooley into anger he had never felt.

Dooley stepped toward the one-eyed outlaw, who also had sprung quickly to his feet. Dooley side-stepped the man's left and sent a right fist into the man's nose.

Blood spurted and cartilage gave way. The already twisted nose became even more crooked, and the man gasped like a girl and staggered back. Dooley hit him again, twice, a left that broke some of the man's teeth, and a right that glanced that bloodied ear.

Dooley kept coming, fists into the man's head. The man staggered back, grunting, turning his head right and left, sending blood and saliva sailing. When he finally brought up his arms to shelter his bloodied face, Dooley went to work on the man's ribs, his stomach, and he was even so angry, he stopped just long enough to kick the man in the balls.

Cowboying all those years had made Dooley tough, wiry, and determined, but the past two years he had spent on the farm—forking hay, pushing a plow behind a mule, carrying sacks of grain and corn, and sweating in Iowa from sunup to sundown—had made Dooley Monahan stronger than even Ole, and especially stronger than a miserable swine like this fellow with the patch over one eye, who was too lazy to work for an honest man's dollar.

Somewhere behind Dooley, Blue barked out encouragement.

The kick to the groin brought something out of the outlaw, something menacing and brutal. As the big man came up, lowering his arms, Dooley slammed two rights into the man's face, an uppercut left to the jaw, and another right that glanced off the man's shoulder. Then that big fellow swung a fist that sent Dooley sailing. He landed on his back, rolled over, but got only to his knees when the man's fist caught him again. Dooley went down, rolled over, and kept rolling because he glimpsed the man jumping up, trying to land on Dooley with all his weight. A blow like that would have crushed Dooley's spine into splinters and dust. But the man landed hard, too hard, and fell to his knees. Dooley took that advantage to climb to his feet.

His lungs ached as his chest heaved. Sweat poured from his forehead, and he blinked away the salty water that burned his eyes. He tasted blood. His nose was busted, but he had to think he looked better than the big man.

This would be something like the end of the first round of a boxing match between a couple of pugilists who had never heard of those Queensberry rules or whatever they were called. Both men sucked in oxygen, deeply, holding it, blowing it out of their mouths, staring at each other with pure hatred.

Blue barked encouragement.

Dooley straightened when the big man began

walking toward him. Then he saw the man scramble and pick up that grubbing hoe.

This was Nebraska, and Dooley knew what a grubbing hoe could do to a person. He had heard a fellow over in North Platte some years back say that Wild Bill Hickok had not killed Dave McCanles at Rock Creek Station with a pistol. The man had even sworn that there never had been a McCanles gang and that Wild Bill had shot most of the people from ambush. He had said it was basically a fight over a strumpet, and the strumpet had picked up a grubbing hoe and finished off Dave McCanles.

Dooley dived to his left, catching another glimpse of poor Ole, and he landed short of the Smith & Wesson .32., but Blue was charging again, ducking underneath the swinging hoe, landing and tumbling in the dust. The man righted himself and brought up the hoe, prepared to swing it like an axe and cleave in Dooley's head.

But the .32 was in Dooley's hands by then, and he was ready. The rimfire pistol bucked, and Dooley's mind flashed back to Cheyenne, Wyoming.

CHAPTER EIGHT

That night in Cheyenne was when his memory came back.

Saloons, gambling parlors, and brothels still crowded Fifteenth Street in the territorial capital. That's the way things had always been—ever since the Union Pacific laid down its first iron rails and pitched its first tents—and that's how things, everyone in Cheyenne said, would always be.

Fifteenth Street was crowded that night when Dooley rode from his hotel after supper to find a friendly game of poker. Every now and then, his head would ache from where the man had clobbered him in San Francisco and shortchanged his memory, but he knew one thing for certain about this here Dooley Monahan that he was supposed to be.

Dooley Monahan liked poker. He understood the game pretty well, and he didn't even need to bury his nose in one of Hoyle's books explaining all the rules and all the types of poker, and other games of chance played with fifty-two cards.

Dooley had outfitted himself since San Francisco.

He carried a short-barreled Colt in .44-40 caliber—the same shells would also fit in his Winchester carbine—and had bought a fine new pair of boots in Boise, some good duds in Bozeman, Montana—gray-striped britches and a matching vest with a black string tie—and now wore a new blue silk shirt that he had bought in Cheyenne, along with a new gray hat with a pinched crown and satin headband. He had a stomach full of elk steak, beans, potatoes, and corn bread, with a slice of vinegar pie for dessert. He had capped off his supper with a snifter of brandy.

Now he had a mind for a relaxing night of cards.

The place he chose was Vanwy's Gaming House. Stenciled in the big window facing Fifteenth Street, cursive letters proclaimed:

> ### Honest Dealer
> *A Fair Chance*
> *—Pretty Ladies—*
> *Watch 'em Dance*

That's not why he chose Vanwy's establishment. This was Saturday night in Cheyenne, and the only open spot he found anywhere on Fifteenth Street was at the rail in front of that gaming house. He squeezed between a sorrel and a dun, looped the reins over the rail, which he ducked underneath.

"I'll be out in a jiffy," he told General Grant. "With enough money to get us to Alaska."

He stepped onto the boardwalk, put a hand on one of the batwing doors, and paused, turned back toward the bay gelding, and asked out loud. "Alaska?"

What did he mean by that?

A bald man with whiskey on his breath grunted angrily, and Dooley turned back toward the saloon, saw the bald man with whiskey on his breath, and stepped aside to let the man stagger out onto the boardwalk and weave his way toward oblivion.

Dooley pushed back his new gray hat and stepped through the batwing doors, stopping to take in the scene. It was crowded, and the spinning of roulette wheels and the rolling of dice on felt made him smile. Music pounded away from the corner, and he saw three girls, scantily dressed, doing the cancan. Glasses clinked, whiskey poured, and the place smelled of bourbon and cigars. He squeezed through a crowd of railroaders and made his way to the bar.

Luck was with him. Just when he reached the end, a woman led a cowboy away toward the stairs, and Dooley made his way to the opening before a man in a bowler hat could get there. The bartender, with a thick gray mustache, was already waiting.

"Whiskey," Dooley said.

The bartender kept waiting.

Dooley pulled out a coin and slapped it on the bar.

The coin disappeared, a shot glass took its place, and a moment later amber liquid splashed into the container.

Dooley smiled and lifted the glass in a toast, but the bartender had already moved down to another customer. Dooley sipped the whiskey.

Eventually, he found his way to the poker layouts, but had to wait through one more whiskey and half a mug of beer before one of the games opened up. Dooley managed to find a seat between the house dealer and a woman in a red dress. A bearded cuss in buckskins, a stringy-haired man with a yellow brocade vest, and a man with a vaguely familiar face—appeared to be a cowpuncher—filled out the game.

The man in buckskins left after two more rounds, and no one took his place. Dooley took advantage of the break in action to ask the saloon girl—she had been one of those cancanning when he first entered this joint—for a new beer.

"If you gents, and you, Miss Stephenson, don't mind," the dealer said, "I'm going to take this moment to pee."

The woman in red did not even blush.

"Good idea," said the man with the stringy hair. "I'll go fetch me another whiskey."

The cowpuncher leaned over, crushed out his cigarette, and studied Dooley hard. "You look familiar."

"So do you," Dooley said.

"Ever worked in Arizona?" the cowhand asked.

"I don't know," Dooley said.

Which pretty much ended that conversation, and the woman in red stared at Dooley as if he were a simpleton.

"Got hit in the head," Dooley told her.

She nodded as if she understood, waited for the dealer and the man with the stringy hair to return, before she rose, collected her chips and cash and the man in buckskins' Crow scalp, and said, "I'm turning in, too, Dave. Nice game, boys. Good luck."

A tiny man who spoke with a French accent replaced her seat. As soon as he sat, Frenchy said, "Perhaps the luck of this chair shall continue with me instead of Miss Stephenson."

It didn't. Luck moved to Dooley's seat.

Two hours later, as the clock chimed midnight—early for Cheyenne's gambling element—the familiar-looking cowboy took the jack of spades, stringy hair the three of spades, Frenchy the eight of clubs, Dooley the eight of hearts, and the dealer the queen of spades.

The dealer bet five dollars. Everyone, even stringy hair with his lousy three, even Frenchy with his eight, even Dooley with an eight despite another eight already showing, saw the bet. At least nobody raised, although Dooley considered it. He had the ace of spades in the hole.

The game was five-card stud. "Manly poker," Miss Stephenson had said. "For manly men. And a girl like me."

The cowboy got the three of diamonds, which caused stringy hair to groan, and groan even more when his card turned out to be the four of spades. That told Dooley that stringy hair wasn't going for a straight and maybe had a pair of threes. Frenchy got a king of spades. Dooley took the ace of diamonds, but his eyes and face revealed nothing. The dealer dealt himself the two of hearts, which made Dooley think that maybe Vanwy's did offer honest poker.

Dooley bet ten dollars. The dealer, even though he was playing with Mr. Vanwy's money, folded. The cowboy stayed in. So did the man with stringy hair, who maybe was looking at a straight. Frenchy looked again at his hole card and sighed as he pushed in a $10 gold piece.

The hand continued. The cowboy got a three, which gave him a pair. Stringy hair took a two of clubs—straight still possible, but no longer a flush—

but Frenchy took the cowboy's three—clubs—and Dooley landed the eight of clubs. Two pair. He didn't think stringy hair was going for a straight—for he had made some noise when the cowboy had taken a three earlier in the game. All the threes were out, so the cowboy could not beat Dooley's two pair. He didn't know why Frenchy remained in the game.

One more round of cards.

The cowboy got the jack of diamonds. Which changed a few things in Dooley's mind. If that familiar face had a jack in the hole, Dooley might be in trouble. Stringy hair landed the two of diamonds, which could also turn his game around if he had a two in the hole. Frenchy was dealt an absolutely worthless four of diamonds. He would stay in the game only if he were an utter fool. Dooley waited, reached for his beer as if he had no worries in the world, and swallowed as the dealer showed him the ace of clubs.

"You're high," the dealer said.

Dooley smiled good-naturedly at the other smiling faces. He thought: *How did I learn to play poker?* Dooley bet twenty-five dollars. The cowboy matched, and raised fifty. Stringy hair folded. Frenchy, showing he was no fool, did the same.

With a sigh, Dooley called the cowboy's bet and raised fifty dollars. And when the cowboy reached for the leather poke in his vest, Dooley said softly, "You don't want to do that, mister. I have you beat. Trust me."

The cowboy swore, and raised Dooley another fifty. This time, Dooley called.

"You show," the dealer told him.

Slowly, Dooley turned over the ace of spades, his hole card.

The cowboy swore bitterly and shoved his losing hand—probably a full house, jacks over threes—but Dooley never saw the hole card.

"You did get the lady's luck, sir," said Frenchy.

"I guess so," Dooley said, "but I've had enough. I'll leave her luck with one of you guys." He rose. So did the cowboy, whose right hand dropped near his belted revolver.

Stringy hair and Frenchy slid their chairs back. The dealer gathered the cards and gave the cowhand a familiar stare.

"Mister," he said icily, "we won't brook no trouble here. That was an honest game, and the man here, he won honestly."

"I ain't saying he cheated," the cowhand said. "I just want to know his name. I know I know this fellow."

"Mister," the dealer said softly, "if you want to tell this man your name, that's fine by me. And if you don't, that's fine by me, too. This is the West. Your name's your business."

Dooley, of course, saw nothing wrong with saying his name. And if that cowboy with his hand hovering over the ivory grips of a Colt knew him, maybe he could tell Dooley something about Dooley that Dooley did not know about himself—which was a lot.

"My name's Dooley," Dooley said. "Dooley Monahan."

The man stepped back, shoving against a man in a plaid sack suit, who was playing poker at the next table. "Dooley . . ." The word came out like a gasp. "Dooley . . . Monahan."

"Yeah," Dooley said, and could not contain his excitement. This cowhand did know him.

"You . . ." The cowhand's face turned white, then his eyes narrowed, and he straightened, before dropping into a gunfighter's crouch.

Which caused Dooley to think: *How do I know that's a gunfighter's crouch?*

"You the same Dooley Monahan who killed all the Baylor boys?"

Dooley answered honestly. "I don't know."

That's when the cowboy said, "They was cousins of mine." And if that were not enough reason. "*First* cousins."

At that moment, the dealer, Frenchy, the man with the stringy hair, a cancan girl who saw what was happening, the man with the sack suit at the opposite table, and just about everyone in Vanwy's Gaming House were diving to the floor. All except Dooley Monahan and Jason Baylor's first cousin.

The Colt leaped into Dooley's hand, and he was firing. He didn't have to be a good shot—not at that distance. All he had to do was keep fanning the hammer and keep his finger pressed tight against the trigger.

CHAPTER NINE

All I have to do, Dooley told himself, is keep fanning the hammer, *and keep my finger pressed tightly against the trigger.*

He was on the ground on the Nebraska homestead.

The first shot caught the man with the eye patch square in the chest. The second just an inch below. A .32 caliber slug isn't the strongest chunk of lead, but it did the job. The man staggered back, and Dooley, thinking about Doug Wheatlock—first cousin to the Baylors—but mostly thinking of Ole Something-another-dorf, came up and kept shooting the rimfire pistol.

In the dust, and through the white stinking cloud of gun smoke, Dooley kept firing. He saw the bullet turn the big brute around, then saw blood spurt from the man's back, and then the man was gone. He just disappeared. But Dooley fanned the hammer and kept his finger on the trigger. Even when the hammer was landing on empty cylinders, even when the flesh of Dooley's hand was bleeding from fanning that sharp piece of iron that causes a gun to shoot. He kept dry-firing until he heard Blue's whimper.

Then reason took a firm hold on Dooley, and he stopped.

He remembered shooting Doug Wheatlock to death in that saloon and gambling den on Fifteenth Street in Cheyenne. Which had triggered—a bad pun, he knew—that flood of memories. Butch Sweeney and young Julia, Buckshot Bob and George Miller—and all of those damned Baylors—and even the Dew Drop Inn in San Francisco and the want, the need, to go to Alaska. He had even remembered Des Moines and Corydon and Monty's Raiders and he remembered and cried over David and Janine Monahan, his loving parents.

Everything.

He remembered everything now.

Dropping the burning hot, smoking Smith & Wesson in the dirt, he clasped his bleeding hand and stared at the emptiness. Blue charged to him, jumping up and down, whimpering, and Dooley said, "It's all right, Blue."

He saw the well, but did not see the one-eyed murdering robber. He blinked, and finally he understood. That last bullet had sent the killer into the well. Vaguely, he even thought he had heard the splash of water as the dead man hit—but that had to be his imagination, for his ears still rang.

"Blue." Dooley turned, pulled the bandanna off his neck, and wrapped it around his bleeding hand, wrapped it tightly, and then he was hurrying to the farmer, Ole from Norway—or somewhere. Dooley saw the big man lying in the dirt. He stopped, fell to his knees, brought his fists to his eyes, and cried without shame.

The blue-eyed dog whimpered, until Dooley lowered his hands and rubbed the dog's dirty coat of matted hair. "It's all right, Blue. It's all right." He made himself stand and walked over to the big, kind farmer.

The outlaw's bullet had caught Ole in the throat. Maybe the bullet had shattered the man's neck, Dooley thought, maybe death had been quick. Blood flooded the ground all around the dead farmer, and Nebraska's soil quickly soaked up the sticky moisture. It was already congealing and blackening in Ole's throat, and had poured out of his mouth. He had bled from his nose, and, naturally, from the hole in his throat.

The poor immigrant's eyes remained open, staring at the harsh sky. Dooley slowly put his fingertips on the lids and closed the eyes.

His body began aching as he pushed himself to his feet. Muscles screaming, the scratches and cuts the brutal outlaw had inflicted burning, his body tensing over everything he had endured, but Dooley Monahan knew he had a job to do, though it was not one that he really wanted to do.

Apparently, the now-dead outlaw in the well had not lied. Dobbs or Handley had made him walk to find the money and General Grant. It made no sense to Dooley, because even though he had not counted what was in the saddlebags, it seemed like a whole lot of money.

If I had robbed a bank, he said to himself, *I would have sent some men on horseback after a runaway horse.*

But . . . He had reached the dugout.

"I ain't an outlaw," he said, this time, out loud.

He did find two canteens, which the man with the eye patch must have brought with him. Dooley shook one container, then the other. One was full, the other maybe a quarter full. He unscrewed both tops and sniffed. Water. Not whiskey. That was a good thing, because there was no way in hell he planned on drinking from that well.

He could not remember seeing any spade, shovel, or posthole diggers—anything of that nature—inside the farmer's home. But a farmer needed something more than a grubbing hoe.

He went to the corral. The mule looked skittish. Dooley figured his face wasn't the most comforting sight to anything, man or beast, right then. General Grant came up to the poles, and Dooley reached over with his hand that was not bandaged with the bandanna and rubbed the bay's neck.

The plow he found on the other side of the corral. He walked up the hill to where the roof had collapsed inside the dead Ole's home. He looked down and shook his head. It would take a man days to dig through that earth if he had a shovel, and all Dooley had were two hands and a grubbing hoe. From here, Dooley had a fair view of the land, but no toolshed, no barn, nothing could be seen.

Well, maybe Ole Something-another-dorf had not been much of a farmer.

Cellar? Potato bin? Dooley saw nothing. The only place he had not looked inside was the privy. And, come to think of it, Dooley's kidneys and bowels began strong suggestions that it was time.

Which is where he found the shovel. Some magazines. A pencil. An axe. A woolen blanket. A ball-peen hammer. An empty tin cup filled with rusty nails. Even two sacks of potatoes, which made Dooley a bit nauseous when he remembered all those potatoes Ole had fried.

He knew one thing. If the gold in the Black Hills did not pan out, Dooley would return to his farm near Des Moines and understand that he would never move to Nebraska to farm. On the other hand, he had told himself that he was done with the West after he had gunned down Jason Baylor's first cousin, and here he was, back in the lawless frontier again. It was a hard land.

The dirt was hard. The sun was hot. The wind was bitter.

It took him well into the afternoon before he had the grave deep enough. Slowly, he then rolled poor Ole onto the scratchy blanket he had fetched out of the outhouse. Even more slowly did he drag the body on the blanket to the shaded side of the house where Dooley had dug the grave.

By the time he had Ole there, Dooley had to stop to drink from the canteen. The water was tepid, brackish, but it slaked his thirst and gave Dooley enough energy to drag the dead farmer into the grave. Dooley climbed into the grave and struggled, but finally managed to roll Ole over so he would be looking up, not down. You only buried bad men facing down—so they'd have a good look at where they were going. Carefully, he covered the dead man's body with the blanket and pulled himself out of the grave.

Blue, that loyal dog, knelt at the side of the grave and whimpered appropriately.

A horse. A mule. A dog. A stranger.

It seemed like any man deserved more at his funeral. Dooley stood, trying to think of words, but none came. So he sighed, whispered, "Amen," and began shoveling the Nebraska sod onto poor Ole something-another-dorf.

From the outhouse, Dooley tore off a chunk of wood. Thought about what else he should do, and used the axe to knock off another. He brought the nicest piece and laid it beside Ole's grave. The other, he brought to the well. Then he knelt by the well, pulled out his pocketknife, and began carving. It was crude, but Dooley felt reasonably sure that he had spelled everything correctly. Using the hammer and two nails that he had fetched from the outhouse, he secured his signpost on the side of the well. Just to make sure no one would be tempted, he removed the well bucket and tossed it inside the opening. The splash was muted, probably by the dead outlaw's floating body.

Dooley stepped back, and pitched the hammer to the ground.

POISON WATER
(DEAD VARMINT
IN WELL)

It was more than an evil killer like that brute with the eye patch deserved, but Dooley had not done that for him. He had done that to save any passerby from some horrible sickness one got by drinking foul water.

He spent more time on the next chunk of wood.

When he finished, he folded the pocketknife and slid it back into a vest pocket, then placed it at the head of the grave, and secured that with a few stones.

Ole
Farmer
R I P

Sure, it wasn't fancy, and maybe the sign he had nailed on the well was more important, but the letters were even, and he had carved them wider and deeper into the wood so that the tombstone might last longer. He rose, looked at his handiwork, and the words that he could not think of earlier finally came to him.

"You were a good man, Ole." Dooley wasn't about to butcher the man's last name, so he let the first name do. He looked across the homestead. "I bet, had God granted you a little more time on our earth, at this here farm, you would have turned it into a really good place. I appreciate all you did for me, and am sorry you got killed. I hope it wasn't on my account. I mean, like as not, that fool killer would have stopped here anyway—if just to steal your mule. I'm sorry I couldn't do much better for a headstone, or a grave, but this is the West. You know that. Life's hard. Dying's hard. But you're in a better place now, and I have to think our good Lord's welcoming you home now. You're in peace. That's a good place to be." He smiled. "I bet Saint Peter enjoys a nip of potato hooch, too. But I bet it isn't anywhere near as good as yours."

Blue began growling, but Dooley paid little attention. He felt worn out, and the merle-colored shepherd often growled at spiders and snakes and grasshoppers. Dooley heard no horse, or horses, or metallic sounds of guns being cocked.

"Shut up, Blue," he said, "and show some respect for the dead."

The wind felt cool on his neck as he stood over Ole's grave. He looked to the west and saw the sun beginning to disappear. Dusk, but he saw no reason to stay here. The mule brayed, and Dooley looked toward the corral.

"Yeah," he said, "I reckon I'll have to take you with us. Not much to pack, though." He thought that maybe he could buy some more grub and things he'd need for the trail to the Black Hills, but quickly rejected that. This wasn't his mule. He was no thief.

Blue still growled.

"I'll leave you at the sheriff's or the marshal's or whatever law they have in Dutch Bluff," he told the mule. "If they have any lawman in that town. If I can find that town." He turned toward the saddlebags. "And I'll take the money back to the bank." He wet his chapped lips. "Then I'll be on my way."

The plan satisfied him. Honest. And Dutch Bluff appeared to be in the general direction of the trail he would take to the Black Hills. He had his horse back. He had his dog. He had his life. Which made him look again at Ole's grave.

Blue stopped growling.

"It could've been the other way around, Ole," he said. "I'm real sorry it was you. Hope you believe me."

Now Blue began barking, and not a friendly bark. The hair stood up on the dog's dirty neck, and the loyal dog bristled, backed up, barked some more.

Then he heard something else. General Grant's whinny, which was answered by another horse. That made Dooley regret not listening to his blue-eyed dog, not thinking about danger. His stomach tossed and turned a bit, and the hairs on Dooley's own neck began tingling. Slowly, Dooley turned around to spot the lightest-stepping roan gelding he had ever seen. The rider in the saddle held another double-barreled shotgun, and those barrels were pointed right at Dooley Monahan.

CHAPTER TEN

Something else caught Dooley's eye, and he let out a sigh of relief.

"You're a sight for sore eyes," Dooley said, and nodded at the six-point star pinned to the chest of the linen duster the shotgun toter wore.

"Am I?" The long face of the man with the keen pale eyes and the Roman nose said he did not tolerate nonsense. So did the sawed-off shotgun he held.

"I'm Dooley Monahan," Dooley said.

The lawman did not care. He did not lower the shotgun. He did not even tell Dooley his own name.

Blue growled some more, but Dooley told the shepherd to hush. He didn't want Blue to take any buckshot. He didn't want to take any buckshot himself.

"There's been trouble here," Dooley said.

"Appears so," said the lawman. For a peace officer, this man did not say much. On the other hand, most men holding sawed-off shotguns—the dead man in the well, for instance—usually did not have to say much.

"That fellow," Dooley began, and pointed at the well. He stopped. The lawman might think Dooley was crazy as a loon. He wet his lips. He pointed at the corral. "My horse got stole," he said.

"The one in the corral?" the lawman asked.

"Yes, sir." Dooley sighed. Certainly, he was sounding like a madman. "Can I explain . . . everything?"

The lawman kicked free of one stirrup.

"Here's what's going to happen," he said. "I'm going to swing down off Blue here—"

"That's my dog's name!" Dooley sang out.

The shotgun came to the man's shoulder, and he leaned his head so he could sight down perfectly on Dooley Monahan.

"I won't do anything, sir," Dooley said. "I don't even have a gun." He tilted his head toward the dead man's Smith & Wesson in the dirt.

Slowly, carefully, the man came to the ground. He had experience doing that kind of thing. Dooley could tell. And he was really good at it. One moment he was sitting in the saddle, shotgun in his arms, one boot hanging out of the stirrup, and a second later he was on the ground, shotgun up and aimed, ready for anything. The blue roan did not even move.

"All right," the lawman said. "Speak your piece."

He stood ramrod straight, like someone had replaced his spine with a telegraph pole. And he was just about the size of a telegraph pole, maybe six feet six inches high, and the heels of his stovepipe boots weren't high at all. He wore black woolen pants, a black gun belt with a nickel-plated Colt revolver holstered on his left hip, but the butt pointing outward—making him most likely a right-hander. Black suspenders. A yellow and blue polka-dot shirt, green bandanna with all sorts of designs on it, and the low-crown, wide-brim black hat. The face had been bronzed in the sun, and the beard on his cheeks and chin seemed just stubble from some days on the trail. The mustache and the underlip beard, both gray with a few touches of black, appeared permanent. His hair had been soaked with sweat, but it was salt-and-pepper, and well groomed, too.

No fat that Dooley could tell. No softness. Probably two hundred and thirty pounds of chiseled muscle and sinew. He stepped away from his horse, spread out his legs, and kept the barrels of the scatter-gun aimed at Dooley's midsection.

Dooley sucked in a deep breath, slowly exhaled, and tried to tell the lawman everything that had happened.

He told about Omaha. He even mentioned the plump blonde. He said he hailed from a farm near Des Moines, Iowa, and that he was bound for the Black Hills up north in Dakota Territory. He gestured toward the Platte River, and said how he had been swept into the gang of outlaws as they fled Omaha, blocking him in, leaving him no choice but to gallop with them. He told about fording the Platte, and gave vivid descriptions of the faces of Hubert Dobbs, Frank Handley, and Doc Watson—much better likenesses, Dooley felt, than any wanted posters he had seen or any article in the *Register* or *National Police Gazette.* He related how a mean hombre, now dead, had knocked him into unconsciousness with a shotgun, now buried underneath a quarter ton of dirt in what had been a homesteader's soddie. He went on about how he had followed the trail of the killers for days and days.

"On foot?" The lawman had finally spoken.

"Yes, sir," Dooley said. "On foot."

He waited, but the lawman had no more questions, so Dooley went on with his story.

About the hunger he had endured. About the quail eggs. And about seeing the smoke from the farmer's chimney and crossing the river and finding the farmer named Ole Something-another-dorf. He said how brave and kind Ole was, and how Dooley himself now regretted ever stopping here and bringing harm to the poor man who had fled Norweigeway for a better life in the West of America.

He explained about spending the night, and finding one of Dobbs's and Handley's outlaws here this very morning. He gave much detail about the fight inside, that had destroyed the farmer's home, and the fight outside, the cowardly shooting of Ole by the man with the eye patch, and how Dooley had then killed the killer, with the final bullet carrying the beast into the well.

"That the money?" the lawman asked when Dooley finished. The man's eyes make a quick glance toward the saddlebags.

"It's in the left side," Dooley said. "The other side has my stuff. Extra long johns, socks, those kinds of things."

The lawman nodded. "So that's your take from Omaha."

Dooley spit. He had spent a half hour talking, and now it was getting dark, and that fool lawman had not heard anything Dooley had told him.

"Not Omaha," Dooley said. "Dutch Bluff. The gang robbed that bank after they robbed the one in Omaha."

"I'm supposed to believe that hogwash?"

"It ain't hogwash," Dooley said. "It's pure gospel."

"Yeah. I saw you in Omaha."

"You did. Then you know—"

"I saw you riding right with those killers. I saw someone in that crowd shoot poor Milton Mitchum off the hotel roof. For all I know, that killer was you."

Dooley frowned. He thought. He sweated. "If you find that plump blonde who was walking on the boardwalks, she saw me. She saw me riding alone— for the Black Hills—before those bandits took off down Front Street. You just ask her."

"Boy," the lawman said, "do you know how many fat blond women live in Omaha?"

Dooley didn't answer. He tried another tack.

"Would I make up a story like that?"

"Maybe."

"You think I rode with those vermin?"

"Yep." This time, the man kept talking. "And you might have murdered Ole, too."

Frowning, Dooley shook his head furiously. "If I was a bank robber," he said, "do you think I'd shoot a man into a well and then take time to nail a warning about the well being polluted with a corpse and also bury the farmer and even put a headstone on his grave?"

"Maybe," the man said. "Bounty hunters do strange things. They're strange birds, killing men for money."

"I ain't no bounty hunter," Dooley said.

"Tell that to the Baylor brothers," the lawman said. "Or Doug Wheatlock, their cousin."

Dooley's heart pounded against his chest. "You've heard of me?"

"Enough," the lawman said.

"I'm not a bounty hunter. Those shootings . . . they were more accident than anything else." The man's eyes revealed he didn't believe anything Dooley told him. He tried something else. "If I was a bounty hunter, would I shoot an outlaw like that gent with the eye patch into a well?"

"More accident," the lawman said, throwing Dooley's words back in is face, "than anything else." He pointed the shotgun at Dooley's midsection. He spoke what would be a regular speech for a man like him. "Here's what's going to happen now. Getting too late in the day to travel. You're going to sleep in the outhouse. With that dog. If any one of you pops out—and it'll be a full moon tonight and I don't sleep—I'll shoot you both dead and give that gent in the well some company. Then tomorrow morning, you'll ride the mule, and I'll pull the bay behind me. And we'll take that money you stole back to Omaha."

"That money," Dooley said, "is from the bank in Dutch Bluff."

The man gestured with the shotgun. "I can just shoot you dead now."

He was a thorough lawman. Before he sent Dooley and Blue into their jail for the night, he looked inside the outhouse. The tools he took out. He even dumped the nails through the hole and tossed the tin can in behind it. He left most of the newspapers and magazines, and two potatoes for Dooley's and Blue's supper. The rest he took with him.

* * *

The lawman did not make breakfast. No potatoes. Not even coffee. Dooley, once he was given permission to leave the privy with Bluc, had decided that the lawman did not even cat. He wasn't human.

Sometime during the night, or maybe when the sky got light enough this morning, the lawman had thrown Dooley's Navajo blanket and saddle over the mule, and had fashioned a lead rope that he secured to General Grant. He did not waste time. The shotgun's twin barrels pointed toward Ole's worn-out mule.

"Get on," the lawman said.

Dooley obeyed.

Not much for talking, the leathery-skinned man tossed Dooley a pair of manacles, the cuffs opened, and waited. Dooley knew what to do, and fastened one bracelet on his left wrist and the other on his right. When he had finished, he looked down at the lawman for approval. All he got was a scowl, so Dooley tightened the iron cuffs and shot the tall man a less friendly look.

He must have put on the handcuffs to the lawman's satisfaction, because all the tall man said was: "If that dog tries something, I'll kill him, you, the mule, and your horse."

"Blue won't try anything," Dooley said. "He's a good dog."

When they neared the Platte River, Dooley began thinking that everything would turn out fine. The lawman hadn't killed him, but was taking him in. People got fair trials in the West—even in Omaha. All he had to do was find that plump blonde, no matter how hard the lawman said that might prove. She'd tell the truth. So would anyone else who had seen him. He had done business in Omaha. Bank robbers didn't spend money. They stole it.

His stomach soured. Not everyone got a fair trial in the West. How many lynchings had he read about? How many had he seen?

They came to the Platte, which looked wider now but even shallower, if that could be. Dooley prepared to cross, but the lawman eared back the hammers on the shotgun.

"Upstream," he ordered.

Dooley looked back at the big man, but did not argue. Maybe the man knew a better crossing, though even a toddler could cross this river without drowning. Perhaps he had decided that Dooley wasn't lying, and that he should take his prisoner and the money to the bank in Dutch Bluff. Dooley did not ask anything. He just rode.

They rode toward a lot of green on the riverbank.

That was one thing about the plains, about most of the West that Dooley had seen. Trees could be scarce here and there, but you usually could find them growing along creeks and rivers. The Platte was no different. Dooley had found mostly ash in this country, or trees that looked like ash, but he could tell the big trees in this bunch were cottonwoods. He had always liked cottonwoods. Big, massive, sprawling, green.

"Hold up," the lawman said, and Dooley reined in.

"Get down," the lawman said, and Dooley dismounted.

Turning around, the lawman admired the largest of the cottonwoods. "Yes," he said, more to himself, mostly a whisper.

Maybe, Dooley thought, he just wants some shade.

"Yes," the lawman repeated. "This'll do. This'll do just fine."

Keeping the shotgun in his right hand, he used his left to remove the lariat hanging underneath his saddle horn.

CHAPTER ELEVEN

Dooley wanted to swallow, but his mouth had turned to sand. His throat felt dry. Beads of sweat popped about his forehead like pimples, and his heart began racing. The lawman sailed one end of the lariat—the one with a loop already coiled—over the stoutest branch. The rope dangled in the wind, the noose just about the height of Dooley's head.

"Mister . . ." Dooley began, only to realize the lawman had not introduced himself.

Ignoring Dooley, the man busied himself wrapping the other end of the rope around the cottonwood's massive trunk before tying a knot and testing the rope and branch to make sure both could support weight—about one hundred and seventy pounds.

"There." The man grinned and wiped his hands on the legs of his pants. After picking up the shotgun he had leaned against a smaller cottonwood while he secured the lynching rope, the silent, tall man with a badge walked toward the mule and Dooley Monahan.

"You can't hang me," Dooley said. "Without a trial."

"Trials are a waste of time."

"But I'm innocent."

Smiling, the lawman shook his head. He grabbed the bridle and pulled the mule toward the noose. Dooley hoped the mule would turn into what many mules turned into—stubborn—but this one was so placid, he eased Dooley's head straight in front of the hangman's noose.

It wasn't really a hangman's noose, though. No coils. Just a loop through a honda. But Dooley figured it would sure enough do the job on a bona fide hangman's knot. Maybe not break his neck outright, until Dooley did some kicking as he strangled.

The man stopped, stepped away from the mule, and lifted the shotgun. The barrels did the talking. Dooley, fighting down the terror in his stomach, lifted his shackled hands and slipped the rope over his neck.

Dooley glanced at Blue, who had slaked his thirst from the river while the lawman manufactured his gallows, and now rested in the shade of the cottonwood. The lawman's eyes hardened, and he turned toward the dog, bringing the shotgun's stock to his shoulders.

"Don't . . ." Dooley pleaded.

"Sic that dog on me," the lawman said, not taking his cold eyes off the blue-eyed dog, "and he'll be feeding buzzards."

"I wasn't going to do anything," Dooley said. Which was the truth. If Blue started attacking that lawman—maybe even if Blue only started barking—chances seemed likely that the mule would bolt, and leave Dooley dancing about a foot off the ground, kicking until his face turned blue, his tongue purple, and his heart stopped beating.

"Good." The hangman tugged the rope, tightening the noose over Dooley's throat.

"Now . . . you got anything to say?" the lawman asked.

"You can't do this," Dooley told him.

"That all you got to say?"

Dooley managed to summon up just enough saliva to swallow.

"You're a lawman," Dooley reminded him. "You took an oath."

"Said I'd uphold the law. Hanging a no-good killer and robber is doing that."

"I told you the truth."

The man waited, nodded, and took a step toward the back of the mule, pushing the shotgun to his left hand, raising his right as if to whack the mule's rump.

Dooley decided that he had better do some more talking.

"That money," Dooley said. "When you turn it in to the bank in Omaha, they'll say that it's not theirs." Dooley did not know how the bankers in Omaha would be able to tell that, but he figured maybe some of those notes said Bank of Dutch Bluff on it, or depositors might see some gold coins that weren't theirs. It was just something to say, something that might give the taciturn lawman pause.

The lawman stepped back, looked up at Dooley, and for the first time since Dooley had seen him, he did something odd.

He smiled.

"What money?" the lawman said. It came out as a mocking joke, a sinister sneer, and right then Dooley Monahan knew that this lawman did not give a whit about law and order or Dooley Monahan. He was going to take that money for himself and leave Dooley

Monahan hanging. He knew that because the lawman, seeing what little color Dooley had left in his face drain instantly, began what appeared to be a veritable monologue.

"I'm going to leave you here, Dooley Monahan, hanging high and dead. I'm going to pin a note on your shirt—sort of like the markers you left at that hardscrabble homestead—only instead of being a grave marker or a warning about bad water—this note will be simple. All it will say is something like, *This Is What Happens to Rustlers in This Country.*"

Dooley said, "Rustlers? There ain't no beef or horses to steal in this country. This is farmland."

"Whatever," the lawman said.

"But I tell you I'm innocent," Dooley said again.

"And I tell you . . . I'm rich." He laughed. Dooley didn't find anything funny, and he sure did not like the way the man giggled at Dooley Monahan's expense. Again, the lawman moved toward the mule's rump.

"You'll take care of my horse, won't you?" Dooley said, resigned now to his fate.

"Figure to sell him in Omaha."

"And . . ." Dooley somehow managed to swallow again. "My dog?"

The lawman sighed. "I leave him to mourn over you."

"Promise?"

"Do I look like a low-down snake who'd kill a dog with no cause?"

Dooley tried one last plea. "But you'd hang an innocent man."

"Big difference," the tall man said, "between killing

a man and killing a dog." He raised his hand to strike the mule.

"Give me a few minutes," Dooley said. "To make my peace with the Lord."

It stood to reason. A man that would not kill a dog without good reason would at least grant the last request of a man he was about to murder, to lynch, especially if that request was to pray for redemption. The lawman swore bitterly, but he raised his hand, reached for his gray hat, and he pulled it off, dropped the hat to his thigh, and even bowed his head.

"Make it quick," he whispered.

Dooley prayed. Rarely had he been what you might call a regular churchgoing man, but his mother had educated him on the Bible. He had learned to read that way before the first schoolmaster set up in Des Moines, and, as a child, he had attended the gatherings at Mr. Witherspoon's barn whenever the circuit-riding minister came to preach. Even as a drifting saddle bum, Dooley had managed to sneak out of a poker game or a smoke-filled saloon to find a tent revival now and again. He hoped that his Almighty God would remember those times a few minutes from now.

He prayed that he would be able to see his mother and father—and those little siblings he had never gotten to know because the Lord, for his wisdom and reasoning that Dooley surely did not question, had taken them when they were but babies. He prayed that the Lord would be welcoming Ole Something-another-dorf into his Kingdom. He prayed for good weather and plenty of rains to bless the farmers in this country. He prayed for General Grant. He prayed for Blue, that he might be guided to a good family with plenty of boys and maybe even a couple of girls and a she-dog that would bring forth multitudes of baby Nebraska shepherds. He even prayed that the Lord would forgive the reticent lawman for the crimes he was about to commit.

"Give it an amen, buster," the lawman said, his head still bowed in prayer. "It's getting hot, and it's a long ride to Omaha."

"I'm just about done," Dooley said. He wet his lips. He glanced at the lawman, whose head was still bowed, who faced the north while Dooley Monahan looked at the dust rising on the far side of the Platte River. "Let me see," he said, "where was I? Oh, yes."

He prayed that the West would be rid of men like the Baylors and Doug Wheatlock and that men and women and children and horses and dogs could live in peace. He prayed that Miss Julia Cooperman would find warmth and riches in Alaska. He prayed that the Lord would smile down on Butch Sweeney and provide him with a good horse, a good saddle, and a camp cook who was no belly-cheater. He prayed for fat beef and good water. He prayed for Fifteenth Street in Cheyenne, Wyoming. He was about to pray for Tempe, Arizona, and even San Francisco, California, when the tall lawman stepped back and slammed his hat on his head.

"That's amen, damn it," the man said.

Dooley Monahan smiled. "Amen," he said.

Because by that time, the riders had reached the Platte River. Nine riders splashed across the wide, shallow river, and the lawman whirled around, bringing his shotgun up, but stopping. The men had spread out, taking their time, studying the scene as they rode slowly across the river.

"Say one word," the lawman whispered, "and I use one round on the dog, and the other blows your head off before they gun me down."

Dooley couldn't nod his agreement or understanding because the rope was too tight against his throat. He had to be patient, but this appeared to be the one chance he needed to avoid a necktie party. His only chance to live through this day.

The riders neared the bank. That's when Dooley frowned. He knew those men, well, at least, three of them.

They must have seen the lawman's badge reflecting in the sunlight, because five of them instantly filled their hands with their revolvers. The lawman must have recognized them, too, because he started to bring the shotgun up again, but a cannonade sounded from the Platte, and the taciturn lawman danced this way and that, bullets peppering his duster, sending dust flying in the air, followed by blood. The lawman, likely dead by then though still standing, squeezed both triggers and sent buckshot digging into the dirt a few feet from his boots.

By that time, Dooley no longer smiled. The dog barked. The lawman's horse bolted away from the river. The gunmen crossing the river cursed and whooped and kept right on shooting. The mule brayed, bucked, and began to follow the lawman's blue roan. Dooley tried to tell the mule, "Whoa," but he couldn't manage a word, not even a grunt. He tried to squeeze the mule's sides so hard that the dumb plow animal would stop, but that just made the mule run harder. Then Blue, sensing the danger, started yapping at the mule, trying to keep it from running. Which only made the mule bolt, and Dooley felt himself slipping off the rear end of the mule, and the rope tightened across his neck.

Then, he was kicking the hanging man's death dance.

CHAPTER TWELVE

His eyes bulged out of his head. He felt blood trying to push through the veins and arteries in his throat. His lungs screamed for air. His brain told him to die. Dooley tried to stop kicking, fearing that would just hasten his demise, but his feet and the muscles in his legs would not listen. He bounced up and down. His heart wanted to explode. No longer could he hear anything but Satan's laughter.

The last thing he thought he would see on this earth was Hubert Dobbs, standing in the stirrups on his big black horse, one hand pressing down on the saddle horn, the other aiming a long-barreled .44 caliber Remington at Dooley's head. Dooley saw the muzzle blast, but heard not a pop. The world turned suddenly black.

"Ouch," said Dooley.

His eyes opened. He must be in Hell. Doc Watson's gaunt, white face stared down at him. Vaguely, Dooley understood that his head was off the ground. The gunman coughed as he jerked the noose off Dooley's head. Dooley's head slammed against the ground.

This time, he didn't say *ouch*. What he said caused a bunch of men to laugh.

"'Pears he don't care much fer yer bedside manner." The voice sounded nasal and twangy, but oddly feminine.

More laughter.

Dooley slowly reached over and rubbed the back of his head that had made contact with hard dirt. He remembered his name, and remembered hanging by the neck, so he knew he had not lost his memory. He knew he must not be in Hell, but still on the banks of the Platte River in Nebraska. His hand moved from the back of his head to his throat, gingerly touching the raw flesh, already scabbing over from a hideous rope burn. He sucked in a deep breath, which burned his throat but satisfied his lungs. He blew out. Repeated the process. Beside him came a familiar noise, and Dooley smiled, but quickly regretted that. It made his throat hurt.

"I'm all right, Blue," he told the shepherd. That hurt, too.

"Bear grease," said the nasal, girlish voice. "Do the trick. Rub some on that scratch, Doc."

"Scratch," Doc Watson said. "Any deeper and his head would've been cut off. And that's one thing I know about . . . cuttin' off heads."

"I've cut meself worser shavin' me armpits," the voice said.

"Forget the damned bear grease," roared the voice of Hubert Dobbs. "Get that feller up on his own legs. Now."

Doc Watson and another man each took one of Dooley's arms and jerked him to his feet. The world began spinning, and if the second man had not kept a firm grip on Dooley's left arm, he would have spilled onto the Nebraska sod again.

"Start talkin'," Hubert Dobbs ordered.

Dooley waited until the dizziness passed. He shook his head, swallowed painfully, and looked at the men. His mouth opened, but no words escaped. Impatiently, Hubert Dobbs drew the big Remington and cocked it, pointing the barrel at Dooley's midsection. The man let go of Dooley's left arm and took a few steps off to the side. Doc Watson moved closer to the Platte River.

"I give you the benefit of a doubt, feller," Hubert Dobbs said. "I can always string you up again."

"He just cain't talk right now, Pa," said the female voice. "Hell's fire, he just got hung."

Dooley blinked. Yes, that slim rider in buckskins with a wild mane of brown hair spilling from underneath a wide-brimmed straw hat was a woman. Her breasts pushed hard against the greasy buckskin shirt she wore. She also carried a brace of Navy Colts, butt forward, in a green sash. A woman. Yes. Definitely a woman. Sort of.

He finally managed to say something

"Your daughter."

"Don't get no manly desires, mister," Hubert Dobbs said, waving the gun angrily.

"Shucks, Pa," his daughter said. "You spoilt all the fun. He ain't that bad-lookin'."

"Quiet. Don't shame your ma. Don't shame me. I—"

The Remington lowered, and he swung down from the big black stallion, tossing the reins to his daughter. Hubert Dobbs stepped until he was practically standing on Dooley's toes.

"I know you," the outlaw leader whispered.

Doc Watson coughed, spit, and gestured vaguely to some point across the Platte River. "He's the gent from Omaha. The one Zeke coldcocked and taken his horse."

"Only, that's the horse there," said Frank Handley. He pointed to General Grant.

"Which means . . ." The daughter of Hubert Dobbs laughed. ". . . that he up and stole back that horse."

Dobbs leaned even closer to Dooley.

"That right? You stole Zeke's horse?"

Dooley swallowed. He tried to speak as loudly as he could, but all that came out was a hoarse, painful whisper. "It was my horse."

That was an honest answer, but one that did not set well with Hubert Dobbs. A backhand sent Dooley crashing to the ground. It also sent Blue's jaws clamping on the big outlaw's arm. Dooley knew what would happen, and he jumped up, hearing the sounds of hammers clicking and Doc Watson giggling. He moved fast, ignoring the pain in his throat and cheek, and dived, pulling the shepherd off the big man with the thick beard, and taking Blue to the ground, shielding the dog with his own body.

"Easy," he whispered. "Easy, Blue. It's all right. It's all right."

It wasn't. Dooley figured that both he and his dog would be dead soon.

"Kill 'em both!" Hubert Dobbs bellowed.

"No," his daughter contradicted. "You always said

a man that does right by his dog is a man to ride the river with, Pa. Don't kill that cowboy. Not yet."

Blue stopped growling. Dooley squeezed his eyes shut when he heard the outlaw leader say, "I never said that."

"No," his daughter agreed. "What you said was, 'Think afore you kill a man.'"

"So?"

"We come here to find Zeke. And to find that money. Didn't we?"

Dooley opened his eyes.

"So?" the skinny, filthy girl's daddy said again.

"He got his horse back, Pa. Do I have to spell it out for you?"

Silence. Then Doc Watson was kneeling by Dooley. "Stand up, mister," the deadly gunman said. "Just keep your dog calm. Stand up. You might get out of this day alive."

"Easy, Blue," Dooley whispered. "Everything's going to be fine." He sat up, rubbed the dog, scratched its ears, and tried to give the blue-eyed dog that this-is-all-funny-some-joke-ain't-it-good-dog look before he wearily managed to stand on his own two legs once more. He sucked in a painful breath of air, exhaled, and looked at Hubert Dobbs, whose daughter had dismounted and was tying a filthy bandanna over her father's bloody arm.

Dooley wasn't so certain either he or Blue would live much longer.

"Zeke?" the big man asked.

"I killed him," Dooley said.

A few of the men whistled. "That takes some doin'," one of them said.

"How?" That question came from Doc Watson,

Hubert Dobbs, Frank Handley, and Dobbs's dirty daughter.

Dooley didn't answer at first. He couldn't. Then Hubert Dobbs nodded, looked at another of his men and said, "Fetch some bear grease."

It did work. At least the bear grease took the pain out of Dooley's throat. And the dirty girl showed a kind hand at nursing as she wrapped the sleeve of one of the outlaws' spare shirts—and it was a clean shirt—over the grease and the skin cut deep by a hangman's rope.

Some of the men gathered the bloody corpse of the quiet and now dead lawman and propped him up against the big cottonwood. Naturally, they went through the dead man's pockets, but every now and then—when Dooley's story got really interesting—they would stop their thievery to listen closer to Dooley's story.

It was, Dooley came to think a few hours later, a pretty good story—and Dooley didn't even have to exaggerate. Dobbs and Handley and Doc Watson and the boys—and girl—believed everything Dooley said, and Dooley told the truth, where that dead lawman stiffening up underneath the cottonwood had scoffed at Dooley's tale. Oh, that corpse might have actually believed Dooley's story, but he planned on murdering Dooley for the money Dooley'd planned on returning to its proper owners.

Which led Dooley to a dilemma as he got deeper into his story. Would Dobbs and Handley and the others let greed trump their morals? Would they kill Dooley Monahan, and Blue, for that wealth?

Well, Dooley decided to gamble.

He pointed to the saddlebags on the lawman's blue roan. The one two of the outlaws had ridden off after and fetched back.

"Money's in the saddlebag," Dooley said. "That saddlebag, by the way. But the money's from the bank at Dutch Bluff." Dooley ran his fingers over his bandaged neck. "Not that side," he instructed. "The other. Yeah."

The leather cover flapped open. Dooley saw the outlaw's eyes widen.

"Whoopee!" he cried.

Hubert Dobbs shook his head, drew the big Remington, and walked over to the dead lawman. He emptied his revolver into the dead man's head, turned around, shucked the empties from the cylinder, and filled the holes with fresh loads.

"One thing I despise," Dobbs said, "is a dishonest man. A lawman at that. Sworn to uphold the law."

Dooley wanted to vomit, but he managed to say, "I told him the same thing."

The leader of the outlaw gang shoved the smoking .44 into his holster. "Gnaws inside my gizzard, it does." He came back to Dooley and stuck out his hand. "Put it here, mister. Why, you brung tears to my eyes when you told us what you done." He turned around. "You heard him, boys. Heard what this gent done. He's a bona fide hero, yes, sir." The man's big arm went around Dooley's neck, and Dooley almost fainted from the pain from the rope burn that had almost severed his windpipe. "How many of you would've done what this boy did? Nary a one. That be my guess. Hell, I wouldn't have thought to do it my ownself." He squeezed, bringing Dooley closer to the man's stinking clothes. "Kill a swine like Zeke. Shoot his arse into a well. But then have the decency to bury a good, honest, foreigner who come to this state to farm. Bury him with his own hands, mind you. And not only that, he nailed up a sign to save any wayfarers who might have drunk from that well, got sick to their stomach from the disease Zeke put in that water. Boys, this is a good man. This is a man we need. He's what they say is 'a man to ride the river with.' And we're in luck, boys. 'Cause Dooley Monahan is riding with us."

The man's death grip released Dooley, who turned, wet his lips, and said, "I am?"

"You are, Dooley, my amigo."

"Well . . ." Dooley tried to think of a way to decline the invitation.

"Or we leave you swelling up beside that dead hombre." Dobbs nodded his big head toward the gory body of the dead lawman.

That's how Dooley Monahan, who had once ridden with Monty's Raiders, became a member of the Dobbs-Handley Gang. It wasn't so bad, not at first. They let him take his saddle off Ole's mule, which they turned loose to graze underneath the shade of the cottonwoods—and the stink of the dead lawman—and let him put his Navajo blanket and saddle on General Grant. They loaned him a Colt .44-40 and a Winchester carbine. They tossed corn dodgers to Blue, who ate them with relish.

"I'm glad you're with us," Hubert Dobbs's daughter, Zerelda, said, and winked.

"Uh. So am I," Dooley lied.

They rode west.

CHAPTER THIRTEEN

It didn't start off so lousy. For Dooley Monahan, riding with the Dobbs-Handley Gang rang similar to that time long ago—when he was practically still a kid—when he had been a member of Monty's Raiders. After all, back then, before he sneaked away from the outlaws a few weeks before most of them were shot dead near Davenport in ambush, and a few days later the ringleaders were busted out of jail by several Iowa citizens for an old-fashioned lynching, all Dooley had to do was hold the horses and keep a lookout, or cook, do laundry, and wash dishes in camp.

There was no laundry for Dooley to wash with any of the Dobbs-Handley boys, or Zerelda Dobbs herself, and nobody ever asked him to cook or wash dishes. Mostly, their grub consisted of hardtack, soda crackers, stale biscuits, or beef jerky—washed down by whiskey. Certainly, neither Frank Handley nor Hubert Dobbs trusted Dooley enough to let him serve as a lookout. Besides, that's how Dooley had managed to leave the employment with Monty's Raiders.

So what he did was ride.

That was one thing the men—and Dobbs's daughter—who rode with this band of outlaws excelled at. Riding. They rode hard. They rode long. They rode . . . and rode . . . and rode.

Through washes and dried creek beds. Down creeks or rivers to make it hard for any scout or lawman or posse to trail them. On the treeless expanse that was this part of Nebraska—where it appeared that a man on a good horse (and General Grant was as good a horse as Dooley Monahan ever owned) could see forever—Dooley learned that a savvy person could find places to hide or camp for a night. They spent one night in a buffalo wallow, which proved to be a great spot to stay out of view, but not so good to sleep. Buffalo left not only dung in the sandy pits, but they wallowed away their fleas and ticks. Dooley spent the next two days scratching, but then a thunderstorm blew in to wash off the fleas, and pea-sized hail knocked off the remaining ticks and left Dooley with a few bruises on his arms and back. Thunderheads—especially those that cut loose with hail like grapeshot—were another way to avoid lawmen and posses, according to the philosophy of Hubert Dobbs.

The gang members didn't really accept Dooley Monahan as one of their own, but they certainly admired his horse. In fact, more than a couple of the outlaws asked Dooley for permission to take General Grant once Dooley was dead. Dooley just shook his head and whispered, "Do that, I'd likely be dead

quicker than the good Lord has planned for me,"
which got chuckles from the requesters and the lis-
teners. Dobbs's daughter usually laughed the hardest,
and asked, "How 'bout you will the Gen'ral to me,
sweetie pie?"

"Then I'd be dead even sooner," Dooley would
answer.

Every evening, that conversation happened. The
gang seemed to enjoy the same joke.

But the outlaws especially enjoyed Blue. They
wanted Dooley dead and wanted General Grant to
ride, but they certainly swooned over the shepherd,
feeding him bites of jerky or stale biscuits, letting him
drink their coffee or maybe just a sip of whiskey. Blue
never got drunk, though, and always—to the dismay
of the men and Zerelda Dobbs—Blue would curl up
beside Dooley when they finally called it a night and
turned in.

Of course, you needed a really good scout—
someone who knew the lay of the land and locations
of creeks and rivers and buffalo wallows and trails
that a flea could not have passed through—to navi-
gate Nebraska, and Dobbs and Handley had one of
the best scouts between Nebraska City and Denver
City.

"What do ya see there, Dooley?" Zerelda Dobbs
asked. She snorted, spit out some juice from the
copious amount of snuff she had packed between
the gums below her brown front lower teeth and
bottom lip.

Zee—she kept telling Dooley to call her Zee and
drop that Miss Zerelda stuff—nodded toward the
northwest.

"I don't know, Miss—um—I mean—er—Zee," he

said, and glanced nervously behind him. They had to be a mile or more ahead of Hubert Dobbs, Frank Handley, Doc Watson, and the rest of the bad men, for Dooley could see no sign of the gang.

That was something Dooley had learned about the Great Plains. The country looked flat, but it wasn't that flat. A man could disappear, or a herd of cattle, or a little less than a dozen murderers and rapists and robbers and cheaters at cards. The land rose and fell, so that men could actually hide in the country.

Dooley turned back toward Zerelda, who swung one leg over the horn and waited. She tilted her head toward the northwest. Dooley studied the land and blue skies.

He shrugged.

"Don't you see nothin'?" she asked.

Dooley stood in his stirrups and concentrated. Tall grass rippled like waves in the wind. Low on the horizon he saw a few small dots of clouds.

"Grass," he said. "Some clouds." He repeated his shrug.

Zerelda laughed, and pointed a crooked finger to the southeast.

"How 'bout yonder?"

The land and sky looked the same. Rolling grass. Small clouds.

"Same," he told her.

"Clouds?" she asked.

Dooley nodded his head.

She slid her leg back into position, found the stirrup, and gathered her reins.

"Them ain't clouds, you dumb oaf. They's smoke."

Dooley looked to the southeast first, and realization struck him like a jenny's kick in the gut. He could see now, one puff that certainly was no cloud, rising slowly toward the heavens, breaking up, dissipating, followed by another that did the same, and another. Jerking his head around, he found almost a reflection in the northwestern skies. White wood smoke, one . . . two . . . three . . . rising from the Nebraska plains, whipped into oblivion by the winds.

"Smoke . . ." His voice started out as nothing more than a whisper, but the next word he said with loud emotion—stomach-churning fear.

"Signals!"

As in confirmation, an arrow cut a few strands of hair.

General Grant bucked at the shrieks, and two Sioux warriors galloped their pinto ponies from out of nowhere—the Indians knew even more hiding places in this country than Zerel—er, *Zee*—Dobbs. Something roared, and as Dooley felt his rump leave the saddle and the tops of his boots catch the tops of his spurs, keeping him from being pitched to a sure and ugly death but sending his rump crashing hard back on the saddle and shooting spasms of pain up his backbone, Dooley saw the first warrior fly off his pinto. Zee had shot him dead.

She shot the second one, too.

"Ride fast, hombre! I'm faster than a bolt of lightnin', and if you ain't no faster, you're deader than a skunk!" Zee Dobbs did not need to tell Dooley twice. General Grant had recovered, ceased his bucking, and Dooley gave the bay all the rein he wanted. He took off after the woman, looked behind him, and counted at least six more Indians chasing him.

Dooley leaned forward, held out the reins, tried to breathe, and between curses, muttered a few prayers that his parents and that circuit-riding preacher had made him memorize years earlier, and a few he came up with on the spot.

Dear God, don't let General Grant step in a prairie-dog hole.

Wind whipped the side of his face.

An arrow flashed through General Grant's mane and underneath Dooley's reins.

Lord, if I am killed, please let it be mercifully quick.

Hooves of their horses cut down grass like reapers and churned up clods of dirt and sod. They rode in a southerly direction, but turned this way and that, dodging arrows. The Sioux warriors yipped, shouted, and one even blew a cavalry bugle that sounded more like squeaky, panting groans than some signal. Another arrow flew past. Dooley followed Zee. Even as fast as General Grant was, the gelding could not keep up with the outlaw's daughter's mount.

They turned east. Dooley held his breath, his rump pounding the saddle, his boots bouncing in the stirrups. A Sioux brave with a pockmarked face painted vermillion and green came alongside him, raising a tomahawk over his head. The handle was studded with brass tacks and hawk feathers. The warrior swung the war axe, missed, brought it up to swing again. Dooley shot at the brave, missing him, but killing the horse. The warrior yelped, pitching the tomahawk to his left, crashing hard and swallowed by the grass. The dead horse rolled over and over, before landing on its side, but causing two other warriors to lose their seats as their ponies became caught up in the wreck.

Dooley looked at the Colt in his hand. He did not even remember ever drawing it.

A bullet scratched his chin, and Dooley looked to his left. Beside him rode another Sioux, this one holding an old Remington cap-and-ball pistol. This one's face was younger, his black braids flapping in the wind, his thumb earing back the hammer of the old .44.

Dooley's right hand swung around, and he raised his left arm out of the way. He squeezed the trigger, felt the muzzle blast, and caught just a glimpse of the blood that sprayed from the Indian's stomach, just beneath the ivory-white bone breastplate he wore. The Indian was gone, falling from his horse, and Dooley kept riding.

Kept following Zee Dobbs.

Kept praying.

Somehow, his luck held. He turned, surprised to find that they had put some distance between themselves and the still-yipping, screaming, shooting Indian warriors.

Dooley looked off to the east, hoping to find Zee's father and his partner and the rest of the killers riding hell-bent for leather, like the United States Cavalry galloping to the rescue.

He saw only grass and sky.

"Dagnab it!"

Somehow, Dooley managed to hear Zee Dobbs's cry. She was pulling hard on the reins, turning her horse—still at a gallop—toward the southwest. Dooley understood her reasoning and urged General Grant to follow the leader.

More Sioux warriors—somewhere between four and eight—were loping hard from the south. The ones, Dooley told himself, who had been sending up the smoke signals from that direction.

They splashed through a creek, went up, down, up again. Dooley felt the sweat already drenching his shirt, but he could see the foams of lather appearing on General Grant's withers. He could feel something else, too, and that made him uncomfortable. The great bay gelding was beginning to tire. Oh, Dooley knew the horse would ride, ride till his valiant heart broke. He looked behind him, saw the Indians keeping their distance but not turning back. They were playing it smart, having lost a few more warriors than they had expected to while chasing a white woman and a white man.

Zee cut back north, then east, riding hard, but Dooley knew her horse was about played out, too. They kept going, and Dooley looked back. Those Indians weren't giving up the chase, not by a damned sight.

Shoot Zee. Then yourself.

The thought flashed through his head, but Dooley quickly shook it off. For one thing, he didn't think he'd be able to shoot the girl, not with her bouncing in the saddle on a fast horse and himself doing the same.

Suddenly, Zee was jerking hard on the reins, pulling her gallant beast to a stop, and leaping off the saddle. Before her boots hit the ground, she had jerked out her revolver and put a bullet into her horse's head.

Down, crashed the dead beast, and the woman jumped behind the animal, shouting to Dooley as she slid behind the horse's stomach and snapped a shot at the charging Indians behind them.

"Shoot yer bay, boy! We'll fort up an' make our last stand here!"

"Keep running, General!" Dooley screamed. "Run as hard as you can!"

Dooley leaped off the bay, landed hard, rolled over six or seven times, but somehow managed to keep a grip on his pistol.

He came to his feet. An arrow sliced his left thigh. He whirled, and saw the Indian coming right at him, holding a lance, and Dooley wondered what it would feel like to be skewered.

The red-skinned warrior's nose disappeared in an eruption of blood and gore, and the lance went between Dooley's legs, just missing his manhood. He tripped over the ash lance, and staggered as another arrow tore off the hat that somehow had not come off his head. A second later, and he was diving over Zee's dead horse, sliding between the saddle and the horse's tail. He came up, surprised to find the Colt still in his hand. The revolver bucked in his hand, and he tasted and smelled gun smoke, and thought he saw an Indian slammed into the grass.

"Yee-hiii!" screamed Zee.

Dooley came to his knees, thumbed back the hammer, found another target. The gun roared, and another Sioux somersaulted over the back of his horse.

At any moment, Dooley knew that his body would resemble a pincushion, that arrows would tear into his body. His ears roared and rang, and dust stung his eyes, but he saw most of the Sioux braves chasing after General Grant, who had kept running northeast.

The Indians seemed more interested in catching that horse than in taking Dooley's scalp. Most of them. But not all.

"Good thinkin', Dooley!"

Zee had the wrong impression of Dooley Mona-han. He knew she had wanted him to kill his horse, the way she had done, which made sense. Fort up. Hold them off for as long as they could. Die bravely. Only, most of the Indians went galloping after the bay gelding. That's not what Dooley had expected. He just did not have it in his heart to kill that fine horse.

Zee had tossed her empty pistol beside her dead horse's head, and now worked the lever and trigger on her Winchester carbine. One Indian went down. Then another's horse. That Indian jumped to his feet, but Dooley shot him dead.

"Yeee-hiiii!" Zee bellowed. "Let's die game!"

Let's not die at all, Dooley thought. But he knew that hope was forlorn.

The hammer of his Colt fell, but he felt no buck, heard no report. He thumbed back the hammer, tried again, then tossed the empty revolver toward a charging warrior. That one ducked to his left as the Colt sailed past him. The Indian smiled, but then Zee shot him out of the saddle.

"I'm empty!" Zee shouted.

"Me, too!"

Dooley braced himself for death. A tall Sioux had pulled his brown mustang to a stop and brought up a lever-action rifle. The Indian drew a bead on the center of Dooley's chest, but Dooley refused to cower, to run, to cry. He told himself that he would die like a man.

CHAPTER FOURTEEN

Not his life flashing before his eyes. Not the flash of gunpowder sending a leaden bullet through his heart. No instant blackness. All Dooley Monahan saw was a blur.

A streak of darkness leaped out of the grass and slammed against the Sioux warrior, sending the rifle sailing end over end, and the mustang snorting, kicking out with its hind legs, and moving quickly out of the way. The Indian shrieked like a girl and let out a groan as he landed on the hard sod with the blur still atop him. Suddenly, Dooley heard the growl.

Reality hit him hard.

I'm still alive! he thought. And then he shouted: "Blue!"

Yes, his loyal shepherd was tearing through the Indian's flesh, fierce, savage, protecting his master. Zee ran to help, a butcher knife in her hand.

Dooley recovered instantly and bolted for the Henry .44 the Indian had dropped. He looked quickly for Indians—but found none—and he thought that the rest of the war party must have gone off after

General Grant, leaving the young braves to count coup and take scalps and torture and whatever the hell else Sioux warriors did. He lifted the rifle, checked the barrel to make sure it was free of dirt, and turned to the east.

He half expected to see Hubert Dobbs and Frank Handley leading the gang of cutthroats like cavalry to the rescue, yet all he saw was waving grass and blue skies—no clouds, no smoke signals this time.

The Indian's mustang danced a few stutter steps a few yards away, frightened but staying close to its master. Dooley looked southwest, saw the dust, and used his left hand to grab the horsehair hackamore. The brown mare pulled away, but Dooley held firm, shot a final glance at the back of Zee Dobbs as she lifted the butcher knife over her head and prepared to bring it down, and then Dooley was turning, leaping into the rough Indian saddle.

"Stay here!" he shouted, either to Blue or Zee, or maybe both.

Later, it struck him: Where else would they go?

Slamming the Henry's barrel against the brown pony's side, he leaned forward and felt the burst of locomotion as the Sioux's horse galloped after the dust . . . after the war party . . .

After General Grant.

Over the pounding of the mustang's hooves, Dooley heard Blue bark and Zee call out, "Where the hell are you off to, Dooley?"

In all his years cowboying, Dooley had ridden a lot of horses, used a lot of different types of bridles and reins, and forked various kinds of saddles, yet never had he ever . . .

1) Ridden an Indian pony.
2) Sat in an Indian saddle.
3) Used a hackamore.

The brown mustang wasn't a bad horse. Far from it, Dooley had to concede, though a bit small for Dooley's liking. The hackamore was all right; just took some getting used to. The saddle? Well, that was something different, but Dooley had ridden bareback before, and he had sat in some lousy saddles. He kept thinking about something Old Man Buckshot Harrigan used to tell him back when Dooley was riding for the 5-Bar-Double-H outfit in the South Texas brush country.

"Ain't the saddle. Ain't the bridle. Ain't even the rider. It's the hoss. The hoss is all that matters."

The brown mustang was a mighty good horse.

Dooley figured the horse knew this country better than he did, for he assumed that the Sioux Indians had ridden across this country a few times before this day. The mare also knew where she was going, or where Dooley wanted her to go. She just followed the trail of dust.

After a couple of miles, however, two of the Indians must have realized they were being followed, and they gave up on trying to catch General Grant and turned back toward their pursuer. Dooley saw them loping easily toward him, saw them stop, and saw them kick their mounts into a gallop.

One swung off to Dooley's right, the other to the left. Their war whoops reached his ears.

He had little time to think, which reminded him of another thing Old Man Buckshot Harrigan used to tell the greenhorns who wanted to become cowboys.

"Don't think. React."

Dooley reacted. The Indian on his right had a bow and quiver full of arrows. The one to his left waved a long gun. Dooley couldn't tell for sure, but it certainly looked to be an old single-shot muzzle-loader. Maybe a shotgun. Maybe a rifle. It didn't really matter that much to Dooley.

Still gripping the hackamore in his left hand, he raised the Henry rifle with his right, pointing, not even aiming, letting his instinct guide him. He squeezed the trigger and saw the Indian with the bow catapult over the back of his pinto.

Shoot that one first, Dooley had told himself. *The other's got only one shot.*

Besides, he had seen how fast a Sioux could fire those arrows—almost as fast as Dooley could squeeze a trigger.

He was, of course, shocked that he had actually hit the Indian, but did not marvel over his luck or accuracy. The kick of that old Henry almost ripped his arm from the elbow socket, and he kept the .44 in his hand only through some sort of miracle. He heard a roar, but felt no bullet, and wheeled the brown pony toward the remaining brave.

That warrior had covered a lot of ground quickly, and Dooley barely had time to duck as the gray-headed Sioux swung the barrel of the rifle—it was not a shotgun, but it was a single shot—that glanced off Dooley's back as he ducked. The Indian rode past, cursing in what Dooley thought was French, and Dooley sucked in a deep breath, the air burning his lungs, and turned the brown mustang around.

Through the dust, he spotted the Indian wheeling his pinto, pitching the empty rifle to the dust, and kicking the pony's sides hard with his moccasins as he charged again, this time bringing a tomahawk up over his head.

The brown mustang was already galloping without waiting for Dooley's command, ready to meet the charge like one of those Knights of the Round Table Dooley had read about in a line shack seven or eight winters back. As the horse carried him into duel, Dooley jerked his wrist, sending the stock of the Henry forward. He kept a fierce grip on the repeater's lever, and then jerked forward. The motion brought the rifle back, fully cocked and loaded—providing at least one round remained in the Henry. He swung the rifle up, over the saddle, ducked as the Indian swung the hatchet, and squeezed the trigger.

The Henry roared like a cannon, and it kicked as if Dooley were holding a cannon. This time, he could not keep the rifle in his hands, and felt the heavy .44 tear free and fall into the grass. It almost ripped Dooley out of the seat of the Indian saddle, but he did the old cowboy's version of pulling leather— which was much harder on an Indian saddle than a slick fork.

He came up quickly, grimacing as he turned around, fully expecting to find the Indian there, swinging that war axe into Dooley's brain. What he saw, however, was another riderless Indian pony galloping away. Dooley blinked, looked around, and this time found the gray-headed brave lying faceup in the sun. The .44 slug had caught the Indian in his side, blown through the old man's vitals, and torn a fist-sized hole in his other side.

The Sioux had had no time to sing his death song. Dooley steadied the brown mare, who wanted to run after the other ponies. He caught his breath and swung down from the brown, keeping a firm grip on the hackamore. Refusing to let go of the hackamore, he knelt and grabbed the Henry. After slowly levering another cartridge into the magazine, he eased down the hammer and climbed back onto the pony's back.

Dooley stared off in the direction of the two ponies, riding straight for Wyoming or the Black Hills or some parts unknown. Maybe to a Sioux encampment. Would those horses bring back other warriors?

He didn't know. Actually, he didn't care, although he hoped that that Indian village was a good three- or four-day ride from here. Make that, three- or four-week ride from here.

Dooley blinked, swallowed, and wet his lips. He was alive. Somehow, he was alive. He glanced over his shoulder, but saw no dust, no sign that Zee and Blue, or the rest of the Dobbs-Handley Gang, might be following.

"Come on, girl," he said, his voice hoarse, his throat parched, every muscle in his body aching. But he was game. And so was the mare.

He kicked the mustang's sides and started off in a lope, heading after General Grant and however many Sioux warriors were trying to steal Dooley's horse.

CHAPTER FIFTEEN

Uncertain about the land and how long he might have to chase those horse-thieving Indians—or if any more might be riding back toward him—Dooley Monahan slowed the mare to a lope, and then a trot. After another mile, he let the brown even walk as he looked around. The land was just one big bunch of nothingness as far as anyone could see. By now, even the dust had settled, so he just followed the trail of trampled grass and hoped he was following the right trail.

For the next hour, he took his time, guessing more than tracking. Every now and then, he swung down to the ground and walked the mustang. He seemed to recall an old army sergeant telling him that the 4th Cavalry spent a lot of time walking their horses. If it was good enough for the United States Cavalry, then it seemed sound logic to Dooley Monahan. He didn't want to run the mustang to her death and be caught afoot in Nebraska—especially with Sioux warriors around.

When he came to a shallow creek, he felt better,

and since the mare had cooled off some from the walk, he let her drink. Stepping upstream from the brown, Dooley then lowered himself onto his belly and dropped his face into the cool water. It revived him instantly, and he drank his fill, soaked his head, and splashed water onto the back of his neck. Eventually, he rolled onto his back, and looked at the sky.

His muscles still ached, and his stomach let him know that it had been a hard day and he had eaten nothing since jerky for breakfast. He sat up. The horse snorted, and Dooley pushed himself to his feet. Suddenly, the horse's head went straight up, and her ears bent forward.

Something had alerted her, or at least pricked her interest. Dooley stared off in the direction the mare kept looking. Her front left hoof pawed the banks of the stream, and she snorted. Before the horse could whinny, however, Dooley quickly shot out his free hand and muzzled her.

"Shhhhhhh," he whispered.

He wet his lips, which were already wet, and thought for a moment.

The wind blew toward him, and he knew the mare had caught the scent of something. But what? Wolf? Snake? Indians? General Grant? All four? Or something else?

A man can think hisself into doin' a whole bunch of nothin'. The words of Old Man Buckshot Harrigan ran through his mind so clearly that Dooley almost thought the grizzled Texan stood right behind him, but Buckshot never whispered anything in anybody's ear, and Dooley didn't smell Bull Durham tobacco, just Nebraska grass and the stink of his own sweat and the pleasant odor of a fine mustang.

He swung into the Indian saddle.

"All right," he told the mare, "let's see what it is."

Slowly, letting the mustang pick her own path, Dooley followed the creek, rifle across his lap, the hammer of the Henry already eared back so the .44 was ready to fire.

He felt the horse begin a climb, not that it was a climb like heading over the Sierras, but the mare left the creek, and snorted again. Dooley could hear the shouts now, the songs of Sioux warriors, and the whinnies that only a bay gelding named General Grant could make.

Dooley ran his tongue over his lips, which had quickly lost all the moisture from that creek. What rolled down his spine was not creek water, but sweat. His heart beat. He ground his teeth. And then he saw them.

Three of them. Three Sioux braves. Two had ropes over General Grant's neck, the hemp burning the leather of their shirts as the two warriors struggled against the might of a fierce horse. General Grant reared, snorted, his eyes flashing anger, the front hooves slashing down toward the third Indian, who waved a blanket at the gelding and ducked.

One of the Indians with a rope yelled something at the blanket-shaker, who stumbled back, scrambled to his feet, and barked out something in his native tongue at the roper, who had lost his footing and was now being dragged across the ground on his knees. The other Indian with the rope pulled hard, and the one on his knees managed to regain his footing.

The blanket-shaker caught his breath and charged, waving the blanket, letting it sail, but General Grant ducked his head, and the blanket missed, landing on the other side. The ropers pulled, steering the gelding away, giving the third warrior time to gather up the blanket for another try.

Dooley knew what the Indian wanted, needed, to do. Put the blanket over the General's head. A horse that could not see became, more or less, docile. That's how many a bronc-buster worked. Blindfold the horse, get on the saddle, release the blindfold, and let 'er buck.

He pressed the stock of the Henry against his right shoulder and touched the trigger with his index finger as he lined up the sights. It would be easy enough, he told himself. The Indians didn't hold any weapons. Shoot all three—just be careful you don't hit General Grant by accident—and catch up the gelding. And put the spurs to that bay and get the hell out of Nebraska, as far away from the Dobbs-Handley Gang, and up to the Black Hills as quick as you can.

Yet he couldn't pull that trigger.

Yes, the three Indians were unarmed—for the time being—but they were trying to steal Dooley's horse, and the laws of white men—and, most likely, the laws of any Indian tribe—had decreed that stealing a man's horse in the West meant a death sentence.

Dooley had seen a few horse thieves strung up.

But he had never strung any of them up. Certainly, he had never shot any of them dead.

Don't think. React.

Dooley started to lower the rifle. He should just

ride down there. He'd have the drop on them. He could get his horse, and ride off at a hard lope, leaving the Indians afoot.

Afoot?

That stopped him. Brought him back to sound reasoning. Those Indians had to have horses nearby. And he had heard singing a while back, and those Indians were too busy trying to stop General Grant from smashing their heads with hooves to be doing any singing.

Dooley swung around just in time to see one of the Sioux braves nocking an arrow on his bow. He spun the horse, brought the Henry back up, and this time had no trouble pressing down on that trigger. The Henry roared, the Indian dropped his bow and arrow, and doubled over, gut-shot.

Another arrow flashed past Dooley's left ear, and he felt himself leaving the Indian pony. He hit the ground, rolled over, and shouldered the Henry as he worked the lever. The next brave came right at him, with another right behind him, and Dooley cut loose. Firing. Cocking. Firing. Cocking. Firing and cocking.

He forced himself to his knees, saw that he had put two more Sioux braves down, and he swung back toward General Grant and the three others. Those warriors had dropped ropes and blankets. Two were heading for their weapons, which he now saw a few yards away in the grass. The third had unsheathed a bone-handled knife and came at him, his face masked with war paint and grim determination.

Dooley aimed at the charging Indian's chest, touched the trigger, and heard the almost deafening, heart-stopping click of the hammer striking . . . nothing.

He was empty.

Quickly, as the charging warrior shouted in triumph, Dooley brought his right hand out of the case-hardened lever, gripped the hot barrel. His left hand slid up from the walnut forestock, and he brought up the rifle, swinging it across, the stock catching the Indian's head.

The blow brought down both Dooley and the Sioux, but only Dooley rose. He knew he had crushed that man's skull. He did not try to pick up the rifle, but instead reached down and snatched the dead brave's knife.

Dooley had never been in a knife fight. Oh, he had seen one or two, but that would do him no good now. Nor would the knife. Those two Indians were twenty or thirty yards away, and they were going for rifles. Dooley couldn't throw a knife with any accuracy, and even if luck smiled on him, he would take out just one of the two men left.

He threw the knife anyway, watched it sail. It did not hit an Indian's heart. It did not cover twenty or thirty yards. It went blade over handle a few arcs, before it landed in the dirt—maybe six feet in front of him. It didn't even stick in the sod, but skimmed across the ground on its side.

Dooley came up to his feet, and, even though he came from a Yankee state, he let out the old Johnny Reb cry that Old Man Buckshot Harrigan screamed when he was drunk or having nightmares. He charged the two Indians with only his fists. He knew he'd be killed.

Guns roared. Dooley kept screaming, kept charging, and slowly began to stop, then hit the brakes, and felt himself tumbling.

The first brave jerked upright, turned around, and two more shots drove him to his knees, a final shot blew off the top of his head. The second warrior turned the old Sharps buffalo gun away from Dooley and roared. Then, seeing his comrade fall, understanding that he had fired his one shot, he tossed the empty rifle aside, folded his arms, and met his death like a brave Sioux warrior.

He started to sing his death chant, but he barely got out two or three words.

Bullets shattered the brave's bone breastplate and drove him back. He tripped over the dead lookout's body and landed on his butt, his legs out in front of him, and more bullets dropped his torso to the ground. As he rolled over onto his bloody back, maybe six or seven more bullets tore through his body.

By then, the Indian felt nothing.

Nor did Dooley as he turned around and sank to his knees.

He heard the hooves of horses, the curses and shouts of men—and one woman—and Dooley sighed, closing his eyes, sucking in air to fill his lungs.

"Hooray for ya, Dooley Monograms!" Zee Dobbs cried. "Don't ya fret, boy, I'll fetch yer hoss up right quick. I'm faster than lightnin', ya know!"

Air rushed past him as Zee Dobbs lived up to her word.

"By thunder!" came a man's voice, and over the curses and jokes and the scalping of the dead warriors, Dooley almost broke into tears. He knew that voice. He knew what it meant.

"You's the bravest cur that ever rode with me, boy!" Hubert Dobbs slapped Dooley's back so hard, Dooley almost toppled over himself. "Do you gots any notion how many scalps we've done took off the bucks you left behind? Hell, Dooley, the army don't need that pettifoggin' blowhard Custer to kill no Sioux and send 'em bucks back to the reservation. They should hire you! You'd lick 'em all afore Independence Day!"

Dooley sighed, shook his head in defeat, and fell back on the grass.

"You see him, boys!" Dobbs bellowed. "This is the kind of men I needs to ride fer me. Brave and loyal and a deadlier shot than Doc Watson. Hooray! Hooray for Dewey Mulligans!"

Something wet and scratchy slapped his face. Dooley heard the whimper, the excited bark, and felt Blue's tongue on his cheek again. Somehow, Dooley found the strength to lift his right arm and find the fur, to rub the dog.

Blue barked again.

At least, Dooley thought, I've got Blue with me. And as soon as Zerelda's back, I'll have General Grant, too.

CHAPTER SIXTEEN

The Dobbs-Handley Gang celebrated that night . . . well, after they had covered a lot of ground to get as far away from any other Sioux warriors, or Cheyenne, or Pawnee, or lawmen that might be riding across Nebraska.

When the moon rose, they kept riding, but stopped around midnight and broke out the whiskey.

This wasn't rotgut, but bona fide bourbon and rye that they had liberated from a gristmill on a river.

"That's what kept us, boy," Frank Handley said. "Else we woulda come ridin' to save your hide and hair before then. Nice mill. Brick buildin', good brush dam, a couple run of stone burrs. We even got us some grain for biscuits."

"Dooley don't care 'bout grain, Frank!" Hubert Dobbs said.

"Sure he do," Handley argued. "No cowboy alive don't care 'bout biscuits and corn bread."

"He ain't no cowboy," Dobbs said. "He's a gunfighter. A killer. A proud rider of the Dobbs-Handley Gang."

"Well," Handley relented, "it was as fine a mill as I've ever laid eyes on in this part of the country."

"And Dooley don't care nothin' 'bout no gristmill, neither."

"Neither do the owners of that mill," Doc Watson said with a low, lifeless chuckle. "Not no more . . . since we paid 'em a visit."

With a sigh that grew into a moan, Dooley put his right forearm over his eyes. He felt bone-tired, and did not need the rye to help him sleep, but he kept a grip on the bottle, just in case. He was riding with the worst bunch of killers in the West. Sure, he had ridden with Monty's Raiders, but they said they were fighting for the Southern cause in the North, long before the Civil War actually broke out and even before John Brown started hacking slaveholding folks to death in Kansas and Missouri or John Reid's Missouri bushwhackers started sacking Kansas towns like Lawrence.

Even the worst of Monty's bunch was not a patch on the most timid killer who rode for Hubert Dobbs.

He brought the bottle to his mouth, managed to swallow some rye without drowning or coughing, and lowered his arm and the bottle. Someone took it from his grasp, and Dooley did not object. Not long after, when Zee broke out the mouth harp and her father began playing the spoons while Frank Handley sang "Old Dan Tucker," Dooley Monahan went to sleep.

He wished those Indians had killed him. At least then he would know peace.

* * *

The boys slept in. They had had a hard day, a rough night, and a lot of good whiskey that their stomachs were not accustomed to.

Dooley's eyes opened. His arm remained across his forehead. He realized he had slept on the ground and not in his bedroll. Not that he had been drunk. Just utterly exhausted. After wetting his lips, he looked at the sky. From the sun's position, he guessed it to be eight or so in the morning—late for a cowboy, even later for a wanted man.

He could smell Blue's rancid dog breath, and feel the air blowing against his ear. The loyal hound softly snored, and Dooley laughed softly, and turned around to look at the blue-eyed dog.

"Holy—" He sat bolt upright, his chest heaving, and watched as Zee Dobbs snorted, spit, and opened her eyes.

"Hey there, Dooley, my sweetheart," Zee said, and hacked up some snot, spit it onto the spot where Dooley's head had been resting, and pushed herself to a seated position as she farted, burped, and began to scratch one of her armpits.

I was not that drunk. I was not that drunk. I was not that drunk . . .

Dooley kept telling himself that. Hell, he had only had two or three slugs of rye. He felt better, though, realizing that his pants remained on and all of Zee's filthy duds had not been removed.

"You sleep all right, precious?" Zee asked, and she pulled herself to her feet.

"Yeah," Dooley answered, and looked around for his dog. Blue, whose breath did not stink as bad as Zee's, lay curled in a ball near General Grant.

Other men began stirring, and Doc Watson started poking the embers and ashes of the fire.

"Monahan," the gunman said as he stifled a cough. "Go fetch some dried dung. We got coffee to make before we ride."

As they moved north, the land began to change more abruptly. You didn't find many trees, but the land turned sandier, and hills sprang up and down, rivers flowed with grace, and they even camped ponds whose banks were green with cattails and canebrakes. The air felt cleaner here, crisper, though the wind still blew with a harshness and a raw, cutting edge that reminded Dooley of the danger around him.

It had been a long time since Dooley had ridden in the sandhill country. If he remembered right, if he could figure out his bearings, he guessed the Niobrara ran to the north, and beyond that the Missouri.

He must have guessed right, because when they settled in that afternoon to make an early camp, Hubert Dobbs made a vague gesture over his shoulder.

"Yankton's yonder way," he said. His head bobbed to the west. "Ogallala's a fer piece that way. What do you boys think?"

Dooley tried to do some thinking himself. Yankton lay across the Missouri in Dakota Territory. It would have law, plenty of law, plenty of lawmen. It might be a good way for Dooley to get away from the rough crew he found himself among. Besides, Dooley remembered Ogallala all too well. Dobbs was not exaggerating by saying Ogallala was far from here. Ten days. Two weeks. But Ogallala could be wild and woolly, lawless as the Kansas City stockyards or Fort Worth, Texas, on a Saturday night. There might be a lawman in that cattle town, but probably not one with enough sand (or a lack of brains) to try to capture Frank Handley, Doc Watson, or Hubert Dobbs. On the other hand, Dooley remembered that there was an army post somewhere between here and Ogallala. Hartford? No. Hartstuff. That was it. Fort Hartstuff.

"We robbed the bank in Yankton two years ago, Hubert," someone said.

"Yeah, but the bank would have more money by now," another outlaw countered.

"What did the whores look like in Yankton?"

"Better'n you, Mort."

"And cost the same as 'em wenches in Ogallala."

"Ya see how democratics my pa is?"

Zee Dobbs had sidled up close to Dooley, who had smelled her before she got too close, but he had frozen, the way you did when you heard a rattlesnake whirling just under your boots. "Lets the boys takes part in the votin', kinda like regular citizens does when they's pickin' a president or somethin'. Kinda nice, ain't it, Doosey?"

"Uh . . . yeah. I reckon."

"Not as nice as you is, though, love." She giggled.

"Well," Dobbs said. "I reckon y'all've decided then. Ogallala it is."

The men cheered, although Dooley could not recall anyone raising an arm or drawing lots or saying aye or nay.

He turned away from Zee and stared off to the north, toward Dakota, toward Yankton, toward possible salvation. Of course, Ogallala would be on his way

to the Black Hills . . . like he had a snowball's chance
in Zee Dobbs's hot breath of ever getting there.

"All right," Dobbs said. "Atkinson."

"Yeah, boss," came a low drawl.

"You ride to Yankton. We'll meet you on the South
Fork of the Elkhorn. Take . . . um . . . take . . . er . . ."

"Let him take Doobie," Zee said.

All chatter stopped. Everyone turned to stare at
Zee Dobbs as if she had lost her mind. Then they
looked at Dooley as if they were seeing a dead man.
Finally, they turned to Ewing Atkinson. Dooley
looked at him, too.

Six-foot-six, maybe, two hundred and fifty pounds.
Dressed more like a farmer than a cutthroat, in bib
overalls and a muslin shirt and two boots that did not
match. His hat was straw, most of the brim ripped to
shreds, and his beard was black and thick. The man's
face that was not covered with hair was free of scars.
His massive fists, however, were covered with scars.

Across the denim of his overalls he wore two gun
belts, and each belt held two holsters—all of them
Walker Colts converted to take brass cartridges. Walk-
ers were like cannon, in size and weight, and Dooley
had seen only one of those ancient six-shooters
before. And that owner had carried his in a saddle
holster, not on his waist.

"You sure you want Dooley to go with Atkinson?"
Hubert Dobbs asked softly, almost as if he were beg-
ging for his daughter to suggest someone else.

"Yep." Zee placed her hands on her hips.

"But . . . well . . ."

"We've seen how Dewey can handle dumb red savages, Pa," Zee said. "We've seen that he forks a horse
right well, he ain't afraid, and he's got one smart

dog and a real fine horse. We've seen he's got the gumption to go after his horse and his dog when anybody else would find somethin' better and safer to do. Ain't that right?"

Heads bobbed. Dooley only saw that in the corner of his eye. His focus trained on Ewing Atkinson, whose black eyes—even the one that was always wandering—locked dead on Dooley's nose. It was Dooley who finally had to look away. He turned to stare at Zee.

"If we really want to see if we can trust this gent," Zee said, "and I mean trust him with our lives, see if he's one of us or just some yellow-livered chicken turd who wants our heads . . . well . . ." She tilted her head toward the massive bull of a brute named Ewing Atkinson. "Then I figure we find out exactly what he's got in his craw. Don't you, Pa?"

Hubert Dobbs frowned for the longest while. At length, he lifted his head and turned toward Frank Handley, who rubbed his chin as he considered Zee's reasoning. Dooley looked back at Ewing Atkinson, a quiet cuss who Dooley had paid scant attention to before now. He had seen buffalo smaller than this man. He had seen a herd of buffalo smaller than this man.

Some sort of fringe fluttered from the braces of his overalls.

When Dooley looked away from the behemoth, his stomach knotted. Handley's head nodded in agreement, while Doc Watson merely chuckled, coughed, and squatted again by the fire to pick up the coffeepot.

"Then it's settled." Hubert Dobbs strode toward Dooley, but barked his orders at the towering giant.

"Steal a wagon, Atkinson, but don't kill nobody. Unless you ain't got a choice. But see Zee for the money. You're buyin' supplies. Buyin'. Not stealin'." The leader stopped in front of Dooley and lowered his voice.

"Atkinson's loyal as a coonhound, but he ain't got the sense God gave a turnip. Make sure he don't kill nobody in Yankton. Don't want no posse raisin' dust after us all the way to Ogallala. You understand that, Dooney?"

Dooley didn't understand a damned thing, but he said in a dry voice, "I reckon I do."

The outlaw reached over and his big hand gripped Dooley's shoulder, giving it a firm, almost collarbone-crushing squeeze.

"Zee's got her notions. Up to me, I wouldn't have done this to you, pard, but . . . I reckon it's fer the best. South Fork of the Elkhorn. I'll see you there in three days."

What struck Dooley was how Hubert Dobbs said that, and how he could not look Dooley in the eye.

I'll see you there in three days.

Hubert Dobbs didn't mean it. He acted and sounded as if he were speaking to a dead man.

CHAPTER SEVENTEEN

To Dooley Monahan's way of thinking, everything started off well enough. After all, Ewing Atkinson did not kill anyone when they stole the farm wagon.

Oh, sure, Dooley had heard Hubert Dobbs bark, preach, and order that no one was to be killed to get the wagon, but Dooley didn't believe that Ewing Atkinson would obey any orders. All the big man did as they rode east and then north toward the Missouri River was hone the edge of the biggest bowie knife Dooley had ever seen against the whetstone he kept in one of the pockets of his overalls. The knife, of course, did not look that big in Atkinson's enormous hands.

First, that wasn't fringe stitched into the braces on the killer's overalls. They were scalp locks, and not just scalps from those recently killed Sioux warriors. Sure, most of the scalps on the front of the giant's denim duds were black, as though lifted from Indians, or Mexicans, or maybe even Dooley's great-uncle Joseph, whose oil-black hair was one thing Dooley's mother always bragged about, how it glistened like a crow's wing, and how she sure hoped Joseph had made it to California and the goldfields all those years ago. He had never written. Then again, Joseph had never learned his letters. The back of Ewing Atkinson's clothes were decorated with scalps of all colors: auburns and carrottops and blonds, brunettes and sandy browns and dirty blonds, grays and silvers and salt-and-peppers.

Dooley knew that the silent leviathan planned to add Dooley's own hair to his grotesque collection.

But not the farmers from Rose Creek. That's because Dooley had heard the singing and commotion and preaching and all those *amens* when they rode past the creek near the turn of the Missouri.

"Camp meeting," Dooley told Atkinson, who did not blink, did not nod, did not even part his lips. The man did not even glance at the gathering of farmers and homesteaders and one fire-and-brimstone preacher dressed in black broadcloth and a straw hat that was not well chewed and practically falling apart like Ewing Atkinson's.

Dooley felt better after seeing practically every family this side of the big river listening to the Word of God. So they had ridden to a nice-looking farm about two miles due east. The house wasn't much— though a mansion compared to the sod hut of the late Ole Something-another-dorf—but the corrals were well built, the privy a two-seater, and two other wagons parked near the barn.

Atkinson took the largest wagon, and Dooley harnessed the sorriest pair of mules he could find. Maybe the farmer wouldn't miss those animals too much. Perhaps, Dooley tried to tell himself, he was even doing those folks a favor.

"Well," he said out loud but in a whisper, "I am saving their lives."

"You," Ewing Atkinson said when the wagon and team were ready to ride. "Drive that." The man's huge head nodded at the farm wagon.

Up until then, Dooley half thought that big Ewing Atkinson was a deaf-mute. For a moment, Dooley thought about arguing, but decided against it. He surprised himself by even considering drawing his Colt and filling Ewing Atkinson's overalls full of bullet holes. But that would be murder. If the bullets somehow managed to put a dent in the giant's chest.

"All right," Dooley said, and gathered the reins to General Grant. He led the gelding to the rear of the wagon and tethered the bay to the wagon. He thought Atkinson would want to ride the General—and that likely would have led Dooley to palm his Colt—but the killer merely nodded, waited for Dooley to climb into the driver's seat, gather the lines, and release the brake. Atkinson grunted, kicked his big horse's sides, and rode alongside the wagon as Dooley whistled nervously.

When they had made it about two or three hundred yards from the farm, the huge man unsheathed his bowie, brought out his whetstone, and resumed his sharpening.

Keep that up, Dooley told himself, *and he won't have any blade left to sharpen.*

Which, he thought a mile later, *would not be a bad thing . . . not in the least.*

Mosquitoes buzzed, bit, and whined, and gnats tried to fly into Dooley's mouth, nose, ears, and eyes, as they waited for the ferry to arrive on the Nebraska side of the Missouri. The owner of the ferry considered Dooley with skepticism but Ewing Atkinson with fear. He took the fifteen cents Dooley offered him, pocketed the coins, and went back to his spot in the shade, near the smoking fire that would keep the insects away, and much, much closer to the double-barreled shotgun that leaned against the outer picket wall of his shack.

A salesman in a light-colored suit and gray derby, and a woman carrying a parasol and wearing a blue-and-white-checked dress rode up together a few minutes after Dooley and Atkinson had arrived. The ferry docked a few minutes later. The man and the lady decided they would wait a while, take in the sights, and admire the lovely river. They weren't very convincing liars. They just didn't want to cross the ferry with Ewing Atkinson. Dooley Monahan didn't want to, either.

The Missouri ran wide and swift, but the ferry did not capsize, and it did not sink. Eventually, it bumped onto the landing in Dakota Territory, and Dooley climbed back into the stolen farm wagon and followed the giant on the big dun horse onto the road to Yankton. At least the mosquitoes and gnats had stayed on the Nebraska side of the river.

They rode to Yankton.

E-Hank-Ton-Wan. That's what the Nakota Sioux Indians called the place. It meant "People of the End Village," or something like that. Translating Indian words into English didn't always turn out right.

Anyway, that's what the clerk at the general store

in Yankton told Dooley. The man kept right on talking, telling Dooley about the Yankton Treaty of 1858, and how that gold strike in the Black Hills was making Yankton, the territorial capital since President Buchanan had created Dakota Territory back in 1861, boom like it had never boomed before.

Dooley had known that long before they had forded Rhine Creek and driven into Yankton. Steamboats and every other kind of ship or boat that Dooley had ever seen lay moored or anchored along the northern banks of the Missouri. Black smoke belched out of some of the smokestacks, and men and women, of all sizes, shapes, and skin colors, lined the wharves, the levees, and the boardwalks. Music belched. Men hawked their goods and commodities. Horses, donkeys, mules, pedestrians, and wagons churned the muddy streets into a quagmire.

Yankton was a lot larger than Dooley had expected.

The store sprawled across several lots on Fourth Street, down from the two-story wooden capitol. Burly men carried the sacks and crates from the back of the store to Dooley's stolen wagon parked out front, while Dooley let the clerk clip off the end of the cigar and fire it up with a long-stemmed match.

"I saw some saloons down—what was that— Broadway?" Dooley said, dreaming of the time when he could have gone to one of those places, sipped on a beer or a whiskey, and played a friendly game of poker. Of course, Dobbs and Handley had not given Dooley enough money to gamble with—just enough to buy plenty of grub and grain for the horses.

And ammunition.

"You sure carry a lot of guns," the clerk said as he

brought out the last four boxes of .44-40 cartridges. "Must be a whole army you're outfitting."

Dooley removed the cigar, blew smoke, and grinned his fakest grin. "Bunch of my neighbors from Des Moines," he lied, "decided we'd light out for the Black Hills."

"You and everybody else in the United States and her territories," the clerk called out. Then yelled, "Gomer, see if we have any more boxes of .45-60s and .50-95s in the back room!" He glanced back at Dooley. "I know we've got the .45-70s and plenty of .38s, .44s, and .45s—and all the shotgun loads you asked for." He checked the list Dooley had given him, the one Doc Watson—whose handwriting was the most legible of anyone who rode with Dobbs and Handley—had written out for Dooley. "You wouldn't think a bunch of farmers from Iowa would carry so many different calibers of bullets."

Dooley returned the cigar to his mouth. "You should see the size of the mercantile in Des Moines," he said.

Down the counter, Ewing Atkinson looked at a bolt of calico as his teeth smashed a peppermint stick into oblivion.

"I wish I could get to Deadwood in the Black Hills," the clerk said.

Dooley sighed. "How is that gold strike going?"

"Wouldn't know firsthand," the clerk lamented, "but I've seen hundreds of people coming through here, bound for Deadwood, and nary a one to come back. At least, not yet."

Dooley shook his head. "How far are the Black Hills goldfields from here?"

"Depends on how you get there. I hear a lot of

folks are going to Cheyenne down there in Wyoming Territory. Taking wagon trains or stagecoaches there. That is, if the Sioux don't jump you and lift your hair. From here, best way is to take a packet upriver to Fort Pierre Chouteau. That's the trading post and strong-hold old Pierre Chouteau's boy founded on the north side of the river's mouth back in '32. You remember Chouteau, don't you?"

"Sure," Dooley lied. He wouldn't know Pierre Chouteau—junior or senior—from Hubert Dobbs's wife and mother of Zerelda.

"Then you just head west to the Black Hills. If the Sioux don't jump you and lift your hair."

The clerk barked out a few more orders. "Or you just head upstream to the confluence with the White, cross the river, follow the White into the Bad-lands and then make your way into the Black Hills. That is . . ."

Dooley joined him: ". . . if the Sioux don't jump you and lift your hair."

The two men laughed, and the clerk handed Dooley the bill. Dooley pulled out the stolen green-backs and stolen gold pieces that Dobbs had given him, counted out enough money to foot the bill, and dropped what little money he had left into his vest pocket.

"If you want a good place to eat," the clerk said, "Ma Vérendrye puts on a good feed at her place over on Sixth Street."

"Thanks," Dooley told him, and they shook hands. "But I reckon my pard and me should get back to our outfit on the other side of the bluff. Enjoyed talking to you."

The man leaned over the counter and whispered

in a conspiratorial voice as he tilted his head toward Ewing Atkinson. "That's your pard? I thought that was your woolly mammoth."

Dooley laughed, though he found nothing amusing about the joke, shook hands with the clerk, and walked toward the stolen farm wagon parked outside and now loaded with supplies.

He climbed into the wagon, released the brake, and flicked the lines. The mules struggled with the weight and mud, and people cursed Dooley and the big brute called Atkinson as Dooley tried to turn the wagon around in the wide street.

Atkinson reached for his large bowie knife, but Dooley told him, "Remember what Hubert told you."

Reluctantly, the giant shoved the knife back into the sheath.

Dooley wondered if he could somehow elude Atkinson, take the wagon, follow one of the trails the clerk had suggested, and finally make his way to the Black Hills . . . without being jumped and having his hair lifted by the Sioux.

Instead, he signed and guided the wagon and mules back toward the ferry on the Missouri River. They were crossing the little creek again when the big man rode up alongside the wagon.

"What is it?" Dooley asked.

Ewing Atkinson did not answer. He merely thrust out his right hand, grabbed Dooley by the shirtfront, pulled him off the driver's seat, and slammed him hard into Rhine Creek.

CHAPTER EIGHTEEN

The water was shallow, and Dooley hit a rock at the bottom that smashed his nose. He rolled over, coughing and spitting out blood and water, blinking the murky water out of his eyes, and came up quickly. The leviathan killer had surprised him, but Dooley knew he had to react quickly. For some reason, Ewing Atkinson wanted to kill him.

"Are you crazy?" Dooley shouted, backing up in the little creek, reaching for his Colt only to discover that it had fallen out of his holster. He saw the gun on a rock that wasn't completely submerged in the water. Then the revolver disappeared underneath Ewing Atkinson's massive boot—the tan one, not the black one with the mule-ear pulls.

The big man had taken his time getting off his horse, but men that size usually did not move—as Zee Dobbs kept saying—"quicker than lightnin'," although the big galoot had moved fast when he had jerked Dooley off the wagon.

Remember that, Dooley told himself as he wiped his

bloody nose with the soaking sleeve of his left arm. *He can be fast when he needs to be.*

The mules had stopped on the other side of the creek, the wagon's rear wheels still in the shallow water, with General Grant tethered to the back of the Studebaker, looking curiously at Dooley and the giant. Atkinson's horse had not budged from where the big cuss had stopped, and now lowered its head to start slurping up the muddy water.

Dooley looked down the road that led to the ferry, but saw no one. He didn't dare take a chance to glance down the road that led to town. He knew better than to take his eyes off Ewing Atkinson, for the big man had pulled that razor-sharp bowie knife that looked more like a cavalry saber.

Atkinson grinned.

Dooley stepped back a little more and spread his arms out.

"I must kill you," the giant said.

"Why?" Dooley asked.

"You know why."

"If I knew why—" He had to jump back as the man swung the knife blade toward Dooley. Dooley kept his feet. The water was soaking his socks. The big killer laughed, for the knife had not even come close to Dooley.

"If I knew why," Dooley repeated, "I wouldn't ask."

The big man stepped forward, and Dooley looked but no longer saw the rock, and no longer saw his Colt.

He gestured wildly toward the wagon. "We need to get those supplies to Hubert Dobbs and the boys."

The blade slashed again, but this time it came a little closer.

The two men circled, dangerous, sizing each other up. Dooley came out of the water and onto the grassy, slippery bank. Run? Take a chance and make a mad dash for the ferry? He remembered the ferryman's large shotgun. But if he turned his back on Atkinson, that knife blade might find its way in Dooley's liver, lungs, or heart. And he didn't want any innocent bystander killed, although he certainly would not begrudge one who happened along right now, especially if he carried a .50 caliber Sharps rifle or maybe a mountain howitzer with him.

That got Dooley thinking some more as he stepped back in the water. The back of the wagon didn't just carry food and supplies and a few hundred pounds of ammunition in various calibers and makes. Two kegs of gunpowder for the boys who still used cap-and-ball muzzleloaders, and maybe to blow up the vaults in a bank or Wells Fargo office, along with six sticks of dynamite. The clerk at the general store had not questioned such purchases. After all, he was selling to an outfit bound for the Black Hills gold camps, where dynamite and gunpowder were needed for tunneling through hard granite. And a new-model Winchester repeating rifle in a caliber meant for killing buffalo.

So all Dooley had to do was make it to the wagon, jump into the back, rip off the canvas, find the Winchester Centennial, find the box of shells that fit the Winchester lever-action rifle, load the rifle, cock it, aim it, and shoot Ewing Atkinson between the eyes. Or find the dynamite, cap it, find a match, light the fuse, hurl the stick underneath the huge killer's legs—and duck. He patted his vest pocket and felt the wetness. His matches would be worthless now—not that he would even consider such a foolish idea.

"You got designs," Atkinson said as he taunted Dooley with the big knife. ". . . on Miss Zerelda."

Dooley stopped, his mouth dropping open, then arced away from the slashing blade. He backed up against the side of the wagon.

"I got what . . . ?" he shouted.

"I seen you," Atkinson said. "You're after my sweet-heart."

"Is this why . . . are you . . . Zerelda Dobbs?"

He ducked again as the knife went over his head, and fell to his knees, came up, remembered where he had dropped the Colt, and reached under the dark water, groping and praying, and coming up fast and away from the knife as Atkinson slammed it down.

It splashed and disappeared in Rhine Creek, and Dooley turned around, watching the big man on his hands and knees in the creek. Dooley looked at his own right hand. It held no Colt, but he had managed to snatch up a fair-sized rock.

As Atkinson looked up and brought both hands out of the water, Dooley reared back his right arm, let it windmill a couple of rotations, and let the rock fly. It smashed perfectly underneath the giant's nose, and although the thick black beard cushioned the blow, Ewing Atkinson fell backward, his feet stretched out in the water before him. His face seemed stunned, as blood drenched his beard. With his left hand, he touched his smashed lips. He frowned, then spit out blood and a couple of rotten teeth, and quickly climbed to his feet.

"I'll kill you for that," he said, and spit out more blood.

"You were going to kill me for some nonsense that I wanted Zerelda," Dooley reminded him.

"I kill you," the giant said, and shook water off his big bowie. "Twice."

Dooley had always heard that buffalo could run incredibly fast, which most people would not expect for such cumbersome-looking shaggy beast. But Dooley knew that Ewing Atkinson could move with blazing speed when he wanted to, and right then, Dooley knew that the mountain-sized man wanted to. He sprang forward, the knife held low near his waist, his eyes now burning with seething hatred. Dooley didn't wait long, but held his place just long enough, then dived to his left as Atkinson brought the blade up with a grunt. The knife cut nothing but air, and Atkinson fell onto the bank of Rhine Creek.

Dooley had landed in the water, and he also leaped to his feet. He had tried to find another rock to hurl, but this time all his two hands came up with were globs of mud. He threw those in the general direction of Ewing Atkinson, but mostly the mud just splashed into the creek.

As Dooley shook most of the remaining grime from his hands, he thought about making a dash for the place where his Colt lay submerged. That would be a gamble, though. Certainly, water filled the barrel and chambers by now, and maybe even a lot of mud.

The killer's horse looked up from the water, snorted, and began urinating in the creek.

That gave Dooley another idea, and he backed up,

spreading out his arms again, shooting a glance at the wagon, then focusing again on the killer.

"Your scalp," Atkinson said, trying to taunt Dooley, but his busted mouth just made the threat sound more comical than threatening, "will look good on my overalls."

Dooley smiled. "A man's scalp?" He shook his head. He had learned how to taunt, too. "Tell me something, you dumb ox. Did you ever take the scalp of a man you actually killed? I mean . . ." He pointed at the wet scalps. "I guess you killed the women, maybe, and the kids. Even the dogs. Well, maybe not the dogs. Hell, maybe not the kids. Yeah, now that I think on it, I figure Doc Watson or even Zee killed most of the people. You just lifted the scalps. Hell, you probably even had to get someone to tie those locks to your overalls."

The roar sounded like a volcano erupting, and Ewing Atkinson charged, but now rage blinded the killer, and Dooley easily sidestepped the charging man as he slammed into the rear wheel of the wagon, which shuddered, and even lifted partly off the ground before the wagon settled back and sank a little deeper into the muddy bottom of the creek. That disturbance caused General Grant to snort and flatten his ears.

Atkinson had to grab hold of the spokes to keep from slipping into the wagon. He shook his head, spraying snot and saliva and blood this way and that, and spun around, but that blow had staggered him, and it took a moment for him to push himself to his feet.

Again, Dooley looked back toward Yankton and

down the road to the Missouri River. Again, nobody appeared anywhere. He cursed his luck. Here he was, spitting distance from a ferry and one of the most navigated rivers in the western United States and even closer to the territorial capital of Dakota Territory, which was filling up with gold seekers by the score. And nobody—not one damned person—was here when he needed a little help.

Atkinson took a step, brought the blade up again, and slowly approached Dooley, who stepped back and to his right. He moved again, barely lifting his boots, pushing against the fast-flowing creek. Dooley stepped back. Atkinson came forward. Dooley moved to his side. Atkinson did the same.

A standoff. Stalemate. Each man waiting for the other to make a mistake.

Dooley wet his wet lips. He moved again, back, and then upstream. Upstream.

That, he told himself, should be just right. He moved to his right.

"I kill you," Atkinson mumbled. "Then Miss Zerelda will love me. Only me."

"I would not interfere with your bliss," Dooley told him, and stepped to his right one last time.

He waited. Atkinson made the same move, and brought the knife up over his right shoulder.

"Yeeeeee-hiiiiii!" Dooley screamed. "Yippie, yippie, hoooo-rraaaaahhh!!!!!!"

He couldn't see behind the behemoth, but he got a glimpse of General Grant. When Atkinson had crashed against the wheel, the violence had pricked the bay gelding's nerves, and Dooley's sudden shouts and screams made the horse kick out with both of his hind legs.

"Ummmph!"

The hooves caught Ewing Atkinson square in his back and propelled the giant toward Dooley. That, Dooley had not actually considered when he had concocted the plan. Actually, he had hoped the gelding's hooves would have come up a little higher, catching the giant's neck or head, smashing both to cinders. Instead, the bowie knife whirled dangerously close to Dooley's head. He heard and felt the rush of air as the blade sliced just a few inches from Dooley's ear. And then Ewing Atkinson—no bashed-in brain, no broken neck, and very much still a living, breathing menace—came crashing straight into Dooley Monahan, driving both men into the murky, now bloody, Rhine Creek.

CHAPTER NINETEEN

It hurt to breathe . . . perhaps because Dooley could not breathe. He got his head out of the water, blinked away pain and water, and understood that Ewing Atkinson straddled him, crushing his chest, his lungs, and dripping blood and mucus into Dooley's face. He could just make out the man's bloody, bearded face, and saw two hands the size of a baby whale come toward Dooley's throat.

Dooley brought his right hand up. He knew he couldn't stop the man. He knew he was dead. Yet his hand felt different, and as he slammed it into Atkinson's solid stomach, he heard the big man cry out like an alley cat.

Air filled Dooley's lungs. By thunder, he thought, none of his ribs had even been cracked and snapped like twigs. He sat up, surprised to find that the giant had fallen off of Dooley.

No time to think. No time to do anything. Dooley used his left arm to push himself to his knees, and then jumped to his feet. He staggered back a few paces, caught his breath, shook his head, and came up, prepared to face Ewing Atkinson one final time.

The big man was on his hands and knees, his back to Dooley. Charge? Dooley considered it. Jump on the man's back. But then what? Dooley's chest heaved as his lungs worked for air. He looked down the road toward Yankton, but the pike remained deserted. Quickly, he faced Atkinson again. The killer had managed to stand, though unsteady, and slowly turned around to stare at Dooley.

That's when Dooley understood what had happened. He stepped back, but his boots slipped in the mud, and back he fell into the creek.

Blood streamed from Atkinson's mouth, drenching the beard, as the man brought both hands to the handle of the bowie that stuck just below his ribs. The right hand missed, but the left hand caught the handle, and tugged. Strong as he was, even Ewing Atkinson could not pull the big knife free with one hand.

Dooley's stomach churned. He had not even realized he held the knife, couldn't recall touching it, grabbing it, or anything. He had thought he was hitting the killer, not stabbing him deep.

Now Atkinson brought his right hand up again, and the massive fingers wrapped around his left hand. He staggered, almost fell, but righted himself, and looked again at Dooley as both hands tugged hard. The knife tore free, and blood rushed from the ugly hole.

The killer's lips moved, but he only coughed up more blood. He could not speak, but he did not have to, for Dooley knew exactly what the man wanted to say.

I'm dead . . . but I'm taking you with me.

Dooley tried to get to his feet, as the killer raised the bowie over his head and lurched toward him, gurgling as his eyes began to glaze over. Just then, something roared, and the top of Ewing Atkinson's head disappeared in an explosion of gore and blood. Dooley rolled over and over, heard the gargantuan splash into the creek, and then Dooley was standing, staring down at the dead fiend for just a moment.

That's when Dooley's own legs buckled, and he was sitting on the bank. He could see the dead killer, the creek carrying the blood and gray bits of brain—and two of the scalps that had come loose—downstream and into the Missouri River. He shook his head and looked at the wagon. General Grant remained tethered, and no longer kicking. Atkinson's horse had moved out of the water and onto the bank, to graze on spring wildflowers. The wagon remained where it was, the mules waiting sleepily on the road.

It occurred to him that he could mount General Grant and ride away . . . or even take the supplies Dobbs and Handley had purchased for him—and be off to Deadwood and the Black Hills. But that would mean leaving Blue with a pack of cutthroat vermin. Dooley had not been willing to let a bunch of Sioux Indians take his horse. He certainly wasn't going to abandon a loyal dog to the likes of Hubert Dobbs and his kind.

Not that he had a choice. Not now anyway.

"I swan, Doosey," a nasal drawl sounded in his ear. "Never thought I'd live to see anybody kill ol' Ewin'. You done good, love. Killed him fair and square and deader than Moby-Dickens."

Zee Dobbs knelt in front of Dooley and kissed him full on the lips.

She tasted like snuff.

"You killed him." His voice sounded hollow.

"Nah." Zee spit into the stream. "You stuck him plumb center." She tapped the spot with a small, dirty fist. "He likely had jus' 'bout bled out. I just prevented him from takin' you to hell with'm. It's what lovers do, Dewey. Good thing for you, though, that I's faster'n lightnin'."

Rising to her feet, she holstered her revolver and held out both hands toward Dooley. He had no choice but to accept the offer, and she pulled him to his feet and let her lead him to the side of the wagon.

A quick glance told him that Zee was right. She had shot him, and Ewing Atkinson was dead, and his attempt to kill Dooley had been the actions of a dead man.

"How long have you been here?" Dooley asked.

Zee withdrew a pewter flask from one of her pockets, unscrewed the lid, and held the container under Dooley's nostrils, like they were smelling salts. The whiskey in the flask smelled worse than smelling salts, but did the job, and Dooley took the flask, brought it to his lips, and took two fast swallows.

Coughing, he returned the flask to Zee, who chuckled, downed a few swallows herself, and began fastening the lid as she answered his question.

"Oh, I was in the woods yonder. Waitin'. And watchin'. Right fair fight. Best I'd ever seen with ol' Ewin'. Figured he'd try to kill you before you reached the big muddy."

"He could have killed me in town," he told her.

"That was a possibility, but crowds ain't in—wasn't in, I mean—Ewin's nature."

"He's done this before." It was a statement from Dooley, who felt anger suddenly replacing utter exhaustion and contemptible disgust.

Zee's dirty head bobbed. "But you's the first who's kilt him." She shook her head and let out a coyote cackle. "Land sakes, Dooney, you're somethin' else."

Dooley found his hat, walked through the muddy water, knelt, and probed the shallow but dark depths until he finally located his Colt. It was soaked and caked with mud, useless until it had a good cleaning, and maybe fresh cartridges. The brass might have kept the powder dry, but Dooley wasn't in a position to take any chances. He dropped the weapon into the driver's box, turned around, and again knew he needed to lean against the wagon for support.

"He seemed to think I was wooing you. Seemed to think you belonged to him."

She nodded, spit, and wiped her mouth with a sleeve.

"Done that 'em other times, too. Felt like he owned me, which nobody—not even you, Mr. Manningans—does. Pa'd hire on some new killer, I'd chat with him—friendly, is all—and then next thing you'd know, Ewin' would be takin' him to town, guttin' him like a catfish, and addin' a scalp lock to his collection." She batted her eyes. "But all that's changed now, thanks to you, Doolin."

Dooley stepped away from the wagon, and raised his right arm, pointing angrily at the wretched girl in the creek.

"This was your idea," he said, his voice rising. "You

suggested that Atkinson and I go to fetch supplies. You knew this would happen." He shook his head. "So did your father. So did every single man in camp."

She nodded honestly, and if that was not confirmation enough, said, "Yup."

Dooley removed his hat, ran his fingers through his waterlogged hair, shook his head, and swore under his breath.

"And then you followed us?" he asked.

"Course. Pa still don't trust you like he would one of his own. And ol' Ewin' wouldn't have sense enough to find his way to the South Fork of the Elkhorn had he done you in."

"You little . . ." He cut off the insult.

"Remember, love, if I wasn't here, you'd be lyin' underneath that locomotive yonder. He might not've had enough life left in him to tear offen yer head, but I does believe that his weight—dead weight— would have pushed you underneath the water. It ain't deep, but his weight would've had you drownin' sure enough."

That he could not deny. He started to look again at the dead behemoth, but knew he did not want to. Instead he found the killer's horse and walked to it, just to keep moving, to keep busy, to keep from letting his mind realize all that had just happened.

"Good idea, love," Zee said. "Folks in this part of the country knows to mind his own business, but that shot I fired is like to arouse some curiosity. I'd say we'd best be on our way."

Dooley did not answer. He walked the horse to the rear of the wagon and tethered the reins to the gate on the opposite side of General Grant. As Zee walked to the woods to fetch her own mount, Dooley looked down the road toward the capital city, but again saw only an empty street. He stepped around the dead man's horse, rubbed the skin of the gelding as he eased past General Grant, and stared off toward the Missouri River and the ferry. Nobody was coming. Nobody was going.

Except Dooley and Zee, who rode out of the woods, splashed across Rhine Creek, and reined to a stop beside the mules.

"Did you buy me a pretty dress or a nice silk handkerchief whilst you was shoppin' in Yankton?" she asked.

"No." Dooley walked to the front of the wagon, gripped the side, brought his foot to the wheel cap, and started to climb into the seat, but Zee Dobbs chuckled and swung a leg over the saddle horn.

"Love," she said, "ain't you forgettin' somethin'?"

Dooley lowered his leg into the water. He blinked, shook his head, and asked in an angry voice. "Like what?"

She pointed past the wagon at the dead man lying facedown in the creek. "Why, Ewin' Atkinson, of course."

Dooley stepped back, turned, and looked at the corpse, and again moved his head.

"Bring . . . him?"

"Well," Zee said with a little laugh. "Not all the way to the South Fork of the Elkhorn. But my bullet didn't tear off all of his head, so he's still identifiable, most likely."

"You want me to turn him in?" Dooley couldn't believe it. "For a bounty?"

"He's wanted, dead or alive," she said. "Three hundred dollars, last I heard."

"You must be joking."

"No." Her voice and expression turned serious. "It's policy. That's all. Thcm boys ol' Ewin' killcd. They got turned in, too. Didn't fetch more than a hundred and twenty-five between 'em, but it's what Pa always tells us. Outlawin' is a hard way to make a livin', and you got to take money when and where it comes." She swung off the saddle and splashed through the creek toward the dead man.

"C'mon," she said. "Like as not, you'll need a hand loadin' that big oaf into the back of the wagon."

Among the supplies purchased in the general store in Yankton had been a stout rope, some harness, and a winch. That helped them get the dead body into the wagon, where he was wrapped in four saddle blankets and laid over the crates of ammunition. The tarp was lowered, and Dooley found himself in the driver's seat and Zee on the back of her horse.

"Let's make for that ferry," Zee said. "I love ridin' in a ferry. It's so romantic."

"Shouldn't we take Atkinson to the law in Yankton?" Dooley asked. "For that reward?"

"Shucks, no, love." She wheeled the horse around, rode up to the side of the Studebaker, and said in a whisper—although still nobody had dared to set foot on the road from the ferry or from the territorial capital. "Don't you think the law might suspicion why you'd be bringin' in the body of a wanted man that was shoppin' for groceries and gunpowder with you just an hour or two afore?"

Dooley's head shook at that logic. After a sigh, he said, "Don't you think the ferry man might be suspicious as to why I'm traveling with a girl in buckskins when I crossed that same ferry just a few hours afore with a man as big as one of those steamboats lining the wharves in town?"

She laughed again, turned the pony around, and dashed up the bank.

"Hell, no, love. Folks in this part of the country minds their own business. Wagon, ho-oooo!"

CHAPTER TWENTY

All of the ferry workers did eye the wagon, the riderless horse, the dirty woman, and Dooley Monahan with both suspicion and trepidation, but nobody said anything, and no one came close to the wagon. Dooley paid the toll, and they rode south—but only for a short ways.

Dooley had to remind Zee that the wagon that was loaded down with supplies and a ripening corpse had been stolen from a farm just a ways south, and the owners might want it back.

So they turned east, sticking close to the southern banks of the Missouri River for a few miles before the mosquitoes and gnats drove them about a hundred and fifty yards farther south.

As dusk fell, they rode back to the Missouri, where they made a cold camp that night, too close to both the farm and Yankton to risk a fire. Zee fashioned a couple of fishhooks, and they sat on the banks while Zee fished, watching a stern-wheel riverboat make its way up the river, showering the night sky with sparks from the smokestacks like fireworks on the Fourth of July.

Zee landed two fair-sized catfish, and the hunger in both of their stomachs caused them to forget about Yankton and the farmers. They gutted, cleaned, and roasted the fish quickly, doused the fire, and ate.

"Pretty good eatin', ain't it, love?"

Dooley nodded, and licked his fingers.

"Like mine with paprika, though," Dooley added. She looked up, "Hey, did Pa ask you to buy some paprika whilst you was in Yankton?"

"No. Sorry."

"Hell. That's a shame."

Dooley tossed the bones into the ashes of the fire. "What did you use for bait, by the way?" he suddenly asked.

"Ol' Ewin's brains," she answered. "What else?"

Dooley spent the rest of the night on his knees, puking into the wide, muddy river.

The next day brought them into the Niobrara Reservation, which made Dooley worry that maybe the Santee Sioux confined here had been family and friends of the Indian war party that had attacked Dooley and Zee what seemed like an eternity ago. Zee, however, told Dooley that those dead Indians had been Brulé Sioux from up north of there. He didn't know why, but he believed her.

They made it through the reservation, too, and that night camped on the banks of the Niobrara. They made a fire this time without much worry, and Zee fried up salt pork for supper, but Dooley stuck with black coffee and some soda crackers. His stomach had not completely recovered from the catfish dinner.

By the next afternoon, Ewing Atkinson was beginning to smell and draw flies.

"Maybe we should bury him and forget about the reward," Dooley said. He spoke through his bandanna, which he had pulled up over his mouth and nose to reduce the stench and awful reminder of part of the cargo they were hauling in the back of a wagon stolen from churchgoing farmers southeast of here.

"Huh?"

Dooley repeated his suggestion.

"Nah." She spit out brown juice and tilted her head south. "Little town called Maple Grove about two miles from here. Ain't no grove to it. And no maples this side of the Missouri. But they's a lawdog there. And a bank. I know. We robbed the bank four years back. Maybe five. No, four. Well, four and a half."

Maple Grove—all seven buildings, one corral, and no maple trees or any trees for that matter—was more than two miles, but fewer than twelve, and the wagon pulled up beside a building with a sign nailed to the post in front of the hitching rail. The sign read:

BAR
BANK
CONSTABLE

Dooley set the brake and wrapped the reins around the handle. He nodded at the sign. "Is that in order of importance?"

After a short chuckle, Zee shook her head. "Allfeebetickal."

"Bank comes before bar," Dooley pointed out.

"It did four and a half years ago." She moved her horse to the other side of the wagon, pulled her hat down low over her forehead, and pulled the bandanna up. "You best do all the talkin'," she said. "In case it's the same lawdog and banker who was workin' four and a half years back."

It wasn't. Zee must have forgotten that Doc Watson had killed the banker four and a half years ago, and that Frank Handley had trampled the constable to death. The bank had not recovered and had been forced to shutter its doors a month after the raid. The bartender had replaced the constable, but he had not been working that morning four and a half years ago.

He gave Dooley a whiskey on the house.

"Ewing Anderson?" the barkeep/lawman asked.

"Atkinson," Dooley enunciated, and then spelled out the name. The lawman worked through one drawer, closed it, opened the other, and made it halfway through it before he pulled out a weathered, crumpled piece of parchment.

"Ewing Atkinson," the man read. He was slight of build, with bloodshot eyes, beard stubble on his chin but a well-groomed mustache. He wore red sleeve garters to push up the arms of his pink calico shirt, and an unbuttoned vest. He wore no star, no badge, or any sort of identification, but, then, Dooley did not expect a lawman had much business in a town like Maple Grove.

"Six foot seven inches tall, two hundred and seventy pounds. Uses a bowie knife with deadly accuracy and is known for decorating his person with scalps."

Dooley nodded. "That would be him."

"And it says he's wanted for." The man's lips moved, but no words escaped as he read and read and read before finally passing the wanted poster to Dooley. "Been easier had they just listed what that dude hadn't done." He poured himself a bracer, downed it, smiled with pleasure, and asked, "That him?"

"It's certainly his likeness." Dooley slid the paper across the bar. "You want to identify him?"

"Guess it comes with my other job." The man grabbed his hat and a notepad, stuck a pencil over his ear, and held the door open for Dooley.

They stepped outside, and the bartender/constable spotted Zerelda Dobbs. He studied her, looked curiously at Dooley, and said, "Who is that?"

"I'm his fiancée," Zee called out, and laughed so hard she had to slap her thigh, sending clouds of dust up toward the buzzing flies.

"What the hell is that smell?" the bartender/constable asked.

"Ewing Atkinson," Dooley answered, and led the young man to the wagon. He climbed into the back, unloosened the tarp, flung it over, and pulled away the blankets covering the bloated face of the corpse. It was harder to do than Dooley had imagined, and quite grotesque, for the blood had dried and stuck to the wool. Skin ripped. Dooley's bowels and stomach began to trouble him, but he looked away as the blanket tore free.

"Close it," the man said in a gasp. "Close it. It's him. I'll swear to it. I'll swear to anything just as long as you cover him back up."

Dooley did not need any further instructions.

The bartender/constable stared again at Zee as he made his way back to the bar/insolvent bank. This time he did not hold the door open for Dooley but made straight for the bar, uncorked the bottle of gin, and drank it down greedily. Dooley closed the door behind him and went to the bar, hooking his boot on the brass rail and leaning onto the rough, warped pine.

He hoped the bartender/constable would offer him some gin, or anything, and Dooley was willing to pay.

The man just drank, until he finally let out a heavy sigh and tossed his hat onto the bar. It slid down to a bunch of empty beer mugs.

"Well?" Dooley asked.

"I'll have to write you out a receipt," the man—now acting as a town constable—said. He pointed to the open vault, still hanging off one hinge from that robbery not five years ago. "Don't have the funds to pay you the three hundred and thirty-six dollars you got coming."

"All right," Dooley said. He remembered the receipt he had carried for the first outlaw, Jason Baylor, he had killed. He had carried that one for a long, long time.

The lawman pulled the pencil from his ear, found that note tablet, and began writing. He had nice penmanship, too, though not quite as pretty as Doc Watson's.

"What's your name?" the constable asked.

"Dooley," Dooley said, and spelled it, too. "Dooley Monahan. That's M-o-n-a-h-a-n."

The middle-aged man stopped writing and lifted his face to stare Dooley right in the eye. "*The* Dooley Monahan?" he asked.

"Don't know about that *the* part, but I'm the only Dooley Monahan I know."

"The Dooley Monahan that wiped out the Baylor brothers?" the constable asked.

Dooley sighed. "And their cousin," he added with regret.

"You're the most famous bounty hunter we've ever had in these parts, Mr. Monahan," the constable said, and held out his hand to shake.

Considering what Dooley had seen of Maple Grove, that did not sound like great praise.

They left the ripe body of the late Ewing Atkinson at the undertaker/barber/land agent's office in Maple Grove, Dooley using the brute's horse and rigging to pay the bony, bald, pale gent with the thick spectacles for the burial of the dead outlaw. The old undertaker demanded more on account of the deceased's size and smell—the last of the money Hubert Dobbs had given Dooley to spend on supplies in Yankton.

Then Dooley and Zee followed the Niobrara River on its northwesterly course for a couple of days until the river began to bend. At that point, Zee Dobbs told Dooley they needed to turn south.

Two days later, they crossed the Elkhorn River, made camp, ate salt pork as they caught no catfish, and rode on the next morning. Around dusk, Zee told Dooley to stop the wagon. He obeyed, and Zee rode on ahead roughly two hundred yards. There she stood in the stirrups, proceeding to call out like a turkey, then a duck, and finally she made a bunch of grunts like a buffalo in heat. As she settled back into the saddle, four riders appeared out of the brush. Three of them stopped in front of Zee, but the fourth rode straight up to the side of the wagon.

Hubert Dobbs stuck out his right hand and grinned.

"By thunder, Dimly Monograms, I knowed you could do it. Sure as shootin', I knowed you'd be the one to put Ewin' Atkinson, that fat, worthless turd, under. Knew it as well as I knowed anything. It's great to see you, pard. How much reward did that tub of lard bring?"

CHAPTER TWENTY-ONE

A few days later, Dooley cashed in his voucher for Ewing Atkinson at the town marshal's office at Plum Creek. Not that he got to hold on to the greenbacks for long. Hubert Dobbs took the money out of Dooley's hand as soon as Dooley came to the bar in the town's one saloon. He did buy Dooley a beer, though. Just one.

When the bartender moved to the far end of the bar to serve three cowboys, Frank Handley suggested that they rob the bank, but Doc Watson pointed out that a bunch of army troopers were drinking across the street, and the telegraph wire would likely be singing if they made it out of town.

"The army, eh?" Dobbs scratched his beard. "Maybe we can rob the blue-belly paymaster."

"I think," Dooley said, "the paymaster has already been through this month."

"How can you know that?"

"Because soldiers are drinking in the saloon across the street."

Dobbs snorted and wrapped his thick arm around

Dooley's neck, pulling him close, and pounded the top of the bar to bring the beer-jerker back to that end of the bar. "I like you, boy," Dobbs said as he released his grip on Dooley. "You ain't dumb like Ewin' Atkinson. You got a head on your shoulders. You'll do fine by me and Frank . . . and even Zee."

The bartender had arrived.

"Four beers," Dobbs ordered. "Pay the man, Doomey. This is yer round."

Three rounds later—Hubert Dobbs had bought only one round, and that was before Frank Handley and Doc Watson joined them—the leaders of the gang decided that Plum Creek offered little opportunity for any robberies, and they seemed to be well funded anyway, thanks to the reward Dooley collected for Ewing Atkinson. Anyway, they did not want to stick around for another month to wait on the next army paymaster, so that evening they rode out of town and followed the wide, dusty trail on the north side of the Platte River, which seemed twice as wide as it had been down around Omaha, and maybe even shallower.

They camped that night in an abandoned log cabin that had once served as a Pony Express station and, before that, as a trading post along the old Oregon Trail. It was nice to have a roof over his head—and a real roof, not a bunch of dirt like that time at Ole Something-another-dorf's sod hut. This was a regular log cabin, sturdy—because it would have to be solid for Pony Express riders, Dooley figured—with a couple of windows and one door. Dooley spent the night in the northwest corner, as far away from Zee Dobbs as he could possibly be. It prohibited any chance of escape during the night, because he would have had to sneak over the bodies of eight well-armed, lightly snoring, desperate characters who slept with guns in their hands. Not to mention past Zee herself, who slept in front of the doorway. Besides, Blue was sleeping in the southeastern corner, with a rope affixed to the dog's neck and the other end wrapped around Doc Watson's gun hand. Doc Watson, it appeared, did not trust the dog or Dooley Monahan.

A wagon train lumbered past around noon the following day, but Hubert Dobbs, Frank Handley, and Doc Watson saw no need to rob any wagon train. They had enough supplies in the stolen farm wagon—even after everyone had collected his, or her, ammunition. A Union Pacific freight steamed past them, heading west, two hours later, and the boys considered robbing it, but by the time they had reached any decision, the train was practically in Ogallala.

On the following morning, they left the wide trail and began to skirt a very wide loop north, away from the Platte, away from the well-traveled road, but mostly as far away as possible from Fort McPherson.

The next morning they rode into the town of North Platte from the north.

Grenville Dodge had platted the town a year or so after the Civil War had ended, when the Union Pacific was building the first transcontinental railroad. North Platte had started as a regular "hell on wheels," rough and rowdy, and the town's reputation had not changed much over the past decade.

"Fall and Parker," Handley ordered, and two gunmen nodded. "You two'll stay with the wagon and the dog. Don't worry. You'll be the first into town when we hit Ogallala. The rest of you, don't get too drunk, don't get in no fights, don't steal nothin', and don't kill nobody. We'll save all that fun for Ogallala, too. Do yer drinkin' on the south side of Front Street. They's a U.S. marshal, a county sheriff, a judge, a jail, and a town law on the north side. Nobody knows the Handley-Dobbs Gang is—"

"It's the Dobbs-Handley Gang, Frank," Hubert Dobbs interjected.

"When you say it, Hubert," Frank Handley told his partner, and then nodded at the gathering of gunmen. "We pull out at first light."

Everyone entered the Red Dog Saloon on the south side of Front Street, but quickly split up to the bar, tables, roulette wheels, faro layouts, or the hurdy-gurdy girls working the floor. Dooley hung back, watching a dice game, but not betting, and when six railroaders pushed through the batwing doors, and four army soldiers from Fort McPherson staggered inside while singing "The Battle Hymn of the Republic," Dooley took advantage and slipped out onto the boardwalk.

"Too noisy in there for ya?"

Dooley stiffened. That nasal voice made his skin crawl. He turned around to see Zee Dobbs sitting on a trash barrel at the corner of the saloon, puffing on a pipe instead of dipping snuff.

"More than one saloon on this side of the street," Dooley said. Actually, he had hoped to cross to the other side, find that U.S. marshal, that county sheriff, and that town lawman.

"That's so." She climbed down off the trash barrel,

removed her pipe, dumping the tobacco and ashes onto the boardwalk, and slipped the pipe into the pocket on her canvas jacket.

"Why aren't you in one of the saloons?" Dooley asked.

Cackling as she approached Dooley, she raised a bony arm and put it around Dooley's neck, pulled him close, and kissed him on the cheek. "You fool boy. Ladies ain't allowed in saloons."

She released him. "Let's take us a stroll, love," she said. "I ain't never seen no real city in Nebraska."

"What about the bank you robbed in Omaha?" Dooley asked. "Or Dutch Bluff."

"That was work. Work don't count. This is pleasure. Let's have some pleasure."

She linked their arms and led him down the boardwalk to the edge of town.

Zerelda Dobbs was twenty-four years old, an old maid by her standards, and itching to get hitched. This was the gang's first foray into Nebraska, having been driven out of Kansas, and as she told Dooley, Zee's pa wanted them to make for Wyoming, maybe rob that Cheyenne Social Club there before heading up to Deadwood in the Black Hills.

"Deadwood?" Dooley's stomach started feeling queasy again.

"That's where the gold is," Zee answered.

"Sioux Indians, too."

She leaned closer. "I done seen how you handle Sioux braves, love."

Queasier. The stomach got even queasier.

"I hear Buffalo Bill Cody's got hisself a ranch just west of town," Zee said. "Maybe we could go pay him a visit. Sure like to meet him."

"So would I," Dooley said. Of course, he was thinking that if anyone could bring down the likes of Doc Watson, Frank Handley, and Hubert Dobbs it would be a man like Buffalo Bill Cody.

But they weren't walking west, but east, and now that he thought about it, he seemed to recall reading that Buffalo Bill Cody was acting in some play back East. On the other hand, Dooley had also heard that Wild Bill Hickok was in Cheyenne, maybe even in Deadwood by now, and Wild Bill, the prince of pistol fighters, would be even a better famous Westerner to bring the Dobbs-Handley (or Handley-Dobbs, depending on who was doing the speaking) Gang to justice.

Dooley just had to live to see Cheyenne. Or Deadwood. Or, hell, even Ogallala. Even tomorrow morning in North Platte, Nebraska.

They had reached the train yard, which was practically a city in itself.

A flat-switched yard with twenty tracks, the darkened yard must have covered acres and acres. A locomotive, belching smoke, hissing, squeaking, and churning, bumped two boxcars and sent them coasting down the "lead" to a resting place.

"Ain't this romantic, love?" Zee asked.

She had to shout. The noise of engines and iron and cursing railroaders had turned deafening. Dooley could not hear clearly, but the lights from the headlights of locomotives and the lanterns of railroad men made seeing everything a little easier, and Dooley saw clearly.

"Look out!" He pushed Zee aside just as the knife flashed past.

"What the . . ." Zee tripped over the rails and

landed sprawling on the track. Dooley leaped back as the knife turned toward him.

A giant hand held the knife, although the hand was nowhere near the size of the late Ewing Atkinson's, and the knife was a jackknife and not a bowie the size of a cavalry saber.

The hand belonged to a man in brogans, striped denim trousers, a plaid shirt, dirty red bandanna, and railroaders cap. Gray stubble lined his cheek, and a scar crossed from the corner of his left eye, over his nose, and across his right eye—if he had a right eye—to the forehead and disappeared into the man's gray hair and blue cap.

Dooley could not help but stare at the hole in the man's head where an eye should have been. But he quickly jumped back as the knife came toward him again.

"Right nice-lookin' lady you got with you, mister," the man said in a panting Irish brogue. "I think I'll take her after I gut you like a fish."

Dooley ducked away from the knife again.

He chanced a quick glance toward another engine bumping another U.P. freight car, this one a flatbed, down another track, and wanted to call out for help, but knew how fruitless that would be. No one could hear him, and even though Dooley could see the workers several tracks away clearly, he knew they couldn't see him, or Zee, or the one-eyed man with the knife.

"I appreciate ya bringin' that sweet-lookin' thing here fer me to enjoy, laddie," the man with the knife said. And Dooley wondered if having just one eye could ruin a man's vision.

Dooley tripped over another rail, landed hard on the crossties, and saw the man shift the knife quickly, into a throwing position, and Dooley reached for the Colt on his hip—wondering why he had not thought to pull his revolver before—and then a whistle screamed.

Bracing himself for the searing pain of a knife entering his belly, Dooley brought the gun up, but before he even pulled back on the hammer, the one-eyed man's good eye was closing, and the railroader was dropping to his knees, the jackknife slipping from his fingers, and he was turning his head, and then he was falling, crashing against the other rail with a sickening thud. The man's legs shuddered, and he pulled himself into a ball like an infant. He stopped moving.

Dooley pushed himself to his feet, holstered his Colt, and saw Zee Dobbs rushing to his arms, hugging him tightly.

"Love, oh, love, oh, Dooley-Dooley-Dooley . . ." She buried her face into his chest and squeezed him hard. "You saved my life, love. You sweet, brave, boy. You saved poor little me."

The barrel of her revolver—the one she had used to put a bullet in the railroader's back—burned Dooley's side.

CHAPTER TWENTY-TWO

"Mr. Dobbs . . ." Dooley tried again back in front of the Red Dog Saloon.

"Hubert, boy. Any cur that saves my onliest daughter from a fate worser than death can call me Hubert."

"Yes, but, see, it was more like Zee saved my bacon . . . Hubert."

"Nonsense," Zee said. "You shoulda seen Doosey, Pa. How brave he was. We oughts to celebrate."

Dobbs shook his head. "No time fer that, sweetie pie. But I's beholden to ye, Mannihan. I's truly beholden to ye." He stuck out his right hand. Sighing, Dooley shook it.

Dobbs turned to his daughter. "This man y'all kilt. Did he have any money on him?"

"Nothin' but a jackknife, Pa," Zee told him. "Dooney insisted that we leave it, and leave him."

"Good jackknife?"

"Fair to middlin'."

Dobbs's stare turned harder as he considered Dooley, but softened as Dooley began to explain.

"The engine's whistle drowned out the gunshot,

but I figured it would be best to leave the body where it fell, and get Zee to safety. The knife would be evidence for the U.S. marshal, or the county sheriff, or the local lawman, or the U.P. railroad officers. They'd likely figure that the man had met his death while trying to commit a crime." He paused. "I mean, they certainly won't attribute that to the Dobbs-Handley Gang."

"Smart thinkin', son. But we best gather up the boys and get out of North Platte before they find that low-down dirty dog."

And so they left North Platte, Nebraska, under the cover of darkness and made their way along the South Platte River west, did not stop when the sun rose, barely stopped for a noon meal and to rest their horses and stolen mules, and made another ten miles before camping that night.

There, Zee told her version of what had happened, and how Dooley had saved her from a fate worse than death, and Dooley felt men coming over to shake his hand, pat his back, or just give him that nod that said more than words or handshakes or pats on the back ever could. He had been accepted into the gang of cutthroats, for even the worst of the killers who rode with Hubert Dobbs and Frank Handley (now that Ewing Atkinson was dead and buried and his reward paid off) would never, ever, have ill designs on a woman—especially one that looked like Zerelda Dobbs.

Well, one man did not come over to shake Dooley's hand, or offer any word of praise, or pat his back, or give him that all-knowing look.

In his bedroll near the stolen farm wagon, Doc
Watson merely sipped coffee and cleaned his revolver. He did look at Dooley when all the praisers
and patters and head-nodders had returned to their
plates of salt pork and beans, and it was an all-
knowing look, too, but Doc Watson knew the truth.

Ogallala had also been founded when the Union
Pacific was pushing rails westward to link the oceans,
but it had never amounted to much until a year or so
back. That's when the town had been laid out and
when the first cattle from Texas began arriving. The
city had grown with the cattle industry, and so had
the city's cemetery, a well-used patch of ground called
Boot Hill. It was even on a hill, a real hill, because this
far west, the land began to rise.

Front Street in Ogallala was longer and wilder than
the one in North Platte, and the cattle pens sprawled,
but the rail yard was not nearly as complex as North
Platte's.

A trail herd from Texas had arrived, so the town
was booming. The gang rode past the livery stable,
the Cowboy's Rest Saloon, the undertakers, the
lawmen, the hotel, the stores, the brothels, the gambling parlors, the cafés, the hotels, but before they
got to Boot Hill, they pulled into a wagon yard.
There, Frank Handley and Doc Watson negotiated a
reasonable price for the crew to spend the night, feed
and grain the livestock, and have a pretty fair night.

"Fall, Parker," Hubert Dobbs said while the men
unsaddled their mounts and unhitched the team of
mules from the stolen farm wagon. "You boys can go
to one of the saloons first. On account you didn't get

to in North Platte. Nobody else leaves this wagon yard, though. Till I get back."

"Where you goin', Pa?" Zee asked.

"Post office. Then find me a newspaper. I want to make sure that dead man Dooley killed . . ."

Dooley instinctively started to raise his hand to correct the outlaw again that he had killed nobody in North Platte, but lowered it when he realized how fruitless that would have been.

". . . ain't caused no stir."

Zee stood next to Dooley. She leaned her head close to his and whispered, "He always does this, Doomey. Thinks of some reason to go see the wanted posters, see which one of the boys is on the rise, so to speak. What all is you wanted fer, love?"

"I'm not wanted for anything," he told her.

She snorted as her father continued. "Now, as soon as I'm back, we'll do us some drinkin' and gamblin' and whorin', but we ain't robbin' nothin' here, neither. No shootin', no killin', no stealin', no nothin'. Too many damned cowboys in this burg, and cowboys can clutter up anythin'." He pointed at Fall. "You recollect what happened that time in Ellsworth, don't you, Parker?"

"I'm Fall," Fall said.

"Sure, you recollect. Damned cowboys. Liked to have gotten us all killed." He eyed Dooley. "We was ridin' out after robbin' the bank, and those damned waddies was ridin' right at us. Not to stop us. They was just shootin' out the street lamps. Hoorawin' the town. Damnedest hoss wreck you ever seen. Barely got out of that burg afore the law was upon us." His head shook. "So none of that. We lost Fall that day."

"We lost Smalls," Fall corrected. "I'm Fall."

"Besides," Dobbs concluded, "I've been doin' some considerations and I've decided that we don't rob nothin', don't kill nobody, we become peaceable citizens till we gets to Cheyenne. Then, maybe we get ourselves a stake by robbin' that club or a bank, or a U.P. express, and then we set up an operation in Deadwood that'll make the James-Younger Gang look like a bunch of nuns on Easter mornin'."

With that, he checked the loads in his revolver and nodded at Fall and Parker. They walked out of the wagon yard, and the trail dust from two thousand longhorn cattle quickly swallowed them.

There wasn't much for Dooley to do except tend to General Grant—and the stolen mules, since no one else in the gang volunteered. He led the mules to the water trough, dropped some grain in a feed bucket, and rubbed down the gelding, cleaned the hooves. The horse nuzzled him as he fed the bay a sugar cube.

"You haven't had a good run, have you, General?" Dooley said softly. "Been hitched to that wagon for so long. But don't worry. We'll get you out of here somehow, some way. You and Blue."

The blue-eyed dog had come over, and so Dooley patted the horse's neck and squatted to rub Blue's fur. The dog rolled over, and Dooley rubbed his belly. He stared through the fence posts of the wagon yard at the cattle town in western Nebraska.

A town like Ogallala could offer Dooley plenty of opportunities, more than he had seen since Dodge City, Kansas. Some herds just stopped in Ogallala on their way to the Powder River range in Wyoming, or maybe even Deadwood in the Black Hills. After all, miners had to eat, and a savvy cattleman could make a small fortune selling a herd in a town like that. Providing, of course, they weren't jumped by Sioux and got their hair lifted.

Or Dooley could stay in town, gamble. He didn't need to get to the Black Hills, especially if Hubert Dobbs, Frank Handley, and Doc Watson planned on settling in that area to rob and steal and kill and plunder. Ogallala seemed peaceful compared to Deadwood.

And Dooley might even find a job on some cattle drive, drift on to Wyoming—but not the Black Hills— or hire on with a kindly rancher, and head south to Texas or Kansas or New Mexico or Colorado or any-where that was far, far away from Zee Dobbs, her father, and the killers she rode with.

Or, hell, Dooley figured even if he could wind up back in Des Moines, Iowa, alive, that would suit him right down to the ground.

Hubert Dobbs returned two hours later. He turned the boys, and his daughter, loose, after reminding them about the restrictions on killing, stealing, and other criminal acts. He did not, however, let Dooley go with them.

"You stick with me, sonny," the outlaw leader said. "Get a good rest. I got me an idea, and I want you to ride out a ways with me come first light. You can ride that fine bay you got, kid. And bring that smart dog of yourn, too."

That got Dooley hoping. Was Dobbs serious? Or would someone else ride out with them—Zee, for in-stance? He refused to get his hopes up, until the next morning. After breakfast in the wagon yard, Hubert

Dobbs saddled the big horse he rode, and Dooley saddled General Grant.

"We'll be gone two, four days," Dobbs told Handley, Zee, and Doc Watson. "I heard there might be somethin' goin' on in Julesburg. Y'all sit tight. Enjoy the town. I'll be back directly and we can light out for Cheyenne."

Zee waved as they rode out of the yard. "Be careful, love. Bring me back somethin' fancy from Julesburg!"

They crossed the Platte and rode at a gentle southwesterly direction, walking the horses at first before picking up into a trot. Blue barked happily as they rode, and it felt good to ride, feel the saddle underneath him, feel the air in his face. General Grant kicked into another gear, and they were loping, but only for a few hundred yards. Then Dooley reined in, and let Blue and Hubert Dobbs catch up.

The last thing he needed was to catch a bullet in his back from Dobbs, who might think that Dooley was trying to escape. Which, of course, was Dooley's intention. He wouldn't get a better chance than this.

"What's in Julesburg, Mr. Dobbs?" he asked.

"You'll see. It's a good idea I come up with. Yep. Real good one."

Julesburg. Dooley had never been there, although he had heard of it. It lay in the northeastern corner of Colorado, and had played a big part in the Pony Express days. But from all Dooley had heard, the town was small. If it had a bank, it would not carry enough cash to entertain a greedy outlaw like Hubert Dobbs.

"I'll fill you in when we make camp this eve," Dobbs said.

So they rode, in the sage and grass and wind, and

Dooley kept glancing back over his shoulder, toward Ogallala, thinking he might see dust from the rest of the boys, and girl, in the gang. Yet all he saw were blue skies, until they made camp.

They had probably covered half the distance between Ogallala and Julesburg, Dooley figured, though he still had no idea what a town like Julesburg had to offer a robber and murderer like Hubert Dobbs. But the evening had turned nice, not much wind to speak of, the smell of sage intoxicating, and flat, soft, sandy ground in which to make camp. Dooley picketed the two horses, while Dobbs busied himself getting a small fire going between some clumps of sage.

Dooley filled the coffeepot with water from his canteen, and brought it to the fire.

"Thanks," Dobbs said. "You tend the fire. I'll fetch us some grub."

So Dooley busied himself with adding branches of dead sage, and—after he had dropped some coffee beans into the pot, of course—dried buffalo dung to the fire.

They had outfitted themselves fine indeed, Dooley thought. Dobbs had already set a cast-iron grate over the fire and had laid out his skillet and some utensils at the side. They had not shot any game for supper, but Dooley had packed some beans in his saddlebags while Dobbs had brought some bacon and an onion with him.

Coffee. Fried onion and some bacon. For outlaws always on the run, that seemed to be mighty fine grub for a one-night camp.

"Hey, Doolski," Dobbs called out. "Stand up, will ya?"

Leaving the pot on the side of the fire, Dooley

obeyed. He found himself staring down the barrel of a double-barreled shotgun Hubert Dobbs had brought out. The killer thumbed back both barrels and grinned.

Shotgun wedding? That was Dooley's first thought, but he knew that couldn't be what this was all about. After all, Zee was back in Ogallala.

"I found somethin' mighty interestin' on the post office wall, boy," Dobbs said with a sneer. "You've got quite the price on yer head, boy, and I's aimin' to collect."

CHAPTER TWENTY-THREE

"I'm not wanted for anything," Dooley told the leader of the Dobbs-Handley Gang.

"Shuck yer Colt over yonder," Dobbs told him, and Dooley obeyed. It wasn't like he had any choice in the matter.

That at least made Dobbs relax a little, although he did not lower the double-barrelled shotgun.

"You sure you ain't wanted for nothin'?" Dobbs asked.

Dooley nodded.

That caused the old man to chuckle, which in turn caused Dooley to grimace because he did not like to see a man laughing when he was holding a shotgun pointed straight at Dooley's midsection. If he laughed too hard, he might touch off a trigger, or both triggers.

"Well," Dobbs said, "then how do you explain this?"

Without lowering the barrels of the scattergun, Hubert Dobbs let his left hand slip into a pocket. The right hand kept the double-barrel braced against his hip, and Dooley knew better than to make a play with two rounds of double-ought buckshot looking him in the face. When the right hand reappeared, it held a folded-up placard, which the outlaw flapped open in the wind, and tossed it to the ground. The wind carried it about halfway between Dooley and Dobbs.

Of course, the piece of paper landed facedown, snagged on a clump of sage.

"Pick it up," Dobbs instructed. "Turn it over. Man should know what he's done and why he's gotta die."

Slowly, Dooley moved forward, squatted, never taking his eyes off the shotgun and the man holding it. He turned the paper over and read:

WANTED
BANK <u>ROBBER</u> & <u>KILLER</u>

There was no name, no artist's rendition of a likeness, but nobody could deny that the description below the bold uppercase and underlined words didn't fit Dooley Monahan to a T.

On the 8th of May, 1876, the Second State Bank of Omaha was robbed of $3,182 by the Dobbs-Handley Gang, which left a teller and a deputy marshal slain on the streets of this fine Nebraska city. One newcomer to the gang is believed to have murdered in cold blood our beloved county sheriff, Noble James Brazile IV, devoted to upholding the law and good order of our fine state, who was

found brutally shot to death on the banks of the
Platte River a few days later.

The newcomer is described as dressing like a
common saddle tramp—probably to deceive citizens
from knowing the true, cold-blooded nature of his
character—of medium build, slightly above average
height, no noticeable scars, and fairly dull in
personality. Yet he happens to be mounted on a
strong, fast, and impressive bay gelding, and is
accompanied by a splendid blue dog.

$750 REWARD
DEAD OR ALIVE.

There was more, but that seemed enough for
Dooley's stomach to twist and turn and his throat to
run drier than a South Texas creek in the middle of
a four-year drought. Dobbs chuckled, and Dooley
looked up.

"But I didn't kill that sheriff," Dooley told him.
"Y'all did."

He also remembered that Sheriff Noble James
Brazile IV, before he was cut down by a hail of lead,
wasn't exactly so "beloved" and certainly not "devoted
to upholding the law and good order of our fine
state." He had planned on lynching Dooley and
taking the money from the Dutch Bluff bank for
himself.

"Read that little type underneath that big seven
hunnert and fifty dollars," Dobbs instructed.

Dooley read.

The posse, consisting of some of Omaha's finest
citizens that discovered the butchered body of the
great Sheriff Brazile, reports that near our gallant

hero's corpse were prints left by cowboy boots, plenty of horses, and not only dog tracks but dog dung, thus revealing the true identity of Sheriff Brazile's murderer.

POSITIVE IDENTIFICATION REQUESTED

Money Guaranteed

Body May Be Turned In to Any Duly Elected Sheriff in Nebraska or Surrounding States or Territories

Preston M. Garland, President,
Second State Bank of Omaha (Neb.)

"None of the boys ridin' with me never brung me more'n four, five hunnert bucks tops," Dobbs said. "Well, I reckon Frank's head's worth twenty-five hunnert now, and Doc'd bring in seventeen seventy-five, but they's like family. You're a good hand, Dummie, but well, this is policy, like I've always said. I figure seven hunnert and fifty bucks will get us to Cheyenne and Deadwood in high style. Hope you understand."

Dooley's mind kept racing, but every plan that came to him would seemingly end with his body leaking from a dozen buckshot holes in his middle. But one idea might just work.

"You'll do me the favor of taking care of Blue and General Grant, won't you, Mr. Dobbs?"

The killer chuckled. "Oh, I sure hope the sheriff in Julesburg lets me keep that horse. You got mighty fine taste in horseflesh, son. But I figure to kill the dog. Less trouble. And his carcass would kinda seal the deal, don't you think? I mean, his body, yourn, and your horse . . . that would be . . . what did that poster say? . . . 'Positive identification requested'?"

"No, Blue!" Dooley shouted, and pointed at the dog.

Dobbs merely smiled. "I ain't no dummy, Dumpy." He started to bring the shotgun up to his shoulder, and Dooley moved his finger from pointing at Blue to pointing at Hubert Dobbs.

Which was all Blue—and Dooley—needed.

He heard the growl, of course, but Dobbs hesitated— which is the first thing outlaws were supposed to be taught never, ever, to do—uncertain if he should shoot Dooley first or swing the barrels to kill the dog. Eventually, he decided that the shepherd posed the worse threat, and he began to turn. That moment of choosing took only a second, but that was all it took.

Both barrels of the shotgun roared, spraying the sage and the Colt that Dooley had shucked a few minutes before with buckshot, as Blue's teeth tore into Hubert Dobbs's forearm. The shotgun, now empty, toppled into the ground as the weight of the big shepherd brought the big killer down. He crashed with a thud, shouted, cursed, and brought his other hand up to grab for Blue's throat. Blue released his hold on the bloody arm and bit off Dobbs's thumb on his other hand.

The outlaw gang leader's curses grew stronger.

Dooley ran to help Blue, but the outlaw and dog rolled over, the outlaw now on top of the shoulder, and Dooley tripped over them, bouncing over brush that shredded the left sleeve of his shirt.

"Arrghhh!"

Dobbs fought to protect his neck. Blue was typically

a mild-mannered dog, but the killer had brought out plenty of aggression in him. Dooley came up, feeling a lot of anger in his own body, and went back to the melee. Dobbs was using his left forearm, letting the dog rip the sleeves and hair and flesh with his fangs, while his right hand lowered. Dooley feared the man was bringing up a knife to gut the dog.

He kicked Dobbs in the head.

The blow turned the man over and sent Blue flying off into the sage. It also caused Dooley to lose his balance, and he fell straight back on his hindquarters. Breath shot out of his lungs, but he had no time to be dazed or out of breath. He came up quickly and saw Dobbs, his left arm hanging loose at his side, useless except for irrigating the Nebraska sage with blood, but his right now going for, not the knife, but the six-shooter in his holster.

Dooley could have sworn that he had kicked Dobbs right in the temple. It should have killed the murdering fiend, or at the very least, knocked him out cold. The gun came up, but Blue dived again, biting, growling, his white fangs vicious, and snapped at the killer's hand.

The pistol fell, and Dobbs had to spin to his side.

Dooley was diving for Dobbs's revolver, but when Dooley came up with the big weapon, he saw that Dobbs had picked up Dooley's Colt.

"Confound it!" Dobbs bellowed.

The buckshot from Dobbs's shotgun had riddled the pistol—Dooley didn't know exactly how badly, but Dobbs could not get the piece to cock. Dooley was having trouble himself with Dobbs's six-shooter, for the cylinder was now caked with a gritty, cementlike mixture of Nebraska sand and Hubert Dobbs's blood.

Dobbs hurled Dooley's pistol, and Dooley cut loose with Dobbs's.

The big man ducked as Dooley's throw missed just to the right, while Dooley felt his mangled Colt slam straight into his chest. He fell backward, blinked out the pain, heard Blue barking, Dobbs cursing, then the dog yelping. His hair singed, and Dooley felt the heat and that awful stink of burning hair. He knew he must have fallen right next to the fire he had been building to cook supper. It could have been worse. He could have landed in the fire, on that heavy iron grate.

Swatting at his burning hair, Dooley tried to get to his feet.

He knew Dobbs had kicked his dog, but he saw the dog limping around, cutting a wide path around the killer. Stunned. But still game. Still alive, at least.

Dobbs had brought out his knife. He spit out blood, laughed, and charged.

There was no time to think. Dooley had no weapon.

Dobbs was running, and again Dooley remembered that saying that a buffalo, despite its size, ran fast when it had to.

Dooley reached. His hand burned. He ignored the searing in his palm. He let the coffeepot sail.

The pot missed the charging man-killer and landed on some sage. The scalding water and not-quite-ready coffee did not miss, however, but soaked and steamed and scarred Hubert Dobbs's battered face. He screamed and fell to his knees, dropping the knife, and reaching with both hands at his miserable face.

Blue barked, started to charge, but stopped, uncertain. Was Dobbs out of it?

Dooley didn't know himself, but he figured he needed to find a weapon. As in . . . immediately.

He turned, tried to lift the grate, but buffalo dung and sage burned really hot. His skin sizzled, and he cursed, let go. Tears broke free. Blue barked, growled, and helped again.

"Get away from me, you damned cur!" Dobbs shouted.

Dooley looked back, saw the big man, again on his feet, staggering toward Dooley. He had been battered, half blinded, ripped to shreds, and practically beaten by a dog and a cowboy. Yet Hubert Dobbs had been an outlaw for many, many years, and he was far from finished.

"I'm gonna kill you," Dobbs yelled. "I'm gonna kill you and your dog and your horse, Dooley Monahan, you swine!"

He had gotten Dooley's name right. And he also held his pistol, which he had managed to cock. He brought the big revolver up, and aimed it at Dooley.

CHAPTER TWENTY-FOUR

With just a few yards separating him from Hubert Dobbs, Dooley knew that there was little chance a killer like Dobbs would miss from that range, and he couldn't pray that the gun might misfire. Instinctively—that primal fear of death—caused him to reach for whatever was closest, something to protect himself, something that was not a clump of sage. His right hand found something—Dooley didn't know what—and he brought it up, before the deafening report of Dobbs's pistol caused Dooley to flinch.

Something whined, and Dooley felt hard metal slam into his chest, knocking him back onto the sage. He landed with a grunt, pain jarring his chest and sending spasms up his legs and all the way to his neck. Yet Dooley knew that he had not been hit by a bullet, and felt no new blood leaking from his body.

No time to think, to relax, to realize he wasn't dead . . . yet.

Dooley reached up, grabbed the iron handle of the skillet that lay on his chest, slid it to the ground, and sat up instantly. With all his strength, he brought

up the frying pan, intending to throw it at Hubert
Dobbs. A cast-iron pan like this, which strained
Dooley's arm muscles, was no .44 but could be lethal
in the right hands.

It was.

Dooley blinked, lowered the skillet to his side, and
sucked in a painful breath of air.

Hubert Dobbs lay faceup, spread-eagle in the sage
and sand. Blue danced around his unmoving body,
barking, yipping, and growling. Dooley could see that
the outlaw still grasped the revolver in his right hand
and that his eyes kept blinking.

As Blue kept barking and the killer just lay there,
Dooley glanced at the skillet. It had been blackened
by so much use over the years, yet he saw a gray or
silver spot in the lower end of the pan, near the
handle. Dooley shook his head and put the skillet on
the ground. His finger touched the dent, felt the
traces of lead, and he brought himself to his knees,
understanding what had happened.

"Blue." His voice sounded raw, but it had gotten
the shepherd's attention. "Sit. Stay." Blue turned
quickly toward Dooley, growled as he faced the blinking, breathing Dobbs, and began backing away a few
feet before lowering himself to the ground. He didn't
exactly obey Dooley's commands, but that was close
enough. The good dog refused to take his eyes off
Dobbs, though, and kept up that low growl, hackles
on his neck stiffer than Dooley's tightening muscles.

Cautiously, Dooley walked over to Dobbs.

The killer stopped blinking, and his eyes found
Dooley.

"Help . . . me . . ." the outlaw pleaded. Just those

two words tormented Dobbs, and blood frothed his lower lip. Every time the man's chest moved up or down, a terrible sucking sound escaped from the hole in the right side of his chest.

Dooley could sort out what had happened, but he couldn't understand why it had happened. By all accounts, Dooley Monahan should be the one lying dead beside the fire. Yet when Dobbs had pulled the trigger, the heavy bullet had slammed into the cast-iron frying pan that Dooley had just brought up for protection. A couple of inches lower, and Dooley would have been gut-shot. A couple of inches higher, and the leaden slug might have still hit the skillet, but the ricochet would likely have missed Hubert Dobbs completely, allowing the murdering thug another chance at shooting down Dooley Monahan.

Dooley wanted to look at the sky. Maybe he would find an angel flying overhead, smiling down on him. Perhaps he would see God himself, and his hair would turn white, and he would grow a beard like Moses. But Dooley knew better than to take his eyes off Hubert Dobbs, who still held that pistol, no longer cocked, in his right hand but didn't seem to be aware of it. Dooley refused to look at the gun, lest he remind the killer that he could still do what he set out to do, and kill Dooley Monahan.

Actually, that was only part of what Dobbs had planned, but from the amount of blood on the killer's shirt, and on his lips and cheek and chin, and considering how awful that hole snorted and sang with the outlaw's every breath, Dooley knew that Dobbs wouldn't be able to collect any reward in Julesburg. If he lived another five minutes, it would be the second miracle of the evening that Dooley had witnessed.

He knelt beside the badman.

"Dooley," Dobbs managed. "You've . . . kilt . . . me . . ."

Dooley had to work his mouth and wet his lips before he could speak. "Well, you killed yourself, I think."

The man laughed, but that proved painful, and he almost doubled over, and then soiled his britches.

Dobbs recovered, opened his eyes again, and muttered an oath.

"Yes, sir," Dooley said. "That's what you just did."

"A gypsy . . ." Dobbs began, spitting out saliva and bloody sputum. "She said . . . cards said . . . I'd die . . . at my . . . own . . . hand." He coughed slightly. "Never figured . . . me to . . . blow my own head off . . . hang myself . . . some other . . . suicide." His face tightened in pain for the longest while, and Dooley thought those might have been the last words of Hubert Dobbs. A moment of stillness passed, and Dobbs recovered.

"I tol' her . . . she was . . . crazy. Shot 'er dead. Taken . . . her rings . . . and silk . . . kerchiefs." He managed to shake his head slowly, and now blood leaked from both nostrils. "Reckon . . . the bitch . . . was . . . right."

Another lengthy quietness.

Then.

"After . . . all."

Dooley tightened his lips. The killer's cold eyes locked on Dooley, waiting for some response, but Dooley decided he had nothing to say to this despicable waste of a man. It wasn't the way the circuit-riding

preacher back in Iowa said folks should think, but
Dooley just wished that Hubert Dobbs would hurry
up and die.

"Doo . . . mey . . ." Dobbs said, and coughed again.
"Lean closer . . . I . . . gots . . . somethin' . . . to . . .
tell . . . ya."

Dooley thought about denying the killer's request,
but couldn't quite do that. He told himself it would
be the right thing to do, that, well, Hubert Dobbs had
saved him from a lynching on the Platte River. And
Hubert Dobbs would be dead soon enough. He
leaned down toward the man's bloody mouth.

And felt the barrel of the six-shooter pressing
against his temple.

"Kill me . . ." Somehow, Dobbs had summoned up
enough hatred, enough energy to hold that .44
against Dooley's head. "I . . . can . . . take you . . .
with . . . me . . ."

A few yards away, Blue growled and began barking,
and Dooley wished that he had not ordered the shepherd to stay, that his dog would not obey Dooley's
command for the first time ever. But no luck. Was that
angel or God himself laughing at Dooley right now?

Dooley waited, before he realized that Dobbs
wasn't pulling the trigger. Slowly, he lifted his left
hand until he gripped the gun's barrel, and even
more carefully, he pushed the barrel away from his
own head.

"Damn me all to Hades' hottest fires," Dobbs managed to sing out. He coughed again and dropped the
big revolver on his bloody chest.

"Doo . . ." The sucking sound grew even louder.
"Do . . . me . . . a kind-ness." Dooley waited. "Cock . . .

my . . . pistol. Ain't . . . got . . . strength . . . no . . . more."

Dooley didn't think he'd be able to get that .44 to fire again, at least no time soon, and he wasn't about to help Hubert Dobbs.

He waited. The revolver remained on the killer's chest, and Dobbs's hand and arm fell off, onto the blood-soaked ground.

Birds chirped in the distance, and the sun began turning into a beautiful orange ball as it slipped toward the western horizon.

"Boy." Again, Dobbs had summoned strength. "Ain't you . . . got . . . nothin' to . . . tells me . . . afore . . . I'm . . . dead?"

Dooley looked the killer in his deadly eyes.

"Go to hell," Dooley said.

Only Hubert Dobbs was already there.

CHAPTER TWENTY-FIVE

Dooley's first thoughts were to mount General Grant, pull Blue up into the saddle with him, and raise dust for anywhere that wasn't Nebraska. Yet the sun was sinking, and Dooley didn't want to run into any party of Sioux or Cheyenne or even Pawnee or tenderfeet. He kept telling himself that Hubert Dobbs could not harm him anymore, and that he had a nice fire already going. That reminded him to add some sage and dried dung to the fire.

After that, he just worked to stay busy, to take his mind off the pain, his wounds, all that had happened to him over the past weeks, and the fact that he had a dead man lying in his camp.

After checking the pickets, he decided to hobble Dobbs's horse, but left General Grant saddled, just in case he needed to ride fast and hard in the middle of the night. He tied Dobbs's hands together, and his feet, with some pigging string. Not that he knew exactly why he needed to do the precaution, but it certainly made him feel better. He thought about fingering the corpse's eyes closed, but couldn't do it. He did wrap the dead body in a woolen blanket, and then proceeded to police his camp.

His Colt was ruined, and although he managed to wipe the grime and sand from Dobbs's revolver, Dooley didn't trust it to fire, so he dropped both pistols in one of Dobbs's saddlebags, where he discovered another weapon.

It was a Colt, too, although with a shorter barrel and the sight filed down, nickel plated and ivory grips. Too fancy for a cowboy like Dooley, but he thumbed a cartridge out of his shell belt, opened the Colt's chamber gate, pulled the hammer to half cock, and rotated the cylinder. His shell fit perfectly, and Dooley laughed at his good fortune. He filled the six-shooter with four more cartridges, keeping the chamber under the hammer empty. The pistol slipped easily into Dooley's holster.

He had to rinse out the coffeepot and find more coffee. The salt pork he just wiped off with his gloves, which he then ran around the inside of the cast-iron skillet, mostly to clean off the remnant tracings of the bullet. The dent in the lower edge of the pan went deeper than Dooley had originally thought, and when the salt pork was sizzling in its own juices, grease leaked through the bottom of the pan and caused the fire to flame up every now and then.

But Dooley could understand that. Dobbs had packed his loads with a lot of gunpowder, and they had been at, not quite but close enough, point-blank range. Dooley felt even luckier than he had earlier that evening.

He ate with his fingers, straight out of the pan after it had cooled, and drank coffee until the pot was empty. He let Blue have the last two pieces of pork and lap up all the grease, which cleaned the pan good enough for breakfast—if Dooley wanted any breakfast.

After dousing the fire, he took the reins to General Grant, told Blue to follow, and led his dog, his horse, and his bedroll about two hundred yards from the camp. Just to be safe. There, in a buffalo wallow that the fleas had deserted ages ago, Dooley made his camp.

It wasn't the best night's sleep he ever had, but at least he wasn't as dead as Hubert Dobbs.

Before first light, Dooley returned to the camp.

No coyotes, no buzzards or other raptors, had bothered the corpse, and no Indians or night raiders had stolen Hubert Dobbs's horse. Dooley thought about breakfast, but decided that hardtack and jerky would be even better than scrambled eggs, fried pickles and ham hocks and corn bread at Charlie's Eatin Place in Newton, Kansas.

The morning was cool, so Dooley did build a fire, making sure there was not much smoke, and warmed his hands over the flames before resuming his work.

Dooley packed the cooking grate, the skillet, coffeepot, and other items, and started to police the camp. He found the wanted poster stuck on some sage, read it again, frowned—his stomach roiling— and moved to the fire, where he held the parchment until it ignited, and then let it burn with the dung and sage.

When Dobbs's horse snorted, Dooley walked over to feed the big horse.

"I'll turn you loose," he whispered. "And . . ."

That's when Dooley remembered another piece of paper in Dobbs's saddlebags. He walked back to the saddle, and blanket, and leather bags, opened one side, and withdrew the paper.

Hubert Dobbs always carried the wanted posters that described the likenesses and crimes—but mostly the offered rewards—of his men, but Hubert Dobbs was also a vain, vain man.

Dooley held out the piece of paper and read, not all of it, just the description and the pertinent details.

WANTED
Dead or Alive
HUBERT DOBBS
$4,500.25 Reward.

Blue wagged his tail. General Grant snorted contentedly. The blanket-covered corpse of Hubert Dobbs did not move.

I was going to leave Dobbs here, Dooley thought. *Turn the horse loose. Mount up and ride hard and fast. Get as far away from this place as possible. Forget the Black Hills. Forget Iowa. Hell, maybe even forget the United States. Try Canada. Or Mexico. Or Argentina if I could find it.*

His eyes fell back on the wanted poster.

"But why?" he said aloud.

With a stake of $4,500—and twenty-five cents, for some reason—Dooley could try anywhere. Black Hills? He wouldn't have to mine, but open a saloon—or buy one—and watch his money grow. Or even head west to San Francisco. Or Canada, Mexico, or Argentina if he wanted to see what life was like up or down that way. Besides, he had earned this reward. He had displayed the presence of mind to lift a cast-iron frying pan to his midsection to deflect a bullet and send Hubert Dobbs to a place where he could torment decent folk no more.

Dobbs had told Zee and the boys that he and Dooley would be gone for four days. They had traveled one. Another day's ride to Julesburg. Turn in the body. Claim the reward. Tell the lawmen that the rest of the Dobbs-Handley Gang was hiding out in a wagon yard in Ogallala, Nebraska, and that Dooley didn't want any of that reward, that it was all for the lawman and whoever he got to shoot and kill with him. Dooley wouldn't have to worry about the gang members seeking revenge. They'd all be dead, or in prison. Zee would be arrested, too. Maybe not killed. He didn't hate her that much. Just put in prison . . . for the rest of her life. That would mean Dooley was free. Free to ride west to Denver or Cheyenne or Santa Fe. Or disappear in the Black Hills.

"I've already got the reputation of a bounty hunter," Dooley told General Grant. "I'd have a two-day start on Handley and Watson and Zee even if the Julesburg lawman didn't kill them all. General, you could put a lot of miles between us and those vermin if . . ."

He jerked the wanted poster out of the bay gelding's mouth.

"Don't eat this!"

Dooley folded the paper—missing just the upper left-hand corner and the *W* in *Wanted* and the *Dea* in *Dead*, which didn't seem too important—and shoved it into the back pocket of his trousers. He went back to work, saddling Dobbs's horse, shoving the blanket-covered corpse over the saddle, and securing that dead outlaw with Dobbs's own lariat.

It was still early in the morning, before most people—especially notorious bank robbers like Doc Watson and Frank Handley—were even finished with their breakfasts, when Dooley Monahan rode off toward Julesburg, Colorado. He pulled the dead Hubert Dobbs on Hubert Dobbs's horse behind him.

The trail that ran to Julesburg was wide and with deep ruts. He certainly shouldn't get lost.

For most of the way, he kept the horses at a trot if not a gentle lope.

He spotted the dust, and, cursing softly, he reined General Grant to a stop. Behind him, the big horse carrying the body of Hubert Dobbs began to urinate, and Blue, panting, walked off the side of the trail and found a patch of grass between some clumps of sage.

After exhaling slowly, Dooley let out a little sigh. Well, the road from Julesburg to Ogallala and points east was typically well traveled, so the chances of not meeting anyone seemed to be a bit out of reach. And the riders were coming from the west, not Ogallala, and that made Dooley feel better, if just slightly better.

The horse finished its bodily function, snorted, and shook its head, tugging on the lead rope. Dooley turned and looked back.

On the other hand, explaining the corpse he was carrying might be troublesome.

He looked again at the dust. The riders were making a good clip.

"Maybe it's a stagecoach," Dooley told Blue. His head nodded as if that would make Dooley's wish

come true. "Stages have to keep their schedule."
Another nod. "So the driver ain't likely to stop. Just
keep going."

He frowned. Keep going to Ogallala, where the
driver would tell his boss who would tell one of his
workers who would hurry into the saloon to tell every
drunk and drinker there that so-and-so had seen a
rider on a bay horse carrying a big dead man on the
back of another horse bound for Julesburg, which
would be overheard by Doc Watson or Frank Handley which . . .

"Hell," Dooley said.

He glanced to his left, then right, and saw the
hopelessness of his situation. In this country, he
would need to find a really deep buffalo wallow to
hide in, and that didn't seem likely. Especially when
he considered just how close that dust kept coming.

So he drew the Colt from its holster and filled the
sixth chamber with a bullet. Sometimes, you listened
to your gut. Sometimes, it paid to be careful.

He wet his lips and swung down from the saddle,
keeping the reins to the General in his left hand. He
tested the new Colt, making sure he could draw it
quickly, without snagging. He looked at the barrel
and wondered why in hell any fool would file down
the front sight. Oh, sure, that might prevent it from
catching in a cut of the leather, or something else.
But it would make it damned hard for a man to take
a good aim at a stomach he wanted to put a bullet
into.

The Colt fell back into the holster, and Dooley
inhaled deeply, and exhaled rapidly.

"It's not a stagecoach!" he told Blue.

But then he thought: *That's not necessarily a good thing.*

And it wasn't. Four riders stopped their horses about fifty yards from where Dooley waited. One rose in the stirrups to give Dooley, the General, Blue, and the trailing horse and its package scrutiny. The men talked among themselves, although Dooley couldn't make out any of the words. Finally, the four men tested the revolvers in their holsters, too, before putting their horses into slow, deliberate walks.

They spread out, two on the main road, the others flanking out a good ten yards off the trail.

They rode straight toward Dooley.

He shifted his reins to his right hand, which he kept close to his Colt, and lifted his left in a friendly wave that could not be mistaken for friendly, just cautious. Actually, nervous.

The riders did not return the wave, and Dooley lowered his hand, took the reins, and let his right hand hover just above the Colt's handle.

"Halllooooo!" he called out. "I come in peace."

The words made him feel like a greenhorn idiot, like he had learned how to talk by reading dime novels.

The men did not *halllooooo* him back.

Ten feet in front of him, they stopped, still spread out, still keeping their hands on the handles of their six-shooters.

The leader of the men, or so Dooley assumed, nodded. He wore a dusty white hat and trail duds, and sported a thick mustache and underlip beard.

"You've had trouble, I see." The accent sounded Scottish.

Dooley just glanced at the other men, two young,

one old, all leathery and sharp nosed. Mostly he took in the horses, which were well lathered and already laboring for breath. They had been ridden hard, too hard, and as an old cowboy, Dooley knew that men who abused horses like that were in a hurry. Running for something. And in need of fresh mounts.

Like General Grant and Hubert Dobbs's horse.

"No," Dooley said. He decided he could sound like a dime novel some more, only the tougher hero in the dime novel, and not someone who was coming in peace.

He gestured with his shoulder toward the late Hubert Dobbs.

"He's the one who had trouble."

The man in the white hat laughed.

Off the trail to Dooley's left, the one on the buckskin, the one with the black hat and stringy black hair, who had hooked a leg over the horn of his pinto pony, whipped his big Schofield from the holster.

It should have occurred to Dooley that a gun that belonged to a killer like Hubert Dobbs would have a fast action and hair trigger. The Colt leaped into Dooley's hands, and he had cocked it and touched the trigger in a blaze of speed. But too fast. The bullet hit the pinto, killing the horse, and sending the man with the Schofield somersaulting off his saddle, the big revolver falling on the other side.

Dropping the reins, Dooley let General Grant run west—right toward the man in the brown hat on the brown horse, which caused the brown horse to buck. Stepping away from the trailing horse carrying the late Hubert Dobbs, Dooley fanned back the hammer of the Colt. He ignored the man on the bucking brown horse for the time being and shot the man in the white hat square in the forehead.

He had been trying for the man's chest, but didn't have a front sight to guide his aim.

That one got off one shot before he was blown out of the saddle, but the bullet just punched a hole in a cloud above. Dooley stepped away from the dun horse as it bolted toward Ogallala, dropped to a knee, and shot the man off the brown horse. He hit him just above the missing button on his calico shirt, which was more or less where he had intended to shoot him.

This Colt's all right, Dooley told himself, and tripped over sagebrush as he stepped off the trail.

The brown horse leaped over him, and Dooley shouted, swallowed the panic, and raised his head, and the Colt in his right hand.

By then, Dooley figured that the man in the black hat on the dead pinto had recovered his Schofield, and he knew he was right, because as he had been falling, he heard the report of a pistol and felt the hot air as the bullet whizzed over his back.

"Take this, you dirty cur!" the man in the black hat shouted, and punched two more shots from the Schofield. One clipped the sage to Dooley's left. The other spit sand into Dooley's nose and mouth. Dooley brought the Colt up and squeezed the trigger.

The bullet caught the man in the side, spun him around, and dropped him to his knees. Yet he still gripped the big .45, and grimacing, brought the pistol up with both hands, desperately trying to push back the heavy hammer.

Dooley shot him again, and that bullet finished the man, and dropped him dead into the dirt.

The last man, the one on the palomino with the Mexican sugar-loaf sombrero, Dooley had ignored—mainly because he saw a flash of dark fur and knew Blue had gone for him. Sure enough, the shepherd had leaped up, knocking the man from the saddle, sending his revolver flying into the sage, and sending the horse running farther into the sage.

Standing, Dooley cocked the gun in his hand as he ran across the road, leaped over one dead road agent, and stopped. The man had lost his sombrero, and Blue had torn great gashes in his left arm, which now hung useless by his side. Blue was charging at the man, who was turning his old Navy .36 at the dog.

"Hey!" Dooley yelled.

The man spun around, tried to bring the old Colt up at Dooley's midsection.

If Dooley had counted right, he had one bullet left in his Colt.

CHAPTER TWENTY-SIX

It wasn't much of a settlement, and Dooley would not have known he was in Colorado Territory instead of Nebraska, had the sign not informed him:

You're in **JULESBURG**
(Colorado Terri)
Good Luck!

The sign on the other side of the Union Pacific railroad tracks hung crooked on a post that had been splintered with bullet holes. For that matter, so had the sign. The dot over the *i* in *Terri* appeared to have come from a .38, while what Dooley guessed once spelled the rest of *Territory* had been blown off with a shotgun or heavy buffalo rifle.

The depot, nothing more than an old boxcar with the wheels removed and sitting on a log foundation, was also pretty much ventilated with bullet holes. So was the sign nailed above the door. It read:

JULESBURG DEPOT
Union Pacific

Those *i*'s had also been dotted with bullet holes. Nobody was at the depot.

Cottonwoods and other trees grew along the South Platte, south of town, but that's about all that grew in this country, other than sagebrush and grave markers. Dooley rode slowly past the cemetery. He counted a dozen or so buildings, not including outhouses and lean-tos, most of those structures on the northern side of the main, and only, street that ran on southwest toward Camp Wardwell, long abandoned by the army, and on toward Denver City.

A dog crawled from underneath a porch, growled, then disappeared back under the partly rotted, mostly warped planks of an abandoned building on the southeastern edge of town.

Julesburg seemed to lean a little to the southeast, probably because all the buildings had been blown that way from cold winds. There didn't appear to be anything to blunt the force of the winds from here to the Rocky Mountains to the northwest.

Dooley saw the Julesburg Store, the Julesburg Hotel, the Julesburg Bank, the Julesburg Saloon No. 1, the Julesburg Tonsorial Parlor, the Julesburg Express Station, the Julesburg Marshal and Jail, the Julesburg Livery, the Julesburg Saloon No. 3 (apparently, the Julesburg Saloon No. 2 was the abandoned building with the dog under the porch), and the Julesburg cabin that was for sale. The other buildings, on the opposite side of the street, were cabins and sod huts for the residents.

People began stepping out of the buildings—and the cabins and soddies—to watch Dooley Monahan as he rode into town. He couldn't blame them. They did not say anything, did not nod their heads or wave their hands, or even whisper among themselves. They just watched.

He rode into Julesburg with a nickel-plated, ivory-handled, short-barreled Colt on his hip, a panting dog walking alongside his bay gelding, leading a string of four horses behind him.

The big black carried the blanket-wrapped body of Hubert Dobbs. The brown packed the body of the man with the brown hat and the man with the Schofield whose horse Dooley had accidentally killed. The dun carried the corpse that had worn a white hat. The palomino carried its rider, the one with the left arm ripped to shreds and Dooley's last bullet (for that gunfight) in his heart.

Had he his druthers, he would have reined in front of the Julesburg Saloon No. 1 or the Julesburg Saloon No. 3 to slake his thirst and put something in his stomach so he wouldn't feel so damned empty. But he knew whiskey would just worsen that sickness he felt.

Instead, he rode up to the Julesburg Marshal and Jail. One arm pressed against one of the posts that would have held up an awning (had there been an awning or a second post), the town badge-wearer eyed Dooley. He smoked a cigarette. His suspenders fell loosely beside his legs, and a tin star remained pinned, heavily pulling at the one pocket on his solid gray shirt. He wore a black hat, but no belted six-shooter. He didn't need a revolver, because Dooley could see the double barrels of a shotgun poking through the window to the left of the doorway. No panes of glass were left, making it easy for Dooley to see the bald man who tried, but failed, to keep the shotgun steady.

"Marshal," Dooley said as he reined in, keeping his right hand far from the holstered Colt.

"Deputy," the man replied as he removed his cigarette and blew smoke that the wind carried away.

Dooley nodded, and tried to think of how to begin. With a sigh, he gestured toward the load he pulled behind his horse.

"That's Hubert Dobbs on the first horse," Dooley said. The mere sentence made him feel as if he needed to sleep through two nights and three days.

The cigarette fell onto the boardwalk, and the deputy marshal stepped back.

Even with the blowing wind, Dooley could hear the whispers that grew too loud for whispers ranging from the Julesburg Saloon No. 3 all the way to the Julesburg Store. News spread faster than a fire that could have reduced Julesburg to ashes.

The old-timer holding the shotgun rose from his kneeling position, and he stepped outside, leaving the shotgun sticking out of the window.

"The hell you say," the man said. He was bald, but solid, wearing spectacles, gray boots, gray pants, a gray shirt, and a gray vest. He also wore a tin star. Only his read *Julesburg Marshal.*

His thick mustache was gray, but not as dark gray as his clothes.

Slowly, Dooley stood up enough to bring the reward poster out of his back pocket. After flipping it open, he held it in the wind, and the deputy stepped into the street.

"Check him out, Dewitt," the marshal told the deputy. As the deputy obeyed the order, the marshal looked at the other bodies. "And the others?"

Dooley shrugged and let out a sigh that felt more

like a moan. "I don't know. Never saw them before. I was on my way here when they rode up. Started shooting."

"Friends of Dobbs?" the old man asked.

"I don't think so. Dobbs didn't have any friends, and they couldn't have known it was Dobbs that I was carrying." He looked back as the deputy pulled up the blanket. The population crowded the boardwalk. Even the women did not turn their heads as the deputy made his inspection.

"Their horses were pretty much worn out," Dooley went on. "My guess is that they meant to steal my bay and . . ." He swallowed down the bile. "Dobbs's . . ."

He didn't finish because now he saw newcomers. Men in black broadcloth and women with their hair in buns and children . . . children! . . . walking from what at first Dooley thought must have been a wagon yard, only it seemed too far off to the north, too far out of Julesburg proper—if one could call this place proper.

A stout woman with red hair and more rouge on her face than Dooley had seen in entire brothels stepped off the boardwalk and made a wide berth around Dobbs's horse. She waved her fat arms over her head and shouted at the men and women coming toward them.

"Stop. You all stop it right now. This ain't no sight for no damned tenderfeet!"

The procession stopped. The women took their children by their hands or swept them into their arms. They did not turn back, however, but kept watching from the distance. Waiting.

"Well?" the marshal asked his deputy.

"Fits the description on the dodger, Maximilian," the deputy said, "but I . . . I don't know."

"Let me take a look at that scoundrel," the fat woman with the rouge said, and she waddled to the horse, pushed the deputy aside with her right hand, grabbed Dobbs's dirty hair, and jerked up the dead man's face.

"Well, I never thought I'd live to see the day that ol' Dobbsy got hisself shot deader than my first five husbands," the big woman said. She let go of the corpse's hair and backed away, wiping her hands on her dress, and moving around General Grant. "It's him, Maxxie. Hubert Dobbs his own shot-dead self. I'll swear to it."

"You knew Dobbs, Sheila?" the lawman asked.

"Knowed him." Sheila's laugh sounded like a mountain lion's cry. "I knowed ever' inch of him, at Maude's Place in Denver, at my own crib in San Antone, one night in one of 'em healin' baths in Eureka Springs, an all-night poker game in Abilene back in '69, and . . ."

Marshal Maximilian cut her off. "I'll let you sign an affidavit. Maybe you know the other three dead men."

"Four," Dooley corrected, and nodded at the brown horse. "That one's carrying two bodies."

"Hell's bells, I gots to see this." A little man with a waxed mustache ducked underneath a hitching rail and came to the palomino before Sheila could reach the dun horse.

"Hell's bells," he said again as he looked at the corpse. As he stepped away from the horse, he asked Dooley, "Was this one wearin' one of those big Mexican hats?"

Dooley considered him before his head nodded.

The wind had carried the hat away, across the South Platte, and Dooley had not figured chasing down the hat of a dead man was worth the effort.

"Hell's bells." It seemed the only thing the little man could say, but everyone—including the men and women and the kids who weren't supposed to be looking upon such a ghastly scene even from afar— let the little man move to the brown horse carrying the two dead men, and the dun with the man who had worn a white hat that Dooley had managed to pick up before the wind blew it away.

"It's them, Marshal," the little man said, and now others were coming to investigate. The townsmen and women, not those with their hair in buns or wearing black pants, coats, and hats. Dooley could catch snippets of conversation, not that the talk would have been stimulating.

"Yes."

"See."

"Remember?"

"Yes."

"Didn't that one?"

"I think so."

"I know so. I was this close to him."

"Well, I'll be . . ."

"God have mercy on his soul."

"Do you think . . . ?"

"Dead."

"Golly."

"Where the hell's the money, mister?"

Dooley turned in the saddle to find a man with a pale blue shirt and black sleeve garters pointing a long finger at Dooley's chin.

"What?" Dooley asked, and told Blue to be quiet when the shepherd began to growl and show the man in the sleeve garters his fangs.

"The money these bushwhackers stole."

Dooley stared, blinked, and turned back to find that the marshal had pulled the shotgun through the window and now had the big bores trained on Dooley's midsection.

"Money?" Dooley asked. "These men jumped me on the trail."

"Before they done that," Marshal Max said, "they robbed the Julesburg Store the other day and killed poor Budd Totter, who was clerking that morn." Deeming Dooley no threat, the lawman lowered the shotgun and stepped off the boardwalk. "How much did they get, Horace?"

"Thirteen dollars and seventeen cents," Horace shouted from behind two of Sheila's girls.

"You didn't take no money off their persons, did you, stranger?" the marshal asked as he moved to the first horse trailing the one carrying Hubert Dobbs.

"I didn't even look through their pockets," Dooley said. "Or their saddlebags."

It was in the left-side satchel of the saddlebags on the palomino that Horace and Marshal Maximilian found the thirteen dollars and seventeen cents.

CHAPTER TWENTY-SEVEN

If you could get across the boardwalk without breaking your leg, and through the batwing doors without riddling your hands with splinters, the Julesburg Saloon No. 3 wasn't that bad of a watering hole. The beer came in a clean glass and was pretty cool, thanks to a deep basement in the back of the log cabin that the proprietors kept filled with ice chopped out of the South Platte during the winter. And the whiskey served was honest-to-goodness pure Monongahela rye from Pennsylvania.

Dooley Monahan sat at a green felt–covered table in the corner, near a window that actually still had panes of glass, and sipped his rye. Marshal Maximilian dropped his shot glass into the mug of beer and drank down half of it while the suds foamed over his gray mustache that looked even lighter after the lawman wiped off the foam with the sleeve of his shirt.

"So how did you catch Hubert Dobbs with no gun?" Maximilian asked.

"He had a gun," Dooley said, "his own gun. I didn't have a gun."

The lawman smiled that smile that said, *That's a good one, boy. You ought to perform in the Denver Opera House.*

"He was going to shoot me dead," Dooley explained. "Only I grabbed up a skillet—the bullet meant for me hit the pan." He rubbed his chest. "Still hurts. Probably a bruise from the impact."

"Of the bullet?" Maximilian inquired.

"No. The skillet hit me. The bullet ricocheted and gave Hubert Dobbs a mortal wound."

Maximilian drained his mixture of beer and rye, wiped his mouth again, and flagged the bartender over for another round. Dooley saw that the beer-jerker was bringing two more mugs and two more shot glasses, so he finished his rye and sipped some beer.

When the new beverages arrived, Maximilian did not dump his rye into the beer, but downed it with one quick shot, stifled a cough, and leaned forward, both elbows on the green felt and his hands folded to make a table for his chin.

"You're serious, ain't you?" the lawman asked.

"Yes. That's exactly what happened."

Maximilian reached for his beer. "I'll be damned," he said, and finished it off in three gulps.

The lawman took down Dooley's statement, let Dooley read over it and make any corrections, then had the paper "notarized" by Sheila and the bartender, although the bartender could make only an

X and had Maximilian write his name, Jude Smith, neatly underneath the rough-drawn *X*.

Dooley and Maximilian left the Julesburg Saloon No. 3, maneuvered their way safely past the boardwalk, and walked down the dusty street to the Julesburg Café, but were interrupted by the owner of the Julesburg Store, who needed to speak to the Julesburg marshal about some important business. So Dooley waited in the street and stared down at the encampment. The women with the buns in their hair and the men in the black pants, black coats, and black hats had taken their children back to the line of wagons. Only one man had ventured into town as soon as the bodies of the dead men had been positively identified, and he had just offered to pray at the funeral of the deceased and maybe preach a sermon or two.

Dooley turned back and stared at the cemetery, where the marshal's deputy and two other men—one from the livery and the former owner of the Julesburg Saloon No. 2—were busy digging the graves. The ground here must have been right hard. The preacher—Dooley at least assumed that man had been a preacher as he sure had the face of one, as well as a Bible—had returned to the wagons to wait until it was his time.

Hearing bits and phrases of the conversation between the marshal and the store owner, Dooley looked back at the wagons. He could see the oxen picketed probably too far away from the wagons. Indians—if any Indians were around—could easily steal those animals during the night. Some girls played roll-a-hoop in their muslin dresses. The men busied themselves greasing the axles of their wagons or doing other camp chores. The women cooked or worked on a quilt. If they were old enough, the boys did their chores, which pretty much amounted to collecting dried buffalo dung for fires. Younger boys taunted the girls with the stick and the hoop, or tossed a ball to each other.

To his surprise, Dooley found himself envying those greenhorn tenderfeet. The scene away from Julesburg seemed idyllic. He could picture himself among those people, probably heading west to farm. Yes, that would be just fine, and some of those younger women—the ones working on the quilts or listening to the bossy old crone who stirred the stewpot—didn't look bad at all. At least, from this distance. But, compared to Sheila or any of the girls who worked for her, Marshal Maximilian looked good.

"You hungry, Dooley?" the lawman asked. He had stepped out of the store and returned to the street.

"I can eat," Dooley said.

"Well, let's see how much."

"So you're the man who killed Doug Wheatlock," Marshal Maximilian said.

Dooley finished forking the last bit of steak, coated with mashed potatoes, into his mouth. He chewed, swallowed, washed the grub down with coffee, and set the cup by his cleaned-over blue-enamel plate.

The food, while not the best or even close to the best that Dooley had ever eaten, was filling, and tasty, and satisfying. He wiped his mouth with a napkin and looked at the grinning lawman. Dooley decided he wouldn't let Maximilian spoil his appetite.

"And his cousins," Dooley said.

"Huh?"

"Jason Baylor," Dooley said. "And the Baylor brothers."

"I see," the lawman said, and lifted his glass of water.

"I killed Ewing Atkinson, too," Dooley added. "Well, no. I didn't really kill that one, but I got the reward. Dobbs took it from me, though, but that was fine with me."

"So you killed Dobbs for the reward of Jason Baylor," Maximilian said.

"No. Ewing Atkinson."

"Who'd Atkinson kill?"

"I don't know. Plenty of people. Almost me."

"Well, the world and the West won't miss the likes of Hubert Dobbs, Dooley. That's for sure. But I want to know just how you came to kill a man like Dobbs."

So Dooley told him. Told the lawman everything. Then he started to keep talking. It's amazing what a plate of steak, onions, mashed potatoes after two ryes and two beers can do for a man's tongue. Yet after he had finished with the shooting of Hubert Dobbs and the killing of the robbers of the Julesburg Store, Marshal Maximilian raised his hand.

"I don't need to hear anything else, Dooley," he said. "You tell me where you're going, well, I might just tell someone who undoubtedly would tell Frank Handley."

Dooley's stomach started doing one of those dances that it had been doing quite often since he had ridden into Omaha, Nebraska.

"What . . . why . . . ?"

"Oh, they wouldn't want to, son. Whoever told

those murdering fiends about you. Talk to Handley. Or Doc Watson. Or that daughter you told me about. Dobbs's girl. Wouldn't want to. On account that they like you. I like you. But . . . well . . . you got to think that men like Frank Handley and men like Doc Watson have ways of getting information they want to know out of men like . . . well . . . even womenfolk . . . hell, anyone in this town. Don't you think?"

Dooley wished the Julesburg Café served rye whiskey, or any liquor. He narrowed his eyes as he focused on the lawman.

"But you wouldn't tell them."

The marshal laughed and rocked back in his chair. "On account that I won't be here, son. No. No, sir." The chair came back to the floor, and Maximilian put his elbows on the table, folded his hands into a table, and rested his chin on his hands.

"It's a little more than thirty miles from Julesburg to Ogallala. You covered that in two days, and that's after killing five men dead, loading their dead carcasses on four horses, and riding fairly easy. Typical. Two-day ride here. Two-day ride back. Meaning that Frank Handley and those others'll be expecting you to return to Ogallala in two days. And when you don't show up, well, the United States Cavalry says they can make forty miles a day. Forty miles on beans and hay, ain't that how that goes? So I think those murderers will be here in three days. And probably not that long. Killers like Doc Watson and those of his ilk, they don't have much use for patience. So . . . let's see . . . today's Tuesday." He counted on his fingers. "Wednesday. Thursday. Yeah. Friday afternoon, maybe even Friday morning if they left at dusk Thursday. That's when I figure they'll be arriving in Julesburg.

Since, as you've already told me, Hubert Dobbs said he was coming here. And when they come . . ."

He made that cutting motion with his finger across his throat.

"Well," Dooley said, after easing the dryness in his throat and mouth with a few swallows of water, "I thought you could send a telegraph to the marshal at Ogallala. Maybe even the commander at Fort McPherson. And . . ."

Dooley stopped. Maximilian sadly shook his head.

"You saw the telegraph poles, didn't you?" Dooley didn't have time to answer. "Poles are still standing, but the murdering scum who you brought in along with Hubert Dobbs cut down the lines, east and west, after they robbed the store and done their killing. Haven't been able to reach anybody at the U.P. to fix 'em."

"And the trains?" Dooley asked but without much hope.

"Eastbound, which I could send somebody on, is due Friday, probably about when Dobbs's avengers ride here. So wouldn't be no need to send word to Ogallala that late in the day. Westbound, if the bridge ain't washed out forty-nine miles east of here, should pull in Monday at noon, or midnight."

Dooley felt hopeless, and Marshal Maximilian went on without lifting Dooley's spirits.

"Now, we do get a stagecoach through here, eastbound or westbound, once every two weeks. So that don't do you, or Julesburg, any good. I guess I could send out a rider, my deputy maybe, but that bay gelding of yours is the best horse I've seen in Julesburg since those bandits you killed rode in here. And those fools run those horses down so much, before you sent them to Perdition, that they won't be much good for walking, let alone a full gallop, for . . . my best guess . . . a week or two. And not only that, my deputy don't ride worth a damn."

He sighed. "So, no, Dooley Monahan, we can't get the word to any lawman or army officer in Nebraska. Hell, we can't even get word to Denver until the west-bound comes through . . . and that's not due till Sunday, the stage I mean, and the train, like I've already pointed out, on Monday, maybe Tuesday, but no later than Wednesday."

"I see."

The marshal chuckled and pulled out a yellow piece of paper. "Naturally, the Julesburg Bank doesn't have the funds to pay off the reward for Hubert Dobbs, so this is a voucher. Let me explain how these work . . ."

Dooley raised his hand. "I know how those work, Marshal."

"Oh." He slid the voucher across the table. "Next time, Dooley, kill your man in a big city. Denver. Hell, Denver's got its own mint."

As he slid the voucher into his trousers pocket, Dooley mumbled, "I'll try to remember that, Marshal."

"And here's something else." The marshal slid a twenty-dollar gold piece across the table.

"What's this?"

"That's the reward," Maximilian said.

"Reward?" Dooley studied the coin, picked it up, bit it, assured that it was indeed a real double eagle. "For what?"

"That's the reward Mr. Posnanski offered after those killers you killed robbed his store."

Dooley put the coin beside his empty plate. "But they only took seventeen dollars and thirteen cents."

"Thirteen dollars and seventeen cents," Marshal Maximilian corrected. "It's policy, is all. Besides, they also murdered poor old Budd Potter."

"Totter," Dooley corrected.

"*P* or *T*, nobody'll remember him next month. Hell, I'd already forgotten the handle he was using. So it's policy. A man gets killed who works for you and your store gets robbed, you post a reward."

Which, if Dooley could do his ciphering correctly, meant that the owner of the Julesburg Store thought Budd Totter's life was worth six dollars and seventy- or eighty-odd cents.

"And," Marshal Maximilian added, "someone kills your partner, or your gang's boss, or your daddy, and, well, you come after the person who done the plugging."

"The way it struck me," Dooley said, "being with the gang for a while . . . neither Frank Handley nor Doc Watson cared one whit for Hubert Dobbs. And I'm not altogether certain Dobbs's daughter would lift a finger to save, or avenge, him."

"Like ain't got a danged thing to do with it, son," the marshal said. "It's principle, like I've already said. A man's gotta do what he's gotta do. Principle, you see."

He pointed at the double eagle. "Best take that, Dooley, and raise dust."

Dooley put the gold coin in his pocket. "You're asking me to get out of town."

"I'm not exactly asking, Dooley."

"I'd planned to go anyway, Marshal. Thanks."

"When you go, son." Maximilian stayed in his chair as Dooley rose. "Try for Denver, maybe. Cheyenne. Or south, though the Cheyenne will likely lift your hair. Just stay away from Scottsbluff. That's where I'm bound."

"You're leaving?"

The old man laughed heartily. "Son, I sure ain't planning on being here when Frank Handley and his boys ride in. They'll burn this town and everyone in it looking for you."

CHAPTER TWENTY-EIGHT

Marshal Maximilian was right, the way Dooley saw things. Handley, Doc Watson, Zee Dobbs, and the rest of the gang would ride after Dooley, if not for revenge then for all the money that Dobbs had been carrying that the gang figured needed to be divvied up among the surviving outlaws. Even before Dooley had arrived, he had never considered staying long in Julesburg anyway. Now that he had seen Julesburg, he knew nothing could keep him here.

He still had two days. Two days before the killers came looking for him. Even at a hard pace, he knew he couldn't make it to Cheyenne in two days, but he probably would be able to get there well ahead of the ruffians chasing him. But that would likely mean waiting for one of the U.P. trains. If the westbound arrived in Julesburg on Monday . . . ? Dooley swore underneath his breath. Hopeless.

On the other hand, Denver held some promise. A hundred and eighty, two hundred miles? Five days of hard riding, six or seven to keep General Grant—and

Dooley himself—fresh. Besides, Denver had a mint. In Denver he could cash in that voucher.

"But I've never ran away from anything," he said aloud. He opened the door, stepped delicately onto the boardwalk, and laughed at the absurdity of his statement. The door closed. "You've run from your responsibilities," he reminded himself. "From Ma and Pa. From the Baylors. From Des Moines. From Monty's Raiders. And you wanted to run from Dobbs, from Ewing Atkinson."

He stepped off the boardwalk, looked back toward the railroad tracks. Yeah, Marshal Maximilian had not been lying. No telegraph wire could be seen against the darkening sky. Darkening sky. Dusk was fast approaching. He had been in Julesburg for maybe two or three hours. He could put a few more miles between him and the Dobbs-Handley Gang now if he saddled up and rode away.

"Yes," he told himself, and turned back to head toward the livery. He stepped right on the blonde's brogans, heard her scream, and he fell right on top of her on Julesburg's dusty lone street.

She smelled of lilacs. Lilacs and . . . he couldn't help but sniff. Her hair held the aroma of yucca, but Dooley hadn't seen anything but sage in this part of the country. And her hands, which had reached up to grip his shoulders, reminded him of vegetable soup. He thought he had eaten enough vegetable soup back on his farm in Des Moines, thought he never wanted to get a whiff of that odor again, but now . . . well . . .

"I'm sorry." Dooley rolled off her as fast as he would a rank bronco that had just pitched him in a bucking corral. He came to his knees, gasping, terrified, and held out his hands. "I . . . didn't . . . see you."

She blinked. He knew she was not one of Sheila's girls, and, from the looks of her, had to belong to that wagon train parked on the north side of town. He thought he might have crushed some of her bones, but she sat up, eyes still wide with terror, and turned to face him.

"Are you . . ." Dooley even had trouble speaking. "All right?"

Her mouth opened. It was a pretty mouth, white teeth—most teeth a man saw in this country were yellow, sometimes brown, even black, and often quite a few missing. As far as Dooley could see, she had all of hers, and there was this splendid little gap between the two big ones up front in her upper gums.

She raised a hand and brushed away a lock of blond bang that had fallen from underneath the red bonnet. Red. Most of the women Dooley had seen appeared to be wearing blue bonnets, a few gray, one yellow. Hers was not only red, but red and white polka-dot calico—just like Dooley's bandanna.

"Ma'am . . ." Dooley looked at her, then up and down the boardwalk, but no one had appeared from any of Julesburg's businesses. The store was even closed.

She laughed. Dooley sank back onto his buttocks. Maybe she had lost all her reason. Had she struck her head on something hard? She bent over, she laughed so hard.

"Ma'am?" Dooley tried to figure out how did you help a person who had just gone loco.

"Ohhhhh," she said, and her voice sounded so

musical. At length, she stopped, wiped the tears rolling down her cheeks, sniffed, and looked at Dooley as her chest heaved up and down.

Dooley held his breath. He waited. She stared at him with those wonderful blue eyes. Freckles coated her nose. Her dress was buttoned close and tight against her neck.

"Ohhhhhh," she said again, and started laughing again.

Dooley stared off toward the wagon train and raised his hat, hoping to get someone's attention. He didn't think Julesburg had any doctor. At least, he had seen no sign saying JULESBURG DOCTOR anywhere in the town limits.

"That . . ." At last the woman had said something else. She caught her breath. "Can you believe that?" she asked, and began her insane laugh again.

Dooley put his hat back on his head. She stopped again, looked at him, and this time when she began howling like a crazy woman, Dooley accompanied her.

When they finally finished, Dooley rose to his feet and held out his hand. She accepted, and let him pull her to her feet.

"You sure you're all right, ma'am?" Dooley asked.

"Yes." Now her voice turned formal. "I am, kind sir."

"I didn't see you."

"I should hope not."

"Well."

"Well." She grinned.

He swept his hat off his head again. "Sorry, ma'am. My name's Monahan. Dooley Monahan."

He stiffened. If she said something like, *The Dooley*

Monahan who killed the Baylor boys, he would just turn to dust and blow away.

Only she did not say, *The Dooley Monahan who killed the Baylor boys.* She said, "It's a pleasure to meet you, Mr. Dooley Monahan." She held out her right hand. "I am Sabrina Granby."

His hand dwarfed hers, and he feared his calluses would scar her permanently, but she had a firm grip, a sturdy shake, and when she lowered her hand to her side, she did not attempt to wipe off the dirt on her apron or in the folds of her dress.

"Ummmm." Dooley didn't know what to say.

"I am bound for the funeral," Miss Sabrina Granby told him.

He squinted. "Oh," he said, and turned around to look at Julesburg's sprawling cemetery. The deputy and the two other Julesburg citizens had gotten the graves six feet deep, or deep enough for the likes of Hubert Dobbs and four poor-shooting store robbers and clerk killers. The tenderfoot who had offered to do the preaching stood under the lone cottonwood that grew away from the South Platte River, holding his black hat by his black trousers in his left hand and his big black Bible in his right hand.

"Would you care to accompany me?" she asked, and crooked her arm as a signal.

Dooley sighed. "I reckon I should see them planted," he said, and thought, but did not add, *seeing how I killed all five of them.*

He ran his arm through the opening between her arm and waist, and led Miss Sabrina Granby down the dusty Julesburg street and turned left into the cemetery that had no gate. He let Miss Sabrina

Granby go stand beside the tall, gangly man in black, and Dooley again removed his hat and got ready for the funeral.

The deputy marshal matched coins with the blacksmith from the livery and the former owner of the Julesburg Saloon No. 2 to see who would stay behind to cover the graves after the funeral. The smithy lost, so the deputy and the other townsman walked off, leaving a crowd of two, not counting the preacher, to pay their final respects—though it wasn't actual respect—to Hubert Dobbs and four men whose names would not be recorded.

Since it was growing dark, the parson kept the funeral fairly short. He quoted from the Beatitudes and quoted from some other Bible books that Dooley couldn't quite put his finger on, said "Ashes to ashes," and led Miss Sabrina Granby in "Shall We Gather at the River." Dooley just mouthed the words that he remembered and those words that he did not remember.

After that, the preacher bowed his head and prayed:

"Merciful Father, hear our prayers and comfort us. Renew our trust in your Son, whom you raised from the dead. Strengthen our faith that all who have died in the love of Christ will share in his resurrection, who lives and reigns with you now and forever. Amen."

Dooley knew the amen part.

"And thank you, God, for bringing this stranger, this good man, this intelligent man, into our midst. We are not worthy, Lord, but you in your infinite wisdom, must truly love us to bring this good man to us."

Dooley wanted to look around to see who the preacher was talking about, but didn't dare lift his head until the preacher said again, "Amen."

Miss Sabrina Granby said "amen," as well.

CHAPTER TWENTY-NINE

As soon as the preacher put on his black hat and took two steps toward Dooley Monahan and Sabrina Granby, the burly blacksmith began covering the blanket-wrapped corpses with Colorado sod.

"Did you know the deceased men, sir?" the preacher asked in a solemn voice.

"Not well," Dooley answered with a certain measure of discomfort.

"I saw you bring their bodies in," the preacher said. "You are a lawman?"

"Well . . . not . . . um . . . exactly."

"But I must guess that you have experience in . . . such . . . ahem . . , delicate matters of . . . how should I put this?" He looked at the darkening sky for guidance. "Surviving in this rough, lawless land," he said as if given the words through divine intervention.

Dooley said solemnly, "Well, I'm alive." He thought: *For the time being*.

"I am Robert James Granby the third," the reverend said, and held out his right hand.

Dooley shook, and introduced himself. The parson's

hand was cold like a cadaver's, but firm, and for a tenderfoot, he sure knew how to keep a handshake short and to the point.

"You're Miss Sabrina's . . ." Dooley started but did not finish.

"Uncle," Miss Sabrina Granby filled in.

"And, you, Mr. Dooley Monahan, will do us the honor of dining with us in camp tonight, sir," the preacher said.

Dooley grimaced. "Well . . ." he started, but the parson was already walking away, and Miss Sabrina Granby had taken his arm in escort.

"Nonsense, sir," the preacher said. "I insist."

A tall man, the Reverend Robert James Granby III moved at a fast gait and did not give Dooley any time to tell him that he had already eaten, and not just eaten but had a steak and mashed potatoes and corn bread and fried onions. Dooley watched Miss Sabrina Granby's dress bounce and sashay and decided that a full stomach would not hurt him and he could still make good time if he left at seven or eight o'clock, that the moon would be bright enough, and even if he left at first light, he would still be able to put a lot of trail dust between him and the late Hubert Dobbs's bunch back in Ogallala. Besides, who was he to argue with a man of God?

The good news was that they were serving soup and sourdough bread for supper, and the soup was not vegetable after all but something fairly tasty and creamy, and the women who had been in charge of the bread had seasoned it with sage and cheese, and that tasted just absolutely wonderful.

Before eating, they gathered in a circle, reached out, and held their neighbors' hands, bowed their heads, and had a nice little prayer, led by, naturally, Miss Sabrina Granby's uncle. After that, they formed a line, women and children first, and collected their grub.

"Just a little soup and a small slice of bread, please, ma'am," Dooley told the gray-haired woman in charge of parceling out the eats. She didn't listen. Nor did the silver-haired woman who wore no bonnet but still had her hair up in a big bun. She was in charge of the coffee or tea, and when Dooley told her he'd just have some water, she slid to him a mug of thick brew that had been doctored with goat's milk—Dooley could hear the goats picketed over by the oxen—and sweetened with honey.

It turned out to be the best coffee Dooley had ever had.

Dooley stood off in the center of the camp, trying to figure out where he should go with his food and drink.

"Over here, Mr. Monahan!" the Reverend Mr. Granby said, and waved him to an old Conestoga wagon. Dooley made himself smile and walked to the preacher. He had hoped to have been made to join Miss Sabrina Granby, but he saw her over with a bunch of other young women in bonnets. Miss Sabrina did, however, smile at him and wave her hand.

At the Conestoga, Dooley found himself introduced by other men in black pants, black coats, and black hats—Mr. Franco, Mr. Jones, Mr. McCreery, Mr. Hentig, and some other misters, although Dooley could not put a face to a name five minutes after the introductions.

Penguins. That's what he thought. Six years back, when he had been working a line shack on the north forty of the Circle 79 Ranch in Idaho, all he had had to read for three lonely months was a copy of *Harper's Weekly*. He did not remember much about the article written about the great continent of Antarctica and a desperate try at reaching the South Pole, but he did remember those illustrations of the birds with wings that could not fly but could swim like a shark and eat more fish than a Baptist. Black-and-white birds. That's what all of these men reminded him of. Penguins.

The men asked Dooley the usual questions. Where he came from. How did he like the soup? How long had he been in the West? The Widow Kingsbury sure knew how to make bread, didn't she? What was his line of work? Did he know that the sourdough starter the Widow Kingsbury used had been in the Renick family—that was the Widow's maiden name—since they had arrived in Massachusetts in 1697? What was the weather like in Iowa? Was Des Moines anywhere near St. Louis? How did his crops fare last year? What did he think of Julesburg? How did he manage to kill four men in a gunfight and not take even one bullet? Was Hubert Dobbs as evil as the *Commercial Gazette of Cincinnati* said he was?

"Ain't you got a dog?"

Dooley put the last piece of sourdough bread, which he had used to wipe up the last of the soup that was more chowder and sure hit the spot after steak and rye whiskey, in his mouth. Before him stood a freckle-faced boy wearing a hat that Dooley thought had been made for a girl.

After he swallowed, Dooley wiped his mouth and fingertips with the ends of his bandanna and picked up the coffee cup to wash down his supper. He kept nodding, though, so the tyke would not think Dooley rude.

"Yes, boy, I got a dog," Dooley told him.

"I thought so. Seen it. Don't tell my ma. I wasn't supposed to be looking."

Dooley's head just kept bobbing.

"Where's that dog?"

Dooley smiled. One of the penguins—maybe it was Mr. McCreery but it could have been any of those who was not the Reverend Granby—called out from the wagon tongue where he was sitting, "Madison, don't you be bothering Mr. Monahan any!"

"He's no bother, sir," Dooley said, and told the boy, "My dog's in the livery."

"Liveries is for horses and mules," Madison said.

"Yes. My dog's keeping my horse company."

"Oh. You didn't want to bring him here."

"I didn't know Blue was invited."

That made the boy's eyes light up. "Blue? Is that what you call your dog?"

"That's what I call him. His coat looks blue. His eyes are blue."

"The hell you say!"

Dooley shot a quick glance toward the wagon tongue and over by the neighboring wagon, which wasn't a Conestoga but a heavy farm wagon. None of the men in black had heard the boy's curse.

"A blue-eyed dog. You ain't fooling me?"

"No." Dooley laughed. "His eyes are blue. Bluer than yours even."

"On account mine's gray."

Dooley drank some more coffee.

"If I had a dog, I'd have brung him here. So I'd have a dog to play with."

"Well," Dooley said, "had I known . . ."

A woman in a red calico dress with a muslin apron and a yellow bonnet appeared. "Madison," she said, but her voice did not appear to be scolding, even when she took the boy's hand and pulled him to her side. "You should not be bothering our guest, son."

"He's no bother, ma'am," Dooley assured her.

"Just asking him about his dog, Ma," Madison told the woman. She was a young woman, and quite pretty, though not on the scale of beauty as Miss Sabrina Granby.

Dooley started to rise, but the boy's mother said, "Oh, please, Mr. Monahan, don't stand on my account. Come along, Madison."

She led the boy away, who whined, "If I had a dog, Ma, I'd have brung him up to play with me. I wasn't pestering him none."

For a moment, Dooley wondered if maybe he could head down to the Julesburg Livery and bring Blue up to play with the boy, even though Dooley did not think the dog had ever played with any boys since he had found that dog all those years ago in Arizona.

Maybe he would have, but by then, three of the men in black pants, coats, and hats had brought out their musical instruments, and everyone was gathering in that circle in the center of camp again. The Reverend Granby had walked over to Dooley and said, "Come along, Mr. Monahan. Join us in our dance."

"You all dance?" Dooley asked.

The minister chuckled. "We're not Baptists, sir."

They danced, all right, and the men on the banjo,

fiddle, and harmonica sounded better than plenty of musicians Dooley had found on the frontier. Miss Sabrina even stood up with them to sing, and her voice reminded Dooley of angels. "Onward, Christian Soldiers" and "Dear Old Skibbereen." No one danced to the first song, of course, but they waltzed to that old Irish ballad. Miss Sabrina Granby did not sound Irish, though. She just sounded beautiful.

When she had finished, everyone applauded, and the fiddler broke into "Put Your Little Foot," and most of the men found a woman, and even some of the boys found girls, and, Dooley's mouth hung open, as Miss Sabrina Granby came up to him, extended her hands, and said, "Isn't this our dance, Mr. Monahan?"

He liked the dance, since it was mostly a waltz but sometimes a mazurka and a bit of a polka. Not that Dooley had ever been much of a dancer, but he never once stepped on the beautiful woman's toes. He even felt . . . dare he say . . . graceful?

Alas, the song ended too soon, and the banjo player said he needed time to tune, and the harmonica player said he needed to wet his windpipe. Dooley had hoped he might stay out on that prairie dancing with Miss Sabrina Granby until some low-down snake tapped him on the shoulder and asked to cut in.

He walked her to her wagon.

"Are you having a nice time?" Miss Sabrina asked.

"Yes, ma'am."

"Don't *ma'am* me, please, sir. You make me feel old."

"All right. You don't have to call me sir, either, Miss Sabrina."

They had reached the Conestoga. She turned and

looked him right in the eye. "Why don't you forget the *miss,* too, Mr. Monahan. My name is Sabrina."

Dooley wet his lips. He looked over his shoulder, but the reverend was talking to one of the penguins.

"Sabrina," he said.

"That's better." Her eyes twinkled.

He pushed his luck.

"My name's Dooley. Mr. Monahan was my pa."

His luck held. His heart beat faster. "Dooley," she said. "That's such a nice name."

His throat turned dry. No one had ever told him that he had a nice name. Usually, men said, *What kind of name is Dooley?* Or, *Who in his right mind would name his kid Dooley?*

"Well," she said.

Darkness had covered northeastern Colorado Territory by that time, but the fires were going all across the camp, and Dooley could see the reflection of the flames in her eyes. He could have stared at her eyes forever, and maybe he would have, if the voice behind him had not said:

"Mr. Monahan, mayhap we can have a word with you. A word of the utmost import."

CHAPTER THIRTY

For a while, after Dooley had been led away from Miss Sabrina Granby and her beautiful eyes and those freckles he really wanted to kiss, Dooley thought the important discussion had to do with Mrs. Abercrombie's apple pie. They gave him a slice, and a glass of goat's milk to wash it down.

"What do you think?" asked one of the penguins as Dooley chewed.

"Criminy, Fred, let the fella at least swallow."

"Nobody makes better apple pie than Beatrice," another penguin stated.

"Because of her crust. It's her crust that seals it."

"Crumbly top. With cinnamon."

"Never tasted anything better."

Dooley had to nod. It was pretty good pie. Made with apples from a can, but that had to be expected because it was too early for any fresh apples and Dooley did not think they had brought any apples they had stored in a cellar back from wherever it was that they hailed from before landing in Julesburg, Colorado Territory.

"It's good," Dooley said, and realized he probably should say a little more because at least a dozen penguins were staring at him with beady penguin eyes.

"Best I've ever had."

The twelve pairs of eyes widened.

"I told you."

"Beatrice is a blessing."

"Because of the crust."

"And the cinnamon."

"And how she makes that top so crumbly and delicious."

"You like the goat's milk, Mr. Monahan."

He nodded. That didn't need any more explanation. They let Dooley finish his pie and milk in peace while they polished off the rest of Beatrice Abercrombie's apple pie.

"Well," the Reverend Granby said. "How about a nightcap, Dooley?"

As Dooley turned, he saw the leader of the penguins had produced a brown earthen jug, which he unstoppered, rested the bottom in the crook of his arm, and lifted the opening to his mouth. His Adam's apple bobbed a few times, and then the preacher lowered the jug and wiped his mouth with the back of his other black sleeve.

The jug was extended to Dooley, who quickly set down his plate and empty glass and took the heavy container.

"You drink?" he asked the preacher.

That got chuckles from all of the penguins.

"Certainly, Dooley," the minister said. "Like I told you earlier, we're not Baptists."

"We're Episcopalians," said the penguin with the

bushy eyebrows. That had to be Mr. Abercrombie, because he was collecting the empty pie tin.

"I see." Dooley saw. He took a sip of whiskey, and it was certainly whiskey, but not rotgut. It had that taste and smell of Scotch, which Dooley had never been particularly fond of, but Scotch would do in a pinch, and as night had come full on and brought with the darkness a certain chill, the Scotch—if indeed Episcopalians drank Scotch and not Episcopal whiskey— warmed his mouth, throat, stomach, and settled over his entire body.

Mr. Hentig—Dooley was getting to tell the penguins apart, at least some of them—cleared his throat, and Dooley passed the jug to him. He watched the jug make its rounds in the circle of men in black, and nodded at the questions and answered a few of those that required more than nods, and thought that he really should get down to the livery, pay the livery man, saddle General Grant, and load up Blue, and start out for Denver or Cheyenne or maybe even turn south, because Doc Watson and Frank Handley probably would not expect him to go that way on account of the Cheyenne Indians who might be looking to lift any white man's hair.

It was too dark now, though, to ride anywhere. He would have to wait for the moon to rise.

"Did you train that dog of yours to fight?"

"He's a real fighter, isn't he?"

"But he would be gentle around our children, wouldn't he?"

"That's a Colt Peacemaker on your hip, isn't it?"

"What caliber?"

"And is that the only weapon you own?"

"We're not prying, just new to these Western ways.

Did they carry six-shooters on their hips in Des Moines?"

"Beatrice made another pie. Not apple, but peach. Canned peaches. Would you care for a slice of peach pie, Dooley?"

"Are you sure?"

"Well, the children will appreciate that, Dooley. Mrs. Abercrombie made the pie for them, you see."

"But the whiskey is all ours."

"And it's back around to you, Dooley."

The reverend smiled as he handed Dooley the jug.

He took only a small sip this time, barely enough to wet his lips and tongue, and let the jug make its way across the circle once more. This time, when it reached the Reverend Granby, the minister returned the stopper and set the jug back inside the Conestoga.

"It's getting late," one of the penguins said.

Another penguin yawned.

Silence. The fires were dying down, but Dooley could see the women in pretty dresses and bonnets leading their children away from the remnants of Mrs. Abercrombie's peach pie and to their own bed-rolls underneath various wagons of all shapes and sizes.

The younger women, including Miss Sabrina Granby, began gathering the dirty dishes and taking them to a thick, black pot from which steam wafted in the night air. Dishwashing time. Dooley thought about volunteering to help, but Mr. Hentig said abruptly, "Ask him, Bob."

"We need to get a-moving," said Mr. Jones, or perhaps it might have been Mr. Franco.

"Or we ain't never gonna get to—"

"Shut up, Mark," Mr. Abercrombie barked.

All of the penguins became silent. And all of them looked straight at Dooley Monahan.

"Dooley," the preacher said after a long, awkward pause, "remember I said I had something of importance to bring to your attention?"

The apple pie and goat's milk began fighting each other in Dooley's bowels. He wished he was helping Miss Sabrina Granby wash dishes, and Dooley hated to wash dishes.

Still, he managed to nod his head.

"Then let us find a spot by the fire yonder and have our private conversation." He accented the word *private*, and Mr. Jones and Mr. Abercrombie and Mr. Franco and all the other penguins waddled off to their own wagons and families, except for Mr. Hentig, who had announced that he would check on the goats and oxen before finding his bedroll.

The fire yonder that the Reverend Granby had suggested turned out to be the one at the south-easternmost point in camp. The preacher squatted at the northwestern spot, where all the smoke was drifting toward, and gestured at the other side for Dooley.

Dooley sat and watched as the preacher stoked the fire with a stick and then fed it with pieces of dead sagebrush. From his spot, however, Dooley saw he had a real fine view of Miss Sabrina Granby as she washed dishes with Madison's mother while one of the old silver-haired women watched, spit snuff, and dried with her apron. Then she passed the plate to one of the other older girls who would take the plate or pot or cup or utensil to the proper wagon. Like a military operation.

Mostly, though, Dooley just watched Miss Sabrina.

"Dooley," the preacher said, and, reluctantly, Dooley looked at Miss Sabrina's uncle. "Let me tell you a story."

And he did. This one:

Long ago, the Episcopalian penguins had left Massachusetts and brought the Widow Kingsbury's sourdough starter and their families from Peabody, which before 1868 had been called the South Parish and before that Brooksby and before that The Farms and before that Northfields and before that part of Salem and before that nothing unless the Indians called it something. They left Peabody, Massachusetts, and came to Ohio.

Oh, Cincinnati was a wonderful town, with the Ohio River and the Miami and Erie canals and streetcars. You would not believe the streetcars. Why, those horse-drawn conveyances could take a person anywhere he wanted to go. If he wanted to take a steamboat somewhere, the streetcars could take him right up to the river. If he wanted to board a train, he would be driven to the depot. If he wanted to visit a friend in one of the hill communities, he could board a railcar and go there, too.

"You did know Cincinnati is surrounded by hills, did you not, Dooley?"

Dooley shook his head. He knew nothing about Cincinnati other than it was in Ohio and had streetcars, but was quickly told that the best city in Ohio or anywhere along the Ohio River was also known as "The City of Seven Hills," even though there were many, many more hills than seven. Mount Adams . . .

Mount Harrison . . . the Walnut Hills . . . Fairmont . . . College Hill . . . Vine Street Hill . . .

Rome may have been built on seven hills, but Cincinnati outshone Rome by far.

"The Cincinnati Inclined Plane Company can take you all the way to top of Mount Auburn," the Reverend Granby said.

"Wow," Dooley said just to please the uncle of Miss Sabrina Granby.

Life must have been grand in Cincinnati. Residents could fish or buy fish, they could drink, they could read assorted newspapers, they could go to any church that they desired to worship in—even Mormons, provided they stayed out of the good parts of the city—and if they wanted to watch a baseball game, why, Cincinnati had the best ballists money could buy.

Dooley knew nothing about baseball or ballists.

"And . . ." The Reverend raised his index finger. "Surely you have heard about the Tyler Davidson Fountain."

"No, sir," Dooley whispered. "Tell me."

It was the "Genius of Water," the symbol of that glorious city, located in the center of Fifth Street among all the coffeehouses and stores and hotels and restaurants and finest businesses you'll find anywhere in Ohio and definitely better than anything Pennsylvania has to offer.

Forty-three feet tall, in bronze, inscribed on its base of green granite, *To the People of Cincinnati*, it has brought tourists from all over, even Chillicothe.

It certainly sounded important, but Dooley quickly grew tired of Cincinnati, and after two suppers—one that included a big, thick, juicy steak—and several beers and some Monongahela rye whiskey from

Pennsylvania and finally some Scotch or Episcopalian whiskey and apple pie, but no peach pie, and goat's milk, Dooley Monahan was growing mighty tired. He wanted to sleep, but he certainly did not want to sleep in Julesburg. He needed to be riding. Riding west. Or south. Or anywhere but toward Scottsbluff, Nebraska—and definitely not Ogallala.

The preacher kept talking. For a man who gave mighty short funerals, really short, considering how the funeral had been for five men, the Reverend Robert James Granby could be long-winded when it came to waxing poetic about Peabody, Massachusetts, and Cincinnati, Ohio.

Dooley focused on Miss Sabrina, but all too soon the dishes were finished, and Miss Sabrina was walking toward the Conestoga. Dooley sighed. She climbed into the back of the wagon, and there was nothing left to look at except right across the fire now, at Miss Sabrina's uncle.

Certainly, by now, the parson had finished talking about where these Episcopalians had hailed from. Dooley looked at the man in black, waiting for him to tell him how much money they needed or what kind of investment was needed to restore the Genius of Water, that wonderful, irreplaceable Tyler David-son Fountain, and Dooley could hand him the golden eagle still in his pocket and get the hell out of Julesburg.

"Our travels were hard," the reverend lamented. "Wickedness took two of our great people in St. Louis. Disease claimed four in Kansas. One turned back in Hays City. And we buried poor Rolfes on Frenchman Creek. Our guide got us this far, but then he fell in with bad company."

Dooley waited, but the man did not speak.

"Bad company?" Dooley asked.

The preacher nodded. "His name was Jefferson Chatfield."

The name meant nothing to Dooley, but the description the preacher gave made it all come back to Dooley.

Mexican sombrero. Rode a palomino mare. Had one arm, his left, and hand pretty much chewed down to the bone, and a bullet that must have killed the man instantly, seeing how it hit him right in the heart.

One of the bunch that had robbed the Julesburg Store, killed poor Budd Totter, and tried to murder Dooley Monahan for his horse and the late Hubert Dobbs's horse on the road from Ogallala, Nebraska.

"Oh," Dooley said.

"My niece was betrothed to him."

"Oh." He felt like throwing up.

"But I'm glad we buried the son of a bitch."

"Me, too," Dooley whispered.

"We need you to finish Jefferson Chatfield's job," the preacher said. "We need you to take us to Slim Pickings."

CHAPTER THIRTY-ONE

The Reverend Robert James Granby reached inside his black coat and withdrew two long cigars, thick and tightly wrapped and probably better than any cigar Dooley had ever seen. He held them out for Dooley, who accepted one, and busied himself biting off an end while the preacher did the same. When the preacher lifted a twig out of the fire, Dooley leaned forward to let the minister light his smoke. It tasted slightly of cherry, which made Dooley wonder if Mrs. Abercrombie could make a cherry pie. He preferred cherry pie over apple and even peach and about the only pies he ever ate at a bunkhouse were vinegar pies which were not much to write home about.

When their cigars were glowing red, and the savory smoke was filling their mouths, Dooley and the preacher studied each other across the small fire.

Dooley removed his cigar, blew out smoke, and asked, "Slim Pickings?"

The reverend nodded.

"I've never heard of it," Dooley said.

"And we'd like to keep it that way."

He never knew men of the cloth could be so secretive.

"But how can I guide you there if I don't know where it is?"

"We have a map."

Dooley took another pull on the cigar. You had to suck real hard on the cigar, but it was worth the effort. He looked at the minister, at the wagons, and looked over his shoulder to the few lanterns or candles still glowing in Julesburg. Dooley's head shook as he turned around and told the minister, "Couldn't you follow that map to Slim Pickings yourselves?"

Some tobacco smoke must have gone down the wrong way, because the Reverend Granby coughed slightly, removed the cigar, coughed some more, spit into the fire, and wiped his nose.

"We are not Western people," the parson said. "We hail from . . ."

"Cincinnati," Dooley interrupted. "I know. By way of Peabody, Massachusetts." He was growing impatient because he really needed to get out of Julesburg and get away from the avengers of Hubert Dobbs, and this preacher with the beautiful niece and some quality cigars kept beating around the bush.

"There is no trail to Slim Pickings, and most people do not even know of its existence. I guess I should start from the beginning . . ."

Dooley frowned. The way the preacher talked, Dooley figured that he would never get out of this camp and on the trail west, or south, or somewhere.

* * *

Logan Kingsbury, the Widow Kingsbury's nephew, left Cincinnati before the Tyler Davidson Fountain, that exquisite Genius of Water, had been dedicated in 1871. He wrote his favorite, and only surviving, aunt for a few years, regularly, letting her know where he was, and naturally, where she might remit some money as life kept proving full of hardships and bad luck in Louisville . . . Nashville . . . Memphis . . . Natchez . . . New Orleans . . . Galveston . . . Indianola . . . San Antonio . . . Dallas . . . Fort Griffin . . . Wichita . . . Newton . . . Dodge City . . . La Junta . . . Trinidad . . . Breckenridge . . . Denver . . .

After Denver, the letters stopped coming.

By 1874, the Widow Kingsbury had reached the dreadful conclusion that poor Logan Kingsbury had been called to Glory, perhaps by savage Indians, or disease, or in some terrible accident trying to help the pathetic, homeless, heartbreaking little orphans as he had done in Memphis and Indianola and La Junta and the mining camps around Breckenridge, Colorado.

Or, Dooley thought, *after being caught dealing from the bottom of the deck as he had most likely been doing in Louisville and Natchez and Dallas and Trinidad and Denver . . .*

So the Widow Kingsbury wore black, even stopped baking sourdough bread for four months, and got little pleasure during those dark days from Cincinnati's streetcars or the river or the canals or trips to Mount Auburn on the Cincinnati Inclined Plane Company or even sitting in front of the fountain and marveling over the grandeur of the Genius of Water.

Those were dark times in "The Queen City of the West," which was another one of Cincinnati's monikers, and much better than "The Blue Chip City," which the Reverend Granby considered absurd.

"But . . ." The minister tapped off the ash from his cigar and pointed the stogie at Dooley to let Dooley know that he was about to say something extremely important.

"You know what happened in 1874?"

Oh, yes, Dooley knew something that had happened in 1874. That's when everything that had happened to him in 1872 and before came flooding back into his memories as soon as he had shot dead Doug Wheatlock, first cousin to Jason Baylor and his brothers. Only Dooley did not believe that was what Miss Sabrina Granby's uncle had on his mind. Had there been an election in 1874? Dooley couldn't recollect as he had never been one to follow politics except for that time in 1860 when a fellow had offered him a free beer if he would vote for Stephen Douglas. Dooley had taken the beer, but voted for Abraham Lincoln anyway. He didn't have to answer. The reverend told him after exhaling more cigar smoke.

"George Custer."

Custer. Of course. The Boy General of the Civil War who was making a name for himself as an Indian fighter out West.

"The Black Hills," the preacher said.

And Dooley knew, although the Reverend Granby told him anyway.

"It was Custer who discovered the gold in the Black Hills. Well, perhaps not Custer, but he was in command of the survey party or hunting party or whatever it was they were doing in Indian land, but gold was found. That set off the settlers, and likely will lead to an Indian war in which we white beings will wipe those red devils off the face of the earth."

Dooley wasn't so sure about that, but Episcopalians, it seemed, could be as hard-nosed as Methodists. He tapped his cigar on the heel of his boot, crushing it slightly until the tip was out. A cigar like this, Dooley figured, was worth savoring over two or three more days. And if he put the Cuban in his pocket, maybe the preacher would get the impression that Dooley had places to be—and Julesburg wasn't one of them.

The preacher kept going.

It was in December last when the Widow Kingsbury got an early blessing from the Lord, a gift from St. Nicholas before that jolly old cuss left his home in the North Pole. A letter arrived, crinkled and stained from its miles and miles of travels, but such a letter added years to the Widow Kingsbury's life. She baked a new loaf of bread, added to her famed sourdough starter, and removed the black band she had been wearing for more than a year and a half, and broke out a gray dress and donned a blue hat. Yes, the muffler she wore was black, as was her coat, but it was December, and cold, and the only winter outerwear she owned happened to be black. Yet you could tell by her eyes that she no longer mourned for Logan Kingsbury.

Logan Kingsbury, you see, was not dead. He was very much alive.

And he was successful.

"What do you know about the Black Hills?" the parson asked.

"Well," Dooley said, "it's where I was bound. I read about it, you see. The big gold strike in the Black

Hills. They're in Dakota Territory, those Black Hills, I mean, and the big strike everyone's lighting out for is called Deadwood. Deadwood Gulch."

The minister smoked, exhaled, and nodded. "What else?"

"Well . . ." Dooley didn't know what else to say.

"Indians," the preacher pointed out. "Indians. Savage, heathen red-skinned Sioux devils. The Black Hills are in Sioux land. That's what has those Indians so persnickety, you see."

That explained why those Indians had jumped Dooley and Zee Dobbs.

"The army," the Reverend Granby went on, "was supposed to keep the whites out of the Black Hills, but the army isn't doing that. Why should they? What use would Sioux have with gold? It's for us, the white men, to claim. To take. To make a fortune. And that is our destiny. We will take our people to the Black Hills, to make our fortune, and damn any red devil we meet to Hell's hottest fires."

Dooley's stomach started feeling that poor way again. He had not thought too much about Indians, about being scalped, about maybe even getting himself arrested by an army sergeant for trespassing on Indian lands.

"So . . ." Dooley started with some hesitation. There was a fierceness in the preacher's eyes that Dooley had not seen before, but maybe it was only Dooley's imagination, dark as it was by now, and the fire slowing burning itself out. "You're telling me that the Widow's nephew found himself a claim in the Black Hills."

The reverend leaned closer, and Dooley understood

that he had not mistaken that look in Granby's eyes. "Not a claim, sir . . . *The Mother LODE*!!!!!"

Logan Kingsbury had been among the first to hear about the discovery of gold in the Black Hills on account that a deserter from Custer's expedition wound up in Fetterman City, which probably wouldn't be a settlement Dooley would have picked on account that it existed only because of Fort Fetterman right there on the Bozeman Trail. Be that as it may, the deserter confided in Logan Kingsbury just how rich that land was. So Kingsbury and the deserter, a fellow named Martin Dansforth, had schemed to make their way into the Black Hills, before the rest of the country—the world—learned about it and took most of that fortune for themselves.

In a town like Fetterman City, it was easy to find a few other men willing to trespass onto Indian lands and take out gold by the tons. But they kept it to just a few, four other men whose names Logan Kingsbury did not mention in his letter to his aunt.

After outfitting for a mining expedition, they rode south, just to fool anyone who might try to jump their illegal claims, and then turned east and finally north. Seven days later they reached the Black Hills. Logan Kingsbury had little experience in mining, as he had spent most of his time saving drowning puppies and helping orphans find loving parents who had lost their own child to measles, cholera, syphilis, or some other childhood disease. Martin Dansforth, however, had been a miner during the Pikes Peak rush and two of their hires in Fetterman City knew about gold and pay dirt and where to look.

Unfortunately, the two miners from Fetterman City were jumped by Sioux on the third day in the Black

Hills, filled with arrows, bludgeoned with tomahawks, tortured, scalped, disemboweled, and left as a warning for any other white man in the holiest of all of the Sioux's lands.

The four surviving men of the expedition did find some gold, but in a sad, sad accident, Logan Kingsbury's .44 revolver discharged and put a bullet in the back of the third Fetterman City hire's head. Logan, good soul that he was, did gather up the man's gold dust and nuggets and would have sent it on to the dead man's next of kin, but, well, the man did not have any identifying letters with him, and Logan surely doubted if the man's real name was John Smith and even if it was . . . ?

The shot Logan had fired led to another unfortunate incident.

A Sioux scouting party heard the report of Logan's pistol that had killed the unfortunate Alias John Smith and caught up with the fourth man hired in Fetterman City.

Dansforth and Logan could hear the screams of that man as they galloped west as hard as they could, leaving behind the dead men's horses, the pack mules, and anything else that might have weighed them down. Except for the gold, of course.

"But," the minister said, "as Logan Kingsbury remarked in his letter, they escaped with their lives but nothing more than slim pickings."

CHAPTER THIRTY-TWO

"I don't understand," Dooley said. "If they left—"

"You don't understand, Dooley," Granby said, "because I have not finished this tale."

Dooley sighed. The moon had risen, a good time to start riding, but the way the preacher kept talking the moon would be setting before he ever got around to telling Dooley why they needed him to lead them to someplace that Dooley had never even heard of.

Dansforth and Logan hid in a cave one night, and stayed in that cave all day, sweating, driving themselves mad with fear.

That night they left, but could hear drums beating and see smoke rising above the Black Hills that the Sioux called *Paha Sapa*.

"Logan Kingsbury," the preacher said, "began to wish that he had never heard of Martin Dansforth."

Dooley thought: *Like I'm beginning to wish I'd never heard of the Reverend Robert James Granby; or Cincinnati, Ohio; or Peabody, Massachusetts; or Julesburg, Colorado Territory; or even Miss Sabrina Granby. Well . . . maybe not Miss Sabrina so much . . .*

Thus was how they traveled, nerves taut, sweat pouring out of every pore. Dansforth even began to lose some of his hair. They moved at night, slowly to the point of almost not moving at all. Fearing for their lives, they hid out in the day. Their food was almost nothing, and then became nothing except for the berries they could find, or even the bark on the pine trees. Oh, game seemed plentiful . . . deer and rabbits and even buffalo, but they dared not fire a weapon because one shot might bring Sitting Bull and every Sioux warrior within fifty miles upon them.

And they remembered all too well what they had found left of the first two men from Fetterman City. And the screams of the fourth man still echoed in their ears.

They kept their horses muzzled, until Logan Kingsbury's fine horse played out, toppled over, and died. Two men now, one horse, and the going became even rougher. The Black Hills are not for the feeble, not for the meek. It is rough country, full of black granite, thick briars, freezing streams even in the dog days of August, and perhaps a Sioux warrior behind every pine, every rock, every cattail.

Such an ordeal could drive even the strongest man to the brink of insanity, or push him hopelessly beyond all reason.

At some point, as they moved southwest, the hills became not so towering, the streams not so cold. Oh, the trees remained oppressive with the wind moaning high above them, blocking out the rays of sunlight, as though they were moving through a tunnel. And whenever the wind rustled the pines above them, they thought it was raining. They worried that because of the tall trees, they could not see any smoke signals the Indians might be sending one another.

Madness. It was pure madness.

Yet it was fear that drove the men, that kept them alive.

"It was while they were camping, worried sick, fearing for their hair and their lives, hiding from those fiendish Sioux that they found more gold."

Dooley saw. "I see," he said.

"No," the preacher said, "you don't."

Dooley had no response.

"You were bound for the Black Hills, Dooley," Granby said. "Isn't that right?"

"Yes, sir."

"Deadwood?"

"Well, that's where the gold strike is," Dooley said. "So, yeah, Deadwood. Deadwood Gulch."

"That's where the gold is, sure. It's also where the Sioux Indians are, and the pickpockets and whores and murdering scum who will slit your throat for the gold fillings in your mouth."

Dooley had no gold fillings. He even had all of his teeth, rare for a cowboy. Yet he nodded. The parson could spin a tale, and Dooley found this story a lot more interesting, stimulating, sometimes downright frightening, than all that crap he said about Cincinnati and Peabody.

"But . . ." Again, the parson used his cigar as a pointer. Again, Dooley leaned forward so he would not miss any word. "It's not where all the gold is. It's just the major strike. What the Widow Kingsbury's nephew found was nowhere near Deadwood. Oh, it's in the Black Hills, but not the Black Hills that

has been printed up in every newspaper between
Seattle and St. Augustine. The strike Logan Kingsbury found is not even in Dakota Territory."

"I thought all of the Black Hills were in Dakota,"
Dooley said.

"Wyoming," the preacher said in a whisper.
"Wyoming Territory."

The hills lessened in height and harshness, and
Dansforth and Logan found places that were even
free of pine trees. It had been a day, perhaps two,
since they had seen or imagined any Indian sign, and
once they took a chance and shot a mule deer with
Dansforth's stolen-from-the-army Springfield Trap-
door carbine. Famished, they ate the liver and heart
raw, and quickly vomited, carved out some thick
steaks, and ran as far as they could from the carcass
they left behind. As buzzards and crows appeared
out of nowhere and started circling overhead, the
two men feared Indians would notice and come to
investigate.

On they moved, back into the hills covered with
conifer forest. From a creek they washed the mule
deer's blood from their hands, arms, and faces, and
it was there, in a creek in the southwestern edge of
the Black Hills that Logan Kingsbury made the great
discovery.

As he lay on his belly, lapping up water like a dog,
something in the bed of the stream caught his attention. He blinked away the water and reached forward
into the cold water, found the nugget, and brought it
from the creek to a few inches from his face.

It could not be, he thought.

"Martin," he called out in a shout, and then felt the

dread, the paralyzing fear take hold of him. He rolled over, dropped the piece of stone no larger than his thumbnail, and drew his revolver.

But it was only his imagination, his paranoia. No Indian stood over him. Just another tree.

"Martin," he said again, and looked downstream.

To his surprise, Martin Dansforth sat on a boulder, his worn-out army boots soaking in the stream, as he studied a stone that caught the rays of the sun—for here, in this part of the Black Hills, a man could actually see the sun. It was Wyoming, you see, and not Dakota Territory.

Martin Dansforth slowly turned around. His eyes met Logan Kingsbury's, and Logan dived back into the stream, fished out the nugget he had found, and brought it out, lifting it over his head.

Martin brought his feet out of the water.

"Gold!" they screamed, forgetting their fear, forgetting the ravens and buzzards they had left behind them four miles back, forgetting the four dearly departed partners they had enticed to come with them back in Fetterman City. They ran to each other and danced a jig, then a polka, and then fell onto the grass and laughed and laughed and laughed.

Gold. A bonanza of gold, only it lay far from Deadwood, far from the prying eyes of the United States Army and the Great Sioux Nation. Gold. Gold for the taking. Gold for Martin Dansforth and Logan Kingsbury. Gold. Gold. Gold.

"They named their claim *Slim Pickings.*"

Not that it was an actual, legal claim. No, Martin Dansforth said he had seen what happens to a gold-rich place when claims were made, when people began flocking to steal or just get a slice of that pie. Besides, they had never really studied a map and weren't altogether certain about what the treaty signed by the Sioux and U.S. government designated as Sioux land for as long as the grass shall grow and what was land that was open for white men and women.

It was decided that they would keep the location of the strike a secret.

"But two men can't work a claim of this magnitude," Logan Kingsbury pointed out.

"That's true," Martin Dansforth said.

"We could return to Fetterman City and—"

"No. No. No!" Dansforth shook his head. "That's too dangerous. Men there do not keep secrets. I'm certain we would have eventually had to kill our four partners from there had not the Sioux taken care of them and, well, that unfortunate accident."

"Yes," said Logan Kingsbury. "Do you have any brothers? Sisters?"

"No, alas, as yellow fever took my brother, and a .41 slug from a derringer sent my father from this world."

"And your mother?"

"They hanged her after my father's murder." He paused. "Vigilantes, you see. Bannack City in Montana Territory."

"That's a shame," Logan said.

"How about you?" the army deserter asked. "We need people. This strike is too big for the two of us. And, besides, there's enough gold to go around. But as far away as we are from the Sioux strongholds and burial grounds and the big encampments, we should have men with sharp eyes who can help us defend our riches against the savage warriors."

Logan Kingsbury thought, and he remembered that aunt who doted on him, who helped him take care of all of those orphans, or other unfortunate individuals, who had provided him with money for a meal when he had scarcely a copper or two in his billfold. With tears in his eyes, he thought about all that she had given him, even before he left to find his fame and fortune in the great American West. He could smell the mouthwatering aroma of her kitchen when she pulled sourdough bread out of the oven. And how she might let him steal a pie out of the pie safe, knowing that boys will be boys, and that her pies were not nearly as good as the pies baked by Mrs. Abercrombie, but probably a close second in the City on the Seven Hills.

So he wrote a letter. He told his aunt the secret. He begged her to come to Fetterman City, where he would be waiting to guide her and handpicked trusting families who were willing to sacrifice the comforts of Cincinnati and strike out west. By Martin Dansforth's calculations, the gold they had found in the creek on the edge of the Black Hills would assay at $75 dollars a ton. Logan Kingsbury didn't consider himself a miner, but he had been around mining camps long enough to remember that the highest grade he had ever heard of was $40 a ton.

They left the camp under the cloak of darkness, still traveling cautiously and slowly—with only one horse between them—leaving the hills and forests for the grasslands, across Lightning Creek and down south to the North Platte River and finally to Fetterman City.

Logan Kingsbury posted his letter, which brightened that wintry day of the Widow Kingsbury. And made a few handpicked families in Cincinnati delighted.

The night fell silent. Dooley waited. Waited some more. For a moment, he thought the parson had fallen asleep. At length, Dooley cleared his throat, hesitated, and said, "Well, Reverend, that's a good story. But if the Widow's nephew is waiting for you in Fetterman City, surely you can find that without hiring a guide. You just find the North Platte River, which is thataway, and follow it to Fort Fetterman."

"Yes," said the minister, who was awake. "You would be right, Dooley, except in February the Widow received the second letter."

CHAPTER THIRTY-THREE

By then, Dooley Monahan knew he was doomed. He would not get out of Julesburg until daybreak—if the preacher had finished talking by then. He would sure hate to have to sit through one of the parson's sermons.

Yet when the Reverend Granby reached again inside his black coat and withdrew, not another fine Cuban cigar but a weathered envelope, Dooley held out hope. More relief swept over him when the Episcopalian minister pulled from that envelope a single piece of paper. At least it would be a short letter, unless Logan Kingsbury had really dainty, small handwriting.

After clearing his throat, the parson said, "No date," and began to read:

My dearest Auntie—
    I take pencil in hand in hopes that you are in fine health & received the letter I wrote to you a few months back. With the help of our Lord God Above

in Highest Heaven, you & the Reverend R. J.—
I forget his last name—

Here, the preacher stopped reading, folded the paper slightly so he could look Dooley in the eye as he explained.

"The boy never paid attention. In church. In school. It has been six years since he left Cincinnati, so that might explain his lapse in memory, but I always found him a hopeless cause. However, our Lord works in mysterious ways.

"The rest of the letter is tougher to read, as if written in a rush, which, as you'll hear, is exactly how it was written."

He continued reading the letter.

. . . have found some men who have experience in mining, or at least can hold a pan in cold water, build a sluice, swing a pick-axe but mostly know how 2 keep their mouths shut. No. Mostly they should be able 2 shoot a gun. Have them bring their weapons. & plenty of powder & lead.

There is 1 change in plans from my previous correspondence. Instead of meeting me in Fetterman City, I am enclosing a map 2 my gold strike. Follow it when U reach Wyoming Ty. Don't come 2 Fetterman City. Don't show anyone the map. Don't tell anyone U know me, or King Logan, or Logan King, or John Smith or John Logan Smith, or John Smith King. Don't mention my name, or any of the other names, except, possibly, John Smith.

Do not mention Martin Dansforth's name, either. Please.

*2 quickly explain, Dansforth was no partner
2 trust, & I regret having joined his expedition.
Last night, he caught me in an ambuscade in an
attempt 2 murder me—God have mercy on his poor,
misguided soul—so that he might have the fortune
in gold for his own nefarious designs. As God as
my witness, Aunt, I had no recourse but 2 defend
myself, & Christ in Heaven guided my bullets N2
that scoundrel's ~~back~~ . . . body. As Dansforth has
many friends in this town, I must depart in haste.
I will return 2 Slim Pickings, & living off the land
& what food I have manage 2 procure, until U &
the Rev. & those gallant men come 2 my rescue.*

Hurry, Aunt, please hurry.

*Go with God & go 2 Slim Pickings as fast as
U can.*

> *Tarry not,*
> *Logan Kingsbury,*
> *your most loving nephew*

"His handwriting is quite small, but among the most legible I have ever seen," the Reverend Granby said as he returned the letter to the envelope. "What do you think?"

Dooley hesitated, but you didn't lie to a man of God.

"I don't think I'd trust the Widow's nephew," he said.

The smile that spread across the reverend's face surprised Dooley. "Nor would I." The letter disappeared in the inside pocket of the long black coat, but the hand returned with two more cigars, one of which was offered to Dooley.

He shook his head, and both cigars vanished inside the coat.

"That's the story, Dooley," the preacher said. "That's what brought us to Julesburg."

"Did you tell that fellow that was . . . sort of . . . smitten to . . . your . . ."

"Jefferson Chatfield," Granby said. "Probably as nefarious a scoundrel as the Widow's nephew. No, Dooley, we might be Eastern tenderfeet, greenhorns from one of the jewel cities of our glorious United States, but we are not fools. Chatfield's job was to get us to Fetterman City. Perhaps he would have done that had he not been lured astray by those four other men you shot dead."

"Three," Dooley said. "The other one I shot dead before those boys tried to bushwhack me. And, actually, I didn't shoot him. He sort of shot himself. Dobbs, I mean. I . . ." He was overtired, talking too much, bantering like a gabbing drunkard.

"So all you want is for me to take you to this mining camp?"

The parson's head nodded.

"For which we will pay you in gold."

"A mining camp nobody's ever heard of." He was thinking out loud, but Granby nodded again.

"And nobody knows where it is."

Another affirmation. "Except some dead men, and dead men tell no tales."

Dooley fell silent and looked into the darkness. The moon was not overly bright, but it allowed Dooley to see the outlines of the Conestogas and various farm wagons. A train like that might make ten miles a day, perhaps twelve, and that seemed like mighty slow going when Doc Watson, Zee Dobbs,

Frank Handley, and several killers and thieves were on your trail.

But they likely would not expect Dooley Monahan to be guiding a bunch of families from Cincinnati, Ohio, into Indian country. Would they?

"Those Sioux and Cheyenne could jump us," Dooley tossed out.

"General Custer, General Crook, and more soldiers than I commanded during the late War against the Rebellion should be taking the field to end the red menace, Dooley," the preacher said. "Don't worry about any Indians, lad."

"You commanded a regiment during the war?"

"Well, it wasn't exactly a regiment."

"You saw the elephant?"

"At a circus once."

Dooley groaned. To see the elephant, back in those days, meant to have experienced battle. These days, cowboys said it to mean to see what was over the rise.

"I was with the Queen City Home Guard, son," the preacher said. "My rank was my belief in God Almighty. My command was fifteen volunteers. Don't think us useless, boy, for though we did not fight at Chancellorsville or Gettysburg or Shiloh or Perryville or Bull Run, Cincinnati was just above the Ohio River from Kentucky, and the Confederates were just below Kentucky in Tennessee, and John Hunt Morgan took his rebel horse soldiers out of Tennessee, through Kentucky, and into Indiana and Ohio. By thunder, they rode right through Harrison, and that's just above Cincinnati. No, sir. We were tested. Well, we would have been tested if only—"

"It doesn't matter, sir," Dooley said, regretting that he had brought it up. Wouldn't people say that he was turning yellow, running from Frank Handley and the remnants of the Dobbs-Handley Gang? Probably. They just didn't know that Dooley Monahan didn't like killing people, even murdering outlaws who were wanted dead or alive. It just happened that somehow that was one thing Dooley was quite good at.

"You are familiar with Wyoming, aren't you, Dooley?"

Familiar? That was a good description. Since he left Monty's Raiders, and after he had shot dead Jason Baylor, Dooley had become familiar with quite a few places in the West. He had been a drifting cowboy, working for a season at one ranch, and then riding the grub line until he found another job breaking chuckleheaded horses or roping steers or branding calves. And he had worked his way up from riding drag—eating dust behind a herd of two thousand or sometimes even more Texas longhorns—on cattle drives to Kansas, or other places. He had ridden on the Goodnight-Loving Trail twice—not with either Charles Goodnight or Oliver Loving, but that didn't matter—and that had brought him to Cheyenne, Wyoming Territory, to help feed the Union Pacific workers one time, and the steak-loving population another. And he had killed Jason Baylor's first cousin in Cheyenne, too.

"Yeah, I'm familiar with it," he said, which was no lie.

He had seen the Sweetwater River country, the North Platte, Casper, and the Medicine Bow. He had been across the Red Desert, through Devil's Gate, had stopped at Independence Rock to look at the names of those forty-niners and other wayfarers who had journeyed across this wild country. He had broken some army remounts at Fort Laramie, and once he had thought about even going to Fetterman City but the wind was blowing hard from the north so he had put the wind to his back and drifted back into Colorado.

He knew parts of Wyoming, but he could not honestly say he had ever been too far north of the Platte River. After all, that seemed to be pretty much Sioux country.

"What about the map?" Dooley asked.

The reverend studied Dooley for a long while before at last he pulled a pewter flask from another coat pocket. He unscrewed the lid, had a snort, and offered Dooley the whiskey. Again, Dooley declined.

"Tell me how we get near Fetterman first," the preacher said. "Let me see if you know that territory better than Jefferson Chatfield."

That seemed fair.

"You'll head north from here. Straight north. Two days should put you on the North Platte. Then follow the river to Scottsbluff. That's probably four more days. From there, just keep on the river until you get near Fort Fetterman, or wherever you want to head to Slim Pickings."

"Why not just head along the U.P. tracks awhile, then turn north straight for Scottsbluff?"

"Better water my way. More game, too, to eat. The railroad scares off buffalo and antelope."

"That makes sense."

Dooley waited. "The map?"

Now the preacher smiled. "I don't think you're as low-down as Chatfield, Dooley, but I will show you parts of the map when the time is right. There was one paragraph in Logan's letter to his aunt that I omitted while I read."

That made Dooley decide that the minister wasn't so much a greenhorn after all. He trusted nobody, probably not even the Widow Kingsbury, and maybe that was a good thing. Gold had a funny way with people, and it struck Dooley that all those times when he had set out to make his fortune in mining camps, he had never actually got to those mining camps. Alaska back in '72. And maybe Deadwood this year. Although, well, he had said he was going to the Black Hills, and Slim Pickings might not be Deadwood, but it was in the Black Hills, barely, at least according to Logan Kingsbury.

"When," the Reverend Granby continued, "we get to Rawhide Creek—that's what Logan told the Widow—you will receive part of the map, but just part. Until you've brought us to the end of that map, I shall give you another piece. We shall parcel it out, so to speak, so greed does not get the better of you. I won't have you abandon us the way Chatfield did."

You'd be in a lot worse shape if that happens, Dooley thought, *because being left in Julesburg is one thing. Being left alone on the north side of the North Platte River is really bad.*

Then he thought: *I would never leave Miss Sabrina Granby behind, alone, in Indian country.*

And next he thought: *Where the hell is Rawhide Creek?*

CHAPTER THIRTY-FOUR

After combing the hay out of his hair and brushing some more off his clothes, Dooley found his hat, pulled it on his head, and stood in the stall of the Julesburg Livery. He had slept in the stall. Beside him, Blue raised his head, and in the neighboring stall, General Grant began his breakfast of grain and water.

He buckled on his gun belt, rinsed his mouth out with warmish water from his canteen, and heard the commotion out on the streets of the town. Dooley said, "Come on, Blue," and the dog followed him as Dooley made his way to the daylight shining through the open broad doors of the livery.

The liveryman stood just outside, holding a file in his big left hand, staring as the Conestogas, Studebakers, and other ox-drawn wagons headed toward the trail that paralleled the Union Pacific rails. The Reverend Granby, the Widow Kingsbury, Mr. Franco, Mrs. Abercrombie, and all the other Cincinnatians—including beautiful Miss Sabrina Granby—were leaving town. Riding away. Without Dooley.

"What's happening?" Dooley asked the liveryman who had done most of the burying of the five dead men he had brought to town the previous day.

"They's pullin' out," the barrel-chested, iron-armed man said. "'Em miners."

"Thought they were sodbusters," Dooley said.

The big man, whose arms might have been just smaller than Hercules', shrugged. "Don't make no difference. Green as they is, they'll be back in Ohio come next summer—if they ain't buried somewhere out here."

"I thought they were from Rhode Island," Dooley said.

The liveryman studied Dooley for a second, and without a scowl or any more scrutiny, walked back inside to start shoeing a horse.

"Come on, Blue," Dooley said. "Let's see if we can scare up some breakfast."

He tipped his hat to a woman carrying a basket filled with eggs, and watched the dust settle from the wagons and oxen. The party had no outrider, no guide, no one on horseback—just wagons and mules—and about a half-dozen goats tethered behind the last wagon. The preacher and his niece led the procession in the biggest of the three Conestogas. Dooley stopped to watch. Granby turned his wagon east, not west, which likely meant he would take the trail north and head directly toward the North Platte River.

The parson had decided to follow Dooley's advice.

Stiff and dirty and still covered with hay that had been resistant to his brushing and wiping and slapping, Dooley felt oddly refreshed. He had left the parson at the dying campfire at perhaps midnight or maybe one in the morning, made it to the livery, and slept without bedroll or blanket. Sun rose in these parts at around five o'clock, and the scents of a town around breakfast, and of cook fires at the camp of emigrants, and the stench of goat pee roused Dooley from his slumbers, but he had waited in the hay beside a good dog that was running in his sleep. He had thought about the previous night, and all that the reverend had told him. He had considered his decision, and the question gnawed at him. Had he done the right thing?

The other wagons followed the Conestoga, and before Dooley realized it, the goats had disappeared in the dust and the sage-dotted prairie had swallowed up those tenderfeet seeking gold in the edge of the Black Hills.

Dooley knew he should be getting out of Julesburg, too. He had wasted one night, but he felt that he had a plan now, and that the surviving members of the Dobbs-Handley Gang would not be coming after him until tomorrow night at the earliest. Besides, he didn't know when he might eat again, so he moved down the street, maneuvering across treacherous boardwalks until he slipped inside the Julesburg Café. He told Blue to wait on the boardwalk.

After removing his hat and hanging it on a rack near the entrance, Dooley spied Marshal Maximilian working on a plate of bacon, fried potatoes, and eggs over easy at a corner table. The chair opposite the lawman remained unoccupied, so Dooley moved toward it.

The lawman had just forked a ton of greasy potatoes into his mouth. He stopped chewing and stared in disbelief as Dooley said, "Mind if I join you, Marshal?"

Dooley took the lack of movement as not a rejection, so he pulled out the chair and sat down.

When the lawman still did not move, Dooley opened the Denver newspaper, only three months old, which had been lying beside the cream, and began reading. Out of the corner of his eye, Dooley saw Maximilian's jaws working. The Adam's apple bobbed, and the lawman reached for his coffee cup. After a sip, he said, "Thought you was leaving yesterday."

"So . . ." Dooley stopped. The waitress stood beside him, and Dooley kept his order simple. He pointed at the plate and coffee cup and said, "Same as Marshal Max, please."

When she had gone, Dooley said, "I was. Then decided to light out after breakfast."

The waitress returned with a cup of coffee. She was fast. Maybe because the stove was just a few feet away, but perhaps because Dooley Monahan had brought five outlaws to town for burial.

Dooley added some cream to his coffee, stirred, sipped, and smiled across the table. "And it seems that I recall you saying you were going to skedaddle, too."

The lawman ate some eggs, snapped off a bite of bacon with his hand, and reached for his own coffee cup.

"I intend to. Tomorrow. First light." He drank some of the strong brew. "Figured to let you put some distance between me and you."

"We're not going in the same direction, though," Dooley reminded him. "You're bound for Scottsbluff, same as those sodbusters from Rhode Island. I'm heading toward Denver."

Maximilian tugged his napkin out of his shirtfront and dabbed his mouth before telling Dooley, "They're miners. Going to Fetterman City."

Dooley shrugged.

Maximilian tilted his head and studied Dooley with a lot of suspicion. "You did eat with them last night, didn't you?"

"I did," Dooley said. "That Mrs. Abercrombie makes a mighty fine apple pie."

"Canned apples?" the lawman asked.

"What else?"

"They didn't tell you their sad story?" the lawman asked.

"They did, but I'm a drifting cowboy. Didn't pay attention to what they said. And . . ." He gave his best sheepish look before taking a long pull of coffee that drained the cup. "Well, for religious folk, they can drink liquor with the drunkest waddies I've ever worked with."

That got the lawman to smile. Dooley's plate arrived, and the two men ate in silence. The marshal, of course, finished first, but instead of leaving, he rocked back in his chair and rolled a cigarette. He was smoking his second when Dooley finished eating. The lawman just studied Dooley, a look that made Dooley think that maybe Marshal Maximilian was more than some ten-cent lawman in a two-bit town, that perhaps he did not believe anything Dooley had told him.

When the waitress came by, Dooley brought out his

gold piece and handed it to her. "Pay for my meal," he said, "and Marshal Max's."

She raced off to the cashbox to fetch Dooley's change.

"Generous," Marshal Maximilian said.

"This ain't Delmonico's," Dooley told him, and he rose. "Good luck, Marshal."

"You, too," the lawman said, and asked the waitress for another cup of coffee. The legs of his chair fell back to the floor as Dooley crossed the café, grabbed his hat, opened the door, and stepped carefully onto the boardwalk.

Blue barked, Dooley looked up, and saw the two men who had just dismounted in front of the Julesburg Café.

The one with the patch over his left eye and missing the pinky finger on his right hand was, Dooley thought, called Newton, but he had taken that name, Zee Dobbs had told Dooley, because he had killed his first man at the train depot at Newton, Kansas. He carried two .36 caliber Navy Colts stuck butt-forward in a yellow sash. The blond-headed man with him wearing a dark sack suit was called Miserable Jake. Dooley did not think either man had been baptized with those names.

Miserable Jake spit tobacco juice into one of the holes in the boardwalk.

Newton tilted his head toward the door that Dooley had just closed. The one-eyed badman asked, "Mr. Dobbs in there?"

After wetting his lips, Dooley quickly looked down the street toward the railroad tracks. Nothing. Then down the street near the livery. Clear. His eyes fell back on Newton, then Miserable Jake, back on Newton, back on Miserable Jake, and through the glass in the upper half of the door to the restaurant. When he turned back to Newton, he said, hoping his voice would not crack and betray his utter fear, "Yeah. Finishing his breakfast. Y'all could join him if you want. I'm going to fetch my—our—horses."

Another spit came from Miserable Jake, but not much tobacco juice.

"Where's Doc?" Dooley whispered. "Frank come with you? Zee?"

Newton took two steps back, and Jake slid down the street.

Dooley sucked in a deep breath, held it just a moment, and exhaled.

"What's the matter, boys?" Dooley tried to sound his most relaxed, most friendly, but understood that he had most likely failed miserably.

"Ya seed 'em big mounds at dat boneyard when we rode in, Newton," Miserable Jake said. It was not a question.

"Five." Newton's head bobbed. "No markers. Just dirt."

"Fresh earth."

"Yep."

Newton jutted his chin toward Dooley. "Means you kilt our boss, you low-down cur."

"What . . . why . . . er . . ."

Miserable Jake raised his left arm, fully out-stretched, and pointed a long, dirty finger at Dooley's face.

"Dobbs don't never take no breakfast, ya lyin' boss-killin' bandit. Says it gives 'm indy-gestin'." The gunman's right arm was already reaching across his stomach toward one of the Navy Colts. One-eyed Newton was pulling the long-barreled Remington .44 from his holster.

Dooley was falling.

It had not been intentional. Dooley had just stepped into a hole in the boardwalk. His foot crashed all the way to his knee, and he toppled over to his left as the two men who rode with the Dobbs-Handley Gang were killing the hell out of the front door to the Julesburg Café. Wood splintered. Glass broke. Men and women and the waitress and Marshal Max cried out and dived for cover inside the restaurant.

Dooley's body crashed into the boardwalk, and even over the scent of gun smoke, he swore he could smell the pitch, the turpentine odor of the lousy pine planks that splintered into dust or bits of wood. Blue leaped over him in terror.

The gunmen, professional murderers and thieves, quickly adjusted their aim, and now began riddling the remnants of the boardwalk with lead. But Dooley had disappeared through a haze of smoke and dust and filth. He landed on the ground, saw the brown boots of Newton dancing, saw the legs of Blue on the ground, disappearing as the dog leaped up, reappearing as the dog came down. He couldn't hear Blue's barks, or the curses of the killers, just a ringing in his ears.

He pulled the trigger and saw the left brown boot of Newton explode in a gory mix of leather, bone, and blood.

Dooley did not even recall drawing his Colt, but he must have while he was falling and before he hit the earth because he squeezed the trigger almost instantaneously.

Down went Newton. A bullet from Miserable Jake tore through wood and carved a furrow across Dooley's right calf.

Biting back pain, Dooley thumbed back the hammer, tilted the barrel upward slightly, and pulled the trigger.

"Ummpfh," Miserable Jake grunted. "I be kilt."

Newton was quickly sitting up, finding his other Navy. Dooley heard Blue yelp, caught a few of Newton's curses, and saw the gunman leveling the Navy in Dooley's general direction. The gunman fired first, but the pain from having his big toe and maybe a couple of others blown off spoiled his aim. The bullet lodged in a chunk of boardwalk to the top of Dooley's head. Dooley's round caught the gunman right in the center of his forehead, just as Blue was diving for the outlaw's throat. The dog missed, landed, turned around, and stopped.

Newton had fallen hard to the ground, still clutching one of the old Navy Colts, but not able to do a damned thing with it because he was dead.

Scrambling from underneath the boardwalk, Dooley aimed his recocked weapon at Miserable Jake, only to discover that that blackguard lay spread-eagle in the dust. The two horses had shied away, backing up to the other side of the street. They didn't run, but fear shined in their wild eyes as they skittered about this way and that.

What was left of the door to the Julesburg Café swung open, and Dooley turned his Colt toward Marshal Max, who removed the cigarette from his lips, glanced at the dead man, and the dying one, and Blue, and then Dooley.

"Who are they?" the marshal asked.

"Two of the Dobbs-Handley bunch," Dooley said. He did not holster the Colt, did not even lower the hammer, but moved to the gut-shot Miserable Jake.

"Hell," Dooley heard Marshal Maximilian say, "I guess I'll have to give you another voucher for their bounties, too."

CHAPTER THIRTY-FIVE

Blue growled at the dying man until Dooley told his dog to stop. Kneeling beside the man, he bit his bottom lip and regretted that, once again, it had come to this. One man dead, another about to be, and this time Dooley's leg was bleeding and burning like the hottest hinge in Hades. On top of that, Dooley had splinters in one of his earlobes, in his neck, arm, and the fleshy part of his side. One sleeve had been ripped, and he still tasted pine on his tongue and smelled like he had just bathed in turpentine.

Miserable Jake groaned, and turned his head to look at Dooley. By then, Dooley was squatting, keeping the barrel of his Colt trained on the man's crooked nose while his left hand reached down and removed Jake's uncocked pistol from his hand. There was no resistance. Dooley tossed the gun a few feet into the street. Blue went over to sniff the revolver.

Dooley left the dying killer for a moment, made his way through what once had been a boardwalk, and pulled open the door to the Julesburg Café. It fell off the hinges and crashed at his feet.

The inside made him grimace. A coffeepot had been blown to pieces. Round tables rolled across the scrambled eggs and hash browns and coffee and napkins, and two of those tables had been ventilated with bullets. The waitress poked her head over one table.

"Anybody in here hurt?" Dooley asked, only to understand that the only person having breakfast in the restaurant when Dooley had walked out the door was Marshal Max, and he was standing on the boardwalk, or what remained of it, rolling a smoke. The waitress appeared shaken, but not bleeding.

Dooley yelled, "In the kitchen? Is anyone hurt?"

No one answered, and Dooley felt nauseous as he moved to the door, pushed it open, and found the kitchen empty. The back door was open. Obviously, the cook had run for his life. Dooley didn't blame him.

Dooley walked across the floor, his boots crushing eggs and bacon and hash browns that had been left on the tables by other customers who, luckily, dined early and left before the gunplay. Broken mugs and shattered plates also crunched underneath his weight as he hurried back outside.

"Where are Handley, Watson, and the others?" Dooley asked.

"Go to hell," the man said.

"You'll be there shortly. Where are they?"

The man moved his head and stared at the sky.

"They send you?"

Remorse must have got the better of the wicked

killer, or maybe the assurance that, yes, he would be dead directly with an express ride down to the fiery pits. "My name," he said, as blood trickled out of the left corner of his mouth, "is Valiant. Ain't joshin'. Was my ma's maiden name. Valiant Noble Engledinger. Put that on my cross. Will ya?"

"If it'll fit. How do you spell Engledinger?"

"Hell if I know. Just do yer best, pard." So now Dooley was pards with the man who had tried to gun him and his dog down. "Where are the boys . . . and Zee?"

His head shook.

"That's not the way to go about getting your last request granted, Valiant," Dooley tried.

"No." The man's face tightened in agony. His eyes squeezed shut, and for a moment, Dooley feared they might never open. But the pain must have subsided, because his face relaxed, the eyes opened, and Miserable Jake turned toward Dooley again.

"Mean . . . don't know. Newton an' me . . . just come . . . of our own . . . accord. Thought . . . maybe . . ." He grinned. "Thought Dobbs would kill ya, fer the re-ward . . . Wanted . . . Newton thought . . . if we kilt Dobbs, be a . . . fine joke. Get the money . . . he gots . . . fer ya . . . and collects here that . . . big money . . . on ol' Hubey."

"All you would've gotten here is a voucher," Dooley told him.

If Miserable Jake heard, he did not let on. Instead, he stared at the sky, looking for angels, perhaps, and said, "I think . . . Engle-dinger is *E . . . n . . .*" But that was it.

Dooley reached over and closed the dead killer's eyes. He stood, and saw Marshal Maximilian staring at him. The lawman sighed, shook his head, and said, "Let's go to my office and sort through this."

Sorting did not take long. The lawman had a whole box of posters on the known members of the Dobbs-Handley Gang, which Marshal Max had scratched through the name Dobbs. Apparently, he did not think Zee would take her father's place. He found the posters on Newton and Miserable Jake, slid them toward Dooley, and said, "Bounty on those two might—might cover the cost of the new door and window and all the other damage done to the Julesburg Café. And the boardwalk we'll have to fix."

Dooley did not care.

"So I won't give you a voucher for those two carcasses. We'll just say it's all even."

"Suits me," Dooley said.

"But you'll have to pay for their burial."

"Catch up their horses, Marshal," Dooley said. "Their traps, weapons, bounty . . . that should cover everything."

The lawman grinned. "Pleasure doing business with an understanding bounty hunter, Dooley."

"I'm no bounty hunter. I'm just a cowboy."

The grin turned into a belly laugh. "Yeah. Right."

When Dooley rose, the lawman pointed at the street. "Ride out. You say you're going to Denver?"

"That's what I said."

"Good. I've decided against Scottsbluff. I'm heading south. As soon as I pack up all my possibles."

"What about the Cheyenne Indians down that way?"

The marshal shook his head. "Rather deal with

them redskins than Frank Handley. You've done killed his pard and two of his men."

"Three," Dooley corrected, but did not expand on the death of that big brute in Yankton. He was just relieved that the marshal had not found a wanted dodger describing Dooley's likeness in that batch of posters of known members of the ~~Dobbs~~-Handley Gang.

"I don't care. I'm just getting out of here. When Handley, Watson, and that crowd come here and find out what's happened, this town'll go up like a tinderbox."

The way Dooley smelled right now, he had no doubt about that.

For a few miles, Dooley rode west along the U.P. rails. When he reined up, he stood in his stirrups and looked back toward Julesburg. He held his breath momentarily when he saw dust drifting that had not been raised by General Grant or Blue. The breath exploded out of his lungs with relief as he sank back into the saddle, realizing that that dust was coming from maybe one horse, and it was moving south at a pretty fast lope. Marshal Maximilian had not been lying after all.

Of course, Dooley had.

He never had any intention of going to Denver. Last night, he and the Reverend Granby had concocted what both agreed was a pretty good plan. And it did seem fine . . . until Miserable Jake and Newton showed up outside the Julesburg Café.

The way things were supposed to go was that Dooley would return that night to the livery, sleep in, get up in the morning, and watch the wagon train leave town. Dooley would let folks know that he knew nothing about those gallant Cincinnatians, who were headed straight up the trail toward Scottsbluff, while Dooley was bound to start a hard ride toward Denver. So when Frank Handley and Doc Watson and Zee Dobbs and all those killers who rode with them—less Newton and Miserable Jake, as things turned out—and found out what had happened to Hubert Dobbs, the murderers and dirty, rotten, rabid dogs would light out hard and furious for Denver. After they left Julesburg in flames.

Well, Dooley hoped that wouldn't happen. Besides, Frank Handley had never showed a whole lot of kindness, affection, or even loyalty to Hubert Dobbs, while neither Miserable Jake nor Newton seemed to rank as high lieutenants in the chain of command.

Relaxing, he decided now that Miserable Jake had been telling the truth, meaning that Dooley still had a day or two to pull away from the killers who would be coming after him. Still, he dared not tarry, so he dismounted to answer the call of nature, picked up his loyal shepherd, and got back into the saddle. For another two miles, he walked, with the dog on his lap. He put the bay gelding into a trot for another mile, slowed back to a walk, and guided the horse into the South Platte River. If Frank Handley had any good trackers riding for him, they would find it hard to follow Dooley in a river.

The water remained shallow, and Dooley kept General Grant in the south side of the Platte for a few miles, moved to the middle, and eventually the north side, staying in the water. Often, he would stop and let the mud settle, and peer into the river. Maybe an expert tracker could follow a trail in water, but Frank Handley did not hire expert trackers. He hired expert killers.

Dooley rode a little farther, and kept going until around dusk. That's when he found what he had been seeking all this time.

A herd of buffalo had crossed the river, moving north. He saw the path they had carved, and it had to be a great herd, for the trail covered maybe two hundred yards in width. Dooley let Blue down, and the dog decided to take a bath while Dooley opened the saddlebags and found the soft leather hides and thongs he had packed the previous night. While still in the water, he lifted each one of General Grant's legs and wrapped the hooves in leather, securing them with a thong. Finally, assured that this would work, he called Blue back to him and picked up the sopping wet shepherd and eased him into the saddle. Carefully, Dooley climbed back up, pulled the dog back onto his lap, and moved out of the river and followed the trail left by buffalo.

He rode only about ten yards before he looked back. Relief let a "whoopie" escape, and he laughed and rubbed Blue's wet hair. No obvious trail as far as Dooley could see. As far as most men could tell, only buffalo had crossed the river here and moved north. Dooley put the horse into a trot, stopped, and again looked back. He still saw no sign. The leather was still hiding General Grant's hoofprints. For the next hour, until the light faded so that Dooley couldn't really tell anything in the dirt, the ruse kept working. When the moon rose, Dooley rode with ease. He might have done it. He might have fooled the men who would be coming to kill him.

He decided to ride another hour before stopping for the night and making a cold camp. Although about five minutes later, Dooley realized he had another concern.

No longer did he stink of turpentine.

He smelled like a wet dog.

CHAPTER THIRTY-SIX

Late the following afternoon, Dooley caught up with the buffalo herd and rode easily through that forest of great shaggies. It wasn't as big as some herds that he had seen back in his younger days, for by now the buffalo hunters had killed off most of the beasts, especially those south in Kansas and Texas. He kept one hand on the reins, and one hand holding Blue across his thighs. The dog whimpered. General Grant didn't seem too keen on the idea of riding through buffalo territory, either, but the animals contented themselves with grazing, and after a few tense minutes, they had cleared the gathering of buffalo.

Five miles later, Dooley stopped to remove the soft skins that had served as the gelding's boots. He let Blue jog alongside him now, and when the dog felt like running, Dooley let his horse run, too.

He knew he could make it all the way to Fetterman City easily. After all, he was one man on horseback with a dog that could run pretty fast when he felt like it. Yet Dooley had to pace himself. A wagon train of greenhorns from Ohio would not make good time.

So Dooley kept moving practically lackadaisically, and he kept his eyes often trained to the south and east. So far, everything seemed fine. No dust anywhere, not even from the herd of buffalo he had left back there. Even better, he saw no smoke blackening the sky down Julesburg way.

When he reached the North Platte River, he guessed that Scottsbluff would be to his east. He scouted the area and made camp far off the deeply rutted trails so many emigrants had taken over the years. Finding a perch on a small rise, Dooley had a view of the trail, east to west and west to east. He ran a cold camp, but cowboying had taught him to go for days on stale bread and beef jerky. Blue could fend for himself, and likely ate better than Dooley did on prairie dogs and jackrabbits, and General Grant had plenty of grass to eat, and even a handful of grain that Dooley had bought back in Julesburg.

He did find a creek on one afternoon, and manufactured a hook, used jerky for bait, and wet a line of horsehair. Not that he caught anything, but his father had always told him that you could solve a lot of the problems in the world just fishing. Dooley didn't solve any problems, not the world's and certainly not his, but for an hour or two, he did seem to forget about Zee Dobbs, Doc Watson, Frank Handley, and all the hell he had been forced to endure.

He went back the next day. Didn't catch anything then, either, but on the other hand, he saw no dust rising anywhere on the horizon. Besides, the sun kept shining, he felt warm, and he bathed in the creek so he would not be so rank when the wagon train finally arrived. Naked as a jaybird, he let the sun dry him off, before he dressed and resumed his none-too-serious fishing and problem solving.

It wasn't so bad a life. He was alive, pretty Sabrina Granby was coming his way, and he had a chance to—finally—make that fortune in gold that had eluded him for several years. As a man of independent wealth, he could hang up his guns and, with the good Lord's blessing, that reputation as a bounty hunter and killer of outlaws would fade. People would forget all about Dooley Monahan.

When the morning started approaching the afternoon, he saw the dust, and held his breath. Wagons. Dooley could tell that much, but freighters still used this trail to haul supplies to and from western settlements. So did stagecoaches, but this dust came from no Concord or mud wagon. It moved too slowly, and too thickly, for a stage pulled by six mules. Remaining patient, Dooley kept looking at the horizon, waiting. He had to be sure. He had to be sure.

Not until the wagons came into view, not until he saw that large Conestoga wagon in the front of the train, did Dooley let out that breath of utter relief. He gathered up his belongings, rolled what he could inside his bedroll, and secured that behind the cantle on his saddle. Naturally, he had already saddled General Grant—in case he needed to run for his life.

"Come on, Blue," Dooley said as he swung into the saddle. "Let's join those Cincinnatians." He gave the gelding plenty of rein and let the bay gallop off the rise, across the sage, and to the trail. When the first wagon rumbled along about a hundred yards away, Dooley reined up. He waved his hat, and waited.

The wagons came into view, and the man walking alongside the big Conestoga waved his black hat. Dooley could tell, even from that distance, that the man wore black pants and a long black coat. What's more, he could tell that the young woman sitting in the front of the wagon did not wear black at all.

"Dooley!" Miss Sabrina Granby shouted. "Dooley. Dooley. Dooley. How I've missed you." She wrapped her arms around him and gave him a wonderfully wet kiss on his cheek.

"Oh, Miss Sabrina," he said, blushing. "It hasn't been that long."

He shook hands with several men from Cincinnati, and after much banter, realized that the plan had worked. As far as everyone could tell, they had made it out of Julesburg. Nobody had followed them.

"So all we have to do now," the Reverend Granby told Dooley, "is find Rawhide Creek."

He pulled a piece of paper from the inside of his long black coat and handed Dooley Monahan the first torn page of the map to wealth.

The parallel lines had to designate the main trail, Dooley reasoned, and looked closer at the map. Logan Kingsbury had been rushed when he had drawn the map, and his tiny but neat handwriting did not necessarily make reading the paper that the reverend had torn any easier. For all Dooley could tell, north could be in any direction, but he made a reasonable guess that north would be where the preacher had torn the map at the top.

No river that Dooley could see, but as the trail ran just north of the North Platte, all Dooley had to do was follow the trail. He saw a circle, actually more dot or lowercase *o* than an actual circle, and a waving line that ran from where the paper had been torn to the lines that designated, maybe, the trail.

Dooley looked. The parson and his congregation waited.

Dooley handed the paper back to Granby and pointed at the squiggly line. "Rawhide Creek?" Dooley asked.

"You tell me," the minister said.

"That's the rise." Dooley pointed at the little *o* that ran maybe a half inch from the squiggly line. Logan Kingsbury had not drawn this to scale, but, well, a gambler and killer like the Widow's favorite nephew had no experience as a topographer or cartographer. "I've been camping there, watching the trail." He made a sweeping gesture with his arm to the northwest. The men, and a few women, including Miss Sabrina, looked.

"You can't really see it from here," Dooley said. "That's the beauty of it. The land out here, the terrain, isn't exactly as you'd think. But that's the hill. It has to be. And that's Rawhide Creek."

"You know Rawhide Creek?" one of the Cincinnati men asked.

Dooley did not lie. "I've fished it a time or two."

"Perch?" a woman asked. "Walleye?" asked another.

"Never caught anything," Dooley said. "It runs into the North Platte a few miles west. We follow it?"

"We do." The preacher smiled.

"Plenty of daylight left," Dooley said. "We can be well up that stream long before we have to make camp. That'll put us off this trail, so there will be less chance of any other travelers spotting us."

It's one thing following a wagon trail that has been used for roughly thirty years. It's another thing to be fighting sage and sand and wallows and wind with a bunch of city folk from the Blue Chip City.

On the third day, two of the wayfaring families had had enough.

"We're pulling out, Reverend," Mr. Jones said, and Mr. Franco nodded his consent. Mr. Jones looked at Dooley. "How far is it to the next town?"

"Fetterman City," Dooley said. "Or you can try for Cheyenne." He gave them his best guess at the distance.

"Is it all right if we wait for you there, Reverend?" Mrs. Jones said.

"Of course," the minister said. "And, well, I wonder if you could do us a great service?"

"Anything," Mr. Jones replied.

"Take our women and children with you. This is dangerous country we travel across, and I would feel much more at ease if only righteous men risked our lives to find the Widow Kingsbury's missing nephew."

A dozen wagons became seven, for the wagons belonging to the Jones and Franco families could not carry all of the children and women. The partings were sad. Women cried. Men cried. Children cried. Dooley, on the other hand, felt relief. He did not want to lead women and kids into hostile Indian country, but he felt fairly happy that Miss Sabrina

Granby refused to go along with the gentler sex and the youth to Cheyenne or Fetterman City.

"We will send for you when we are settled," the preacher said.

"You won't send for me," the Widow Kingsbury said. "For I am going with you."

Two women. They wore down the men who did not want the Widow or Miss Sabrina to come along, but the Widow pointed out that it was her nephew they were rescuing and that if not for her, these fine men would be working their businesses and marveling at a sculpture in Cincinnati and not about to make a fortune at Slim Pickings.

The wagons with kids and petticoats and Mrs. Abercrombie and her wonderful pies went back toward the old trail. At least those bound for Logan Kingsbury's mining claim would have sourdough bread.

On the following day, Dooley Monahan ran out of map.

The next torn-up paper was smaller, but Dooley guessed that the upside-down *V*'s off to the right had to be mountains, for he could see the bluish-grayish outline of what might be the Black Hills to the northeast. No more squiggly line could be seen, so Dooley moved the procession toward the upside-down *V*'s.

The land grew tougher. The oxen labored to pull the wagons up steeper inclines. They fell into a ravine that Dooley thought had to be two narrow lines that twisted and turned on its way toward the upside-down *V*'s. When they came out of the ravine, Dooley rode over to the preacher's Conestoga and said, "I think it's time for the next map."

"All right," the reverend said. He climbed into the back of the wagon, and Dooley waited, making small talk with Miss Sabrina. After a long while, the parson returned, and started to hand Dooley an even smaller piece of paper.

"Here," the preacher said. A second later, he started sinking to his knees with an arrow quivering in his belly.

CHAPTER THIRTY-SEVEN

There are some other sounds that, after you've heard them once, you never mistake them for anything but what they are. The bloodcurdling war cry of a Northern Plains Indian brave is one of them.

The war cry shouted by a Northern Cheyenne was echoed by many more, and Dooley Monahan knew that he, Miss Granby, and everyone else in the wagon train were in for a lot of trouble.

Another arrow tore off Dooley's hat as he lunged and knocked Miss Sabrina to the ground. He came up, shocked to find the Colt already in his hand, and yelled something at the young woman as he covered her body with his. He aimed, squeezed the trigger, and saw the skewbald mare carrying one of the braves crash into a somersault, throwing the young Cheyenne who was nocking another arrow onto his bow over the tumbling horse.

Clouds of dust caused Dooley to lose sight of the thrown warrior, and Dooley grimaced, falling back on top of Miss Sabrina to protect her head as the horse Dooley had killed—although he had been aiming for the Indian—kept coming. He braced himself for the horse to roll over him, probably smash his spine, maybe kill both the woman and himself, but the only things that fell on him were sand and pebbles.

He shot back up, this time to his knees, to find the pinto pony lying dead just four feet from Miss Sabrina and him.

Out of the cloud of dust stepped the warrior, his nose twisted into some hideous contortion, blood pouring from both nostrils, his left arm hanging helplessly at his side. No longer did this Cheyenne carry his bow and arrow, but the tomahawk he wielded in his right hand would sure do a lot of damage.

Another Indian rode up, leaping off his buckskin, and ran toward Dooley and Miss Sabrina with a lance.

The injured brave would have to go around the horse, so Dooley turned, aimed, and fired at the one with the lance. This Cheyenne was old, his face scarred with pocks and various wounds from previous battles, and the hair falling in braids from underneath his buffalo headdress was silver. Old, Dooley knew, but tough. The first bullet went through one of his lungs, and the man staggered, twisted, but did not drop the lance. He brought it up to throw, when Dooley's next bullet slammed through the center of his chest, naked except for black and yellow paint. That dropped him and the spear into a quivering heap.

Yet Dooley knew the old-timer had done his job. The Cheyenne had given the wounded young brave with the tomahawk enough time to finish the job. To count coup. To kill Dooley and Miss Sabrina.

Knowing he was dead, Dooley turned, determined to try to save Miss Sabrina for at least a few more minutes. He saw the brave, heard the gunshot, and after Dooley blinked, he watched the young, wounded warrior stagger around the dead horse. The Cheyenne tripped over one of the stallion's broken legs. Another gunshot popped, and Dooley saw the blood spray from the Indian's back as he fell across his dead horse.

Dooley turned. The Reverend Granby, still on his knees, held a shaking Remington derringer in his right hand. The piece of the map had blown away.

More yelps and gunshots sounded. More arrows whipped through the air.

Dooley looked at the Granbys' Conestoga, thinking to make a last stand underneath the big conveyance. Defend themselves as long as they could, and save the last bullet for Miss Sabrina. Now, that plan had to be changed. The orange flames and horrible smoke, white, gray, black, shot from the prairie schooner, a whirling vortex of chaos. Dooley caught a glimpse of a warrior on another pinto. He hurried a shot, shoved the pistol into his holster, and pulled Miss Sabrina over to the dead horse and dead Cheyenne.

"Stay here!" he yelled, but doubted if she could understand anything he had said for the flames from the wagon, the burning, the cracking, the intensity echoed the deafening cannonade being fired by the other men who had left Cincinnati for . . . this.

Dooley caught Miss Sabrina's uncle before he collapsed. The derringer toppled into the dust and blood, and Dooley did not reach for it. A Remington is a two-shot pistol, and the parson had fired both rounds into the brave with the tomahawk. Maybe the reverend had more .41 caliber shells, but Dooley had no time. He dragged the preacher, who now clutched the shaft and feathers of the arrow in his gut, over to the dead horse. There was not time for gentleness, though, just desperation. Dooley let the man's head fall against the sweaty and dusty coat of the pinto, stepped over Miss Sabrina, and leaned his back against the stallion's neck.

Quickly, he flipped open the loading gate of his Colt with his thumb, and rotated the cylinder, plunging out the empty casings. His thumb then pushed fresh loads out of his shell belt, and he filled the Colt with what cowboys called *six beans in the wheel*. Fully loaded. No concern for safety now. The only thing that mattered was survival.

Which seemed hopeless.

Another warrior galloped past, popped a shot with an old Dragoon .44. The bullet slammed into the dead horse's withers, and as the warrior pulled on the hackamore to stop and turn his dun, Dooley brought up the Colt and fired. The Indian cried out and fell near one of the oxen of the flaming Conestoga.

Dead. Dooley saw the horse bolt across the sagebrush. He also saw the big Dragoon.

"Stay here!" Dooley yelled. "Use this." He practically shoved the revolver into Miss Sabrina's right hand, and next he was dashing, ducking, then diving as an arrow tore fabric from his vest. He hit the ground hard, spit out dust, lunged forward, and snatched the old cap-and-ball relic.

That's when the oxen began moving, fast for oxen, panicked by the heat of the burning wreck of a wagon the animals had been hitched to.

Dooley let loose an oath, and rolled out of the way. The oxen stampeded—at least as fast as those beasts of burden could run—and Dooley instinctively covered his bare head with his hands. Hot embers fell all around him as the flaming wagon rolled by. He cried out at the pain, felt his clothes smoldering, and rolled over, grinding his burning back in the dirt and grass.

When his eyes opened, he stared into the vermillion-painted face of another warrior.

The gun came up in Dooley's hand, but he saw the dirt in the cylinder, and realized he could not get the weapon cocked.

That brought a smile to the Cheyenne's frightening face. Dooley shifted the pistol, started to throw it, but before he could even rear back his arm, the Indian was turning, lowering the big Sharps buffalo gun he had in his hands, and a blue blur leaped through smoke, dust, and all the other hell.

The warrior screamed, and dropped underneath the weight of that now-vicious shepherd. Dooley came up. Blue had knocked the warrior onto his back, but the dog had rolled over, before he came up yelping from the burning patch of grass caused by the Granbys' Conestoga.

The Indian was coming up, too, trying to raise his big buffalo rifle, but Dooley straddled him and slammed the butt of the Colt against the Cheyenne's temple. Again. Again. Again. Blood sprayed his face, Dooley's own war paint. Blue came to him, hair on his back and neck raised, growling fiercely at the dead Indian.

"Come on, Blue." Dooley snatched up the heavy .50 caliber rifle and stumbled over burning sage and grass toward the dead Indian pony that had become a fort, perhaps a last stand, for Dooley, the minister, and Miss Sabrina Granby—and now Blue the loyal shepherd.

He dived back, and Blue moved over to the reverend's side.

Something crashed, and Dooley peered over the pinto's neck. The Granbys' prairie schooner had either burned through the traces, or the wagon had toppled over a small incline, or the tongue had broken. Whatever had happened, the wagon had fallen onto its side, rolled over, showering the prairie with sparks and flames and burning trunks, chairs, supplies— whatever the preacher and his niece had wanted to bring with them from their peaceful life in that fine city on the Ohio River.

The oxen kept moving, away from the carnage, and now Dooley saw a couple of young Indians running on foot, chasing the beasts.

Dooley had time to catch his breath. He tasted sweat, gunpowder. The bitterness of battle singed his nostrils. His heart beat against his chest so hard that his ribs ached.

He blew away the sand on the Dragoon's cylinder, untied his bandanna, which he then used to wipe the weapon. Again, Dooley tried the hammer, and this time the cylinder rolled into position. Leaving the old Colt on full cock, he placed the revolver on the dead Indian pony's neck, and brought the .50 caliber Sharps across his back.

It was an old model, not like the new rifles those buffalo hunters had been using for the past few years. This one, like the Colt Dragoon, was cap-and-ball, but the percussion cap remained seated on the nipple, and Dooley eared back the heavy hammer until he thought, above the popping of gunfire, the flames, the whoops, the thundering of hooves, and the screams, that the big Sharps was ready to fire.

He looked over Miss Sabrina's back. She lay on her belly, Dooley's pistol in both hands, her arms stretched out onto the crooked Indian saddle. Her lips moved, but she made no sound. Likely praying.

Keep praying, Miss Sabrina, Dooley thought. *Keep praying a lot.*

Clearing his throat, he raised up just a bit—for he did not want to catch a bullet in his back or head— and started to hand the rifle to the Reverend Granby. But Dooley stopped.

The preacher would not be able to hold such a cumbersome, heavy buffalo gun. Dooley didn't think the Reverend Granby could even hold a Dragoon or Dooley's own Colt that was shaking in Miss Sabrina's hands. As pale as the parson had turned, Dooley did not even think that the Reverend Granby would have been able to raise a .41 caliber Remington derringer anymore.

His lips moved, too, Dooley noticed, and likely in prayer. Only unlike his niece's lips, the parson's were covered with blood, which leaked from one corner of his mouth. The man's chest kept moving, up and down, in shallow gasps, and his fingers clutched the arrow that had gone deep into his stomach.

Dooley dropped back down, rolled over, and brushed the sand and sweat off his mouth and face. Salty sweat stung his eyes, and he smelled smoke, felt more heat, though not as burning as it had been before the oxen had carried away the Conestoga about thirty or forty yards.

Yet there was fire, all around him. The oxen had dragged the prairie schooner off, which had spilled burning wood and cloth and hot embers. There had been little rain in this country of late, and the grass and sage had become thirsty, dry. Now it burned.

"Great . . ." Somehow Dooley heard his own voice. He did not finish what he was about to say. He just thought it:

We might just burn to death.

But all of those Cheyenne braves would likely save Dooley and Miss Sabrina that horrible death.

Dooley got ready, his face hard, his nerves taut.

More whoops. More death songs. More shots and galloping hooves.

The war party was coming back . . . to finish the job.

CHAPTER THIRTY-EIGHT

How many rode their ponies through the sage and smoke, Dooley could not guess. He brought the heavy Sharps up, pressing the stock tight against his right shoulder, and moved the barrel but knew better than to squeeze the trigger. You did not waste lead, especially when you held a single-shot weapon in your hand. An arrow tore through his bandanna, causing the threadbare piece of cotton to pull hard against his throat. Another went so close to his ear he could feel the wind rush by. Behind him came the sickening sounds of arrows and bullets tearing into the flesh of the dead Indian pony he had turned into a fort, a refuge, a last stand.

Yet Dooley had no target at which to aim. He heard the Indians, and their ponies, and maybe he could detect a flash of gun smoke. Mostly, however, all he saw was thick dust that mixed with the smoke from the burning wagon—no, wagons—others from the train, farm wagons and such, were aflame by now—while hot flames licked and spread across grass and sage.

The dust cloud and war party moved on past Dooley, Miss Granby, and her uncle. Dooley fell back to his knees. Blue barked, but did not move.

Dooley wiped away sweat that drenched his face and hair. He tried to wipe his hands dry against his trousers. He wanted to run, but knew he could not do that. Leave Miss Sabrina behind? No, that was something Dooley would not do, but now he regretted that he had not insisted that the Reverend Granby had made Miss Sabrina—and the Widow Kingsbury— travel with the other women and those children to Fetterman City, to Cheyenne. Hell, they should never have left the Queen City of the West.

For that matter, Dooley wished he were back on that farm outside of Des Moines.

The Indians came back, loping, yipping, firing.

This time, however, they rode against the wind, and the smoke and dust had blown away.

Miss Sabrina snapped a shot.

"Aim low!" Dooley yelled. "And stay low."

Ten Cheyenne or thereabouts, Dooley guessed, splitting up. Some rode to Dooley's left, others to the right. Again, Dooley brought up the Sharps, aimed, and lined up his gun sights on a bone breastplate. The rifle roared, slamming Dooley's shoulder so hard he knew he would likely sport a bruise for the short time of life he had left.

He managed only a glimpse as the warrior was slammed off the back of his horse. Dooley started to toss the big buffalo gun aside and reach for the Dragoon, but he had no time, no chance.

Switching his intention, he put both hands on the burning hot barrel of the rifle and brought the rifle up like a club. He reared back, yelling now, shouting something unholy, and hardly human. A black-toothed Indian with his hair cut short—no braids, rare for a Cheyenne, at least the Indians from the only tribe that Dooley had ever seen—leaned over in his Indian saddle, wielding a tomahawk. Dooley swung. So did the brave.

Down went Dooley, sailing over the dead horse, falling on his back in the blood-soaked ground. Blinking away pain and confusion, fighting for his breath, Dooley rolled over, came to his knees. He looked to his left, and then right, trying to find the .50 caliber cannon he had been holding. Yet he couldn't see it, and guessed he had dropped it on the other side of the dead Indian pony. His arm ached, his right wrist throbbed, and he felt blood leaking from two of his fingers. A glance told him one fingernail had been ripped off.

That's when he saw the short-haired Indian, standing up, falling to his knees, coming up again, blood racing from a savage cut across his forehead, so deep and so wide that Dooley could see the Cheyenne's skull.

Dooley had made contact with the warrior after all. Maybe the warrior's tomahawk had hit Dooley as well. He had no idea of knowing, no memory, just pain that could have come from anywhere.

The Indian saw Miss Sabrina, and staggered toward her, before he caught a glimpse of Dooley out of the corner of his eye. Dooley was moving by then, but pain in his left calf caused him to cry out, to fall, and he felt blood soaking his trousers, filling inside his boots, and he knew he had been shot in the leg. Bullet? Arrow? He did not know, and it did not matter.

He fell onto the horse's dead, bullet-riddled body. The Indian drew a knife, and lunged. Dooley gripped the first thing he could, heard the sucking sound as he pulled a Cheyenne arrow from the dead horse. Somehow he managed to turn the weapon, and he jabbed as hard, and as blindly, as he could.

"Aiiyeeeeeee!"

Dooley kept moving, over the horse as a bullet clipped off the heel of his right boot. He saw the Indian, with the arrow now in his belly. The Indian dropped to his knees, and ripped the arrow out, and made a lunge toward Dooley as if to return the arrow, to put it inside Dooley's stomach.

Yet Dooley had picked up the knife that the Indian had dropped. He parried the arrow with the bone blade of the knife, and then turned, slashed, and saw the Indian collapse, his throat cut.

Something slammed into Dooley's back, and he went down, pushing himself up. He saw legs, black, and knew he had fallen across the reverend. As he rolled over, grasping for anything, he found another Cheyenne standing over him, holding a lance, bringing it up to thrust into Dooley, to skewer him.

That's when Miss Sabrina Granby picked herself off the ground and blew a hole in the Indian's cheek with a slug from Dooley's Colt.

The Indian turned, his hideous face out of view, and crashed to the ground. Dooley grabbed the preacher's niece and pulled her back to the dead horse. Reaching up to the horse's neck, he filled his hand with the big Dragoon. He waited, but heard no more hooves, just chanting, and now what seemed to be arguments among the Indians.

"You . . . all right?" Dooley asked, not even recognizing his own voice.

Miss Sabrina choked out: "I-don't-know," almost as one word.

Dooley looked into the dust and smoke, trying to see other men in black hats and black pants and black coats. Two lay on the ground, but that's all he could see, and those two he knew would not be getting up. Even if they still lived, all those arrows and lances in their bodies would have pinned them to the earth.

He turned away from that ghastly sight and chanced a brief look at the reverend. He could not tell if the preacher breathed or not.

"You're hurt."

Dooley saw Miss Sabrina lowering the .45 and moving to Dooley's leg. That's when he looked down and saw the arrow, a bloody black arrowhead poking through Dooley's calf, the feathered shaft on the other end, also stained with blood that leaked out of Dooley's body.

The niece of the preacher took hold of one end of the arrow, and Dooley screamed in pain. Did heroes scream? Dooley did not know, only that it hurt like hell and that he was no hero, anyway, just a man doing what any man would do—trying to stay alive for as long as he could.

"I'm sorry," Miss Sabrina said.

"It's all right," Dooley said, and lowered the Dragoon to grab the Indian knife he had dropped. He put the knife against the point of the arrow, and, yelling again, cut the shaft to a spot just above the bloody hole in his pants.

"Miss . . . Sabrina . . ." He ground his teeth tightly, rolled over, saw Blue lying, quivering, panting, and reached over to rub the dog's fur. "All right, boy. Everything's . . . just . . . dandy as hell. It's . . ."

He cried out, almost fearing that he would pass out, and looked back to find Miss Sabrina holding the feathered shaft of the arrow in both hands. Despite the blinding pain and the tears and sweat in his eyes, he could tell that she had just yanked the arrow from his calf.

"The . . . hell did . . . you do?" he asked.

"I thought that's what you wanted me to do!" she said, her voice two or three octaves higher than normal.

He made himself smile. "No. It's all . . . right."

He fell back down, pressing his head into the hide of the horse. The world spun above him, and he had to fight to stay conscious.

The woman came to him, and he seemed to see her, that gentle, beautiful face covered by sweat and dirt and blood and smut, still lovely, but never had he seen such determination on anyone's face. Her eyes burned as she worked, freeing the knot that held Dooley's bandanna. She brought the kerchief over, and Dooley thought he could feel her as she tied it over the arrow wounds in his leg.

More yips, more songs—Dooley thought he heard women singing now, and maybe he did. Sometimes, he had heard, Indians brought some of their women along, to sing songs of encouragement, to help their warriors. He remembered an old army scout telling him—this was probably Boise or maybe Ogden—that you never wanted to be caught alive by an Indian woman. "A buck," the grizzled old scout had said, "he'll just kill you outright, take your scalp, maybe cut off some parts that you ain't got no use for no more. But an Indian harlot? Well, them gals know more about inflicting pain than ol' Lucifer his ownself."

Dooley rolled over, peered over the dead horse, and saw what looked to be flags waving through the smoke on the prairie. He strained, stared, and buried his face in the horse's stinking flesh, as another round of dizziness almost sent him reeling into a deep black void that had no bottom.

When he straightened, he again saw the waving flags.

Flags? A cavalry guidon? No. No. He had to tell himself to stay awake, to stay focused. Miss Sabrina's very life depended on it.

Then he understood. And he brought up the Dragoon, pulled the trigger. Cock and fire. Cock and fire. Cock and fire. No longer did he taste the acrid smoke, smell the cordite.

"Stop that, you damned curs."

Miss Sabrina must have realized what was happening, too, because now she took up Dooley's Colt again, and her shots echoed Dooley's own.

Bam!

Bam!

Bam!

Indians were just behind the fire, waving blankets—sleeping blankets, saddle blankets, maybe dresses and buckskin shirts. Trying to turn the fire that kept burning sage and grass, fanning the flames, hoping to burn out Dooley and Miss Sabrina and Blue and the reverend.

One of the warriors raised up, and a bullet—
Dooley could not tell if the shot had been fired by
Miss Sabrina or him—must have hit the brave, or
woman, or maybe even a kid, because down went the
figure with a grunt. Two other figures, nothing more
than shadows through the smoke, rushed over,
picked up the wounded Indian, and ran from the fire
and smoke.

"You're not burning us out!" Dooley yelled. "You're
not burning us out! You're not burning us out! We
might see Hell soon enough. But you're not burning us out!"

He was still pulling the trigger, and so was Miss
Sabrina, long after the last round had been fired.
Now all they heard were those hard metallic clicks as
their hammers fell on empty chambers. But it did not
matter. And they did not stop for several minutes.

Click!
Click!
Click!

CHAPTER THIRTY-NINE

When they finally realized what they were doing, when some semblance of sanity returned, they stopped and collapsed against the dead horse. They breathed in and out, deeply, not caring that they sent more smoke and dust into their lungs than air.

At length, they listened.

All they heard was silence.

Dusk came, and darkness soon bathed the prairie, although flames still sparked here and there among the sage and grass, and the remnants of the wagons glowed all around them.

Not trusting his luck—although he had to concede just how lucky he was to still be breathing—Dooley crawled over to where Miss Sabrina knelt, tending to her uncle.

She turned to face him, and from the glowing coals of what had been that giant Conestoga, Dooley could see the trails the tears had left on her dirty face. "I can't," she whispered, "get that arrow out of Uncle Bob."

"Leave it," Dooley said. Pull it out, he knew, and the man might bleed to death. Leaving it in was a risk, too, of infection, of poison, but the shock of the removal of an arrow in that deep might likely kill the preacher. From the looks of the Reverend Granby's face, Dooley didn't think the man would live much longer. He couldn't understand how the man had stayed alive this long, but for the time being, he seemed to be at peace, and Dooley wasn't going to spoil that.

"Are they gone?" Miss Sabrina asked.

He thought about lying, but found no solace in that. "No," he said.

"Will they attack us soon?"

"Not tonight." Dooley read the look on her face, that said she knew he was lying to protect her, even though he wasn't. He explained, "Indians don't attack at night. It's their religion . . ." A quick glance at the sleeping reverend made him question his choice of words. "Superstition," he said, more for Miss Sabrina's and the parson's upbringing. A man of the cloth might not cotton to what an Indian believed, Indians being heathen and all. Dooley wasn't altogether certain that Indians were godless creatures like he had heard the circuit-riding minister back in Iowa preach. "They seem to think that if they get killed, where no one can see them, then they'll have to wander around aimlessly."

"Like Purgatory?"

He shrugged. "Something like that."

Somewhere in the darkness to the south, a voice shouted. "Reverend? Reverend Granby?"

Abercrombie? That's who it sounded like. Dooley bit his lip, not wanting to talk, for he knew the Indians might not attack in the dark, but they could still send arrows or rifle balls in the direction of voices. Yet when the voice kept calling out, Dooley relented. "He can't talk! He's wounded!"

A long pause. Then: "Is that you, Monahan?"

"Yeah!"

"Is Miss Sabrina all right?"

"Yes, Mr. Abercrombie!" Sabrina Granby answered.

"Thank the Lord! How's your uncle?"

Her voice choked, and she could not find the words, so Dooley answered, "Grave."

"We shall pray for him. We shall pray for the deliverance of all of us . . ." Now Mr. Abercrombie's voice broke. ". . . still . . . alive."

"Is Mrs. Kingsbury all right?" Miss Sabrina had recovered from the emotional weight.

"She is well . . . as well as can be expected, but I fear others are with our Lord. Monahan?"

"Yes!"

"All of our oxen are dead, or run off by the savages! All of our wagons have been burned. Only five of us remain—"

That's when the first barrage of gunfire began.

"Down!" Dooley reached over and pulled Miss Sabrina closer to the ground, and he flattened his body over hers and tried to bury his face into the bloating, blood-soaked body of the dead horse. Most of the bullets struck well beyond Dooley and the Granbys, thudding into the ground, the dead oxen, the coals and ashes, and maybe even the bodies of those living, or dead, in the main party. Yet one or two skidded over the sage, and two arrows made that sickening noise as they sliced into the already decimated remains of the horse. Blue crawled over, whimpering now, and Dooley reached over and put his arm over the shepherd, too.

The fusillade lasted less than a minute, although it felt like an eternity. After that, Dooley let out a breath but did not move away from Miss Sabrina or stop holding on to Blue.

"Mr. Abercrombie isn't talking," Miss Sabrina whispered.

"He shouldn't," Dooley told her. "It'll give those warriors something to shoot at." Yet he thought: *If Abercrombie's still alive . . .*

"What do we do?" she asked.

He frowned, a hard frown, one that knew the future.

"Wait for sunrise," he said.

"Couldn't we sneak out at night?"

"They'll be expecting that," he said. "And even if we did, we'd be caught afoot, in open country." If only they had been closer to those forested hills. About four or five minutes later, a scream pierced the night. It sounded, at first, like the wail of a mountain lion, only after another wretched cry, Dooley knew what it was. Bile rose in his throat.

One of the others—Abercrombie, the Widow, Hentig, or one of those men whose names Dooley never could remember—had done just what Miss Sabrina had suggested. Tried to sneak out, escape from what awaited them come morning. Only he had not made it.

His screams, until the Indians tired of toying with him, would keep them awake all night. Not that Dooley could sleep anyway.

* * *

The drums began again in earnest when the skies began turning gray in the east. The screams had stopped about an hour earlier. Now Dooley moved away from Miss Sabrina, and he gathered his weapons, feeding the last shells from his belt into his Colt. When he snapped the loading gate shut, the wailing songs of the Cheyenne warriors, and maybe some women who had made this journey with them, began. Miss Sabrina slid over to her uncle, wiped the blood off his chin, removed a blood-soaked handkerchief wrapped around the arrow's shaft, and ripped off part of her skirt to replace the makeshift bandage.

"He's still alive," she said grimly.

"We have four bullets left," he told her.

"Don't save one for me, Dooley Monahan." Her face hardened, and she moved back toward the stinking corpse of a horse and savagely jerked out two arrows, holding them in both hands. "Just take as many out as you can, and I'll do the same."

The sun began to appear.

"It's been a pleasure knowing you, Mis- . . . Dooley."

For the damnedest reason, Dooley Monahan smiled at her. "Likewise, Sabrina. Likewise."

He heard the pounding of the hooves, and stood to face the thundering horde.

The first wave of riders came from the east, the sun behind them but too low on the horizon to spoil Dooley's aim. He held his fire, though, knowing he couldn't afford to miss any shot, and none of these Indians even held rifles, war clubs, lances, bows. They leaned low in their Indian saddles, and none even paid scant attention to Dooley, Miss Sabrina, or even

Blue. Dooley extended the Colt, cocked, and followed the riders but never squeezed the trigger. They rode past, through the sage and dust and ashes, whooping and yelling, and headed to the west.

"My goodness!" Miss Sabrina said.

"Carrying off their dead," Dooley explained. "Cheyennes—most Indians, for that matter—will do everything in their power to take away their dead." He had heard that from various scouts and soldiers he had played cards with over the years, but never had he seen such a display of bravery—of humanity—until that moment. He wasn't sure if he had ever known a white man who would have risked his hide to save a corpse. Dooley figured he never would have done such a thing, and that shamed him.

The next time the Indians charged, however, Dooley knew they would have no dead to remove from the battlefield. They would be coming to finish the job.

Again, he heard the whoops and cries, and now the Indians galloped back.

"Get ready!" Dooley yelled, and aimed the gun at the dust.

Yet the Indians veered away from Dooley and Miss Sabrina, just before Dooley started to press down on the Colt's trigger. They fired, guns and arrows, and they yelled and screamed above the answering gunfire. They were hitting the rest of the wagon train. Then they would come for Dooley, the dog, the girl, and the dying preacher.

And they did come, but again, not overrunning the makeshift fort commanded by a man, a young woman, and a dog. One arrow sliced over Dooley's head, and he ducked, expecting more. The Indians rode off toward the northeast. Dooley wet his lips, trying to figure out what kind of ruse the Cheyenne were pulling. Suddenly, he heard a voice through the dust, toward the rest of the wagon train.

"Monahan! They've got your horse!"

Dooley stood, watching, and sure enough he saw a young brave on a skewbald mare, pulling General Grant behind him. He never would be able to explain it, what he was thinking—obviously, he had not been thinking—or why he did it, how he even managed to do it, yet Dooley sprang forward, running as fast as he could.

He did hear Blue bark, and Miss Sabrina call out his name.

"No!" Dooley shouted. "No, sir, no, you don't!"

The Cheyenne warrior, not out of his teens, turned and stared in amazement, and quickly brought up his shield as he let go of General Grant's reins.

Dooley had just finished saying "don't" when he sprang up, felt himself as if he were flying like a cannonball. The Indian pony had been running at a pretty good lope, so Dooley had timed his leap, his angle, and the teenage warrior must have slowed down. Perhaps, seeing a crazy white man running at him made him panic. Oh, the horse had not stopped when Dooley jumped, but at least it had slowed down if only slightly.

The mare wheeled as Dooley wrapped his arms— his right hand still gripping the Colt—around the Indian, who dropped the shield, and then both fell into the sage and dust. Sage ripped through Dooley's sleeves, and sand clogged his nostrils, and half blinded him. He tasted blood, knew he had busted his lips, and the Colt had snapped back his trigger finger before it had flown somewhere across the Wyoming landscape. His left ankle hurt.

Yet Dooley Monahan sprang to his feet. He caught a glimpse of the young Cheyenne, who rolled around in the dirt, gripping his left arm, wailing like a newborn calf about to be branded. Dooley paid little attention to the warrior, though, and looked through the dust, left, right, and finally saw General Grant trotting in a circle not ten yards from him.

"Easy, boy," Dooley managed to say, although he spit out those words, and sand, and blood, as he staggered toward the bay gelding. That finger on his right hand was broken. Dooley knew that sure enough, but he reached up with his left hand, and tried to breathe normally, tried to seem relaxed. His horse's eyes were wild with fright, yet the General appeared to recognize Dooley. His left hand came closer, closer, and he wanted to leap at the last second, snatch those reins, get a good grip, and make sure the horse did not bolt his way back to Des Moines.

He did not panic, did not leap or snatch, just wrapped his good hand—or as good as it could be with the scratches, dirt, grime, and dried blood (his own, the dead horse's, Miss Sabrina's, and the reverend's)—around the left rein, and then moved over and took the right.

A sigh escaped, and he almost smiled before he heard the sound of more hooves. An Indian—maybe the whole damned tribe—came back to help the brave, a kid, Dooley had knocked off his horse.

Accepting his death, Dooley turned around to see the Indian who was about to kill him.

Just one Cheyenne, however, rode toward him. He was an older man, silver hair, and a battle-scarred face. He held a long lance in his left hand, but the black point pointed at the ground as he reined in his dapple mare. The ancient warrior turned to the boy, now on his knees, holding a broken arm, tears streaming down his face. The old Indian barked something in a guttural voice, before he kicked his pony into a walk, slowly covering the few yards until he reined up again in front of Dooley.

Dooley tried to swallow but couldn't. He wanted to run away, but knew better. Running was not how a man died. The old man said something, words Dooley could not understand, and he lifted his spear. Dooley held his breath, wondering what it would feel like to be skewered like a pig on the Fourth of July for a barbecue.

Instead, the warrior tapped Dooley on the left shoulder with the blunt edge of the spear, wheeled his horse around, and ran it over to the injured teen, who now stood. The old man shouted something, leaned over, and helped pull the young Cheyenne onto the dapple behind him. Then the horse thundered across the land, joined with the other Indians, and off they rode, away from the remnants of the wagon train, away from Dooley and Miss Sabrina and General Grant and Blue. They just rode away.

Not that Dooley Monahan saw any of that. The last thing he remembered was the Indian's spear touching his shoulder—counting coup, they called it, though Miss Sabrina would later say, "It was just like you were being knighted by King Arthur"—and seeing the grizzled old warrior wheel his horse around and trot away.

After that, Dooley Monahan just fainted.

CHAPTER FORTY

Josiah Hentig, Al Abercrombie, Homer McCreery, and the Widow Kingsbury stood over the Reverend Robert James Granby, while Miss Sabrina pressed down on more torn skirts as Dooley cut through the shaft of the arrow. The minister gasped, but did not open his eyes, did not regain consciousness.

Dooley bit his bottom lip, pulled in as much oxygen as his lungs could hold, and slowly exhaled. He was already sweating.

"Did you search his pockets?"

That stopped Dooley. He must have misheard, but when he looked up at the Cincinnati wayfarers he saw nothing but dead seriousness, a hardness Dooley had not seen since he had escaped from the Dobbs-Handley Gang. Even Miss Sabrina turned around to face her former neighbors.

"Excuse me, Mr. McCreery?" she said.

"I said, 'search his pockets,'" the penguin replied. "For the rest of the damned map."

"Homer," the Widow said, yet Dooley saw that only the woman appeared to show sympathy or empathy and not this crazed lust for gold. "What's gotten into you?"

Dooley looked at the ashes. The dust had settled, and morning had turned calm now that the Cheyenne war party had left. Oh, buzzards had begun circling overhead, and a few wolves were camped about a hundred yards or so to the west. Waiting. Waiting to feast on the dead oxen.

"You really should be burying the rest of your people," Dooley said.

"With what?" Mr. Hentig barked.

"I buried Little Dix Mixson with my own hands," Dooley said, "after he got struck by lightning on the Buffalo River in Arkansas back in '63."

Mr. Hentig opened his mouth, but decided against saying anything else . . . for the time being.

Dooley turned back to the arrow. He knew that the preacher had little chance at surviving, but he most certainly would die if this arrow was not removed. Dooley had waited as long as possible, thinking that the piece of wood would at least stop some of the bleeding. Actually, he had been waiting for the poor man to die, maybe in his sleep, peacefully, mercifully.

A sudden gasp from Miss Sabrina caught Dooley's attention, and when he saw the preacher's face, he realized why Mr. Hentig had stopped from saying whatever words he had been thinking. The preacher's eyes had opened, and he smiled feebly at his niece and turned to Dooley.

"Monahan," he said, his voice somehow carrying above the death rattle that followed. "Save . . ."

"Preacher!" Hentig shouted. "Give us the map!"

The dying man turned away from Monahan and smiled as he brought up his right hand. For a moment, Dooley thought the good man was going to do just that, reach into that pocket in his big black coat and pull out the rest of the map. And then hand it over to a rotten cur like Josiah Hentig.

Instead, the hand landed on his stomach, and a finger pointed at the broken arrow.

"Afraid . . . this arrow . . . took care of . . . that . . ." Dooley tensed as he watched the life leave the eyes of the Reverend Robert James Granby, who had left the Queen City of the West to die in the lawless West.

Miss Sabrina reached over and closed her uncle's eyes, and then Dooley found himself pushed away as Hentig, McCreery, and even Abercrombie dropped onto their knees and began pulling at the dead preacher's clothes.

The Widow said, "Father, forgive them, for they know not what they do."

Dooley knew that they did know what they were doing, and forgiveness was not one of his strong suits. He came up, reaching for his Colt, but Miss Sabrina threw herself against them.

"Let them be, please, Dooley. Uncle Bob wouldn't want this."

So Dooley watched this pack of animals turn a dead man's pockets inside out, and eventually rip out the arrow.

McCreery swore, and Abercrombie laughed the cry of a madman when he picked up a bloody piece of paper that fell apart in his fingers. "He wasn't lying. That arrow . . ." He turned, raising his hands over his head, and falling to his knees. "Those damned Indians!"

Then Abercrombie turned, levering a round into his Henry rifle, and pointing that old .44 at Dooley Monahan.

"You saw the last map. Before the wind carried it away . . ."

"That's right!" Hentig bolted past the dead horse, over the dead oxen, through the ashes, going from sagebrush to sagebrush, looking for a bit of map that the wind had probably deposited miles from here, or had been burned in one of the small grass fires the Indians had tried to turn into a prairie inferno.

McCreery stopped his ranting and stood awkwardly, watching and listening to Abercrombie.

"You can get us closer . . . to Slim Pickings."

Dooley shrugged. "Close don't count . . . not in this country."

"Al, what in heaven's name are you talking about?" the Widow Kingsbury asked.

"Not heaven's name," Miss Sabrina corrected.

"I'm talking about," Mr. Abercrombie said, as though speaking to a four-year-old boy. "About getting you to your darling nephew." He waved the rifle's barrel. "He saw the map. He knows this country. If he can get us close, maybe we can find this place." He cocked the rifle again, even though it was already loaded, and Dooley watched the .44 shell spin up and land in the dirt.

"Josiah!" Abercrombie called out to the crazed map chaser. "Stop that nonsense. Get over here. Get as many canteens as you can carry. We're walking."

His eyes lighted. "To gold. Walking . . ." The barrel waved like the needle on a compass. "That way."

Even Cincinnatians driven mad by an Indian attack and the wicked gold lust have their good points. Or maybe it's hard to take civility out of city folks. They had one horse, and they let Miss Sabrina and the Widow Kingsbury ride General Grant.

And they had even made sure the dead men from the wagon train got a burial. Well, it was only one grave, and only as deep as Dooley could manage with his hands and some broken, burned tools from the heaping mounds of ash that had once been a farm wagon. After that, they had left the massacre site and moved northeast, toward the pine forests, toward the Black Hills, toward—they hoped—Slim Pickings.

It wasn't like Dooley ever played a whole lot of blackjack. Maybe it was because he had never been good at counting cards, remembering what all had been played. And that bout with amnesia back in San Francisco that had held strong till Cheyenne certainly had not improved his memory. But now Dooley could see that bit of map that the late Reverend Granby had shown him, and see it in perfect clarity.

Having three men behind you with guns—they had taken away Dooley's Colt—did wonders for a man's memory.

Of course, remembering the sketchy details in a crudely and hurriedly drawn map was one thing. Trying to figure out what it meant in a place like this turned things sideways and upside down.

They camped that night in a coulee, got up early

the next morning, and continued. Two days later, they began climbing higher, and the air cooled, and the trees from the approaching hills must have stopped the wind. That night, they spent the evening in the trees, hearing the wind rustle above them. It spooked the three men from Cincinnati, but Dooley understood that. You spend what seems like a lifetime in Nebraska and Colorado, crossing these Great Plains, and suddenly you find yourself back in trees, where you can't see forever . . . well . . . it tugs on a man's nerves.

The next day, at Mr. Hentig's and Mr. McCreery's insistence, they left the forest and walked along the grasslands, up and down hills, keeping the trees to their right, never farther than a hundred yards away. They moved along, and then Dooley Monahan stopped.

They were in a clearing, the Black Hills and the forests to the northwest. Dooley looked ahead, like he was staring at a valley. Indeed, that's pretty much what it was. A hill rising off on the southern edge, the timber beginning about halfway up, and to the north, another hill, rougher, though, almost a small cliff before the tree line began not fifty feet up. A creek flowed along the side of the hill, turning, twisting, and disappearing into the forest. Between the two hills, maybe fifty or sixty yards across, stretched this valley. He could see a smaller hill maybe two hundred and fifty yards due east, three trees that could have been those crosslike symbols Logan Kingsbury had scribbled onto his map, and a conical hill far beyond that, green with trees. Beyond that, nothing but blue skies and white clouds. The wind blew, and Dooley wet his lips.

This is it, Dooley told himself, and not just because of what he remembered from the map he had glimpsed.

Dooley did not know how much of the entire map he had seen. Had this been the last piece to the puzzle, or was there more, left bloody and unreadable by a Cheyenne arrow? Yet Dooley knew something else. He had been to many mining camps in the mountains, seen many a town. And he might not have the memory of a grafter in one of those carnivals, but he knew that most of those mining towns had been in country that looked a hell of a lot like this.

"What is it?" Mr. Abercrombie said.

"This is it," Dooley told him.

The Ohioan blinked. "How the hell can you be sure?"

Dooley nodded toward the cliff. "Because there's a white man over yonder with a big-bore rifle aimed right at us."

CHAPTER FORTY-ONE

Later, when they were alone at Slim Pickings, Miss Sabrina whispered into Dooley's ear, "How in tarnation did you know he was a *white* man?"

Dooley could only shrug.

"Keep your hands away from 'em guns of yourn!" the man on the ridge called out in a booming voice. "First one of ya to moves, I blows to hell." The man moved down the cliff, reminding Dooley of a mountain lion, graceful for such a gangly fellow—and that cliff looked pretty steep. As he walked across the flats toward Dooley and the others, Mr. McCreery said in a quiet voice:

"That's an Enfield rifle. He's only got one shot. Means he can only get one of us before we kill him."

"You want to be the one he shoots," Mr. Abercrombie said, "go right ahead."

Mr. McCreery never raised the rifle in his hands, which Dooley decided was a wise play, for Dooley wasn't as blind as McCreery. Sure, the tall man held a single-shot Enfield rifled musket, but a six-shooter

was stuck in his waistband, and Dooley saw another
holster under his left shoulder.

"My goodness," the Widow Kingsbury said as the
man came closer. "Is he . . . even . . . human?"

That, Dooley thought, *is even money.*

If he stood shorter than six-foot-four, Dooley
would have been surprised. Lean to the point that he
practically resembled a skeleton, he took giant steps
over the sage and grass, keeping that Enfield trained
on Dooley and the others. When he stopped at last,
he brought the rifle to his shoulder and studied the
survivors of the Cheyenne attack. He wore no hat, and
Dooley did not think he had ever seen a hat in
any store—even that big one over in Kansas City—
that could have covered his head. Not that this gent's
head was huge, but his hair looked like an osprey
might mistake it for her nest—if any of those big
birds got down this way. It was dark, filthy, thick, and
blown so much by the wind, it went every which way
but loose. Varmints could be living somewhere in that
mane that would break a currycomb. For all Dooley
knew, some rats or mice had made nests inside it.

The face had been burned by the sun and wind,
and plastered with so much dirt that the only white—
not actually white, but more of a gray, and a dark gray
at that—Dooley could see came from whenever he
knotted his brow and cracked some of that paste on
his forehead. Indeed, the only face that Dooley could
see were the stranger's sunburned and pine-sap-and-
dirt-covered nose, the dirty forehead that wasn't ob-
scured by the hair on his head, and those eyes. The
eyes were dark, wild, insane perhaps but more than
likely calculating. His eyebrows were thick, but not as
thick as his hair, or his mustache and beard. That

facial hair had also avoided water, as well as soap and razor, for months. The beard went down to the center of his chest, bristling like cactus spines, so thick and filthy that even the Wyoming wind could scarcely make it move.

Then, of course, there were the man's clothes. Buckskin, maybe, but that was hard to tell as dirty as those duds were, too. Handmade, naturally, but Dooley could not recall anything ever made so poorly. The pants were a patchwork of hides, stitched together with sinew, different shades of brain-tanned hides and even fur pelts from rabbits. The shirt was of an even worse construction, the left sleeve of rabbit fur coming down to maybe his elbow, and the right sleeve of elk skin tied at the middle of his forearm with fringe, the only fringe Dooley saw on the man's outfit. The rest of his arm, not to mention his hands and fingers, was browned from the sun, the dirt, and the grime. And his boots weren't boots at all, nor moccasins, nor brogans or gaiters. No, this man merely wrapped hides over his feet, securing them on his calves with rope.

Dooley had been right, though. A belt—the one bit of his outfit that appeared store-bought or ordered from a mail-order catalog, though purchased many years ago—wrapped around his waist, and a Remington .44 had been stuck around his navel. Dooley had been mistaken about the shoulder holster, however. It wasn't exactly a holster at all, but a makeshift sheath, with the bone handle of a knife sticking out of it, and it was tied across his chest and back with another bit of rope.

The tall man's rifle swung toward Mr. Abercrombie.

"Who are you?" he asked in a voice that told Dooley that this man had not spoken to anyone, other than himself, in a long, long time. Apparently, the stranger with the strange outfit and all-too-familiar rifled musket had pegged Abercrombie for the leader.

"Alvin Sebastian Abercrombie."

"What are you doin' here?"

"We were attacked by Cheyenne Indians some days back." He gestured with a wave of his arm. "South of here."

The Enfield moved to Mr. Hentig.

"Josiah Hentig," Mr. Hentig said without being asked.

"Bound for Deadwood?" the stranger asked.

"Well . . ." Mr. Hentig wet his lips. "For . . . er . . . gold . . . yes?"

"This ain't no trail to Deadwood, fella." The finger tightened on the trigger, and before Mr. Hentig could wet his britches, Mr. McCreery spoke.

"We were not bound for Deadwood, sir, and we don't even know what trail we are on, sir."

His words faded as the rifle swung from Mr. Hentig to his own chest, and he wet his trembling lips with a parched tongue.

"And you be?" the man with the Enfield asked.

"Homer McCreery."

The eyes darted from the three men, passed over the Widow Kingsbury, considered Blue for a second, stayed on General Grant a good while, and landed a fairly long time on Miss Sabrina Granby, before at last stopping at Dooley.

"And you?"

"Dooley Monahan."

Those dark eyes turned darker, and smaller, and the Enfield pulled tighter against the man's shoulder.

"The famous bounty hunter?"

"I'm no bounty hunter," Dooley said calmly, "and I'm far from famous."

"Figgered you was dead."

"Not dead," Dooley said. "Just in Iowa."

"Practic'ly the same. You ain't kilt nobody lately."

You have been away from newspapers, Dooley thought, but made no verbal reply.

He looked at Dooley's hips, then at his shoulder, and Dooley knew that the stranger was wondering why a bounty hunter of Dooley Monahan's renown wore no revolver and carried no long gun or shotgun. Yet next, he swung the rifle back at Abercrombie, and McCreery, and briefly Hentig, then stayed on Abercrombie while his eyes locked on Miss Sabrina.

"You be?"

"Sabrina Granby," she answered. "My uncle was a minister in Cincinnati and now walks the Streets of Gold after an Indian massacre."

"Cin-see-natti?"

Those crazy eyes made Miss Sabrina swallow and her face turn ashen. She could not answer, but did not have to, because the man now swung his single-shot weapon to the Widow Kingsbury.

"And you?" he practically screamed. "What's yer name?"

When she told him, the rifle lowered, and butted against the sod, and he said, no longer screaming, no longer growling like some wild animal, and those once-insane eyes showed relief. Not that he looked like a human being, but he did start acting like one.

"Aunt . . ." His throat rasped. "Aunt . . . H-H-Hhh-hhhh."

"Henrietta," the Widow said. She stepped toward him, raising eyebrows and her arms, searching his face, his lean body, for some recognition. "You can't be . . ."

"I . . . am . . . Logan," he told her, dropped the Enfield, and fell to his knees, sobbing like a lost boy who had just found his favorite auntie.

She told him that he had grown some, and that he looked real different. Dooley almost rolled his eyes, not about the growing taller and thinner because, well, he did not know how short or how fat Logan Kingsbury had been all those years ago. But different? Hell, yes, he expected that lanky cuss to look different. After all, Dooley had seen a lot of hard cases in his day, a lot of strange birds, and real ugly individuals—that brute Ewing Atkinson, late of the late Dobbs-Handley Gang, came to mind—but Logan Kingsbury topped them all.

The Cincinnati contingent seemed to be knocked into total shock, so when the gangling man dropped to his knees and buried his hands in his eyeballs, letting out gasping sobs and crocodile tears, they just stood there. Dooley didn't. He moved like a deer, snatched up the Enfield rifle, and stepped a long way out of Logan Kingsbury's reach. It had to be long, for that man had arms like the tentacles of that big squid Dooley had seen, and even remembered, back when he had been visiting San Francisco on his way to Alaska, where he never even got to.

Dooley did not point the Enfield at Logan Kingsbury, but kept it, more or less, in the general direction of Abercrombie, Hentig, and McCreery. He kept his eyes on those three low-down dogs, too, and positioned himself so that he could see the Widow's reunion with her nephew. Blue came over and lay down at Dooley's side.

Which seemed to be just what Logan Kingsbury was doing, too, for he fell to his side and pulled up his knees until he resembled a suckling infant. The Widow moved tentatively, but eventually knelt beside her poor, suffering son-of-a-cur of a nephew, and ran her hands through that mess of a mane of his. Dooley could not help but grimace. He wouldn't have touched that hair for all the gold in the Black Hills.

"Logan," she said at last.

"Aunt Henrietta," he managed to choke out.

"What happened to you?" his aunt inquired.

"I've been . . . so . . . alone," he wailed.

The sobbing stopped almost as soon as it began, and Logan Kingsbury, after some more gentle strokes from his aunt, came up. He sighed, looked over the three Cincinnati men, stared an uncomfortably long time at Miss Sabrina, and gave Dooley only a sideways glance. He did not even appear to notice that the Enfield was in Dooley's hands. When he looked back at Abercrombie, Hentig, and McCreery, he asked his aunt: "This is all you brought?"

She told him all that had happened, how the party had sent the women and children on to Fetterman City, and how savage Indians had wiped out the rest of those valiant men from the Queen City of the West, but bravely they had walked—although, actually, sometimes, she corrected herself, Mr. Monahan had let Sabrina and herself ride that pretty red horse—for days on end on this treacherous journey to find her favorite nephew.

"Well . . ." The crazy man wet his chapped lips and studied the Ohio contingent again, especially Miss Sabrina, and at length he pushed himself to his feet and looked at Dooley. This time, he appeared to understand that Dooley held the Enfield, perhaps because it was now pointed at his midsection.

"You ain't fer from Slim Pickin's," he said, speaking to his aunt, and maybe the men from the Blue Chip City, but keeping his eyes on Dooley. "We can walk to the camp from here."

Obviously, Dooley thought, unless they wanted to ride General Grant one or two at a time, come back to pick up one or two more, and so forth.

"Is there . . ." Mr. McCreery's Adam's apple bobbed. "Is there . . . still gold there?"

"Not much," Logan Kingsbury answered. "It's pretty much played out." He looked across the grass-lands, concerned now, and turned around. This time, he stared at Dooley. "Best we get out of this open country. Get back to Slim Pickin's. Don't like to be out here. Indians been on the prod." When he faced his aunt again, he smiled. "Now, Aunt Henrietta, I gots to warn you. Slim Pickin's ain't much to look at."

"Like you are?" Dooley said underneath his breath.

CHAPTER FORTY-TWO

Logan Kingsbury's description of Slim Pickings, Wyoming Territory, was an understatement. Not much to look at. There wasn't anything to it.

No streets. No livery stable. No outhouses. Not even a building, unless you counted what once had been a Sibley tent until branches and wind and whatever had ripped off most of the canvas. That's where Logan Kingsbury slept, and Logan Kingsbury had no bedroll. Trash, ranging from broken tools to the unused skins of carcasses, to the bones of those dead animals, and remnants of . . . whatever they once had been . . . were strewn around the campground, which was not even cleared. Blue wandered over and nosed a few bones, but before Dooley could call the shepherd back to him, the dog backed away, turned quickly, and jogged back to Dooley's side. That troubled Dooley because Blue was like most dogs, and would eat anything that was put in front of him or he happened to find in front of him, or buried. What kind of bones would a dog not eat?

A cloud passed over the sun, turning Slim Pickings

into a mighty dark place—not that it wasn't shadowy and eerie before.

The trees here might not be thick, but they certainly were plentiful. Stretching for the clouds, the pines and conifers rustled overhead in the wind. Dooley tethered General Grant to a sapling, and studied more of Slim Pickings.

He could see the gray ash from fires, and decided that was where Logan Kingsbury did his cooking, and that although the demented man had not troubled himself to build a cabin—despite the abundance of trees—he had managed to chop down some firewood. A stack, not enough to get through a winter, not even enough to get to winter, stood beyond his, ahem, tent, and pinecones and other bits of kindling had been piled up against one of the trees that served as a holder for the wood pile.

A creek zigzagged through the area, flowing at a pretty good rate for this time of year. Well, that was a good thing. They had a supply of water, but General Grant would need something to graze other than pine needles, saplings, and old animal bones.

The cloud blew away, and the sun's rays managed to creep through parts of the trees overhead, but to Dooley Monahan, Slim Pickings remained a mighty dark place.

Josiah Hentig, Al Abercrombie, Homer McCreery, and even the Widow Kingsbury spent the next morning along the creek, panning for gold with plates they found strewn about the camp, while Logan Kingsbury slept in. Dooley cleaned the guns, reloaded them, and put together a lean-to for shelter, using the tools Logan Kingsbury had stored—if you would call leaning shovels and axes against a pine "stored."

A rake had been lying on the ground near the trash heap, the prongs facing upward—dangerous, Dooley's pa had always told him—so Dooley picked it up and began cleaning up the mess. He had raked much of the debris that he figured he could not use into the heap when he smelled coffee. He turned to find Miss Sabrina Granby holding two steaming cups. Dooley had been so focused on his work that he had not even seen Miss Sabrina stoke the fire and brew the coffee.

He took the cup she offered him, and drank. Then he thought of something and asked, "Where did you find coffee?"

She gestured toward a sinkhole between rocks and trees. "Over there. I guess that's where he"—she nodded at Logan Kingsbury—"keeps his supplies."

"What else?"

He did not wait for her answer, but set the rake down—prongs down, so no one would step on it and have the handle fly up to break a nose—and walked toward the shallow impression in the ground. Miss Sabrina told him what she had found as he walked, and, sure enough, Dooley found nothing extra, and not much, except the Arbuckles', that would do them any good here.

"What a mess," Dooley said, and drank more coffee.

"I don't see how he lived here for so long," Miss Sabrina said.

"I wouldn't call this living."

She pointed back deeper into the woods. "I found

a corral," she said. "Well, not much of one, but it was definitely a corral. But no horses. Or mules. I guess . . . maybe they ran off . . . or . . . maybe . . . Indians?"

"Maybe," Dooley said. He wasn't going to explain about some of the bones he had found in the trash pile. Dooley drank more coffee to wash down that bitter taste that began to develop in his mouth. Several men had told him that horsemeat wasn't bad, but mule meat was something better.

"Let's put General Grant in that corral," Dooley said.

And that led to the first building put up, if you didn't count the lean-to, in Slim Pickings.

It started out as one log cabin, and not much of a log cabin. But they had axes and hatchets and saws, and Dooley told them later that day that they would need shelter. "It can snow in this country in June and July," he told them, "and we've got just *my* horse." He made sure they understood that it was his horse, and that he had done his job, had gotten them to Slim Pickings, and could leave anytime he chose. Not that he would leave a fine figure of a woman like Miss Sabrina Granby alone in this country.

"But the gold!" Mr. Hentig complained.

Dooley rolled his eyes. They had panned all day and had found maybe a tenth of an ounce of dust— or so the Widow had boasted. Dooley wouldn't argue with the Widow, but he doubted if they had any dust, or if these Cincinnatians would even know gold if it wasn't a double eagle.

"Work in shifts," Dooley said. "Pan in the morning

while others are working on a cabin, then do her the other way around."

"You should be our marshal, Dooley," said Logan Kingsbury, who had finally awakened.

"I'll pick our marshal," Mr. Abercrombie barked.

"Noooooo," Logan Kingsbury said. "Slim Pickin's is my town. Dooley. Yeah, Dooley. He's the marshal."

"Thanks," Dooley said. He was now an officer of the law. In a one-horse town. His horse. That was about to become a one-building town.

It worked out all right. The cabin went up quickly. Not that it would ever compare to that really nice hotel Dooley had stayed in that time in Freemason City, Iowa—back when he was riding with Monty's Raiders—the one the guerrillas had burned down after sacking the town. It wasn't that nice, but it had a roof, sort of, and a window, sort of, and a door, if you could call the saddle blanket a door.

There would be no more buildings, though. Everyone could sleep in the cabin, if on the floor, and that was enough for the people from the Blue Chip City. As soon as the cabin had its roof and its door, the men and the Widow Kingsbury went back to the stream to wash their plates, which was about all they did, because no one ever ran back to Slim Pickings proper saying, "I've found the mother lode."

One person did not pan, and that was Logan Kingsbury. He just slept through the morning, and ate supper with the rest, and shrugged when they asked him about the riches, and reminded them that he had told them, "Slim Pickin's has pert much played out."

"So why," Dooley asked Miss Sabrina Granby one day, "does he stay here? If a gold town isn't producing gold anymore, it usually becomes a ghost town."

"I wouldn't call Slim Pickings a town at all, Dooley Monahan," Miss Sabrina pointed out.

"Still. He's still here."

"He has no horse," she said.

Dooley moved closer to General Grant. This was his time of the day to take his bay gelding out of the woods and to the meadow to graze on luscious grass. It also, he figured, helped him keep his sanity. A man cooped up in thick woods like that might go mad— like Logan Kingsbury. "You can cross this country afoot," Dooley told her. "We did."

"We weren't packing a fortune in gold," she said.

She would make a good lawyer, Dooley thought. "Bury the gold. Come back with wagons or mules, or an escort of heavily armed men, and take it to Denver. Or even Deadwood."

There was no answer. Dooley just liked thinking aloud, especially when he had a woman with such a lovely face and soothing voice such as Miss Sabrina to think aloud with him. You always want to finish a day a bit smarter than you was the day before, his ma had always taught him, or, at least, had tried to teach him.

Dooley led General Grant back into the forest with Miss Sabrina walking alongside him. He was smarter. He had learned something. From here on out, he would sleep in the corral with General Grant. That was the only horse in this one-horse town, and Dooley didn't want Logan Kingsbury, or any of those three other Cincinnati men, to steal the gelding and leave him in this miserable patch of earth.

Two days later, he became even smarter. That's when he discovered the trail.

It wasn't much of a trail, in the woods just behind the little clearing—well, it wasn't actually a clearing—that was big enough for General Grant's corral. It led around the trees and began climbing up the hard granite slope. Dooley had only gone in that direction to answer nature's call, because it would not be polite if Miss Sabrina happened that way after breakfast and caught him with his pants unbuttoned. So he and Blue walked into the woods, a bit deeper just to be safe, and that's when Dooley realized he was following a trail.

You found trails all the time in woods. Usually they were made by animals, and that's what Dooley thought this one was. After all, Blue was using it, and there was this strange-looking footprint on the ground. So Dooley urinated on a tree, and Blue made his own mark on a pinecone, and Dooley rebuttoned his pants, and wiped his hands on some pine needles, and wanted to hurry back to the corral because he still did not trust Logan Kingsbury . . . or McCreery, Hentig, and Abercrombie—or, come to think on it, Logan Kingsbury's aunt.

Yet as he rubbed his hands on the pine needles, he saw the print again, and he put his fingers in the dust, and tried to fathom what kind of wild beast could make such a mark. It did not look human. No boot heel, nothing store-bought had he ever seen that would have left such a print. Not that Dooley was scared yet, but it was still early in the morning, and he did not want to be leaped by some part-cougar, part-grizzly type of beast, with a great big stride from the other prints he saw, but seeing how he could smell coffee back in Slim Pickings proper, he figured he might as well go back and see Miss Granby.

When he reached town, the others were up, eating their boiled corn mush and leftover rabbit. Well, as the group's hunter, Dooley had told them it was rabbit. He believed that they would have balked had they known they were eating marmot. It had a gamey bite to it, and Dooley could not compare it to horse-meat or mule meat, and if he never ever had to eat marmot again he would be satisfied.

Miss Sabrina brought him a cup of coffee and asked if he wanted rabbit or mush.

"Just coffee," he told her.

"Why don't you pan for gold, Logan?" Mr. McCreery shouted.

Logan Kingsbury was up, even this early in the morning, and walking toward the cook fire.

"I did my pannin'," Logan said. "Made my riches."

The men from Cincinnati looked at one another, likely thinking, *Is this how we'll look when we're rich men?*

"Where's your gold, then?" Mr. Hentig said.

"At the First Bank of Ogallala," Logan Kingsbury said.

Dooley sipped coffee and looked at Logan Kingsbury. The Widow's nephew was a liar. Dooley had been in Ogallala, and had ridden past the First Bank of Ogallala one evening with Zerelda Dobbs. The Dobbs-Handley Gang might even would have considered robbing that bank had not the signs on the door knocked off its hinges and hanging above the broken windowpanes announced that the First Bank of Ogallala had gone bust.

"When was that?" Dooley asked, just to make certain.

"Oh, three weeks back, I guess."

Liar, Dooley told himself, and as the tall man made his way to get that cup of coffee, Dooley again found himself studying the man's feet and his makeshift moccasins.

"Why do you stay here?" Miss Sabrina Granby asked.

It was that special time of the day. Dooley knew he should wait until dusk to let General Grant graze, but, well, Miss Sabrina would not accompany a man alone after the sun had set. She wasn't that type of girl. And Dooley couldn't figure any reason to walk out of a dark woods into a dark land. He wanted to see and feel the sun.

So, the gelding contented himself on the bountiful offering, and Dooley chewed on a blade of grass himself, feet crossed at the ankles, leaning against a rock, hands behind his head, talking to Miss Sabrina.

"It's . . ." He did not finish, because, truthfully, he did not really know. He ran the options through his mind.

It's because Frank Handley, Doc Watson, and Zerelda Dobbs would never find me in Slim Pickings.

It's because I couldn't find my way to Deadwood from here.

It's because I can't leave a woman like you behind with a fellow crazier than a bedbug and three men from the Queen City of the West who are closing in on insanity at a right good clip.

"I guess we should go now," he said.

He gathered the reins, called for Blue to quit that digging, and took Miss Sabrina's gentle hand in his, the one not holding the leather reins. He led her out of the meadow, and into the woods, and only once glanced over his shoulder at the vast flatlands to the south.

Miss Sabrina had not spotted the rising dust. But Dooley had.

CHAPTER FORTY-THREE

"You're in an awful hurry, Dooley," Miss Sabrina told him.

Dooley tried to paint a smile, tried to shrug his shoulders, and tried to find some way to laugh off what the late preacher's niece had said, but he could only grunt and practically drag her through the path in the woods.

"Dooley!" Miss Sabrina complained, but by then they were deep in the woods, and Dooley stopped, out of breath, and now found a way to grin.

"Sorry," he said. "Reckon I was hungry."

"For rabbit?" she asked.

Dooley found a way to shrug. Rabbit? Marmot? Porcupine? Possum? Did it matter? It wasn't going to be a T-bone steak anytime soon, and he had not seen an elk, mule deer, or antelope in ages.

"I don't know about you, Dooley, but that rabbit you shot and cooked tasted . . . well . . . peculiar."

He didn't answer, but gallantly waved his arms and let her take the lead. She did not have the fierce intent to reach her destination that Dooley had, but now he could at least watch their backs.

Nothing.

That didn't make Dooley feel any better, but he had another idea. When they reached the one-cabin, one-lean-to, one-something-sort-of-like-a-tent settlement of Slim Pickings, Dooley exchanged a few pleasantries with Mr. McCreery and the Widow Kingsbury, then said he would put General Grant in the corral and maybe try to find something else they could eat.

"Not another one of those rabbits, Dooley," the Widow told him.

He told Blue to stay with Miss Sabrina. He did not see Logan Kingsbury, or Mr. Hentig or Mr. Abercrombie, but decided they must be panning for gold that likely was not here. Picking up the Winchester, he made haste as he pulled General Grant to the corral. His first thought was to leave him in the corral, but he had not seen the Widow's favorite nephew anywhere in the camp that thought it was a town, and did not trust Hentig or Abercrombie or McCreery. Maybe the horse could make it up the trail.

While he had been letting General Grant graze and listening to Miss Sabrina's nice voice, and talking about this and that with her, he had been studying the hill behind them. The tree line ended at maybe a thousand feet in elevation, and Dooley made some calculations that the trail he had discovered behind the General's quarters would likely lead up that ridge, maybe even past the tree line. Above the trees appeared just a lot of black for maybe another five hundred and a thousand feet. Black . . . granite . . . or some hard rock. Black as in the Black Hills.

No one had found much pay dirt in the stream, and maybe Logan Kingsbury and his dead partner had taken most of that out. And maybe the mother lode was higher up.

"Up there," Dooley had told himself. "Up there's where I have to go."

Now . . . he went.

Not for the gold, though. No, Dooley decided that just above that tree line, he would have a good view of not just the meadow and the valley, but those flatlands of sage and sand all the way to Fetterman City, or maybe even Denver. From there, in the right spot, hidden by the black rocks and shadows of the tall trees, he would be able to see without being seen. He'd be able to tell just how many Sioux or Cheyenne warriors had been raising that dust. Or could it even be the leftovers of the Dobbs-Handley Gang?

An hour later, he had renamed the unnamed trail Heart Attack Trail.

He stopped, leaning against a tree that had been splintered years ago by lightning. Sweat streamed down his face, and his shirt was drenched. His lungs heaved. His heart raced. He felt light-headed. He tried to figure out how in tarnation a man like Logan Kingsbury had made this climb. One switchback after another, over rocks and loose shale. Over boulders and fallen timbers. Straight up for a hundred and fifty yards with little handholds.

He couldn't even see daylight, but, still, he kept telling himself. "Up there . . . up there . . ."

After another forty minutes, he decided General Grant might as well just stay here. The Winchester in the scabbard? Dooley considered it, but decided he didn't want the extra weight. The Colt on his hip would have to do, and, well, as many dead outlaws could somehow attest, he was better with a short gun than a repeater. Not that he thought he would run into any outlaw on this climb. He wrapped the reins loosely around a bush, drank water from the canteen still on the horn, and moved on, alone now, up and up and over and over and up and up and up . . .

Then, he saw the blackness of rock, the steep ridge of the mountain, or hill, or whatever it was, and he felt slightly better, despite the screams of his muscles and the shooting pains running from his heels to his hips. He stepped out of the woods, found a good rock to lean against, and looked across the flats.

It was, he told himself, not Iowa.

Beautiful. Rugged. The sun now to his back, casting long shadows across the high prairie. After wiping sweat from his face, he studied the land below. No dust. Nothing at all. No movement, but then only a fool would be moving hard at this time of day. Like Dooley had been doing.

Dooley waited until his breathing did not seem quite as labored. He wet his lips, mopped off more sweat, and looked slowly, left to right, up and down, down and up, right to left. *Make sure you don't miss anything*, he told himself.

He didn't. Nothing was out there. Not now.

Which, he knew, meant nothing. They could have found a hollow to wait out the heat of the day. They could have covered the country in the long, grueling eternity that it had taken Dooley to make it above the timberline. They could have been not Indians, not outlaws, but buffalo or elk or marmots.

"No." Dooley shook his head. "Not marmots."

He was no tenderfoot, no fool. Down below, he

had possessed the presence of mind not to leave that canteen on the horn of his saddle. After unscrewing the cap, he drank more water, wanted to drink even more, but knew better. Refreshed, he looked again at the view below.

Whatever had raised that dust, was gone . . . or at least, out of view.

He corked the canteen, and stood to head back down to Slim Pickings. Dooley Monahan, somehow, still possessed that quick thinking, that instinctive presence of mind. He ducked, and let the machete slice over his back.

"What the hell!" Dooley's momentum carried him forward, and if he had not reached out with both hands and stopped himself against the black, triangular boulder, he would have plummeted over the edge. Instead, he righted himself, and turned to face a wild-eyed Mr. Hentig.

"You're not getting my gold!" Hentig roared, and let the machete fly over Dooley's head again.

"What . . . gold?" Dooley leaped back, as he clawed for the Colt in his holster.

It came out easy enough, but Dooley dropped it when the machete came inches from severing his right hand. And Hentig kept swinging that big knife, driving Dooley away from the six-shooter lying on the ground between two smaller black rocks.

"I found it." Hentig's eyes were even wilder than Zerelda Dobbs's, and Dooley, drained from the hard trek up Heart Attack Hill, was slow. The tip of the machete cut a furrow across his ribs, from nipple to belly button, and Dooley fell against the boulder, which moved under his weight.

He forced himself up, instead of leaning against

the boulder, which shifted and sent pebbles and dirt and rat droppings down a two-hundred-foot drop to more black rocks and long-dead pines.

"I found it!" Hentig said. "It's mine." He swung the machete again. "I put that bridge up." The machete came back around. "I risked my hide." Another swipe that almost nicked Dooley's Adam's apple. "Stay out of that cave." Dooley leaped away from the blade once more. "It's mine!" The machete slammed into the boulder, making an unnerving whine and even sending a few sparks into the abyss.

Dooley moved, leaped back, leaped forward, and tried to tell the insane man from Cincinnati that he was up here to get a look at whoever had been sending dust into the sky.

Hentig, however, did not seem interested in Dooley's excuse. He didn't even seem to have a two-year-old's grasp of English.

After rubbing the bloody front of his ripped shirt, Dooley felt and heard something new. *Avalanche* was his first thought, but then he felt the wind, icy and cold and hard, and the noise was not that of stones rolling over the edge. It was . . .

"Thunder!" Mr. Hentig shouted.

Yes. The crazed fool was right. Dooley chanced one look while Hentig shifted the machete from his left hand to his right. The skies were blackening, and the wind had become fierce. Dooley remembered warning the wayfarers he had been guiding that it could snow this time of year. Snow. Those ominous clouds were more likely to be loaded down with hailstones. Lightning flashed, still far enough away, but scary, foreboding.

That's when Mr. Hentig screamed. What he said,

Dooley could not recall, nor did he want to. He leaped to his side. Well, he didn't actually leap. He tripped over a stone and fell, scraping both knees, and saw only the lower part of Mr. Hentig's pants as the Ohioan charged past. He landed against the boulder that had supported Dooley only moments earlier.

It did not support Josiah Hentig.

Dooley caught only a glimpse. Of the machete blade, of Mr. Hentig's legs, and as Dooley rolled onto his back, he saw the man from Cincinnati slam against the boulder, saw the boulder move, saw it disappear, and saw Mr. Hentig for just a moment before he vanished, too.

After that, all Dooley heard was Josiah Hentig's scream.

CHAPTER FORTY-FOUR

Doolcy sat up, pressing his left hand against his bloody shirt, and with a grunt, made himself stand. Tentatively, he inched his way to the edge, sucked in a deep breath, and looked down. The fall, Dooley told himself, had likely killed Josiah Hentig instantly. The Cincinnatian never felt a thing. Especially not the boulder that had landed a few yards above the dead man, before the impact of Hentig's body must have caused the big rock to roll over and settle atop the dead man.

All Dooley could see were the man's shoes, poking out from beneath the boulder.

"It's sort of like a burial," Dooley told himself. After all, there wasn't much chance of anyone climbing down there and hauling the corpse up even had that boulder not moved over and mashed the dead man down to . . . Hell?

Dooley turned away. Gold. Hentig had said he had found gold. What all had he said? A bridge? A cave? Did the creek that ran through Slim Pickings begin up here? A bridge over a creek? Or . . . ? The cave. Dooley scanned the black rocks trying to find something that looked like an entrance to a cave. This could have been where Logan Kingsbury had found his fortune. But where?

He did not have time to look, because sound carried far in this country, and this high. Below, he heard the reports of gunfire. Somebody, he knew, had launched an assault on Miss Sabrina Granby and the people of Slim Pickings, Wyoming Territory.

Dooley ran.

About fifty yards downhill, he realized he had left the Colt in the dirt between two rocks, but he could not turn back for that weapon now. He didn't need to, for the Winchester remained in the scabbard with the saddle on General Grant. He would have to make that rifle do, and, well, from the roar coming from below, a repeating rifle would be more useful than a six-shooter.

He forgot about that shortness of breath, the pain from the machete cut, the sweat and aching muscles in his legs. Dooley ran, using his arms to push away the briars and low branches, watching the ground to make sure he did not step on some stone, trip over a log or boulder, or step into a hole and snap his ankle.

The thick woods turned darker, despite the midafternoon, and Dooley knew the storm clouds were moving faster than he had expected. He no longer heard gunshots below, but he could not slow down. Miss Sabrina was down there. So was Blue. And, well, those other folks from Cincinnati, too.

His heart pounded, and the wind, now turning cool, made the sweat on his body feel like ice. His throat and mouth begged for water, but Dooley kept pushing himself, and as he leaped over a boulder and turned a corner, he saw General Grant, ears alert, turning his beautiful head to find Dooley, the General just standing there in pure contentment.

Slowing, Dooley came to his horse and practically collapsed against the saddle. The gelding snorted, and Dooley took just a moment to catch his breath before he moved behind the horse, keeping his hand on the bay so General Grant wouldn't kick him in the thigh. When he was on the other side of the horse, he stared at the scabbard.

He held his breath.

The scabbard was empty.

"Hello, Dooley," a voice called from the trees.

Dooley turned around slowly, keeping his hands wide, away from the empty holster on his right hip, away from his left hip. He had recognized the voice.

Still pale as death, Doc Watson stood, not holding a gun in his hand, but holding Mr. McCreery upright, using the Cincinnatian as a shield for some strange reason, one arm around the man's waist, the other on top of the man's hatless head.

Mr. McCreery did not look too good, Dooley thought, although sweat rolled into his eyes, burning them, and blurring Dooley's vision.

"Here," Doc Watson said. "Catch."

The killer lifted Mr. McCreery's head clean off his shoulders, and that's when Dooley saw all the blood, and Doc Watson pitched the head straight at Dooley, those eyes still open, the mouth locked in some eternal, silent scream.

Which is what Dooley Monahan did. He screamed as he instinctively caught the head, and threw it away, slamming against the horse, and falling to the ground.

General Grant stepped this way and that, but did not pull away from the tree, or step on Dooley, who sat up, out of breath, wiping his hands that had touched the head of a man decapitated by the worst killer on the frontier, wiping them furiously on the dirt and leaves and pine needles below.

"You sick son of a—" Dooley did not finish, because Doc Watson pointed the barrel of his six-shooter about an inch from Dooley's nose.

"Insults I don't abide," Watson said, his voice cold and hard. "Get up. Get up and I won't tell anyone that you screamed like a girl."

Dooley fumed, but obeyed. Just because he had screamed did not make him yellow. It was instinct. Anyone, even Frank Handley, Dooley figured, would have screamed if he had seen a head flying straight at him like a crude sort of ball, a ball with eyes open and mouth open and blood dried on the lips and chin and beard stubble.

"Been a while, Dooley." The gun pressed hard into Dooley's spine, forcing him to step forward. "Let's go down to Slim Pickin's, pard. There's some folks down yonder who wants to meet you."

They stopped at the corral as Doc Watson put General Grant, whom he had pulled down the trail, in with the other horses. Dooley looked at the mounts, surprised at the number. Four. Only four horses. He refused to get his hopes up, though. There had to be more than four men. When he and Hubert Dobbs had left the gang back in Ogallala, there had been better than a dozen.

His heart lifted when they reached the settlement, not that it was a settlement, actually, and he saw Miss Sabrina kneeling by the fire, frying up bacon and boiling coffee, compliments of the Dobbs-Handley Gang.

His heart sank, however, when Zerelda Dobbs stepped through the blanket-door of the cabin. She grinned.

"Dooley Monahan, as I live and breathe, it's good to see you, love." She said something else, but thunder drowned out the words. "Get the others out here, Frank."

As Zerelda Dobbs walked over to the cookfire, Dooley saw Frank Handley walk out of the cabin, pulling long-boned, unwashed Logan Kingsbury with him and throwing him toward the trash pile. The Widow Kingsbury and Mr. Abercrombie followed, but neither was pulled nor thrown, but merely lined up against the log wall. One of the outlaws, a thin man with a long mustache and underlip beard, stepped out, and trained a shotgun on the Widow and Mr. Abercrombie. If Dooley remembered right, his name was Clifton.

Inside the cabin, came the constant barking of Blue.

"You tied that dog up good, didn't you?" Handley asked.

"Yeah," Clifton, or whatever his name was, answered.

"Where'd you find him?" Frank Handley turned the conversation to Doc Watson, about Dooley Monahan.

Doc Watson gave a vague wave of his pistol. "Little trail heads up that way. I found his horse. Waited for him to come down."

"And the other one?" Handley looked at Abercrombie. "What did you say his name was?"

"Hentig." Abercrombie's words came out in a hoarse whisper.

"Didn't see him."

Inside, Blue kept on barking.

"Where's . . . Mr. . . . McCreery?" Abercrombie managed.

Doc Watson laughed. "He lost his head."

That made Dooley's stomach sink behind his intestines.

"Hentig?" Frank Handley directed his question at Dooley. "You and him found this ol' boy's mine, eh?" He pointed the barrel of his gun at Logan Kingsbury. "Double-crossing your pards. I can understand that."

Dooley was looking at Logan Kingsbury, seeing the anger in that crazy dude's eyes. He decided that he had better tell the truth. At least that would buy some time, maybe, keep him alive a little longer.

Blue kept barking, and Frank Handley yelled, "Clifton, go inside and kill that yapping cur."

"Blue!" Dooley yelled. "Quiet!"

The dog obeyed, and Dooley felt the relief as Frank Handley grinned. "Never mind, Clifton. Don't kill the dog, as long as Moneymans here tells us what we want to hear."

After drawing a deep breath, holding it a moment before exhaling, Dooley sighed. "I don't know where that mine is. Hentig found it. I was just heading up the trail to get above the timberline, see if I could spot whoever it was raising dust."

"That'd be us," Clifton said.

"Shut up," Zerelda Dobbs snapped.

"Hentig jumped me. He said he had found the mine. Fool tried to kill me."

"And you killed him," Zerelda said. "Like you done

my pa. Tell me, Doomey, was there a reward on this Hentig feller?"

"I didn't kill Hentig," Dooley said. "He fell off the edge. That killed him. Or if it somehow didn't, the boulder that rolled on top of him killed him."

"But you did kill my pa," Zerelda said.

"Well, he was trying to kill me."

Zerelda laughed. "That'd be Pa, all right, the connivin' little horse's arse."

Frank Handley moved to the trash heap, jerked Logan Kingsbury to his feet, and shoved him in front of the cabin.

"All right, Kingsbury, looks like you're the only one who knows where that mine is. Doc, put that gun of yourn again' the Widder's temple." After Doc Watson obeyed, Handley grinned. "You tell us what we want to know," he said, his voice as icy as the wind now blowing. "Or we blow your aunt's head clean off."

"Could I cut off her head, Frank?" Doc Watson asked.

"No, just shoot her . . . unless the boy tells us what we wants to hear."

"He won't do it," the Widow said. "For I'm not his aunt. He's not any kin of mine."

Dooley stared. So did Miss Sabrina, letting the coffee and bacon burn.

Logan Kingsbury swallowed, and his face underneath the dirt paled.

"You called me 'Aunt,'" The Widow told the impostor. "My nephew called me 'Auntie,' and my nephew was nowhere near as tall as you are, nor as ugly and inconsiderate. You're Martin Dansforth, the army deserter. You killed my darling Logan."

Handley looked at the Widow, and at Logan

Kingsbury, but did not seem convinced. Maybe he thought the Widow was a good poker player.

"Really. I don't think so, lady. Why'd you come up here if you knowed this filthy cur kilt yer nephew?"

"Gold," the Widow replied instantly.

That didn't convince Handley, either. "No. Yer lyin', ma'am. All right, what if I tell Doc Watson to kill this here . . . ahem . . . impostor? What if I said, *Doc, take that gun away and blow this filthy dog to hell*?" Doc Watson removed the pistol from the Widow's temple and pointed it at the shivering Logan Kingsbury/Martin Dansforth scoundrel. "What would you say then, Widder?"

"I'd say *Blow that man to hell,*" the Widow said calmly. "He means nothing to—"

The gun roared, and Martin Dansforth, if he wasn't really Logan Kingsbury, went flying into the cookfire, ruining the breakfast, overturning the coffee, and sending Miss Sabrina Granby screaming and running into Dooley's arms.

CHAPTER FORTY-FIVE

"You idiot!" Frank Handley roared.

"She told me to kill him," Doc Watson whined.

Blue started barking again inside the cabin until Dooley yelled for him to be quiet, that he was all right, that nothing was wrong—when, in fact, nothing was right. To his relief, Blue once again obeyed. The barks ceased, but Dooley could hear every now and then the whimpering of the dog above the wind, the rustling of the trees, and Frank Handley's plentiful curses.

"She's not bossin' this outfit, Doc!" Frank Handley kept fuming.

Zerelda Dobbs sniggered as Frank Handley slammed his revolver into his holster and started kicking up dirt, pinecones, and stones across the camp, complaining that of all the men he had lost in Julesburg, why in heaven's name could not Doc Watson have been among them?

That stopped Dooley. He looked at the chastised Doc Watson, at the giggling Zerelda Dobbs, and at the frowning Clifton, while Frank Handley began stringing together profanity and blasphemy in every-body's direction. Dooley had been scouting for the rest of the gang, but now . . . maybe this was all that was left of the once-mighty Dobbs-Handley Gang. Maybe they had tried to sack Julesburg only to find the citizens, after so much violence and outlawry, had been pushed to the point of fighting back. He knew better than to ask Frank Handley what had happened in Julesburg, however.

"He knew where the cave was, you idiot!" Handley roared. "Now what do we do?"

"Oh . . ." Zerelda Dobbs paused just long enough to let the thunder stop rolling. "I imagine Dooley, my love, could find it fer us. Couldn't ya, sweetheart?"

"I can try," Dooley said without pause. It might keep him, and the others, alive. "I'll take you all up there. You just let these three folks go."

"No, no, no, love, that ain't how we's gonna do it." She walked to Dooley, and pulled Miss Sabrina away. "She comes with us. Clifton, you stay here and keep an eye on that widder woman and that fool. Frank, Doc, let's go find that gold."

"And when we've found it?" Doc asked.

"Well, we'll be pards. Share and share alike. Right?"

The outlaws laughed. Dooley knew that once they found the mine, the Cincinnatians and Dooley Mona-han would be killed. Maybe decapitated.

Once again, Dooley climbed up that trail, past the corral with the five horses, over the rocks, between the trees, underneath the low branches. Up, and up, and up, and now they had to deal with the whipping wind, and soon, a drizzling rain, with the skies blackened by ominous thunderheads.

Cold, misting rain covered Dooley's face when he cleared the tree line, and he stopped to lean against a black granite triangle to catch his breath. The others came, too, likewise panting, and lightning flashed overhead.

"Well!" Frank Handley shouted over the roar of wind.

Dooley avoided looking at the rocks where he knew his Colt remained. Instead he turned, and pointed up the slick granite. "My guess would be up there. To that flat little spot. We can crawl along that, see if we find any caves."

"Huh?" Doc Watson yelled.

Dooley repeated his thoughts, louder.

The outlaws looked at one another, then at Zerelda Dobbs.

"Y'all take him with ya!" she bellowed. "I'll stay down here with Miss Pretty Cakes. And I'll kill her if she tries somethin' foolish."

"We'll do the same with Mr. Monograms!" Doc Watson laughed.

Lightning cut through the sky again, followed almost instantly by a roar of thunder, and Frank Handley motioned with his revolver. Dooley began climbing.

His boots slipped three times, and once he slid all the way until he was staring at Doc Watson's revolver. The rain turned from mist to drizzle, and Dooley regained the ground he had lost. When he reached the flat, he rolled onto his back and sucked in thin air and cold rain, and waited for the two outlaws to join him.

"Which way?" Frank Handley bellowed when he made it to the top.

Dooley rolled over, came to his feet, and nodded. They moved . . . into the fierce wind and rain . . . walking, at first, until they had to crawl on their hands and knees.

They came to one crack in the face of the hill, and Doc Watson scrambled up without even being asked, peered inside, shook his head, and slid back down. Dooley crawled on.

He crawled farther until he saw a deeper blackness just ten or twelve yards up. He never would have even noticed it had not he heard a crash to see two long logs, secured together with lariat and rawhide, spinning and then toppling in the wind. They had been leaning against what appeared to be a cave's entrance.

Hentig's words came back to him, and he came up, pointing. "That's it. That's got to be it."

Handley and Watson stared at each other, then at the opening, and looked again at Dooley.

"A marmot, an eagle, nothing tied those two logs together. That was a sign! A sign by Logan King-, I mean, Martin Dansforth."

Dooley was already climbing, trying not to be blown down by the wind, and he stepped just inside the opening. It was a cave, deep and long and dark, and the blowing rounds and dark clouds did not help. Inside, it was pitch-black.

When the outlaws reached the opening, they, too, paused. They looked at Dooley.

"I can't see a damned thing in there!" Handley shouted.

"Can you see this?" Dooley held out the glittering nugget he had found on this side of the cavern.

"Hentig said there were torches just past the entrance," Dooley lied. "On the right."

"You stay here, Monamang!" Doc Watson said, turning to Handley to explain, "If he disappears in that black, I'd never find him to cut off his head."

"Right!"

Excited, fueled by greed, Frank Handley and Doc Watson stepped into the blackness, and disappeared.

Dooley caught only a bit of their screams, and braced himself against the granite, listening. Those two poles strung together had been the bridge Hentig had mentioned. Not a bridge over a creek, as Dooley had suspected at first, but over a chasm. Dooley waited another minute, before sliding down the granite to the flat. He hurried his way back. The rain became a torrent now, and Dooley was soaked to the bone. Shivering, he moved on, closer to Miss Sabrina, closer to Zerelda Dobbs.

When he saw the outline of the granite triangle, Dooley fell to his knees. He crawled, inching his way toward the rocks, hardly breathing, barely moving, just getting wetter and wetter and colder and colder. His hand disappeared inside the rocks, and he felt the barrel of his Colt.

"Hey, love!"

Even with the roar of wind and rain, Dooley heard Zerelda Dobbs. He turned, finding her about thirty yards up the slope, holding a Henry rifle.

"I knew you'd take care of my pards, Doosey!" she shouted. "Now I reckon all that gold's fer my ownself!"

That's when the lightning struck.

It's also when Dooley let go of his metal Colt.

The flash blinded him, and he could feel the heat, but no electricity reached him. When he could see clearly, all he saw was a melting mess, that once had been Zerelda Dobbs, rolling down the hill. Dooley sucked in more air, picked up the pistol, and ran to the triangle, where he saw Miss Sabrina Granby cowering. He took her hand without slowing down, and did not stop until they were deeper in the trees.

"Did . . . ?" Miss Sabrina gasped. "Did you see that?"

"Yeah," Dooley said. "Zee wasn't quicker than lightning after all."

"But . . ."

"Come on," Dooley said. "We've still got Clifton to worry about."

But, it turned out, they didn't.

"When that storm come up strong, he just left us," the Widow said. "Got his horse, and rode out. Never seen a man so chicken-livered of a little thunderstorm."

"Too bad, Dooley," Mr. Abercrombie said. "You'll never find the bodies of Handley or Watson, and no one can recognize what's left of Miss Dobbs. But I guess you can haul in Mr. Dansforth's remains and claim his reward."

"I'm no bounty hunter," Dooley said. He flipped the glittering stone, caught it, and smiled. "We have enough horses to ride off. Back to Fetterman City."

"We're staying here," Miss Sabrina said.

Dooley's heart sank. "What?"

"The mine," the preacher's niece said. "Mr. Abercrombie and Mrs. Kingsbury and I have all decided. We're working the mine."

Mr. Abercrombie, who had been as crazy as the other men? Well, gold had turned enemies into friends before.

Flummoxed, Dooley blinked and leaned against a tree for support. He held up the nugget again, "Miss Sabrina, everyone, it's like I said . . . this isn't gold. It's iron pyrite. Fool's gold."

"We know."

"But it's worthless."

"No," the Widow said. "We'll call this Logan Town, in honor of my brave, late nephew. People will come. Once we have some more buildings up, Mr. Abercrombie will send for his wife and family, and she'll sell pies to passersby. And we shall sell them pieces of Black Hills gold."

Dooley blinked. Had they all gone daft?

"But it's worthless. You can't defraud . . ."

"We won't be defrauding anyone," Miss Sabrina said. "My uncle wanted to make something, riches, yes, and if there's no gold for wealth, he still shall not have died in vain."

"The West will be settled," Mr. Abercrombie explained. "The Sioux and the Cheyenne, they will be defeated, eventually, and the West will be open. It will be tame. And it will bring in people from the East. They can't afford real gold, but they will be hungry for apple pie, and they can afford fool's gold."

"Tourists," Miss Sabrina said.

"There's no trail here," Dooley reminded them.

"There is now," Miss Sabrina said. "And you blazed it, Dooley Monahan. This will be another path to Deadwood, to these stunning Black Hills. Oh, people will come. And they'll owe it—and we'll owe it—all to you."

She walked over and kissed Dooley, not on the cheek, but full on his lips.

EPILOGUE

He helped them for about a week, killed an elk, showed Mr. Abercrombie how to dry jerky, and they had the supplies from the late Watson, Handley, and Dobbs, and Mr. Abercrombie would leave after they had hauled enough iron pyrite out of the mine for stock. Mr. Abercrombie bragged that he thought he might even be able to sell or trade some fool's gold in Fetterman City when he arrived to fetch his wife.

Yet Dooley knew he couldn't stay here, so he saddled General Grant, and led the gelding and Blue out of the woods.

"Are you sure you can't stay with us, Dooley?" Miss Sabrina asked. She had followed him into the meadow, as she had done when he had let his horse graze in the afternoons.

"I reckon not, ma'am," Dooley said. "Running a trading post . . . well . . . I guess I'm just a fiddle-footed cowboy and gambler."

"And bounty hunter," she reminded him.

"Well, sometimes," he had to admit. He held out

his right hand. "It was a pleasure knowing you, ma'am."

She ignored his hand, and kissed him again.

So, Dooley Monahan climbed into his saddle, tipped his hat, and rode away from the Black Hills, and Miss Sabrina Granby. He kept his eye out for Indians, but saw only antelope, until he finally reached that familiar trail. He studied the horizon one way, and then the other.

"Maybe," he said to Blue, who was panting at the General's side, "I just ain't one to find no riches in some mine." He snorted. "Fool's gold." He shook his head, laughed, and looked east. "A man ought to do what he knows best," he said, "and perhaps I'm just an Iowa farmer. What do you think, Blue? Back to Des Moines?"

Blue sprang up, yapped, and took off at a jog.

"Yeah." Dooley smiled. "You're right."

Tugging on the reins, he kicked General Grant into a soft trot.

They rode . . . west.

*Keep reading for a special preview of
the first book in a magnificent new series
by America's bestselling Western writers.*

Here is the towering saga of Breckenridge Wallace,
a new breed of intrepid pioneer who helped forge a
path through the wild American frontier . . .

THE FRONTIERSMAN
by William W. Johnstone
with J. A. Johnstone

In Tennessee, 17-year-old Breckinridge Wallace
knew the laws of nature. When his life was in
danger, he showed a fearless instinct to fight back.
Killing a thug who was sent to kill him got
Breckinridge exiled from his Smoky Mountain
home. Brutally wounding an Indian attacker
earned him an enemy for life . . .

Now, from the bustling streets of St. Louis to
the vast stillness of the Missouri headwaters,
Breckinridge is discovering a new world of
splendor, violence, promise and betrayal. Most of
all, he is clawing his way to manhood behind the
law of the gun. Because the trouble he left back
in Tennessee won't let him go. A killer stalks his
every move. And by the time he joins a dangerous
expedition, Breckenridge has had only a small taste
of the blood, horror, and violence he must face
next—to make his way to a new frontier . . .

Coming March 2017 from Pinnacle.

CHAPTER ONE

Death lurked in the forest.

It wore buckskins, carried a long-barreled flintlock rifle, and had long, shaggy hair as red as the flame of sunset. Death's name was Breckinridge Wallace.

Utterly silent and motionless, Breckinridge knelt and peered through a gap in the thick brush underneath the trees that covered these Tennessee hills. He waited, his cheek pressed against the ornately engraved maple of the rifle stock as he held the weapon rock-steady. He had the sight lined up on a tiny clearing on the other side of a swift-flowing creek. His brilliant blue eyes never blinked as he watched for his prey.

Those eyes narrowed slightly as Breckinridge heard a faint crackling of brush that gradually grew louder. The quarry he had been stalking all morning was nearby and coming closer. All he had to do was be patient.

He was good at that. He had been hunting ever since the rifle he carried was longer than he was tall. His father had said more than once Breckinridge should have been born with a flintlock in his hands. It wasn't a statement of approval, either.

Breckinridge looped his thumb over the hammer and pulled it back so slowly that it made almost no sound. He was ready now. He had worked on the trigger until it required only the slightest pressure to fire.

The buck stepped from the brush into the clearing, his antlered head held high as he searched for any sight or scent of danger. Breckinridge knew he couldn't be seen easily where he was concealed in the brush, and the wind had held steady, carrying his smell away from the creek. Satisfied that it was safe, the buck moved toward the stream and started to lower his head to drink. He was broadside to Breck, in perfect position.

For an instant, Breckinridge felt a surge of regret that he was about to kill such a beautiful, magnificent animal. But the buck would help feed Breck's family for quite a while, and that was how the world worked. He remembered the old Chickasaw medicine man Snapping Turtle telling him he ought to pray to the animals he hunted and give thanks to them for the sustenance their lives provided. Breck did so, and his finger brushed the flintlock's trigger.

The crescent-shaped butt kicked back against his shoulder as the rifle cracked. Gray smoke gushed from the barrel. The buck's muzzle had just touched the water when the .50-caliber lead ball smashed into his side and penetrated his heart. The animal threw his head up and then crashed onto his side, dead when he hit the ground.

Breckinridge rose to his full height, towering well over six feet, and stepped out of the brush. His brawny shoulders stretched the fringed buckskin shirt he wore. His ma complained that he outgrew clothes faster than anybody she had ever seen.

That was true. Anybody just looking at Breckinridge who didn't know him would take him for a full-grown man. It was difficult to believe this was only his eighteenth summer.

Before he did anything else, he reloaded the rifle with a ball from his shot pouch, a greased patch from the brass-doored patchbox built into the right side of the rifle's stock, and a charge of powder from the horn he carried on a strap around his neck. He primed the rifle and carefully lowered the hammer.

Then he moved a few yards to his right where the trunk of a fallen tree spanned the creek. Breckinridge himself had felled that tree a couple of years earlier, dropping it so that it formed a natural bridge. He had done that a number of places in these foothills of the Smoky Mountains east of his family's farm to make his hunting expeditions easier. He'd been roaming the hills for years and knew every foot of them.

Pa was going to be mad at him for abandoning his chores to go hunting, but that wrath would be reduced to a certain extent when Breckinridge came in with that fine buck's carcass draped over his shoulders. Breck knew that, and he was smiling as he stepped onto the log and started to cross the creek.

He was only about halfway to the other side when an arrow flew out of the woods and nicked his left ear as it whipped past his head.

* * *

"Flamehair," Tall Tree breathed as he gazed across the little valley at the big white man moving along the ridge on the far side.

This was a half hour earlier. Tall Tree and the three men with him were hunting for game, but Flamehair was more interesting than fresh meat. The lean Chickasaw warrior didn't know anything about the red-haired man except he had seen Flamehair on a few occasions in the past when their paths had almost crossed in these woods. It was hard to mistake that bright hair, especially because the white man seldom wore a hat.

"We should go on," Big Head urged. "The buck will get away."

"I don't care about the buck," Tall Tree said without taking his eyes off Flamehair.

"I do," Bear Tongue put in. "We haven't had fresh meat in days, Tall Tree. Come. Let us hunt."

Reluctantly, Tall Tree agreed. Anyway, Flamehair had vanished into a thick clump of vegetation. Tall Tree moved on with the other two and the fourth warrior, Water Snake.

Bear Tongue was right, Tall Tree thought. They and the dozen other warriors back at their camp needed fresh meat.

Empty bellies made killing white men more difficult, and that was the work to which Tall Tree and his men were devoted.

Three years earlier, after many years of sporadic war with the whites, the leaders of the Chickasaw people had made a treaty with the United States government. It was possible they hadn't understood completely what the results of that agreement would be. The Chickasaw and the other members of the so-called Five Civilized Tribes had been forced to leave their ancestral lands and trek west to a new home in a place called Indian Territory.

Tall Tree and the men with him had no use for that. As far as they were concerned, the Smoky Mountains were their home and anyplace they roamed should be Indian Territory.

They had fled from their homes before the white man's army had a chance to round them up and force them to leave. While most of the Chickasaw and the other tribes were headed west on what some were calling the Trail of Tears, Tall Tree's band of warriors and others like them hid out in the mountains, dodging army patrols, raiding isolated farms, and slaughtering as many of the white invaders as they could find.

Tall Tree knew that someday he and his companions would be caught and killed, but when that happened they would die as free men, as warriors, not as slaves.

As long as he was able to spill plenty of the enemy's blood before that day arrived, he would die happily.

Now as he and the other three warriors trotted along a narrow game trail in pursuit of the buck they were stalking, Tall Tree's mind kept going back to the man he thought of as Flamehair. The man nearly always hunted alone, as if supremely confident in his ability to take care of himself. That arrogance infuriated Tall Tree. He wanted to teach the white man a lesson, and what better way to do that than by killing him?

He could think of one way, Tall Tree suddenly realized.

It would be even better to kill Flamehair slowly, to

torture him for hours or even days, until the part of him left alive barely resembled anything human and he was screaming in agony for the sweet relief of death.

That thought put a smile on Tall Tree's face.

Water Snake, who hardly ever spoke, was in the lead because he was the group's best scout. He signaled a halt, then turned and motioned to Tall Tree, who joined him. Water Snake pointed to what he had seen.

Several hundred yards away, a buckskin-clad figure moved across a small open area. Tall Tree caught only a glimpse of him, but that was enough for him to again recognize Flamehair.

Tall Tree understood now what was going on. After Water Snake had pointed out the white man to Big Head and Bear Tongue, Tall Tree said, "Flamehair is after the same buck we are. Should we allow him to kill it and take it back to whatever squalid little farm he came from?"

"No!" Big Head exclaimed. "We should kill him."

Bear Tongue said, "I thought you wanted to hunt."

"I do, but Flamehair is only one man. We can kill him and then kill the buck."

"Even better," Tall Tree said, "we can let *him* kill the buck, then we will kill him and take it for ourselves and our friends back at camp."

The other three nodded eagerly, and he knew he had won them over.

Now they were stalking two different kinds of prey, one human, one animal. Tall Tree knew that eventually they would all come together. He sensed the spirits manipulating earthly events to create that intersection. His medicine was good. He had killed many white men. Today he would kill another.

Tall Tree knew the trail they were following led to a small clearing along a creek that wildlife in this area used as a watering hole. Before his people had been so brutally torn away from their homes, so had they.

It was possible Flamehair knew of the spot as well. He came to these hills frequently, and it was likely that he was well acquainted with them. Tall Tree decided that was where he and his men would set their trap. The buck would be the bait.

They circled to reach the creek ahead of the buck and concealed themselves in the thick brush a short distance downstream from the clearing. A fallen tree lay across the creek. Tall Tree had looked at that log before and suspected Flamehair had been the one who cut it down.

As they waited, Tall Tree began to worry that the buck wasn't really headed here after all and would lead Flamehair somewhere else. In that case Tall Tree would just have to be patient and kill the white man some other day.

But he was looking forward to seeing if the man's blood was as red as his hair, and he hoped it was today.

A few minutes later he heard the buck moving through the brush and felt a surge of satisfaction and anticipation. He had guessed correctly, and soon the white man would be here, too. He leaned closer to his companions and whispered, "Try not to kill him. I want to take him alive and make his death long and painful."

Big Head and Bear Tongue frowned a little at that.

They had killed plenty of whites, too, but not by torture. Water Snake just nodded, though.

A few more minutes passed, then the buck appeared. Almost immediately a shot rang out, and the buck went down hard, killed instantly. It was a good shot. Tall Tree spotted the powder smoke on the far side of the creek and knew that if all they wanted to do was kill Flamehair, they ought to riddle that spot with arrows.

Instead he motioned for the others to wait. He was convinced he knew what the white man was going to do next.

He was right, too. Flamehair appeared, looking even bigger than Tall Tree expected, and stood on the creek bank reloading his rifle, apparently unconcerned that he might be in danger. Reloading after firing a shot was just a simple precaution that any man took in the woods. Any man who was not a fool.

The other three warriors looked at Tall Tree, ready and anxious to fire their arrows at Flamehair. Again Tall Tree motioned for them to wait. A cruel smile curved his lips slightly as he watched Flamehair step onto the log bridge and start across the creek. He raised his bow and pulled it taut as he took aim.

This was the first time he had gotten such a close look at Flamehair, and a shock went through him as he realized the white man was barely a man at all. For all his great size, he was a stripling youth.

That surprise made Tall Tree hesitate instead of loosing his arrow as he had planned. He wanted to shoot Flamehair in the leg and dump him in the creek, which would make his long rifle useless and ruin the rest of his powder.

Instead, as Tall Tree failed to shoot, Big Head's fingers slipped on his bowstring and it twanged as it launched its arrow. Big Head's aim was off. The arrow flew at Flamehair's red-thatched head, missing as narrowly as possible.

But somehow it accomplished Tall Tree's goal anyway, because as Flamehair twisted on the log, possibly to make himself a smaller target in case more arrows were coming his way, the soles of his high-topped moccasins slipped. He wavered there for a second and fought desperately to keep his balance, but it deserted him and he toppled into the stream with a huge splash.

Tall Tree forgot about his plan to capture Flamehair and torture him to death. All that mattered to him now was that this white intruder on Chickasaw land should die. He leaped up and plunged out of the brush as he shouted in his native tongue, "Kill him!"

CHAPTER TWO

Breckinridge had good instincts. They told him where there was one Indian there might be two—or more. He knew he was an easy target out here on this log, so he tried to turn and race back to the cover of the brush on the creek's other side.

Despite his size, he had always been a pretty graceful young man. That grace deserted him now, however, when he needed it most. He felt himself falling, tried to stop himself, but his momentum was too much. He slipped off the log and fell the five feet to the creek.

He knew how to swim, of course. Like shooting a gun, swimming was something he had learned how to do almost before he could walk.

So he wasn't worried about drowning, even though he had gone completely under the water. His main concern was the charge of powder in his rifle, as well as the one in the flintlock pistol he carried. They were wet and useless now. The powder in his horn was probably all right, but he figured his attackers wouldn't give him a chance to dry his weapons and reload.

Sure enough, as he came up and his head broke the surface, he saw four Chickasaw burst out of the brush. Three of them already had arrows nocked, and the fourth was reaching for a shaft in his quiver.

Breckinridge dragged in as deep a breath as he could and went under again.

He still had hold of his rifle—it was a fine gun and he was damned if he was going to let go of it—and its weight helped hold him down as he kicked strongly to propel himself along with the current. The creek was eight or ten feet deep at this point and twenty feet wide. Like most mountain streams, though, it was fairly clear, so the Indians could probably still see him.

Something hissed past Breckinridge in the water. He knew it was an arrow. They were still trying to kill him. He hadn't expected any different.

When he was a boy, he had befriended and played with some of the Chickasaw youngsters in the area. The medicine man Snapping Turtle had sort of taken Breckinridge under his wing for a while, teaching him Indian lore and wisdom. Breck liked the Chickasaw and had nothing against them. He didn't really understand why the army had come and made them all leave, but he'd been sorry to see them go.

Not all the Chickasaw had departed for Indian Territory, however. Some of them—stubborn holdouts, Breckinridge's pa called them—had managed to elude the army and were still hidden in the rugged mountains, venturing out now and then for bloody raids on the white settlers. Breck figured he had run into just such a bunch, eager to kill any white man they came across.

He had known when he started into the hills that he was risking an encounter like this, but he had never let the possibility of danger keep him from doing something he wanted. If that made him reckless, like his pa said, then so be it.

Now it looked like that impulsiveness might be the death of him.

His lungs were good, strengthened by hours and hours of running for the sheer pleasure of it. He had filled them with air, so he knew he could stay under the water for a couple of minutes, anyway, probably longer. He had to put that time to good use. Because of the thick brush, the Indians couldn't run along the bank as quickly as he could swim underwater. All he needed to do was avoid the arrows they fired at him, and he had to trust to luck for that since he couldn't see them coming while he was submerged.

Breckinridge continued kicking his feet and stroking with his left arm. Fish darted past him in the stream, disturbed by this human interloper. It was beautiful down here. Breck might have enjoyed the experience if he hadn't known that death might be waiting for him at the surface.

He didn't know how long he stayed under, but finally he had to come up for air. He let his legs drop so he could push off the rocky bottom with his feet. As he broke the surface he threw his head from side to side to sling the long red hair out of his eyes. When his vision had cleared he looked around for the Indians.

He didn't see them, but he heard shouting back upstream a short distance. He had gotten ahead of his pursuers, just as he'd hoped, and once he had grabbed a couple more deep breaths he intended to go under again and keep swimming downstream.

That plan was ruined when strong fingers suddenly clamped around his ankle and jerked him under the surface again.

Taken by surprise, Breckinridge was in the middle of taking a breath, so he got a mouthful of water that went down the wrong way and threatened to choke him. Not only that, but he had a dangerous opponent on his hands, too.

He could see well enough to know that the man struggling with him was one of the Chickasaw warriors. He must have jumped off the log bridge into the creek and taken off after Breckinridge as fast as he could swim. The warrior was long and lean, built like a swimmer. He slashed at Breck with the knife clutched in his right hand while keeping his left clenched around Breck's ankle.

Breckinridge twisted away from the blade. It scraped across the side of his buckskin shirt but didn't do any damage. His movements seemed maddeningly slow to him as he lifted his other leg and rammed his heel into the Indian's chest. The kick was strong enough to knock the man's grip loose.

The Chickasaw warrior shot backward in the water. Breckinridge knew he couldn't outswim the man, so he went after him instead. If he could kill the Indian in a hurry, he might still be able to give the slip to the others.

Breckinridge had never killed a man before, although he had been in plenty of brawls with fellows his own age and some considerably older. This time he was fighting for his life, though, so he wasn't going to have a problem doing whatever he had to in order to survive. Before the man he had kicked had a chance to recover, Breck got behind him and thrust the barrel of his rifle across the warrior's neck. He grabbed the barrel with his other hand and pulled it back, pressing it as hard as he could into the man's throat.

The Chickasaw flailed and thrashed, but Breckinridge's strength was incredible. He managed to plant his knee in the small of the Indian's back, giving him the leverage he needed to exert even more force.

The warrior slashed backward with his knife. Breckinridge felt the blade bite into his thigh. The wound wasn't deep because the Indian couldn't get much strength behind the thrust at this awkward angle, but it hurt enough to make red rage explode inside Breck. The muscles of his arms, shoulders, and back bunched under the tight buckskin shirt as he heaved up and back with the rifle lodged under the warrior's chin.

Even underwater, Breckinridge heard the sharp crack as the man's neck snapped.

The Chickasaw's body went limp. Breckinridge let go of it and kicked for the surface. As soon as his enemy was dead, Breck had realized that he was just about out of air. The stuff tasted mighty sweet as he shot up out of the water and gulped down a big breath.

An arrow slapped through that sweet air right beside his head.

Breckinridge twisted around to determine its direction. He saw right away that the other three Chickasaw had caught up while he was battling with the one in the creek. Two of them were on the bank even with him, while the third man had run on downstream, where he waited with a bow drawn back to put an arrow through him if he tried to swim past.

They thought they had him trapped, and that was probably true. But the realization just made Breckinridge angry. He had never been one to flee from trouble. He shouldn't have tried to today, he thought. He should have stood his ground. He should have taken the fight to the enemy.

That was what he did now. He dived underwater as the two Indians closest to him fired, but he didn't try to swim downstream. Instead he kicked toward the shore, found his footing on the creek bottom, and charged up out of the water bellowing like a maddened bull as the warriors reached for fresh arrows.

The rifle wouldn't fire until it had been dried out, cleaned, and reloaded, but in the hands of Breckinridge Wallace it was still a dangerous weapon. Breck proved that by smashing the curved brass butt plate against the forehead of the closest Indian. With Breck's already considerable strength fueled by anger, the blow had enough power behind it that the ends of the crescent-shaped butt shattered the warrior's skull and caved in the front of his head. He went over backward to land in a limp heap.

The other Indian loosed his arrow, and at this range Breckinridge was too big a target to miss. Luck was with him, though, and the flint arrowhead struck his shot pouch. The point penetrated the leather but bounced off the lead balls within.

Breckinridge switched his grip on the rifle, grabbing the barrel with both hands instead, and swung it like a club. He was proud of the fancy engraving and patchbox on the stock and didn't want to break it, but pride wasn't worth his life.

The Chickasaw dropped his bow and ducked under the sweeping blow. He charged forward and rammed his head and right shoulder into Breckinridge's midsection. Breck was considerably taller and heavier than the Indian was and normally would have shrugged off that attempted tackle, but his wet moccasins slipped on the muddy bank and he lost his balance. He went over backward.

The Chickasaw landed on top of him and grabbed the tomahawk that hung at his waist. He raised the weapon and was about to bring it crashing down into Breckinridge's face when Breck's big right fist shot straight up and landed on the warrior's jaw. The powerful blow lifted the Indian away from Breck and made him slump to the side, momentarily stunned.

Breckinridge rolled the other way to put a little distance between himself and the enemy. As he did an arrow buried its head in the ground where he had been a split second earlier. The fourth and final Chickasaw had fired that missile, and when he saw that it had missed, he screeched in fury and dropped his bow. He jerked out a knife and charged at Breck.

As he rolled to his feet, Breckinridge snatched up the tomahawk dropped by the Indian he had just walloped. He dodged the thrust of the fourth man's knife and brought the tomahawk up and over and down in a blindingly swift strike that caught the warrior on the left cheekbone. Breck intended to plant the tomahawk in the middle of the man's skull and cleave his head open, but the Indian had darted aside just enough to prevent that fatal blow.

Instead the tomahawk laid the warrior's cheek open to the bone and traveled on down his neck to lodge in his shoulder. Blood spouted from the wounds as he stumbled and fell.

Breckinridge would have wrenched the tomahawk loose and finished off the injured Chickasaw, but at that moment the man he had punched rammed him again. This time the impact drove Breck off the bank and back into the creek. He floundered in the water for a moment, and by the time he was able to stand up again the two surviving warriors were disappearing into the woods. The one who had just knocked him in the stream was helping the wounded man escape.

Breckinridge felt confident that they didn't have any fight left in them. He might not have admitted it to anyone but himself, but he was glad they felt that way. He knew how lucky he was to have lived through a fight with four-against-one odds . . . especially when the one was an eighteen-year-old youngster and the four were seasoned Chickasaw warriors.

There was no telling if other renegades might be in the vicinity, so he figured he'd better get out of the hills and head for home pretty quick-like.

He wasn't going back without his quarry, though, so without delay he gathered up his rifle and started for the clearing where the buck had fallen. It would take time to put his rifle and pistol back in working order, and he didn't think it would be smart to linger that long.

When he reached the clearing the buck was still lying there, undisturbed as yet by scavengers. Breckinridge stooped, took hold of the carcass, and heaved it onto his shoulders. Even his great strength was taxed by the animal's weight as he began loping through the woods toward home.

He thought about the four warriors he had battled. Two of them were dead, he was sure of that, and the one he'd wounded with the tomahawk probably would die, too, as fast as he had been losing blood.

What would the fourth man do? Would he go back to the rest of the renegades—assuming there were any—and tell them that he and his companions had been nearly wiped out by a large force of well-armed white men?

Or would he admit that all the damage had been done by one young fella who hadn't even had a working firearm?

Breckinridge grinned. Lucky or not, he had done some pretty good fighting back there. He knew now that in a battle for his life he would do whatever it took to survive. He wondered if he ought to tell anybody the truth about what had happened. Chances were, they wouldn't believe him.

But he knew, and he would carry that knowledge with him from now on.

It was all Tall Tree could do not to cry out in pain as he leaned on Bear Tongue while they hurried through the forest. He was weak and dizzy and knew that was from losing all the blood that had poured out from the wounds in his face, neck, and shoulder.

"We must get you back to camp," Bear Tongue babbled. His voice was thick because his jaw was swollen from the powerful blow Flamehair had delivered to him. "If you don't get help, you will bleed to death."

"No," Tall Tree gasped, even though it caused fresh explosions of terrible agony in his face every time he moved his lips. The pain was nothing compared to the hatred that filled him. "I will not die. The spirits have told me . . . I cannot die . . . until I kill the white devil Flamehair!"

Connect with

U s

Visit us online at
KensingtonBooks.com

to read more from your favorite authors, see books
by series, view reading group guides, and more.

Join us on social media

for sneak peeks, chances to win books and prize packs,
and to share your thoughts with other readers.

facebook.com/kensingtonpublishing
twitter.com/kensingtonbooks

Tell us what you think!

To share your thoughts, submit a review,
or sign up for our eNewsletters, please visit:
KensingtonBooks.com/TellUs.